THE HAUNTING OF LOW FENNEL

— — —

TALES OF SECRET EGYPT

SAX ROHMER

INTRODUCTION BY
MIKE ASHLEY

Stark House Press • Eureka California

THE HAUNTING OF LOW FENNEL /
TALES OF SECRET EGYPT

Published by Stark House Press
1315 H Street
Eureka, CA 95501, USA
griffinskye3@sbcglobal.net
www.starkhousepress.com

THE HAUNTING OF LOW FENNEL
First published in hardback by C. Arthur Pearson, Ltd., London,
1920.

TALES OF SECRET EGYPT
First published in hardback by Methuen & Co., Ltd., London,
1918; and Robert M. McBride, New York, 1919.

"The Mysterious Sax Rohmer" copyright © 2024 by Mike Ashley

ISBN: 979-8-88601-061-9

Book design by Mark Shepard, shepgraphics.com.

First Stark House Press Edition: May 2024

TABLE OF CONTENTS

THE MYSTERIOUS SAX ROHMER

Mike Ashley

It always helps an author if there is an air of mystery about them—who they really are, what experiences they may have had to inspire their fiction—is there anything they're not telling us?

All of that applies to Sax Rohmer, who gained literary immortality with the creation of the insidious Dr. Fu Manchu, one of the world's great fictional villains. We know that Sax Rohmer was a pseudonym and that his name was Arthur Sarsfield Ward—though that wasn't his real name, either. So where did Sax Rohmer come from and, for that matter, Sarsfield?

And how did a writer who achieved worldwide fame for his occult thrillers learn such esoteric material when he started his writing career penning songs and sketches for music hall artists such as George Robey and Little Tich.

He revealed little about his early life. Even Cay Van Ash, who knew Rohmer for over twenty years and worked as his secretary, failed to uncover much about his youth when he collaborated with Rohmer's widow, Elizabeth, on a biography *Master of Villainy* (1972), and clearly Elizabeth didn't know either, even though she had been married to Rohmer for fifty years. The truth is, even Rohmer didn't seem to remember much. He had no idea how old he was. In January 1955 the *Evening Despatch* published a small feature headed "Sax Rohmer Has a Mystery—His Age". Rohmer asked if anyone had known him at school so that he could work out his age, as his birth certificate had been lost. "I'm certainly not 72," Rohmer protested, "I'm in my middle sixties."

In fact, he *was* 72, or just a month short of it when that news item appeared. Surely he couldn't think he was in his mid-sixties when his first stories had appeared in print in 1903 when he would otherwise have been only fourteen or so. Publicity stunt? Maybe, though he hardly needed it. Approaching senility? Unlikely, he remained hale and hearty until his death in 1959 at the age of 76 when he caught a virulent strain of the Asian flu which developed into pneumonia. The sheer pleasure in mystery and make-believe? Quite possibly. Rohmer—or rather Ward—was of Irish descent and delighted in a bit of the blarney.

Arthur Henry Ward, to give him the name with which he was christened, was born in Birmingham on 15 February 1883. His father, William, was of Irish descent, but his mother, Margaret, had been born in Ireland. Her maiden name was Furey, which Rohmer later used as one of his pen names. Rohmer hardly saw his father as a child because William, or Bill as he was always known, worked all hours as an engineering clerk. His absence caused Margaret to become depressed and she turned to the bottle—her own father had been an alcoholic—and the demon drink would soon kill her. She died in 1901 aged about 50.

Young Arthur did not attend school until he was nine and had apparently spent much time reading, as his mother, perhaps surprisingly, had quite a collection of books. His interest in the weird and fantastic was encouraged at an early age and he had even learned how to hypnotize people. This skill, or party trick, changed his career. His father was desperate that his only son have a good job, especially after his wife died, and he managed to secure Arthur a job as a bank clerk. It did not last long because Arthur told his boss that he knew a foolproof way to rob the bank. This involved hypnotizing one of his fellow clerks, but it all went horribly wrong and Arthur was asked to leave. He did not tell his father. Instead he hoped he might find some success as a writer but early attempts all failed. He tried to become a reporter, but that did not last long, either.

His mother's death resulted in two changes in Arthur's life. In some kind of homage to her, Arthur changed his middle name to Sarsfield because his mother believed she was descended from, or at least related to, the first Lord Lucan, Patrick Sarsfield, who had fought in Ireland under King James II and had become something of a local hero. Alas, Sarsfield had only one son, who died unmarried, so Rohmer's mother was unlikely to have been descended from him.

The other event was more significant. The family doctor who attended Rohmer's mother in her final days was Richard Watson Councell—a real Dr. Watson. He was a true student of the occult, with a significant library of esoteric books, and he and Arthur became friends. Arthur regularly consulted the library and it was the source of much of his knowledge of the *outré*, and proved especially useful when he came to compile his book *The Romance of Sorcery*, published in 1914. Councell was a Rosicrucian and therefore probably a Freemason, and it has been suggested that he may have introduced Arthur to the Order of the Golden Dawn, the hermetic society to which W. B. Yeats, Arthur Machen, Algernon Blackwood and Aleister Crowley belonged. However there is no record to suggest that Arthur was ever a member.

Unable to secure a steady job, Arthur tried his hand again at writing and in 1903 he struck lucky. He sent two stories to different magazines and both were accepted. The first, "The Mysterious Mummy", a less than inspiring story of a thief who hides in an Egyptian sarcophagus to steal from a museum, appeared in the Christmas edition of *Pearson's Weekly*, published on 26 November 1903. The second and more interesting tale, "The Leopard Couch" appeared in the rather more prestigious *Chambers's Journal* for January 1904. Both bore the byline A. Sarsfield Ward. "The Leopard Couch", in which the eponymous furniture transports its owner in a dream back to ancient Egypt, shows a more than cursory knowledge of Egyptian history.

These two stories may have started his career, but like a jumbo jet on a long runway, it was still some while before it took off. He attempted a novel but had to admit his knowledge of Egypt was still too limited and it was not until he visited Egypt in 1913 that he at last acquired a deeper understanding of the ancient civilization. Instead, seeking more income, Arthur turned his attention to the theatre and music hall. His gift for the blarney allowed him to write short monologues and songs for the stars of the day, and in this he proved rather successful. Quite how he found his way into this business, I do not know. He was already working on songs before he met his future wife, Elizabeth, who was from a music hall family. It was doubtless through her, or her more famous brother, Teddy Knox—one half of the stage act Nervo and Knox—that he came to know the more famous music hall stars, including George Robey and Little Tich. In 1908 Arthur missed out on an astonishing deal when he failed to take advantage of selling an old painting, which the owner felt might fetch something for the frame, but which later sold for £20,000 (over £3 million today). To vent his frustration Arthur wrote a comedy song, "Bang Went the Chance of a Lifetime", which he sold to George Robey and it became one of his most popular ditties. When the sheet music was published in May 1908 it was credited to Sax Rohmer—the first appearance of that name in print. Where did that come from?

Rohmer's widow, Elizabeth, was certain that when they first met in the summer of 1905, he had introduced himself as Sax Rohmer then, even though his published stories still appeared as by A. Sarsfield

Ward. Arthur had been a gallant hero, rescuing Elizabeth from a man giving her unwelcome advances on Clapham Common. When she first looked up at him she thought he was Sherlock Holmes and in his later publicity photographs Rohmer encouraged that similarity to Sidney Paget's illustrations of the Great Detective. If her recollection was correct, then he must have concocted that name before 1905.

Rohmer himself claimed that the name had come from Sax, or more accurately *seax*, the Anglo-Saxon word for a knife or blade, and 'roamer' (with an 'a') as the idea of a mercenary, or "freelance" blade-for-hire. Perhaps that had entered his thoughts, but it may have been provoked by an early adventure. In late 1904 or maybe early 1905, Arthur had sold a historical story to *Pearson's Magazine*, "The McVillin", a swashbuckler in the style of Alexandre Dumas. The editor of *Pearson's*, Percy Everett, saw the potential in the character and asked Arthur if he could produce a series of stories. Arthur soon found he could not write to order and not a single idea came to him. He panicked and thought he might get inspiration abroad, so he took a rather uncomfortable voyage on an eel-boat to Holland. No one seems to know what he did there. Neither Cay Van Ash nor Elizabeth ever knew. But there may be a clue in a story he wrote afterwards, "A Mission to Grünzburg", even though this did not appear until September 1908 as a two-part serial in *The Graphic* newspaper—still under the name A. Sarsfield Ward. Set at some uncertain period in the late Middle Ages it tells of a Scottish soldier sent to the Castle of Grünzburg to rescue the countess from the clutches of Count Hugo. If Arthur had travelled to Grünzburg, or more properly Günzburg in Bavaria, he would almost certainly have passed through the city of Frankfurt and, if so, he could not have missed seeing the magnificent old house of the ancient Saxon family of Römer. Maybe the name played on his mind, because in "A Mission to Grünzburg" he includes a character called Böhmer. Am I grasping at straws or did his visit to Holland and beyond lead him to the Saxon homes of the Römer family, and he felt a new name and maybe even a new personality emerge? When he rescued Elizabeth from the predator on Clapham Common he seemed so self-assured, no longer the indecisive, uncertain individual who was still struggling to earn a living. There is no doubt that from that time on, Rohmer's fortunes changed—supported by the new love of his life. They were married on 14 January 1909.

Rohmer was still selling songs and sketches as well as writing anonymous articles for *The Globe* newspaper, but he needed to increase his income. Soon after his marriage Rohmer was approached by the publisher Arthur Greening to act as editor and ghostwriter on a collection of essays and sketches by George Robey. The volume appeared in early 1910 under the title *Pause!* Rather oddly it was anonymous, even though Robey was so popular his name would have increased sales significantly. Amongst the miscellaneous pieces were two stories, both with ancient Egyptian connections, "Sebek-Ra" and "The Bronze Mirror", the latter very similar to "The Leopard Couch". It is uncertain whether these were written entirely by Rohmer or whether they were collaborations. Robey was also an enthusiast of Egyptology and had gifted Rohmer a copy of the Egyptian *Book of the Dead*. Either way, this is now a very rare and collectible volume.

It must have sold reasonably well because soon after Greening asked Rohmer if he would help Little Tich write his autobiography. The diminutive Little Tich, or Harry Relph to give him his real name, was a variety act known for his sharp wit, amusing anecdotes and ridiculous shoes, and this book is very much in his style, so how much Rohmer wrote is uncertain. Even the chapter on "My Impression of the Great Pyramid" may have been suggested by Rohmer but has all the hallmarks of Tich's humour. When the book appeared in 1911 there was no credit to Rohmer. Even worse, Greening's went bust and neither Rohmer nor Tich were paid, so although he was being published, neither of these books added to his reputation or bank balance.

But that was soon to change. Rohmer and Greening had become friends and when Rohmer showed him the manuscript of a series of stories he was planning, Greening put him in touch with Newman Flower, the senior magazine editor at the publisher Cassell. Flower was interested and Rohmer sent him the series which began in the June 1912 issue of *Cassell's Magazine* under the Rohmer byline. This series about a Jewish entrepreneur who used various schemes to encourage his rich acquaintances to contribute to the public good, proved popular and formed the book *The Sins of Severac Bablon*, which Cassell published in 1914, by which time Rohmer had become a household name.

Flower wanted to see Rohmer's next series which had arisen from Rohmer's exploits in the Limehouse area of London's docklands, when he was researching for a news story about a crime ring run by a devious mastermind. This became Dr. Fu-Manchu, and the first story began in Cassell's other leading magazine *The Story-teller* in October 1912. It ran through to the June 1913 issue and barely had the last episode appeared than they were rushed into print in book form as *The Mystery of Dr. Fu-Manchu*. The book was an immediate hit and went through a second printing a month later.

As if this wasn't enough of a success, Flower had enticed a different series out of Rohmer featuring his psychic detective Moris Klaw and that began in the April 1913 issue of Cassell's third sister periodical *The New Magazine*. Rohmer was at last earning decent money and he and Elizabeth packed their bags and headed off on a long overdue honeymoon—to Egypt! Although Elizabeth didn't particularly enjoy the country, crawling in one of her best dresses through tunnels in one of the oldest pyramids (she was, in fact, the first woman to ever enter that pyramid)—Rohmer was in his element, soaking up the atmosphere, the history, the culture and the deeper mysteries. His imagination was fired and upon his return he poured his inspiration into the novel *The Brood of the Witch-Queen* which was serialized in Amalgamated Press's new *Premier Magazine* from the opening issue in May 1914.

From here on Rohmer was in constant demand by both Cassell and Amalgamated Press whilst *Pearson's*, who had published some of his first stories, tracked him down for their magazine *The Novel*. Over the next few years, and certainly throughout the First World War, barely a month passed without one or more of the popular magazines boasted his name on the cover, or a new book appeared. He even recounted his and Elizabeth's adventures in Egypt for a series in *Lloyd's Magazine* in 1917 called "Phryné in Pharaoh-Land"—Phryné being one of his pet names for his ever-patient wife.

It was during these inspirational fertile years, between 1913 and 1918, that the stories in this volume appeared in magazines. The series about Abû Tabâh, another mysterious mastermind with supernatural powers, draws directly upon his honeymoon in Egypt, especially the story "The Death-Ring of Sneferu" which uses direct personal experiences. Curiously, the name Abû Tabâh—or in this case Aboo Tabah—had been used by Rohmer as far back as 1909, in a music hall song set in Turkey! Some stories in *Low Fennel* also feature an Egyptian locale whilst others range from England to Burma. Rohmer, fired by the exotic wonder of Egypt, was now writing at the peak of his form, supported by his devoted wife, and helped by the library of his doctor friend Richard Councell—Rohmer would later write an introduction to Councell's rare alchemical volume *Apologia Alchymiae*, published in 1925.

You can sense that inspiration throughout the stories, which were written at a white-hot pace and an exuberance which becomes infectious. Although it was Dr. Fu-Manchu who made Rohmer's reputation it was his entire output that cemented his fame around the world, and it has barely dimmed over a century later. Here are the stories inspired by the power of Egyptian magic.

—March 2024

THE HAUNTING OF LOW FENNEL

— — —

SAX ROHMER

THE HAUNTING OF LOW FENNEL

I

"There's Low Fennel," said Major Dale.

We pulled up short on the brow of the hill. Before me lay a little valley carpeted with heather, purple slopes hemming it in. A group of four tall firs guarded the house, which was couched in the hollow of the dip—a low, rambling building, in parts showing evidence of great age and in other parts of the modern improver.

"That's the new wing," continued the Major, raising his stick; "projecting out this way. It's the only addition I've made to the house, which, as it stood, had insufficient accommodation for the servants."

"It is a quaint old place."

"It is, and I'm loath to part with it, especially as it means a big loss."

"Ah! Have you formed any theories since wiring me?"

"None whatever. I've always been a sceptic, Addison, but if Low Fennel is not haunted, I'm a Dutchman, by the Lord Harry!"

I laughed reassuringly, and the two of us descended the slope to the white gate giving access to a trim gravel path flanked by standard roses. Mrs. Dale greeted us at the door. She was, as I had heard, much younger than the Major, and a distinctly pretty woman. In so far Dame Rumour was confirmed; other things I had heard of her, but I was not yet in a position to pass judgment.

She greeted me cordially enough, although women are usually natural actresses. I thought that she did not suspect the real object of my visit. Tea was served in a delightful little drawing-room which bore evidence of having but recently left the hands of London decorators, but when presently I found myself alone with my host in the Major's peculiar sanctum, the real business afoot monopolised our conversation.

The room which Major Dale had appropriated as a study was on the ground floor of the new wing—the wing which he himself had had built on to Low Fennel. In regard to its outlook it was a charming apartment enough, with roses growing right up to the open window, so that their perfume filled the place, and beyond, a prospect of purple heather slopes and fir-clad hills.

Sporting prints decorated the walls, and the library was entirely, or almost entirely, made up of works on riding, hunting, shooting, racing, and golf, with a sprinkling of Whyte-Melville and Nat Gould novels and a Murray handbook or two. It was a most cosy room, probably because it was so untidy, or, as Mrs. Dale phrased it, "so manny."

On a side table was ranked enough liquid refreshment to have inebriated a regiment, and, in one corner, cigar-boxes and tobacco-tins were stacked from the floor some two feet up against the wall. We were soon comfortably ensconced, then, the Major on a hard leather couch, and I in a deep saddle-bag chair.

"It's an awkward sort of thing to explain," began Dale, puffing away at a cigar and staring through the open window; "because, if you're to do anything, you will want full particulars."

I nodded.

"Well," the Major continued, "you've heard how that blackguard Ellis let me down over those shares? The result?—I had to sell the Hall—Fennel Hall, where a Dale has been since the time of Elizabeth! But still, never mind! that's not the story. This place, Low Fennel, is really part of the estate, and I have leased it from Meyers, who has bought the Hall. It was formerly the home farm, but since my father's time it has not been used for that purpose. The New Farm is over the brow of the hill there, on the other side of the high road; my father built it."

"Why?"

"Well,"—Dale shifted uneasily and a look of perplexity crossed his jolly, red face—"there were stories—uncomfortable stories. To cut a long story short, Seager—a man named Seager, who occupied it at the time I was at Sandhurst—was found dead here, or something; I never was clear as to the particulars, but there was an inquiry and a lot of fuss, and, in short, no one would occupy the property. Therefore the governor built the New Farm."

"Low Fennel has been empty for many years then?"

"No, sir; only for one. Ord, the head gardener at the Hall, lived here up till last September. The old story about Seager was dying out, you see; but Ord must have got to hear about it—or I've always supposed so. At any rate, in September—a dam' hot September, too, almost if not quite as hot as this—Ord declined to live here any longer."

"On what grounds?"

"He told me a cock-and-bull story about his wife having seen a horrible-looking man with a contorted face peering in at her bedroom window! I questioned the woman, of course, and she swore to it."

He mopped his heated brow excitedly, and burnt several matches before he succeeded in relighting his cigar.

"She tried to make me believe that she woke up and saw this apparition, but I bullied the truth out of her, and, as I expected, the man Ord had come home the worse for drink. I made up my mind that the contorted face was the face of her drunken husband—whom she had declined to admit, and who therefore had climbed the ivy to get in at the open window."

"She denied this?"

"Of course she denied it; they both did; but, from evidence obtained at the *Three Keys* in the village, I proved that Ord had returned home drunk that night. Still"—he shrugged his shoulders ponderously— "the people declined to remain in the place, so what could I do? Ord was a good gardener, and his drunken habits in no way interfered with his efficiency. He gained nothing out of the matter except that, instead of keeping Low Fennel, a fine house, I sent him to live in one of the Valley Cottages. He lives there now, for he's still head gardener at the Hall."

I made an entry in my notebook.

"I must see Ord," I said.

"I should," agreed the Major in his loud voice; "you'll get nothing out of him. He's the most pig-headed liar in the county! But to continue. The place proved unlettable. All the old stories were revived, and I'm told that people cheerfully went two miles out of their way in order to avoid passing Low Fennel at night! When I sold the Hall and decided to lease the place from the new proprietor, believe me it was almost hidden in a wilderness of weeds and bushes which had grown up around it. By the Lord Harry, I don't think a living soul had approached within a hundred yards of the house since the day that the Ords quitted it! But it suited my purpose, being inexpensive to keep up; and by adding this new wing I was enabled to accommodate such servants as we required. The horses and the car had to go, of course, and with them a lot of my old people, but we brought the housekeeper and three servants, and when a London firm had rebuilt, renovated, decorated, and so forth, it began to look habitable."

"It's a charming place," I said with sincerity.

"Is it!" snapped the Major, tossing his half-smoked cigar on to a side table and selecting a fresh one from a large box at his elbow. "Help yourself, the bottle's near you. Is it!... Hullo! what have we here?"

He broke off, cigar in hand, as the sound of footsteps upon the gravel path immediately outside the window became audible. Through the cluster of roses peered a handsome face, that of a dark man, whose soft-grey hat and loose tie lent him a sort of artistic appearance.

"Oh, it's you, Wales!" cried the Major, but without cordiality. "See you in half an hour or so; little bit of business in hand at the moment, Marjorie's somewhere about."

"All right!" called the new arrival, and, waving his hand, passed on.

"It's young Aubrey Wales," explained Dale, almost savagely biting the end from his cigar, "son of Sir Frederick Wales, and one of my neighbours. He often drops in."

Mentally considering the Major's attitude, certain rumours which had reached me, and the youth and beauty of Mrs. Dale, I concluded that the visits of Aubrey Wales were not too welcome to my old friend. But he resumed in a louder voice than ever:—

"It was last night that the fun began. I can make neither head nor tail of it. If the blessed place is haunted, why have we seen nothing of the ghost during the two months or so we have lived at Low Fennel? The fact remains that nothing unusual happened until last night. It came about owing to the infernal heat.

"Mrs. Alson, the housekeeper, came down about two o'clock, intending, so I understand, to get a glass of cider from the barrel in the cellar. She could not sleep owing to the heat, and felt extremely thirsty. There's a queer sort of bend in the stair—I'll show you in a minute; and as she came down and reached this bend she met a man, or a thing, who was going up! The moonlight was streaming in through the window right upon that corner of the stair, and the apparition stood fully revealed.

"I gather that it was that of an almost naked man. Mrs. Alson naturally is rather reticent on the point, but I gather that the apparition was inadequately clothed. Regarding the face of the thing she supplies more details. Addison"—the Major leant forward across the table—"it was the face of a demon, a contorted devilish face, the eyes crossed, and glaring like the eyes of a mad dog!

"Of course the poor woman fainted dead away on the spot. She might have died there if it hadn't been for the amazing heat of the night. This certainly was the cause of her trouble, but it also saved her. About three o'clock I woke up in a perfect bath of perspiration. I never remember such a night, not even in India, and, as Mrs. Alson had done an hour earlier, I also started to find a drink. Addison! I nearly fell over her as she lay swooning on the stair!"

He helped himself to a liberal tot of whisky, then squirted soda into the glass.

"For once in a way I did the right thing, Addison. Not wishing to alarm Marjorie, I knocked up one of the maids, and when Mrs. Alson had somewhat recovered, gave her into the girl's charge. I sat downstairs here in this room until she could see me, and then got the particulars which I've given you. I wired you as soon as the office was open; for I said to myself, 'Dale, the devilry has begun again. If Marjorie gets to hear of it there'll be hell to pay. She won't live in the place.'"

He stood up abruptly, as a ripple of laughter reached us from the garden.

"Suppose we explore the scene of the trouble?" he suggested, moving toward the door.

I thought in the circumstance our inspection might be a hurried one; therefore:

"Should you mind very much if I sought it out for myself?" I said. "It is my custom in cases of the kind to be alone if possible."

"My dear fellow, certainly!"

"My ramble concluded, I will rejoin Mrs. Dale and yourself—say on the lawn?"

"Good, good!" cried the Major, throwing open the door. "An opening has been made on the floor above corresponding with this, and communicating with the old stair. Go where you like; find out what you can; but remember—not a word to Marjorie."

II

Filled with the liveliest curiosity, I set out to explore Low Fennel. First I directed my attention to the exterior, commencing my investigations from the front. That part of the building on either side of the door was evidently of Tudor date, with a Jacobean wing to the west containing apartments overlooking the lawn—the latter a Georgian addition; whilst the new east wing, built by Major Dale, carried the building out almost level with the clump of fir-trees, and into the very heart of the ferns and bushes which here grew densely.

There was no way around on this side, and not desiring to cross the lawn at present, I passed in through the house to the garden at the back. This led me through the northern part of the building and the servants' quarters, which appeared to be of even greater age than the front of the house. The fine old kitchen in particular was suggestive of the days when roasting was done upon a grand scale.

Beyond the flower garden lay the kitchen garden, and beyond that the orchard. The latter showed evidences of neglect, bearing out the Major's story that the place had been unoccupied for twelve months; but it was evident, nevertheless, that the soil had been cultivated for many generations. Thus far I had discovered nothing calculated to assist me in my peculiar investigation, and entering the house I began a room-to-room quest, which, beyond confirming most of my earlier impressions, afforded little data.

The tortuous stairway, which had been the scene of the event described by my host, occupied me for some time, and I carefully examined the time-blackened panels, and tested each separate stair, for in houses like Low Fennel secret passages and "priest-holes" were to be looked for. However, I discovered nothing, but descending again to the hall I made a small discovery.

There were rooms in Low Fennel which one entered by descending or ascending two or three steps, but this was entirely characteristic of the architectural methods of the period represented. I was surprised, however, to find that one mounted three steps in order to obtain access to the passage leading to the new wing. I had overlooked this peculiarity hitherto, but now it struck me as worthy of attention. Why should a modern architect introduce such a device? It could only mean that the ground was higher on the east side of the building, and that, for some reason, it had proved more convenient to adopt the existing foundations than to level the site.

I returned to the hall-way and stood there deep in thought, when the contact of a rough tongue with my hand drew my attention to a young Airedale terrier who was anxious to make my acquaintance. I patted his head encouragingly, and, having reviewed the notes made during my tour of inspection, determined to repeat the tour in order to check them.

The Airedale accompanied me, behaving himself with admirable propriety as we passed around the house and then out through the kitchens into the garden. It was not until my journey led me back to the three steps, communicating with the new wing, that my companion seemed disposed to desert me.

At first I ascribed his attitude to mere canine caprice. But when he persistently refused to be encouraged, I began to ascribe it to something else.

Suddenly grasping him by the collar, I dragged him up the steps, along the corridor, and into the Major's study. The result was extraordinary. I think I have never seen a dog in quite the same condition; he whimpered and whined most piteously. At the door he struggled furiously, and even tried to snap at my hand. Then, as I still kept a firm grip upon him, he set out upon a series of howls which must have been audible for miles around. Finally I released him, having first closed the study door, and lowered the window. What followed was really amazing.

The Airedale hurled himself upon the closed door, scratching at it furiously, with intermittent howling; then, crouching down, he turned his eyes upon me with a look in them, not savage, but truly piteous. Seeing that I did not move, the dog began to whimper again; when, suddenly making up his mind, as it seemed, he bounded across the room and went crashing through the glass of the closed window into the rose bushes, leaving me standing looking after him in blank wonderment.

III

Aubrey Wales stayed to dinner, and since he had no opportunity of dressing, his presence afforded a welcome excuse for the other members of the party. The night was appallingly hot; the temperature being such as to preclude the slightest exertion. The Major was an excellent host, but I could see that the presence of the younger man irritated him, and at times the conversation grew strained; there was an uncomfortable tension. So that altogether I was not sorry when Mrs. Dale left the table and the quartet was broken up. On closer acquaintance I perceived that Wales was even younger than I had supposed, and therefore I was the more inclined to condone his infatuation for the society of Mrs. Dale, although I felt less sympathetically disposed toward her for offering him the encouragement which rather openly she did.

Ere long, Wales left Major Dale and myself for the more congenial society of the hostess; so that shortly afterwards, when the Major, who took at least as much wine as was good for him, began to doze in his chair, I found myself left to my own devices. I quitted the room quietly, without disturbing my host, and strolled around on to the lawn smoking a cigarette, and turning over in my mind the matters responsible for my presence at Low Fennel.

With no definite object in view, I had wandered towards the orchard, when I became aware of a whispered conversation taking place somewhere near me, punctuated with little peals of laughter. I detected the words "Aubrey" and "Marjorie" (Mrs. Dale's name), and, impatiently tossing my cigarette away, I returned to the house, intent upon arousing the Major and terminating this tête-à-tête. That it was more, on Mrs. Dale's part, than a harmless flirtation, I did not believe; but young Wales was not a safe type of man for that sort of amusement.

The Major, sunk deep in his favourite chair in the study, was snoring loudly, and as I stood contemplating him in the dusk, I changed my mind, and retracing my steps, joined the two in the orchard, proclaiming my arrival by humming a popular melody.

"Has he fallen asleep?" asked Mrs. Dale, turning laughing eyes upon me.

I studied the piquant face ere replying. Her tone and her expression had reassured me, if further assurance were necessary, that my old friend's heart was in safe keeping; but she was young and gay; it was a case for diplomatic handling.

"India leaves its mark on all men," I replied lightly; "but I have no doubt that the Major is wide-awake enough now."

My words were an invitation; to which, I was glad to note, she responded readily enough.

"Let's come and dig him out of that cavern of his!" she said, and linking her right arm in that of Wales, and her left with mine, she turned us about toward the house.

Dusk was now fallen, and lights shone out from several windows of Low Fennel. Suddenly, an upper window became illuminated, and Mrs. Dale pointed to this.

"That is my room," she said to me; "isn't it delightfully situated? The view from the window is glorious."

"I consider Low Fennel charming in every way," I replied.

Clearly she knew nothing of the place's sinister reputation, which seemed to indicate that she employed herself little with the domestic side of the household; otherwise she must undoubtedly have learnt of the episode of the man with the contorted face, if not from the housekeeper, from the maid. It was a tribute to the reticence of the servants that the story had spread no further; but the broken study window and the sadly damaged Airedale already afforded matter for whispered debate among them, as I had noted with displeasure.

The "digging out" of the Major did not prove to be an entire success. He was in one of his peculiar moods, which I knew of old, and rather surly, being pointedly rude on more than one occasion to Wales. He had some accounts to look into, or professed to have, and the three of us presently left him alone. It was now about ten o'clock, and Aubrey Wales made his departure, shaking me warmly by the hand and expressing the hope that we should see more of one another. He could not foresee that the wish was to be realised in a curious fashion.

Mrs. Dale informed me that the Major in all probability would remain immured in his study until a late hour, which I took to be an intimation that she wished to retire. I therefore pleaded weariness as a result of my journey, and went up to my room, although I had no intention of turning-in. I opened the two windows widely, and the heavy perfume of some kind of tobacco plant growing in the beds below grew almost oppressive. The heat of the night was truly phenomenal; I might have been, not in an English home county, but in the Soudan. An absolute stillness reigned throughout Low Fennel, and, my hearing being peculiarly acute, I could detect the chirping of the bats which flitted restlessly past my windows.

It was difficult to decide how to act. My experience of so-called supernatural appearances had strengthened my faith in the theory set forth in the paper "Chemistry of Psychic Phenomena"—which had attracted unexpected attention a year before. Therein I classified hauntings under several heads, basing my conclusions upon the fact that such apparitions are invariably localised; often being confined, not merely to a particular room, for instance, but to a certain wall, door, or window. I had been privileged to visit most of the famous haunted homes of Great Britain, and this paper was the result; but in the case of Low Fennel I found myself nonplussed, largely owing to lack of data. I hoped on the morrow to make certain inquiries along lines suggested by oddities in the structure of the house itself and by the nature of the little valley in which it stood.

When meditating I never sit still, and whilst marshalling my ideas I paced the room from end to end, smoking the whole time. Both windows and also the door, were widely opened. The amazing heat-wave which we were then experiencing promised to afford me a valuable clue, for I had proved to my own satisfaction that the apparitions variously known as "controls" and "elementals," not infrequently coincided with abrupt climatic changes, thunder-storms, or heat waves, or with natural phenomena, such as landslides and the like.

This pacing led me from end to end of the room, then, between the open door and the large dressing-table facing it. It was as I returned from the door towards the dressing-table that I became aware of the presence of the *contorted face*.

My peculiar studies had brought me into contact with many horrible apparitions, and if familiarity had failed to breed contempt, at least it had served to train my nerves for the reception of such sudden and ghastly appearances. I should be avoiding the truth, however, if I claimed to have been unmoved by the vision which now met me in the mirror. I drew up short, with one sibilant breath, and then stood transfixed.

Before me was a reflection of the open door, and of part of the landing and stairs beyond it. The landing lights were extinguished, and therefore the place beyond the door lay in comparative darkness. But, crawling in, serpent-fashion, inch by inch, silently, intently, so that the head, throat, and hands were actually across the threshold, came a creature which seemed to be entirely naked! It had the form of a man, but the face, the dreadful face which was being pushed forward slowly across the carpet with head held sideways so that one ear all but touched the floor, was the face, not of a man, but of a ghoul!

I clenched my teeth hard, staring into the mirror and trying to force myself to turn and confront, not the reflection, but the reality. Yet for many seconds I was unable to accomplish this. The baleful, protruding eyes glared straight into mine from the glass. The chin and lower lip of this awful face seemed to be drawn up so as almost to meet the nose, entirely covering the upper lip, and the nostrils were distended to an incredible degree, whilst the skin had a sort of purple tinge unlike anything I had seen before. The effect was grotesque in the true sense of the word; for the thing was clearly grimacing at me, yet God knows there was nothing humorous in that grimace!

Nearer it came and nearer. I could hear the heavy body being drawn across the floor; I could hear the beating of my own heart ... and I could hear a whispered conversation which seemed to be taking place somewhere immediately outside my room.

At the moment that I detected the latter sound, it seemed that the apparition detected it also. The protruding eyes twisted in the head, rolling around ridiculously but horribly. Despite the dread which held me, I identified the whisperers and located their situation. Mrs. Dale was at her open window and Aubrey Wales was in the garden below.

The thought crossed my mind and was gone—but gone no quicker than the contorted face. By a sort of backward, serpentine movement, the thing which had been crawling into my room suddenly retired and was swallowed up in the shadows of the landing.

I turned and sprang toward the open door, the fever of research hot upon me, and my nerves in hand again. At the door I paused and listened intently. No sound came to guide me from the darkened stair, and when, stepping quietly forward and leaning over the rail, I peered down into the hall below, nothing stirred, no shadow of the many there moved to tell of the passage of any living thing. I paused irresolute, unable to doubt that I was in the presence of an authentic apparition. But how to classify it?

Slowly I returned to my room, and stood there, thinking hard, and all the while listening for the slightest sound from within or without the house.

The whispered conversation continued, and I stole quietly to one of the windows and leant out, looking to the left, in the direction of the new wing. A light burnt in the Major's study, whereby I concluded that he was still engaged with his accounts, if he had not fallen asleep. Between my window and the new wing, and on a level with my eyes, was the window of Mrs. Dale's room; and in the bright moonlight I could see her leaning out, her elbows on the ledge. Her bare arms gleamed like marble in the cold light, and she looked statuesquely beautiful. Wales I could not see, for a thick, square-clipped hedge obstructed my view ... but I saw something else.

Lizard fashion, a hideous unclad shape crawled past beneath me amongst the tangle of ivy and low plants about the foot of the fir trees. The moonlight touched it for a moment, and then it was gone into denser shadows....

A consciousness of impending disaster came to me, but, because of its very vagueness, found me unprepared. Then suddenly I saw young Wales. He sprang into view above the hedge, against which, I presume, he had been crouching; he leapt high in the air as though from some menace on the ground beneath him. I have never heard a more horrifying scream than that which he uttered.

"My God!" he cried, "Marjorie! Marjorie!" and yet again: "Marjorie! *save me!*"

Then he was down, still screaming horribly, and calling on the woman for aid—as though she could have aided him. The crawling thing made no sound, but the dreadful screams of Wales sank slowly into a sort of sobbing, and then into a significant panting which told of his dire extremity.

I raced out of the room, and down the dark stair into the hall. Everywhere I was met by locked doors which baffled me. I had hoped to reach the garden by way of the kitchens, but now I changed my plan and turned my attention to the front-door. It was bolted, but I drew the bolts one after the other, and got the door open.

Outside, the landscape was bathed in glorious moonlight, and a sort of grey mist hovered over the valley like smoke. I ran around the angle of the house on to the lawn, and went plunging through flower-beds heedlessly to the scene of the incredible conflict.

I almost fell over Wales as he lay inert upon the gravel path. The shadows veiled him so that I could not see his face; but when, groping with my hands, I sought to learn if his heart still pulsed, I failed to discover any evidence that it did. With my hand thrust against his breast and my ear lowered anxiously, I listened, but he gave no sign of life, lying as still as all else around me.

Now this stillness was broken. Excited voices became audible, and doors were being unlocked here and there. First of all the household, Mrs. Dale appeared, enveloped in a lace dressing-gown.

"Aubrey!" she cried tremulously, "what is it? where are you?"

"He is here, Mrs. Dale," I answered, standing up, "and in a bad way, I fear."

"For Heaven's sake, what has happened to him? Did you hear his awful cries?"

"I did," I said shortly.

Standing with the moonlight fully upon her, Mrs. Dale sought him in the shadows of the hedge—and I knew that by the manner of his frightened outcry the man lying unconscious at my feet had forfeited whatever of her regard he had enjoyed. She was dreadfully alarmed, not so much on his behalf, as by the mystery of the attack upon him. But now she composed herself, though not without visible effort.

"Where is he, Mr. Addison?" she said firmly, "and what has happened to him?"

A man, who proved to be a gardener, now appeared upon the scene.

"Help me to carry him in," I said to this new arrival; "perhaps he has only fainted."

We gathered up the recumbent body and carried it through the kitchens into the breakfast-room, where there was a deep couch. All the servants were gathered at the foot of the stairs, frightened and useless, but the outcry did not seem to have aroused Major Dale.

Mrs. Dale and I bent over Wales. His face was frightfully congested, whilst his tongue protruded hideously; and it was evident, from the great discoloured weals which now were coming up upon his throat, that he had been strangled, or nearly so. I glanced at the white face of my hostess and then bent over the victim, examining him more carefully. I stood upright again.

"Do you know first aid, Mrs. Dale?" I asked abruptly.

She nodded, her eyes fixed intently upon me.

"Then help to employ artificial respiration," I said, "and let one of the girls get ammonia, if you have any, and a bowl of hot water. We can patch him up, I think, without medical aid—which might be undesirable."

Mrs. Dale seemed fully to appreciate the point, and in business-like fashion set to work to assist me. Wales had just opened his eyes and begun to clutch at his agonized throat, when I heard a heavy step descending from the new wing—and Major Dale, in his dressing-gown, joined us. His red face was more red than usual, and his eyes were round with wonder.

"What the devil's the matter?" he cried; "what's everybody up for?"

"There has been an accident, Major," I said, glancing around at the servants, who stood in a group by the door of the breakfast-room; "I can explain more fully later."

Major Dale stepped forward and looked down at Wales.

"Good God!" he said hoarsely, "it's young Wales, by the Lord Harry!— what's he doing here?"

Mrs. Dale, standing just behind me, laid her hand upon my arm; and, unseen by the Major, I turned and pressed it reassuringly.

IV

The following day I lunched alone with the Major, Mrs. Dale being absent on a visit. It had been impossible to keep the truth from her (or what we knew of it) and at present I could not quite foresee the issue of last night's affair. Young Wales, who had been driven home in a car sent from his place at a late hour, had not since put in an appearance; and it was sufficiently evident that Mrs. Dale would not welcome him should he do so, the hysterical panic which he had exhibited on the previous night having disgusted her. She had not said so in as many words, but I did not doubt it.

"Well, Addison?" said the Major as I entered, "have you got the facts you were looking for?"

"Some of them," I replied, and opening my notebook I turned to the pages containing notes made that morning.

The Major watched me with intense curiosity, and almost impatiently awaited my next words. The servant having left the room:

"In the first place," I began, glancing at the notes, "I have been consulting certain local records in the town, and I find that in the year 1646 a certain Dame Pryce occupied a cabin which, according to one record, 'stood close beside unto ye Lowe Fennel.'"

"That is, close beside this house?" interjected the Major excitedly.

"Exactly," I said. "She attracted the attention of one of the many infamous wretches who disfigure the history of that period: Matthew Hopkins, the self-styled Witch-Finder General. This was a witch-ridden age, and the man Hopkins was one of those who fattened on the credulity of his fellows, receiving a fee of twenty shillings for every unhappy woman discovered and convicted of witchcraft. Poor Pryce was 'swum' in a local pond (a test whereby the villain Hopkins professed to discover if the woman were one of Satan's band, or otherwise) and burnt alive in Reigate market-place on September 23, 1646."

"By God!" said the Major, who had not attempted to commence his lunch, "that's a horrible story!"

"It is one of the many to the credit of Matthew Hopkins," I replied; "but, without boring you with the details of this woman's examination and so forth, I may say that what interests me most in the case is the date—September 23."

"Why? I don't follow you."

"Well," I said, "there's a hiatus in the history of the place after that, except that even in those early days it evidently suffered from the reputation of being haunted; but without troubling about the interval, consider the case of Seager, which you yourself related to me. Was it not in the month of August that he was done to death here?"

"By Gad!" cried the Major, his face growing redder than ever, "you're right!—and hang it all, Addison! it was in September—last September—that the Ords cleared out!"

"I remember your mentioning," I continued, smiling at his excitement, "that it was a very hot month?"

"It was."

"From a mere word dropped by one of the witnesses at the trial of poor Pryce I have gathered that the month in which she was convicted of practising witchcraft in her cabin adjoining Low Fennel (as it stood in those days) was a tropically hot month also."

Major Dale stared at me uncomprehendingly.

"I'm out of my depth, Addison—wading hopelessly. What the devil has the heat to do with the haunting?"

"To my mind everything. I may be wrong, but I think that if the glass were to fall to-night, there would be no repetition of the trouble."

"You mean that it's only in very hot weather—"

"In phenomenally hot weather, Major—the sort that we only get in England perhaps once in every ten years. For the glass to reach the altitude at which it stands at present, in two successive summers, is quite phenomenal, as you know."

"It's phenomenal for it to reach that point at all," said the Major, mopping his perspiring forehead; "it's simply Indian, simply Indian, sir, by the Lord Harry!"

"Another inquiry," I continued, turning over a leaf of my book, "I have been unable to complete, since, in order to interview the people who built your new wing, I should have to run up to London."

"What the blazes have they to do with it?"

"Nothing at all, but I should have liked to learn their reasons for raising the wing three feet above the level of the hall-way."

Between the heat and his growing excitement, Major Dale found himself at a temporary loss for words. Then:

"They told me," he shouted at the top of his voice, "they told me at the time that it was something about—that it was due to the plan—that it was—"

"I can imagine that they had some ready explanation," I said, "but it may not have been the true one."

"Then what the—what the—is the true one?"

"The true one is that the new wing covers a former mound."

"Quite right; it does."

"If my theory is correct, it was upon this mound that the cabin of

Dame Pryce formerly stood."

"It's quite possible; they used to allow dirty hovels to be erected alongside one's very walls in those days—quite possible."

"Moreover, from what I've learnt from Ord—whom I interviewed at the Hall—and from such accounts as are obtainable of the death of Seager, this mound, and not the interior of Low Fennel as it then stood, was the scene of the apparitions."

"You've got me out of my depth again, Addison. What d'you mean?"

"Seager was strangled outside the house, not inside."

"I believe that's true," agreed the Major, still shouting at the top of his voice, but gradually growing hoarser; "I remember they found him lying on the step, or something."

"Then again, the apparition with the contorted face which peered in at Mrs. Ord——"

"Lies, all lies!"

"I don't agree with you, Major. She was trying to shield her husband, but I think she saw the contorted face right enough. At any rate it's interesting to note that the visitant came from outside the house again."

"But," cried the Major, banging his fist upon the table, "it wanders about inside the house, and—and—damn it all!—it goes outside as well!"

"Where it goes," I interrupted quietly, "is not the point. The point is, where it comes from."

"Then where do you believe it comes from?"

"I believe the trouble arises, in the strictest sense of the word, from the same spot whence it arose in the days of Matthew Hopkins, and from which it had probably arisen ages before Low Fennel was built."

"What the—"

"I believe it to arise from the ancient barrow, or tumulus, above which you have had your new wing erected."

Major Dale fell back in his chair, temporarily speechless, but breathing noisily; then:

"Tumulus!" he said hoarsely; "d'you mean to tell me the house is built on a dam' burial ground?"

"Not the whole house," I corrected him; "only the new wing."

"Then is the place haunted by the spirit of some uneasy Ancient Briton or something of that sort, Addison? Hang it all! you can't tell me a fairy tale like that! A ghost going back to pre-Roman days is a bit too ancient for me, my boy—too hoary, by the Lord Harry!"

"I have said nothing about an Ancient British ghost—you're flying off at a tangent!"

"Hang it all, Addison! I don't know what you're talking about at all, but nevertheless your hints are sufficiently unpleasant. A tumulus! No man likes to know he's sleeping in a graveyard, not even if it is two or three thousand years old. D'you think the chap who surveyed the ground for me knew of it?"

"By the fact that he planned the new wing so as to avoid excavation, I think probably he did. He was wise enough to surmise that the order might be cancelled altogether and the job lost if you learnt the history of the mound adjoining your walls."

"A barrow under the study floor!" groaned the Major—"damn it all! I'll have the place pulled down—I won't live in it. Gad! if Marjorie knew, she would never close her eyes under the roof of Low Fennel again—I'm sure she wouldn't, I know she wouldn't. But what's more, Addison, the thing, whatever it is, is dangerous—infernally dangerous. It nearly killed young Wales!" he added, with a complacency which was significant.

"It was the fright that nearly killed him," I said shortly.

Major Dale stared across the table at me.

"For God's sake, Addison," he said, "what does it mean? What unholy thing haunts Low Fennel? You've studied these beastly subjects, and I rely upon you to make the place clean and good to live in again."

"Major," I replied, "I doubt if Low Fennel will ever be fit to live in. At any time an abnormal rise of temperature might produce the most dreadful results."

"You don't mean to tell me——"

"If you care to have the new wing pulled down and the wall bricked up again, if you care to keep all your doors and windows fastened securely whenever the thermometer begins to exhibit signs of rising, if you avoid going out on hot nights after dusk, as you would avoid the plague—yes, it may be possible to live in Low Fennel."

Again the Major became speechless, but finally:

"What d'you mean, Addison?" he whispered; "for God's sake, tell me. What is it?—what is it?"

"It is what some students have labelled an 'elemental' and some a 'control,'" I replied; "it is something older than the house, older, perhaps, than the very hills, something which may never be classified, something as old as the root of all evil, and it dwells in the Ancient British tumulus."

V

As I had hoped, for my plans were dependent upon it, the mercury towered steadily throughout that day, and showed no signs of falling at night; the phenomenal heat-wave continued uninterruptedly. The household was late retiring, for the grey lord—Fear—had imposed his will upon all within it. Every shadow in the rambling old building became a cavern of horrors, every sound that disturbed the ancient timbers a portent and a warning.

That the servants proposed to leave *en masse* at the earliest possible moment was perfectly evident to me; in a word, all the dark old stories which had grown up around Low Fennel were revived and garnished, and new ones added to them. The horror of the night before had left its mark upon every one, and the coming of dusk brought with it such a dread as could almost be felt in the very atmosphere of the place. Ghostly figures seemed to stir the hangings, ghostly sighs to sound from every nook of the old hall and stairway; baleful eyes looked in at the open windows, and the shrubberies were peopled with hosts of nameless things who whispered together in evil counsel.

Mrs. Dale was as loath to retire as were the servants, more especially since the Major and I were unable to disguise from her our intention of watching for the strange visitant that night. But finally we prevailed upon her to depart, and she ran upstairs as though the legions of the lost pursued her, slamming and locking her door so that the sound echoed all over the house.

We had told her nothing, of course, of my discoveries and theories, but nevertheless the cat was out of the bag; the affair of the night before had spoilt our scheme of secrecy.

In the Major's study we made our preparations. The windows were widely opened, and the door was ajar. Not a breath of wind disturbed the stillness of the night, and although Major Dale had agreed to act exactly as I might direct, he stared in almost comic surprise when he learnt the nature of these directions.

Placing two large silk handkerchiefs upon the table, I saturated them with the contents of a bottle which I had brought in my pocket, and handed one of the handkerchiefs to him.

"Tie that over your mouth and nostrils," I said, "and whatever happens don't remove it unless I tell you."

"But, Addison...."

"You know the compact, Major? If you aren't prepared to assist I must ask you to retire. To-night might be the last chance, perhaps, for years."

Growling beneath his breath, Major Dale obeyed, and, a humorous figure enough, stretched himself upon the couch, staring at me round-eyed. I also fastened a handkerchief about my head.

"It would perhaps be better," I said, my voice dimmed by the wet silk, "if we avoided conversation as much as possible."

Standing up, I rolled back a corner of the carpet, exposing the floor-planks, and with a brace-and-bit, which I had in my pocket, I bored a round hole in one of these. Into it I screwed the tube, attached to a little watch-like contrivance, twisting the face of the dial so that I could study it from where I proposed to sit. Then I took up my post, smothering a laugh as I noted the expression upon that part of the Major's red face which was visible to me.

Thus began the business of that strange night. Half an hour passed in almost complete silence, save for the audible breathing of the Major—by no means an ideal companion for such an investigation. But, having agreed to assist me, in justice to my old friend I must say that he did his best to stick to the bargain, and to play his part in what obviously he regarded as an insane comedy.

At about the expiration of this thirty minutes, I thought I heard a door open somewhere in the house. Listening intently, and glancing at my companion, I received no confirmation of the idea. Evidently the Major had heard nothing. Again I thought I heard a sound—as of the rustling of silk upon the stair, or in an upper corridor; finally I was almost certain that the floor of the room above (viz. the Major's bedroom) creaked very slightly.

At that I saw my companion glance upward, then across at me, with a question in his eyes. But not desiring to disturb the silence, I merely shook my head.

An hour passed. There had been no repetition of the slight sounds to which I have referred, and the stillness of Low Fennel was really extraordinary. A thermometer, which I had placed upon the table near to my elbow, recorded the fact that the temperature of the room had not abated a fraction of a point since sunset, and, sitting still though I was, I found myself bathed in perspiration. Despite the open door and windows, not a breath of air stirred in the place, but the room was laden with the oppressive perfume of those night-scented flowers which I have mentioned elsewhere, for it was faintly perceptible to me, despite the wet silk.

Once, a bat flew half in at one of the windows, striking its wings upon the glass, but almost immediately it flew out again. A big moth fluttered around the room, persistently banging its wings against the lamp-shade. But nothing else within or without the house stirred, if I except the occasional restless movements of the Major.

Then all at once—and not gradually as I had anticipated—the meter at my feet began to register. Instantly, I looked to the thermometer. It had begun to fall.

I glanced across at Major Dale. He was staring at something which seemed to have attracted his attention in a distant corner of the room. Glancing away from the meter, the indicator of which was still moving upward, I looked in the same direction. There was much shadow there, but nevertheless I could not doubt that a very faint vapour was forming in that corner ... rising—rising—rising—slowly higher and higher.

It proceeded from some part of the floor concealed by the big saddle-bag chair—the Major's favourite dozing-place (probably from a faulty floor-board), and it was rising visibly, inch upon inch, as I watched, until it touched the ceiling above. Then, like a column of smoke, it spread out, mushroom fashion; it crept in ghostly coils along the cornices, spreading, a dim grey haze, until it obscured a great part of the ceiling.

Again I looked across at the Major. He was staring at the phenomenon with eyes which were glassy with amazement. I could see that momentarily he expected the vapour to take shape, to form into some ghoulish thing with a contorted face and clutching, outstretched fingers.

But this did not happen. The vapour, which was growing more fine and imperceptible, began to disperse. I glanced from corner to corner of the room, then down to the meter on the floor. The indicator was falling again.

Still I made no move, although I could hear Major Dale fidgeting nervously, but I looked across at him ... and a dreadful change had come over his face.

He was sitting upright upon the couch, the edge of which he clutched with one hand, whilst with the other he combed the air in a gesture evidently meant to attract my attention. He was trying to speak, but only a guttural sound issued from his throat. His staring eyes were set in a glare of stark horror upon the door of the study.

Swiftly I turned—to see the door slowly opening; to see, low down upon the bare floor—for I had removed the carpet from that corner of the room—a ghastly, contorted face, held sideways with one ear almost touching the ground, and with the lower lip and the chin drawn up as though they were of rubber, almost to the tip of the nose!

The eyes glared up balefully into mine, the hair hung a dishevelled mass about the face, and I had a glimpse of one bare shoulder pressed upon the floor.

Wider and wider opened the door; and further into the room crept the horrible apparition....

The light gleamed equally upon the hideous, contorted face and upon the rounded shoulders and slim, white arms, on one of which a heavy gold Oriental bangle was clasped.

It was a woman!

In a flash of inspiration—at sight of the bangle—my doubts were resolved; *I understood*. Leaning across the table, I extinguished the lamp ... in the same instant that Major Dale, uttering an inarticulate, choking cry, sprang to his feet and toppled forward, senseless, upon the floor!

The study became plunged in darkness, but into the long corridor, beyond the open door, poured the cold illumination of the moon. Framed in the portal, uprose a slim figure, seeming like a black silhouette upon a silvern background, or a wondrous statue in ebony. Elfin, dishevelled locks crowned the head; the pose of the form was as that of a startled dryad or a young Bacchante poised for a joyous leap....

Thus, for an instant, like some exquisite dream of Phidias visualised, the figure stood ... then had fled away down the corridor and was gone!

VI

Close upon a month had elapsed. Major Dale and I sat in my study in London.

"Young Aubrey Wales has gone abroad," I said. "He's ashamed to show up again, I suppose."

"H'm!" growled the Major—"I've got nothing to crow about, myself, by the Lord Harry! There's courage and courage, sir! I've led more than one bayonet attack, but I'd never qualify for the D.S.O. as a ghost-hunter!—never, by Gad!—never!"

He reached out for the decanter; then withdrew his hand. "Doctor's orders," he muttered. "Discipline must be maintained!"

"It was the sudden excitement which precipitated the seizure," I said, glancing at the altered face of my old friend. "I was wrong to expose you to it; but of course I did not know that the doctor had warned you."

"And now," said the Major, sighing loudly as he filled his tumbler with plain soda-water—"what have you to tell me?"

"In the first place—have you definitely decided to leave Low Fennel, for good?"

"Certainly—not a doubt on the point! We're leasing a flat in town here whilst we look around."

"Good! Because I very much doubt if the place could ever be rendered tenable...."

"Then it's really haunted?"

"Undoubtedly."

"By what, Addison? Tell me that!—by what?"

"By a grey vapour."

Major Dale's eyes began to protrude, and:—

"Addison," he said hoarsely—"don't joke about it!—don't joke. It was not a grey vapour that strangled Seager...."

"Certainly it was not. Seager was strangled by some wholly inoffensive person—we shall probably never know his identity—who had fallen asleep amongst the bushes on the mound, close beside the house...."

"But man alive! I've *seen* the beastly thing, with my own eyes! You've seen it! Wales saw it! Mrs. Ord saw it!..."

"Mrs. Ord saw her husband."

"Ah! you're coming round to my belief about the Ords!"

"Decidedly I am."

"But what did Wales see—eh? And what did *I* see!"

"You saw the vapour in operation."

The Major fell back in his chair with an expression upon his face which I cannot hope to describe. Words failed him altogether.

"I had come prepared for something of the sort," I continued rapidly; "for I have investigated several cases of haunting—notably in the Peak district—which have proved to be due to an emanation from the soil— a vapour. But the effect of such vapour, in the other cases, was to induce delusions of sight, in nearly every instance (although, in two, the delusions were of hearing).

"In other words, the person affected by this vapour was drugged, and, during the drugged state, perceived certain visions. I made the mistake, at first, of supposing that Low Fennel came within the same category. The classical analogy, of course, is that of the Sibyls, who delivered the oracular responses from the tripod, under the afflatus of a vapour said to arise from the sacred subterranean stream called Kassotis. The theory is, therefore, by no means a new one!"

Major Dale stared dully, but made no attempt to interrupt me.

"There are probably many spots, in England alone," I continued, "thus affected; but, fortunately, few of them have been chosen as building-sites. Barrows and tumuli of the stone and bronze age, and also Roman shrines, seem frequently to be productive of such emanations. The barrow beside Low Fennel (and now under the new wing) is a case in point.

"Sudden atmospheric changes seem to be favourable to the formation of the vapour. The barrow in Peel Castle, Isle of Man, is peculiarly susceptible to thunder-storms, for instance, whilst that at Low Fennel emits a vapour only after a spell of intense heat, and at the exact moment when the temperature begins to fall again. In the case of a sustained heat-wave, this would take place at some time during each night.

"And now for the particular in which the vapour at Low Fennel differs from other, similar emanations. It is not productive of delusions of sight; it induces a definite and unvarying form of transient insanity!"

Major Dale moved slightly, but still did not speak.

"Dame Pryce was the first recorded victim of the vapour. She was accused of witchcraft by a neighbour who testified to having seen her transform herself into a hideous and unrecognizable hag—whereas, in her proper person, she seems to have been a comely old lady. Lack of evidence compels us to dismiss the case of Seager, but consider that of the Ords. The man Ord, on his own confession, had fallen asleep outside the house. He became a victim of the vapour—and his own wife failed to recognize him.

"To what extent the mania so produced is homicidal remains to be proved; the gas is rare and difficult to procure, so that hitherto analysis has not been attempted. My own theory is that the subject remains harmless provided that, whilst under the mysterious influence, he does not encounter any person distasteful to him. Thus, Seager may have met his death at the hands of some tramp who had been turned away from the house.

"As to the symptoms: they seem to be quite unvarying. The subject strips, contorts his face out of all semblance to humanity (and always in a particular fashion) and crawls, lizard-like upon the ground, with the head held low, in an attitude of listening. That it is possible so to contort the face as to render it unrecognizable is seen in some cases of angina pectoris, of course.

"The subject apparently returns to the spot from whence he started and sinks into profound sleep, as is seen in some cases of somnambulism; and—like the somnambulist, again—he acquires incredible agility. How you yourself came, twice, under the influence of the vapour, is easily explained. The first time—when the housekeeper saw you—you had actually been in bed; and the second time, as you have told me, you had gone upstairs, undressed, and then slipped on your dressing-gown in order to complete some work in the study. Instead of completing the work, you dozed in your chair—and we know what followed! In the case of—Mrs. Dale...."

"God! Addison," said the Major huskily, and stood up, clutching the chair-arms—"Addison! You are trying to tell me that—what I saw was

... Marjorie!..."

I nodded gravely.

"Without letting her suspect my reason for making the inquiries, I learnt that on that last night at Low Fennel, feeling dreadfully lonely and frightened, she determined to run along to the new wing—which seemed a safer place—and to wait in your room until you came up. She fell asleep, and...."

"Addison ... can a mere 'vapour' produce such...."

"You mean, is the vapour directed or animated, by some discarnate, evil intelligence? My dear Major, you are taking us back to the theory of Elemental spirits, and I blankly refuse to follow you!"

THE VALLEY OF THE JUST
A Story of the Shan Hills

I

The merciless sun beat down upon the little caravan, winding its way upward and ever upward to the hill-land. Beneath stretched a panorama limned in feverish greens and unhealthy yellows; scarlike rocks striated the jungle, clothing the foothills, and through the dancing air, viewed from the arid heights, they had the appearance of running water. Swamps to the south-east showed like unhealing wounds upon the face of the landscape; beyond them spread the muddy river waters, the bank of the stream proper being discernible only by reason of a greater greenness in the palm-tops: venomous green slopes beyond them again, a fringe of dwarfed forest, and the brazen skyline.

On the right of the path rose volcanic rock, gnarled, twisted, and contorted as with the agonies of some mighty plague, which in a forgotten past had seized upon the very bowels of the world, and had contorted whole mountains, and laid waste vast forests and endless plains. Above, the cruel sun; ahead, more plague-twisted rocks, with sandy scars dancing like running water; and, all around, the breathless stillness, the swooning stillness of tropical midday. North, south, east, and west, that haze of heat, that silence unbroken, lay like an accursed mantle upon Burma.

Moreen Fayne could scarcely support herself upright in the saddle; her head throbbed incessantly, and the veil which she wore could not protect her eyes from the maddening glare of the sun. But although at any moment during the past hour she could have slipped insensible from her saddle, she sat stiffly upright, her dauntless eyes looking straight ahead, her small mouth set with masculine sternness, and her hands clenched—the physical reflection of the mental effort whereby, alone, she was enabled to pursue the journey.

Just in front of her paced Ramsa Lal. His stride had not varied from the lowlands, through the foothills, nor on the rocky mountain paths. He had looked neither right nor left, but had walked, walked, walked. At times Moreen had been hard put to it to choke down the hysterical screams which had risen in her throat; madness had threatened her, as she watched, in dumb misery, that silent striding man. Yet she knew that it was only the presence of this tireless, immobile guide which had enabled her to go on; although he never directed one glance towards her, she knew that his steady march was meant for encouragement.

Behind, like the tail of a scorpion, trailed the native retinue, and on the end of the tail, where the sting would be, rode her husband. This simile had occurred to her at once, and she allowed her mind to dwell upon the idea as an invalid will consider imaginary designs upon the wall-paper of the sick-room.

Sometimes there was a sliding of hoofs and a sound of stumbling; sometimes her own pony lost his footing. On such occasion, there would be mechanical cries of encouragement from the natives, and perhaps a growling curse from the man who brought up the rear of the little company. The road wound through a frowning chasm, where lizards and other creeping things darted into holes to right and left of their progress. Grateful shadow ruled a while, and a stifled sigh escaped from Moreen's lips. Ramsa Lal paced straightly onward, the others came stumbling behind; fifty yards ahead the ravine opened out, and once more the deathly heat poured unchecked upon their heads.

Again Moreen all but lost control of herself; her fortitude threatened to slip from her; so that she bit her lips until the pain filled her eyes with burning tears. The effort to control herself proved successful, but left her white and quivering. She felt impelled to speak to Ramsa Lal, and constrained herself only with a second effort of which her will was barely capable. Then she saw that speech, which would be dangerous, was unnecessary; the man's wonderful intuition had enabled him to hear that crying of the soul, and he was answering her.

His brown fingers were clutching and unclutching convulsively, and as he swung his arm, he would clench his right fist and beat the air. For a moment he acted thus, and then, as if he knew that she had seen, and understood, his fingers hung limply again, and his arm swung loosely as before.

A sort of plateau was reached, and in a natural clearing, where giant bamboos ranged back to the tangled, creeper-laden boughs of the forest trees, the voice of Major Fayne cried a halt. Ramsa Lal was beside Moreen's pony in a trice, and he so screened her exhausted descent from the saddle, setting her down upon an hospitable bank hard by, that she was enabled to maintain her inflexible attitude, when presently her husband came striding along to stand looking down on her, where she sat. His blackly pencilled brows were drawn together, and the pale blue eyes shone out, saturnine, from cavernous sockets. His handsome face was heavily lined, and in the appearance, in the whole attitude of the man, was something aggressive, a violence markedly repellent.

Moreen locked her hands behind her, the fingers twining and intertwining, but she raised a pale face to his, from which by a last supreme effort of will she had driven all traces of emotion.

So they remained for a moment, whilst the servants busied themselves with the baggage; he, with feet wide apart, staring down at her, and slashing at the air with a fly-whisk, and she meeting his gaze with a stony calm pitiful to behold, had there been any soul capable of pity to see her. Ramsa Lal was directing operations.

"Here," said Major Fayne, "we camp."

His voice would have told a skilled observer that which the facial lines and a certain odd puffiness of skin more than suggested, that Major Fayne was not a temperate man.

Moreen made no sign, but simply sat watching the speaker.

"It's a delightful situation," continued he, "and your ambition, frequently expressed in Mandalay, to see something of Burma other than bridge parties and polo-matches, at last is realised."

He spoke with a seeming sincerity that had carried conviction to any, save the most sceptical. But Moreen made no sign.

"Here," continued Major Fayne, "you may feast your eyes upon the glories of a Burma forest. Those flowering creepers yonder, festooned from bough to bough, are peculiar to this district, and if you care to explore further, you will be rewarded by the discovery of some fine orchids. Note, also, the perfume of the flowers."

He twirled his slight moustache, and turned away to supervise the work of camping.

Ramsa Lal already had one of the tents nearly erected, and Moreen watched his deft fingers at work, with an anxiety none the less because it was masked. She knew that collapse was imminent. The cruel march under the pitiless sun had had due effect, but it had not broken her spirit. She knew that she had reached the end of her strength, but she showed no sign of weakness before her husband.

It was done at last, and Ramsa Lal held the tent-cloth aside, and bowed.

Moreen stood up, clenched her teeth together grimly, and staggered forward. As the tent-flap was dropped, she sank down beside the camp bedstead, and her head fell upon the covering.

II

Dusk fell, a quick curtain, and the lamps of night shone out with glorious brilliancy, illuminating the little plateau. The tents gleamed whitely in the cold radiance; there was a dancing redness to show where the fire had been built, with figures grouped dimly around it. On a jagged rock, which started up from the very heart of a thicket, black against the newly risen moon, was silhouetted the figure of Major Fayne. Night things swept the air about him, and rustled in the cane brake below him; the fire crackled in the neighbouring camp; sometimes a murmur came from the group of natives.

But, heedless of these matters, Moreen's husband stood on the rocky eminence looking back upon the way they had come, looking down to the distant river valley.

For many minutes he remained so, but presently, clambering down, heavily forced his way through the undergrowth to the little camp. Passing the tents, he walked back to the dip of the pathway, and paused again, watching and listening; then turned and strode to the fire, grasped Ramsa Lal by the shoulder, and drew him away from the others.

"Come here!" he directed tersely.

At the head of the pathway he bade him halt.

"Listen!" he directed.

Ramsa Lal stood in an attitude of keen attention, and the Major watched him with feverish anxiety, which he was wholly unable to conceal.

"Do you hear it?" he demanded—"hoofs on the path!"

Ramsa Lal shook his head.

"I hear nothing, Sahib."

"Put your ear to the ground, and listen. I tell you that I saw figures moving away below there, and I heard—hoofs, stumbling hoofs."

The man knelt down upon the ground, and, bending forward, lowered his head. Major Fayne watched him, and with growing anxiety, so that, what with this and the pallid moonlight, his face appeared ghastly.

But again Ramsa Lal stood up, shaking his head.

"Nothing, Sahib," he repeated.

Major Fayne suddenly grasped him by the shoulders, spinning him about, and dragging him forward, so that the dusky face was but inches removed from his own. He glared into the man's eyes.

"Are you lying to me?" he demanded, "are you lying?"

"I swear it is the truth: why should I lie to you, Sahib?"

"You want them——"

Major Fayne broke off abruptly and thrust the man away from him. A different expression had crept into his face, an expression in which there was something furtive. He spun around upon his heel and stepped to the tent where Moreen was. Raising the flap slightly:

"Good-night," he called, and turned away.

Ramsa Lal had gone back to the fireside; and Fayne, following a moment of hesitancy, strode with his swaggering military gait to the tent erected in the furthermost corner of the clearing. He had stooped to enter, when he hesitated, remaining there bent forward—and listening.

From the opposite side of the distant fire, Ramsa Lal, though few would have suspected the fact, was watching. Evidently enough, the leader of the little company was obsessed with his delusion that some one or something clambered up the steep path beneath. Suddenly shrugging his shoulders, he stooped yet lower, and dived into the tent.

One of the natives threw fresh fuel upon the fire, and a stream of sparks sped up through the clear air in a widening trail ever growing fainter.

There was a crackling, a murmur of voices, and then a new silence. This in turn was broken by the distant howling of dogs, and in the near stillness one might have heard the faint shrieking of the bats, who now were embarked upon their nocturnal voyagings.

A shrill, wild scream burst suddenly from the heart of the trees in the east, rose eerily upon the night, and died away. But the group about the fire moved not at all, for this dreadful screaming but marked an animal tragedy of the Burma forests. So furred things howled and screamed and moaned in the woodlands, feathered things piped and hooted around and above, and the bats, uncanny creatures of the darkness, who seem to have kinship neither with fur nor feather, chirped faintly overhead.

Once there was a distant, hollow booming like the sound of artillery, which echoed down the mountain gorges, and seemed to roll away over the lowland swamps, and die, inaudible, by the remote river-bank.

Yet no one stirred; for this mysterious gunnery is a phenomenon met with in that district, inexplicable, weird, but no novelty to one who has camped in the Shan Hills.

A second time later in the night the phantom guns boomed; and again their booming died away in the far valleys. The fire was getting low, now.

III

Moreen lay, sleepless, wide-eyed, staring up at the roof of the tent. She had eaten, could eat, nothing, but she was consumed by a parching thirst. The sounds of the night had no terrors for her; indeed, she scarcely noticed them, for she had other and more dreadful things to think of.

Ramsa Lal had been her father's servant; him she could trust. But the others—the others were Major Fayne's. They were no more than spies upon her; guards.

What did it mean, this sudden dash from the bungalow into the hills? It amused her husband to pretend that it was a pleasure-trip, but the equipment was not of the sort one takes upon such occasions, and one is not usually dragged from bed at midnight to embark upon such a journey. It was additionally improbable in view of the fact that up to the moment of departure Major Fayne had not spoken to her, except in public, for six months. The dreadful, forced marches were breaking her down, and she knew that her husband was drinking heavily. What, in God's name, would be the end of it?

Weakly, she raised herself into a sitting position, groping for and lighting a candle. From the bosom of her dress she took out a letter, the last she had received from home before this mad flight. There was something in it which had frightened her at the time, but which, viewed in the light of recent events, was unspeakably horrifying.

During the long estrangement between her husband and herself she had learnt, and had paid for her knowledge with bitter tears, that there was a side to the character of Major Fayne which he had carefully concealed from her before marriage; the dark, saturnine part of her husband's character had dawned upon her suddenly. That had been the beginning of her disillusionment, the disillusionment which has come to more than one English girl during the first twelve months of married life in an Indian bungalow.

Then, perforce, the gap had widened, and six months later had become a chasm quite impassable except in the interests of social propriety. Anglo-Indian society is notable for divorces, and poor Moreen very early in her married life fully understood the reason.

She held the letter to the dim light and read it again attentively. Allowing a certain discount for her mother's changeless animosity towards Major Fayne, it yet remained a startling letter. Much of it consisted in feckless condolences, characteristic but foolish; the passage, however, which she read and re-read by the dim, flickering light was as follows:

"Mr. Harringay in his last letter begged of me to come out by the next boat to Rangoon," her mother wrote. "He has quite opened my eyes to the truth, Moreen, not in such a way as to shock me all at once, but gradually. I always distrusted Ralph Fayne and never disguised the fact from you. I knew that his previous life had been far from irreproachable, but his treatment of you surpasses even *my* expectations. I know *all*, my poor darling! and I know something which you do not know. His father did not die in Colombo at all; he died in a madhouse! and there are two other known dipsomaniacs in Ralph Fayne's family——"

A hand reached over Moreen's shoulder and tore the letter from her.

She turned with a cry—and looked up into her husband's quivering face! For a moment he stood over her, his left fist clenching and unclenching and his pale blue eyes glassy with anger. Then chokingly he spoke:

"So you carry one of his letters about with you?"

The veins were throbbing visibly upon his temples. Moreen clutched at the blanket but did not speak, dared not move, for if ever she had looked into the face of a madman it was at this moment when she looked into the face of Ralph Fayne.

He suddenly grabbed the candle and, holding it close to the letter, began to read. His hands were perfectly steady, showing the tremendous nerve tension under which he laboured. Then his expression changed, but nothing of the maniac glare left his eyes.

"From your mother," he said hoarsely, "and full of two things—your wrongs, *your* wrongs! and Jack Harringay—Jack Harringay—always Jack Harringay! Damn him!"

He put down the candle and began to tear the letter into tiny fragments, pouring forth the while a stream of coarse, blasphemous language. Moreen, who felt that consciousness was slipping from her, crouched there with a face deathly pale.

Fayne began to laugh softly as he threw the torn-up letter from him piece by piece.

"Damn him!" he said again. He turned the blazing eyes towards his wife. "You lying, baby-faced hypocrite! Why don't you admit that he is——"

He stopped; the sinister laughter died upon his lips and he stood there shaking all over and with a sort of stark horror in his eyes dreadful to see.

"Why don't you?" he muttered—and looked at her almost pathetically,—"why of course you can't—no one can——"

He reeled and clutched at the tent-flap, then stumblingly made his way out.

"No one can," came back in a shaky whisper—"no one can——"

Moreen heard him staggering away, until the sound of his uncertain footsteps grew inaudible. A distant howling rose upon the night, and, nearer to the clearing, sounded a sort of tapping, not unlike that of a woodpecker. Some winged creature was fluttering over the tent.

IV

Dawn saw the dreadful march resumed. Major Fayne now exhibited unmistakable traces of his course of heavy drinking. He brought up the rear as hitherto, and often tarried far behind where some peculiar formation of the path enabled him to study the country already traversed. He had altered the route of the march, and now they were leaving the Shan Hills upon the north-east and dipping down to a chasm-like valley through which ran a tributary of the Selween River. Since the dry season was commenced the entire country beneath them showed through a haze of heat and dust.

They had partaken of a crude and hasty breakfast as strangers having nothing in common who by chance share a table. Moreen no longer doubted that her husband was mad, for he muttered to himself and was ever glancing over his shoulder. This and his constant watching of the path behind spoke of some secret terror from which he fled.

Towards noon, they skirted a village whose inhabitants poured forth *en bloc* to watch the passing of this unfamiliar company. A faint hope that some European might be there died in Moreen's breast. Her position was a dreadful one. Led by a madman—of this she was persuaded—and surrounded by natives who, if not actively hostile, were certainly unfriendly, with but one man to whom she could look for the slightest aid, she was proceeding further and further from civilisation into unknown wildernesses.

What her husband's purpose might be she could not conceive. She was unable to think calmly, unable to formulate any plan. In the dull misery of a sick dream she rode forward speculating upon the awakening.

The midday heat in the valley was so great that a halt became imperative. They camped at the edge of a dense jungle where banks of rotten vegetation, sun-dried upon the top, lay heaped about the bamboo stems. None but a madman would have chosen to tarry in such a spot; and Major Fayne's servants went about their work with many a furtive glance at their master. Ramsa Lal's velvety eyes showed a great compassion, but Moreen offered no protest. She was in an unreal frame of mind and her will was merely capable of a mute indifference: any attempt to assert herself would have meant a sudden breakdown. Something in her brain was strained to utmost tension; any further effort must have snapped it.

In the hour of the greatest heat Major Fayne went out alone, offering no explanation of his intentions and leaving no word as to the time of his return. Moreen only learnt of his departure from Ramsa Lal. She received the news with indifference and asked no questions. Inert she lay in the little tent looking out at the wall of jungle, where it uprose but twenty yards away. So the day wore on. Mechanically she partook of food when Ramsa Lal placed it before her, but, although the man's attitude palpably was one of uneasiness, she did not question him, and he departed in silence. It was an incredible situation.

Throughout the afternoon nothing occurred to break this dread monotony save that once there arose a buzz of conversation, and she became dimly aware that some one from the native village which they had passed in the morning had come into the camp. After a time the sounds had died away again, and Ramsa Lal had stepped into view, looking towards her interrogatively; but although she recognized his wish to speak to her, the inertia which now claimed her mind and body prevailed, and she offered him no encouragement to intrude upon her misery.

Thus the weary hours passed, until even to the dulled perceptions of Moreen the sounds of unrest and uneasiness pervading the camp began to penetrate. Yet Major Fayne did not return. The insect and reptile life of a Burmese jungle moved around her, but she was curiously indifferent to everything. Without alarm she brushed a venomous spider, fully one inch in girth, from the camp-bedstead, and dully watched it darting away into the jungle undergrowth.

Darkness swept down and tropical night things raised their mingled voices; then came Ramsa Lal.

"Forgive me, Mem Sahib," he said, "but I must speak to you."

She half reclined, looking at him as he stood, a dimly seen figure, before her.

"The men from the village," continued he, "come to say that we may not camp. It is holy ground from this place away"—he waved his arm vaguely—"to the end of the jungle where the river is."

"I can do nothing, Ramsa Lal."

"I fear—for him."

"Major Fayne?"

"He goes into the jungle to look for something. What does he go to look for? Why does he not return?"

Moreen made no reply.

"All of them there"—he indicated the direction of the native servants—"know this place. They are already afraid, and, with those from the village coming to warn us, they get more afraid still. This is a haunted place, Mem Sahib."

Moreen sat up, shaking off something of the lassitude which possessed her.

"What do you mean?" she asked.

"In that jungle," replied Ramsa Lal, "there is buried a temple, a very old temple, and in the temple there is buried one who was a holy man. His spirit watches over this place, and none may rest here because of him——"

"But the men of the village came here," said Moreen.

"Before sunset, Mem Sahib. No man would come here after dark. Look! you will see—they are frightened."

Languidly, but with some awakening to the necessities of the situation, Moreen stepped out of the tent and looked across to where, about a great fire, the retinue huddled in a circle. Ramsa Lal stood beside her with something contemptuous in the bearing of his tall figure.

"A spell lies upon all this valley, Mem Sahib," he said. "Therefore it is called the Valley of the Just."

"Why?"

"Because only the just can stay within its bounds through the night."

Moreen stared affrightedly.

"Do you mean that they die in the night, Ramsa Lal?"

"In the night, Mem Sahib, before the dawn."

"By what means?"

Ramsa Lal spread his palms eloquently.

"Who knows?" he replied. "It is a haunted place."

"And are you afraid?"

"I am not afraid, for I have passed a night in the Valley of the Just many years ago, and I live."

"You were alone?"

"With two others, Mem Sahib."

"And the others?"

"One was bitten by a snake an hour before dawn, and the other, who was an upright man, lives to-day."

Moreen shuddered.

"Do you know"—she still hesitated to broach this subject with the man—"do you know where—Major Fayne has gone?"

"It is said, Mem Sahib, that a stream runs through the jungle close beside the old temple, a stream which bubbles up from a cavern and which is supposed to come underground from the Ruby Mine plateau. He goes early in the morning to look for rubies—so I think."

Moreen tapped the ground with her foot.

"Do you think"—again she hesitated—"that Major Fayne is afraid of something? Of something—where we have come from?"

Ramsa Lal bowed low.

"I cannot tell," he replied, "but we shall know ere sunrise."

For a moment Moreen scarcely grasped the significance of his words; then their inner meaning became apparent to her.

"Make me some coffee, Ramsa Lal," she said; "I am cold—very cold."

She re-entered the tent, lighting the lamp.

The Valley of the Just! What irony, that her husband should have selected that spot to camp in! She sat deep in thought, when presently Ramsa Lal entered with coffee. He had just set down the tray when the sound of a distant cry brought him rigidly upright. He stood listening intently. The sound was repeated—nearer it seemed—a sort of hoarse scream, terrible to hear—impossible to describe.

Moreen rose to her feet and followed the man out of the tent. Some one—some one who kept crying out—was plunging heavily through the jungle towards the camp.

The men about the fire were on their feet now. Obviously they would have fled, but the prospect of flight into the haunted darkness was one more terrible than that of remaining where they were.

It ceased, that strange cry; but whoever was approaching could be heard alternately groaning and laughing madly.

Then out from the thicket on the west, into the red light of the fire, burst a fearful figure. It was that of Major Fayne, wild eyed, and with face which seemed to be of a dull grey. He staggered and almost fell, but kept on for a few more paces and then collapsed in a heap almost at Moreen's feet, amid the clatter of the strange loot wherewith he was laden.

This consisted in a number of golden vessels heavily encrusted with gems, a huge golden salver, and a dozen or more ropes of gigantic rubies!

Amid these treasures, the ransom of a Sultan, the price of a throne, he lay writhing convulsively.

Ramsa Lal was the first to recover himself. He leapt forward, seized the prostrate man by the shoulders and dragged him into the tent, past Moreen. Having effected this he raised his eyes in a mute question. She nodded, and whilst Ramsa Lal seized the Major's shoulders, Moreen grasped his ankles, and together they lifted him up on to the bed.

He lay there, rolling from side to side. His eyes were wide open, glassy and unseeing; a slight froth was upon his lips, his fists rose and fell in regular, mechanical beats, corresponding with the convulsive movements of his knees.

Moreen dropped down beside him.

"Ramsa Lal! Ramsa Lal! What shall I do? What has happened to him?"

Ramsa Lal ripped the collar from Major Fayne's neck in order to aid his respiration. Then, quietly signing to Moreen to hold the lamp, he began to search the entire exposed surface of the Major's skin. Evidently he failed to find that for which he was looking. He glanced down at the ankles, but the Major wore thick putties and Ramsa Lal shook his head in a puzzled way.

"It is like the bite of a hamadryad," he said softly, "but there is no mark."

"What shall I do!" moaned Moreen—"what shall I do!"

There was a frightened murmur from the entrance, where the native servants stood in a group, peering in. Moreen stood up.

"Hot water, Ramsa Lal!" she said. "We must give him brandy."

"But it is useless, Mem Sahib; he has not been bitten—there is no mark; it may be a fever from the jungle."

Moreen beat her hands together helplessly.

"We must do *something*!" she said; "we must do *something*."

A sudden change took place in Major Fayne. The convulsive movements ceased and he lay quiet, and breathing quite regularly. The glassy look began to fade from his eyes, and with every appearance of being in full possession of his senses, he stared at Moreen and spoke:

"You shall repent of your words, Harringay," he said in a quiet voice. "You have deliberately accused me of faking the cards. I care nothing for any of you. Why should I attempt such a thing? I could buy and sell you all!..."

Moreen dropped slowly back upon her knees again, white to the lips, watching her husband. With the same appearance of perfect sanity, but now addressing the empty air, he continued:

"In my tent—my wife will tell you it is true—my wife, Harringay, do you hear?—I have jewelled cups and strings of rubies, enough to buy up Mandalay! I blundered on to them in that old ruined temple back in the jungle, not five hundred yards from your bungalow. Harringay— think of it—a treasure-room like that within sight of your verandah! There are snakes there, snakes, you understand, in hundreds; but it is worth risking for a big fortune like mine."

"He mixes time and place," murmured Ramsa Lal. "He talks to the Commissioner Sahib in Mandalay of what is here in the Valley of the Just."

Moreen nodded, catching her breath hysterically.

"You see," continued the delirious man, "I am as rich as Midas. Why should *I* want to cheat you! Don't talk to me of what you would do for my wife's sake! Keep your favours, curse you!"

With a contemptuous smile, Major Fayne threw his head back upon the pallet. Then came another change; the look of stark horror which Moreen had seen once before crept into the grey face; and her husband raised himself in bed, glaring wildly into the shadows beyond the lamp.

"You are a spirit!" The words came in a thrilling, eerie whisper. "Oh God! I understand. Yes! I came away from Harringay's bungalow. My wife was asleep and I sat drinking until I had emptied the whisky decanter."

He bent forward as if listening.

"Yes, I went back. I went back to reason with him. No! as God is my witness I did not plan it! I went back to reason with him."

Again the uncanny attitude was resumed. Then:

"I stepped in through the verandah, and there he sat with Moreen's photograph in his hand. Listen to me—*Listen!*" There was an agony of entreaty in his voice; it rose to a thin scream—"My wife's photograph! Do you hear me? Do you understand? *Moreen's* photograph—and as I stood behind him, he raised it to his lips—he——"

Major Fayne stopped abruptly, as if checked by a spoken word; and with wildly beating heart Moreen found herself listening for the phantom voice. She could hear the breathing of the natives clustered behind her; but no other sound save a distant howling in the jungle was audible, until her husband began again:

"I struck him down—from behind, yes, from behind. His blood poured over the picture. You understand I was mad. If you are just—and is not this called the Valley of the Just?—you cannot condemn me. Why did I fly? I was not in my right mind; I had—been drinking, as I told you; I was mad. If I was not mad I should never have fled, never have drawn suspicion—on myself."

He fell back as if exhausted, then once more struggled upright and began to peer about him. When he spoke again, his voice, though weak, was more like his own.

"Moreen!" he said—"where the devil are you? why can't you give me a drink?"

Suddenly, he seemed to perceive her, and he drew his brows together in the old, ugly frown.

"Curse you!" he said. "I have found you out! I am a rich man now, and when I have gone to England, see what Jack Harringay will do for you. I will paint London red! I have looted the old temple, and they are after me, they——"

The words merged into a frightful scream. Major Fayne threw up his hands and fell back insensible upon the bed.

"Mem Sahib! Mem Sahib, you must be brave!" It was Ramsa Lal who spoke; he supported Moreen with his arm. "There is a spell upon this place. No medicine, nothing, can save him. There is only one thing——"

Moreen controlled herself by one of those giant efforts of which she was capable.

"Tell me," she whispered—"what must we do?"

Ramsa Lal removed his arm, saw that she could stand unsupported, and bent forward over the unconscious man. Following a rapid examination, he signed to her to leave the tent. They came out into the white blaze of the moonlight—and there at their feet lay the glittering loot of the haunted temple, a dazzlement of rainbow sparks.

"Only for such a thing as this," said Ramsa Lal, "dare I go, but not one of us will see another dawn if we do not go." He pointed to the heap of treasure. "Mem Sahib must come also."

"But—my husband——"

"He must remain," he said. "It is of his own choosing."

V

The temple stood in a kind of clearing. Grotesquely horrible figures guarded the time-worn entrance. Moreen drew a deep breath of relief on emerging from the jungle path by which, amid the rustle of retreating snakes, they had come, but shrank back affrighted from the blackness of the ruined doorway. Ramsa Lal stood the lantern upon the stump of a broken pillar, where its faint yellow light was paled by the moon-rays.

"It is *you* who must restore," he said.

One by one he handed her the jewel-encrusted vessels and hung the ropes of rubies upon her arm.

She nodded, and as Ramsa Lal took up the lantern and began to descend the steps within followed him.

"No foot save his," came back to her, "has trod these sacred steps for ages, for the secret of the jungle path is known only to the few...."

"How do you—know the way?"

Ramsa Lal did not reply.

They traversed a short tunnel; a heavy door was thrust open; and Moreen found herself standing in a small pillared hall. Through a window high in one wall, overgrown with tangled vegetation, crept a broken moonbeam. Directly before her was the carven figure of a grotesque deity. A long, heavily clamped chest stood before it like an altar step.

She staggered forward, deposited her priceless burden upon the floor, and mechanically began to raise the lid of the chest.

"Not that one, Mem Sahib!" The voice of Ramsa Lal rose shrilly—

"not that one!..."

But he spoke too late. Moreen realised that there were three divisions in the chest, each having a separate lid. As she raised the one in the centre, a breath of fetid air greeted her nostrils, and she had a vague impression that this was no chest but the entrance to a deep pit. Then all these thoughts were swept away by the crowning horror which rose out of the subterranean darkness.

A great winged creature, clammily white, rose towards her, passed beneath her upraised hands and sailed into the darkness on the right. She heard it flapping its great bat wings against the wall—heard them beating upon a pillar—then saw it coming back towards her into the moonlight—and knew no more.

VI

"Mem Sahib!"

Moreen opened her eyes. She lay, propped against a saddle, at the camp beside the jungle. She shuddered icily.

"Ramsa Lal—how——"

"I carried the Mem Sahib! the treasures of the temple I restored to their resting-place——"

"And the—the other——"

"The door that the Mem Sahib opened she opened by the decree of Fate. It was not for Ramsa Lal to close it. That is a passage——"

"Yes?"

"—To the tomb of the great one who is buried in the temple!"

"Oh! heavens! that white thing——" She raised her hands to her face. "But—the camp——"

"The camp is deserted! they all fled from——"

Moreen sat up, rigidly.

"From what?"

"From something that came for what we forgot!"

"My husband——"

"There was a ring upon his finger. I saw it, and knew where it came from, but forgot to remove it."

Moreen stood up, and turned towards the nearer tent. Ramsa Lal gently detained her.

"Not that way, Mem Sahib."

"But I must see him! I must, I *must* tell him that he wrongs me, cruelly, wickedly! You heard his words— Oh, God! can he have——"

"It would be useless to tell him, Mem Sahib,—he could not hear you! But that what you would tell him is true I know well; for see—it is the dawn!"

"Ramsa Lal!..."

"The unjust cannot stay in this valley through a night and live to see the dawn, Mem Sahib!"

VII

At about that same hour, Deputy-Commissioner Jack Harringay opened his eyes and looked wonderingly at a grey-haired, white-aproned nurse who sat watching him.

"Don't speak, Mr. Harringay," she said soothingly. "You have been very ill, but you are on the high road to recovery now."

"Nurse!..."

"Please don't speak; I know what you would ask. There has been no scandal. The attack upon you was ascribed to robbers. You have been delirious, Mr. Harringay, and have told me—many things. I am old enough, or nearly old enough, to be your mother, so you will not mind my telling you that a love like yours deserves reward. God has spared your life; be sure it was with a purpose——"

THE BLUE MONKEY

I

A tropically hot day had been followed by a stuffy and oppressive evening. In the tiny sitting-room of our tiny cottage, my friend—who, for the purposes of this story, I shall call Mr. East—by the light of a vapour lamp was busily arranging a number of botanical specimens collected that morning. His briar fumed furiously between his teeth, and, his grim, tanned face lowered over his work, he brought to bear upon this self-imposed task all the intense nervous energy which was his.

I sat by the open window alternately watching my tireless companion and the wonderful and almost eerie effects of the moonlight on the heather. Then:

"We came here for quiet—and rest, East," I said, smiling.

"Well!" snapped my friend. "Isn't it quiet enough for you?"

"Undeniably. But I don't remember to have seen you rest from the moment that we left London! I exclude your brief hours of slumber— during which, by the way, you toss about and mutter in a manner far from reposeful."

"No wonder. My nerves are anything but settled yet, I grant you."

Indeed, we had passed through a long and trying ordeal, the particulars whereof have no bearing upon the present matter, and in renting this tiny and remote cottage we had sought complete seclusion and forgetfulness of those evil activities of man which had so long engaged our attention. How ill we had chosen will now appear.

I had turned again to the open window, when my meditations were interrupted by a sound that seemed to come from somewhere away behind the cottage. Cigarette in hand, I leaned upon the sill, listening, then turned and glanced toward the littered table. East, his eyes steely bright in the lamplight, was watching me.

"You heard it?" I said.

"Clearly. A woman's shriek!"

"Listen!"

Tense, expectant, we sat listening for some time, until I began to suspect that we had been deceived by the note of some unfamiliar denizen of the moors. Then, faintly, chokingly, the sound was repeated, seemingly from much nearer.

"Come on!" snapped East.

Hatless, we both hurried around to the rear of the cottage. As we came out upon the slope, a figure appeared on the brow of a mound some two hundred yards away and stood for a moment silhouetted against the moonlit sky. It was that of a woman. She raised her arms at sight of us—and staggered forward.

Just in the nick of time we reached her, for her strength was almost spent. East caught her in his arms.

"Good God!" he said, "it is Miss Baird!"

What could it mean? The girl, who was near to swooning and inarticulate with fatigue and emotion, was the daughter of Sir Jeffrey Baird, our neighbour, whose house, The Warrens, was visible from where we stood.

East half led, half carried her down the slope to the cottage; and there I gave her professional attention, whilst, with horror-bright eyes and parted lips, she fought for mastery of herself. She was a rather pretty girl, but highly emotional, and her pathetically weak mouth was doubtless a maternal heritage, for her father, Sir Jeffrey, had the mouth and jaw of the old fighter that he was.

At last she achieved speech.

"My father!" she whispered brokenly; "oh, my poor father!"

"What!" I began——

"At Black Gap!..."

"Black Gap!" I said; for the place was close upon half a mile away. "Have you come so far?"

"He is lying there! My poor father—dead!"

"What!" cried East, springing up—"Sir Jeffrey—dead? Not drowned?"

"No, no! he is lying on the path this side of the Gap! I ... almost stumbled over ... him. He has been ... murdered! Oh, God help me!..."

East and I stared at one another, speechless with the sudden horror of it. Sir Jeffrey murdered!

Suddenly the distracted girl turned to my friend, clutching frenziedly at his arm.

"Oh, Mr. East!" she cried, "what had my poor father done to merit such an end? What monster has struck him down? You will find him, will you not? I thank God that you are here—for although I know you as 'Mr. East,' my father confided the truth to me, and I am aware that you are really a Secret Service agent, and I even know some of the wonderful things you have done in the past...."

"Very indiscreet!" muttered East, and his jaws snapped together viciously. But—"My dear Miss Baird," he added immediately, in the kindly way that was his own, "rely upon me. Myself and my fellow-worker, the doctor here, had sought to escape from the darker things of life, but it was willed otherwise. I esteemed Sir Jeffrey very highly"— his voice shook—"very highly indeed. I, too, thank God that I am here."

II

Five minutes later, East and I set out across the moor, leaving Miss Baird at the cottage. By reason of the lonely situation, and the fact that the nearest house, The Warrens, was fully a mile and a half away, no other arrangement was possible, since delay could not be entertained.

East had managed to glean some few important facts. Sir Jeffrey, whose museum at The Warrens was justly celebrated, had been to London that day to attend an auction at Sotheby's. His Greek secretary, Mr. Damopolon, and his daughter had accompanied him. Returning by train to Stanby, the nearest station, Miss Baird had called upon friends in the village (Mr. Damopolon had remained in London on business), and Sir Jeffrey had set out in the dusk to walk the two miles to The Warrens; for the car was undergoing repairs.

Pursuing the same path later in the evening, the girl had come upon the body of her father in the dramatically dreadful manner already related. He had no enemies, she declared, or none known to her. She did not believe that her father was carrying a large sum of money, nor—although she had scarcely trusted herself to look at him—did she believe that robbery had been the motive of the crime.

Sir Jeffrey had been carrying a large parcel containing one of his purchases, and I remembered, as we silently pursued our way to the scene of the murder, how East's keen eyes had seemed to dance with excitement when Miss Baird, in reply to a question, had told us what this parcel contained. It was a large figure, in blue porcelain, of a sacred ape, and was of Burmese or Chinese origin; she was uncertain which.

Her father had apparently attached great importance to this strange purchase, and had elected to bear it home in person rather than to trust it to railway transport.

"Did you notice if this parcel was there," East had inquired eagerly, "when you discovered him?"

Miss Baird had shaken her head in reply.

And now we were come to Black Gap, a weird feature in a weird landscape. This was a great hole in the moor, having high clay banks upon one side descending sheer to the tarn, and upon the other being flanked by low, marshy ground about a small coppice. The road from Stanby to The Warrens passed close by the coppice on the south-east.

Regarding this place opinions differed. By some it was supposed to be a natural formation, but it was locally believed to mark the site of an abandoned mine, possibly Roman. Its depth was unknown, and the legend of the coach which lay at the bottom, and which could be seen under certain favourable conditions, has found a place in all the guide-books to that picturesque and wild district.

Whatever its origin, Black Gap was a weird and gloomy spot as one approached and saw through the trees the gleam of the moonlight on its mystic waters. And here, passing a slight southerly bend in the track—for it was no more—we came upon Sir Jeffrey.

He lay huddled in a grotesque and unnatural attitude. His right hand was tightly clenched, whilst with his left he clutched a tuft of rank grass. Strangely enough, his soft hat was still upon his head. His tweed suit, soft collar and, tie all bore evidence of the fierce struggle which the old baronet had put up for his life. A quantity of torn brown paper lay scattered near the body.

I dropped on my knees and made a rapid examination, East directing the ray of a pocket-lamp upon the poor victim.

"Well?" rapped my friend.

"He was struck over the head by some heavy weapon," I said slowly, "and perhaps partly stunned. His hat protected him to a degree, and he tackled his assailant. Death was actually due, I should say, to strangulation. His throat is very much bruised."

East made no reply. Glancing up from my gruesome task, I observed that he was looking at a faint track, which, commencing amid the confused marks surrounding the body, led in the direction of the coppice. East's steely eyes were widely opened.

"In heaven's name, what have we here!" he said.

A kindred amazement to that which held East claimed me, as I studied more closely the mysterious tracks.

The spot where Sir Jeffrey had fallen was soft ground, whereon the lightest footstep must have left a clear impression. Indeed, around the recumbent figure the ground showed a mass of indistinguishable marks. But proceeding thence, as I have said, in the direction of the neighbouring coppice, was this faint trail.

"It looks," I said, in a voice hushed with something very like awe, "it looks like the track of ... *a child!*"

"Look again!" snapped East.

I stooped over the first set of marks. Clearly indented, I perceived the impressions of two small, bare feet, and, eighteen or twenty inches ahead, those of two small hands. I experienced a sudden chill; my blood seemed momentarily to run coldly in my veins, and I longed to depart from the shadow of the trees, from the neighbourhood of the Black Gap, and from the neighbourhood of the man who had died there. For it seemed to me that a barefooted infant had recently crawled from the side of the dead man into the coppice overhanging the tarn.

Looking up, I found East's steely eyes set upon me strangely.

"Well!" said he, "do you not miss something that you anticipated finding?"

I hesitated, fearfully. Then:

"Sir Jeffrey carries no cane," I began——

"Good! I had failed to note that. Good! But what else?"

Closely I surveyed the body, noting the disarranged garments, the discoloured face.

"What of this torn brown paper?" snapped my friend.

"Good heavens!" I cried; and like a flash my glance sought again those mysterious tracks—those tracks of *something* that had crawled away from the murdered man.

"Where," inquired East deliberately, "is the Burmese porcelain ape of which we have heard? And, since there are no tracks *approaching* the body, where did the creature come from that made those retiring from it, and ... what manner of creature was it?"

III

At East's request (for my friend was a man of very great influence) the police, beyond the unavoidable formalities, took no steps to apprehend the murderer of Sir Jeffrey. East had a long interview with the dead man's daughter, and, shortly afterwards, went off to London, leaving me to my own devices.

The subject of the strange death of the baronet naturally engrossed my attention to the exclusion of all else. Especially, my mind kept reverting to the tracks which we had discovered leading from the dead man's body into the coppice. I scarcely dared to follow my ideas to what seemed to be their logical conclusion.

That the track was that, not of a child, but of an *ape*, I was now convinced. No such track approached where the victim had lain; no track of any kind, other than that of his own heavy footprints, led to the spot ... but the track of an ape receded from it; and the baronet had been carrying an ape (inanimate, certainly, according to all known natural laws), which was missing when his body was found!

"These are the reflections of a madman!" I said aloud. "Am I seriously considering the possibility of a blue porcelain monkey having come to life? If so, since no other footprints have been discovered, I shall be compelled, logically, to assume that the blue porcelain monkey strangled Sir Jeffrey!”

My friend, East, attached very great importance to the missing curio; this he had not disguised from me. But, beyond spending half an hour or so among the trees of the coppice and around the margin of the Black Gap, he had not to my knowledge essayed any quest for it.

Finding my thoughts at once unpleasant and unprofitable company, I suddenly determined to make a call at The Warrens, in order to inquire about the health of poor Miss Baird, and incidentally to learn if there were any new development.

Off I set, and failed to repress a shudder, despite the blazing sunlight, as I passed the gap and the spot where we had found the dead man. A tropical shower in the early morning had quite obliterated the mysterious tracks. Coming to The Warrens, I was shown into the fine old library. That air of hush, so awesome and so significant, prevailed throughout the house whose master lay dead above, and when presently Mr. Damopolon entered, attired in black, he seemed to complete a picture already sombre.

As East and I had several times remarked, he was a singularly handsome man, and moreover, a very charming companion, widely travelled and deeply versed in those subjects to which the late baronet had devoted so many years of his life. I had always liked Damopolon, though, as a rule, I am distrustful of his race; and now, seeing at a glance how hard the death of Sir Jeffrey had hit him, I offered no unnecessary word of condolence, but immediately turned the conversation upon Miss Baird.

“She has but just hurried off to London, doctor,” he said, to my surprise. “A telegram from the solicitors rendered her immediate departure unavoidable.”

“She has sustained this dreadful blow with exemplary fortitude,” I replied. “Are you sure she was strong enough for travel?”

“I myself escorted her to the station; and Mrs. Grierson, the late baronet’s sister, has accompanied her to London.”

“By the way,” I said, “whilst I remember—was Sir Jeffrey carrying a cane at the time of his death?”

“He had with him a heavy ash stick, as usual, when we parted at Sotheby’s, doctor; but, of course, he may have left it there, as he had a large parcel to take.”

“Ah! that parcel! You can no doubt enlighten me, Mr. Damopolon? What, roughly, were the dimensions of this Burmese idol?”

“The monkey? I don’t think it was actually an idol, doctor; it was, rather, a grotesque ornament. Oh, it was about the size of a small

Moorish ape, hollow, and weighing perhaps six or seven pounds."

"Was it upon a pedestal?"

"No. It was completely modelled, even to the soles of the feet and the nails."

"Extraordinary!" I muttered. "Uncanny!"

Some little while longer I remained, and then set out, my doubts in no measure cleared up, for the cottage. To my surprise—for I had no idea that I had tarried so long—dusk was come. I will frankly confess it—I experienced a thrill of supernatural dread at the thought that my path led close beside Black Gap. However, it was a glorious evening, and I should have plenty of light for my return journey. I walked briskly across the moorpath toward the scene of the mysterious crime, hoping that I should find East returned when I gained the cottage.

Perhaps in a wandering life I have known more thrilling moments than some men; but never while memory serves shall I forget that, when, coming abreast of the coppice, and glancing hurriedly into the shadow of the trees ... I saw a crouching figure looking out at me!

Speech momentarily failed me; I stood rooted to the spot. Then:

"All right, old man!" I heard. "Shall be with you in a moment!"

It was East!

Fear changed to the wildest astonishment. Carrying a strange-looking bundle, he came out and joined me on the path.

"Did I frighten you?"

"Is it necessary to ask!" I cried. "But—whatever were you doing there by the Black Gap?"

"Fishing! Look what I have caught!"

He held up for my inspection the object which he carried, by means of two loops of stout cord bound about it. It was a large china figure of an ape!

"The blue monkey!" he snapped. "Come! I am going to The Warrens."

IV

Again I sat in the fine old library of The Warrens. At the further end of the long, book-laden table, facing me, sat East; Mr. Damopolon occupied a chair on the right, and midway between us, in the centre of the table, presiding over that strange meeting, was the fateful blue monkey.

"You see, Mr. Damopolon," said East, "I knew that Sir Jeffrey was carrying this thing"—he indicated the image—"at the time of his death, and, since it had disappeared, I assumed at first that it had been the motive of the crime. Sir Jeffrey had money and other valuables upon him; therefore we were obviously dealing with no ordinary thief.

"Accordingly, I made inquiries respecting the history of the thing, and found that it possessed but little market value and next to no historical importance. It was of comparatively modern Chinese workmanship, and Sir Jeffrey had bought it, apparently, because it amused him, though why he should have taken the trouble to carry it home, heaven only knows. My first idea—that the curio was a very rare and costly piece—was thus knocked on the head.

"I sought another motive for a crime so horrible and, by a stroke of intuition, I found one. You may not have had an opportunity of studying the mysterious tracks which so puzzled us, Mr. Damopolon, before they were obliterated, but my friend, the doctor, will bear me out. They commenced, then, close beside the body of the murdered man, and they were, as I now perceive, made by the feet of this blue monstrosity upon the table here!"

"Impossible," murmured the secretary incredulously.

"So it appeared to me at the time, when, although I had not then seen the image of the monkey, I perceived, by the absolutely regular character of the impressions, that they were made, not by a living creature, but by the model of one which had been firmly pressed into the soft ground at slightly varying intervals. Since no footprints other than those of Sir Jeffrey were to be found in the vicinity, I was unable to account for the presence of the person who had made these impressions. I devoted myself to a close scrutiny of those footprints of Sir Jeffrey's which led up to the scene of the attack. It became apparent, immediately, that some one had *followed* him ... some one who crept silently along behind the unsuspecting victim ... some one so clever that he placed his feet *almost exactly* in the marks made by the baronet!

"Good! I had accounted for the presence of the murderer. He struck Sir Jeffrey with some heavy implement, but failed to stun him. Then began the struggle, which so churned up the ground that all tracks were lost. The murderer prevailed. He was a man of wonderful nerve. Never once did he place his foot upon virgin ground; not one imprint by which he might be identified did he leave behind him!"

"Then how," inquired Damopolon, who was hanging upon every word, "did he leave the scene if——"

"Listen," snapped East. "I found by the body the torn paper in which the china image had been wrapped—but no string! I went all the way to London to learn if the parcel had been tied with string and if Sir Jeffrey had been carrying a stick!"

"But surely," said Damopolon, "I could have saved you the journey, since I was with the late baronet immediately before he set out for home."

"Quite so—but I had another reason for my visit."

East shot a sudden glance from Damopolon to myself, and there ensued a moment of electric silence.

"Beside the track made by the feet of the image," he resumed slowly, "I found a series of wedge-shaped holes, one on either side of each monkey-impression. Do you follow me, Mr. Damopolon?"

"Perfectly," replied the Greek, taking up and lighting a cigarette. "Wedge-shaped holes, you say?"

"They were the clue for which I sought! I saw it all! The china ape had been used as a *stepping-stone*! The cunning criminal had thus gained the firm ground in the coppice without leaving a footprint behind!..."

"But, my dear East," I interrupted, "I cannot follow you. He stepped from beside the body on to the image, which he had placed at a convenient distance?"

"Yes. Then, by means of loops of string—see, they are still attached!— he lifted it forward with his feet——"

"But——"

"Supporting his weight upon two sticks—Sir Jeffrey's and his own! Hence the wedge-shaped holes beside the track! He had actually reached firm ground when his own stick snapped off short, and he made the fatal error of leaving the fragment and the ferrule, imbedded in the hole! Here is the fragment!"

On the table East laid a fragment of an ebony cane, broken off short some three inches above the nickel ferrule.

"Ebony is so brittle, is it not, Mr. Damopolon?" he said.

"It is indeed," agreed Damopolon, standing up as though he believed East to have finished.

"Yet this stick was made of a particularly fine piece," added East. "Carter!" he cried loudly.

The library door opened ... and Detective Sergeant Carter, of New Scotland Yard, entered, carrying a broken ebony stick. Damopolon dropped his cigarette, and, whilst he stooped to recover it:

"Carter and I went fishing this afternoon," said East, "in the Black Gap. The criminal had sought to hide the broken cane—which bears his monogram—and also the image. He had tied them together, filled the image with clay, and dropped them into the water. Fortunately, they stuck upon an outstanding mass of weeds, and we did not fish in vain. Is there any point, Mr. Damopolon, which I have not made clear? I don't know what implement you used to strike Sir Jeffrey, nor do I know what you did with his ash-stick!..."

Clutching wildly at the table, I rose to my feet, my gaze set amazedly upon the man thus accused, upon the man I had called my friend, upon the man who owed so much to the dead baronet. And he?... He tossed his cigarette into the hearth and shrugged his shoulders. But, now, I saw that he was deathly pale. He began speaking, in a hoarse, mechanical voice:

"I struck him with a broken elm branch," he said. "His hat saved him. I completed the matter with my bare hands. I was desperate. You need not tell me that Olive—Miss Baird—has confessed to our secret marriage, nor shall I weary you with the many reasons I had to hate her father and the pressing need I had for the fortune which she inherits at his death. It is finished; I have lost, and——"

"Carter!" cried East. "Quick! quick!"

But though the detective, who had been edging nearer and nearer to the speaker, now sprang upon him with the leap of a panther, he was too late. The sound of a muffled shot echoed through The Warrens, and the Greek fell with an appalling crash fully over the library table, so that the blue monkey slid across its polished surface and was shattered to bits upon the oaken floor!

THE RIDDLE OF RAGSTAFF

I

"Well, Harry, my boy, and what's the latest news from Venice?"

Harry Lorian stretched his long legs and lay back in his chair.

"I had a letter from the governor this morning, Colonel. He appears to be filling his portfolio with studies of windows and doorways and stair-rails and the other domestic necessities dear to his architectural soul!"

Colonel Reynor laughed in his short, gruff way, as my friend, Lorian, gazing sleepily about the quaint old hall in which we sat, but always bringing his gaze to one point—a certain door—blew rings of smoke straightly upward.

"I suppose," said our host, the Colonel, "most of the material will be used for the forthcoming book?"

"I suppose so," drawled Lorian, glancing for the twentieth time at the yet vacant doorway by the stair-foot. "The idea of architects and artists and other constitutionally languid people, having to write books, fills my soul with black horror."

"He had a glorious time with our old panelling, Harry," laughed the Colonel, waving his cigar vaguely toward the panelled walls and nooks which gradually were receding into the twilight.

"Yes," said my friend. "He was here quite an unconscionable time— even for an old school chum of the proprietor. I hope you counted the spoons when he left!"

Lorian's disrespectful references to Sir Julius, his father, were characteristic; for he reverences that famous artist with the double love of a son and a pupil.

"Of course we did," chuckled Reynor. "Nothing missing, my boy!"

"That's funny," drawled Lorian. "Because if he didn't steal it from here I can't imagine from where he stole it!"

"Stole what, Harry?"

"Whatever some chap broke into his studio for last night!"

"Eh!" cried the Colonel, sitting suddenly very upright. "Into your father's studio? Burglars?"

"Suppose so," was the reply. "They took nothing that I was aware to be in his possession, though the place was ransacked. I naturally concluded that they had taken something that I was *unaware* to be in his——Ah!"

Sybil Reynor entered by the door which, for the past twenty minutes, had been the focus of Lorian's gaze. The gathering dusk precluded the possibility of my seeing with certainty, but I think her face flushed as her dark eyes rested upon my friend. Her beauty is not of the kind which needs deceptive half-lights to perfect it, but there in the dimness, as she came towards us, she looked very lovely and divinely graceful. I did not envy Lorian his good fortune; but I suppressed a sigh when I saw how my existence had escaped the girl's notice and how the world in her eyes, contained only a Henry Lorian, R.I.

Her mother entered shortly afterwards and a general conversation arose, which continued until the arrival of Ralph Edie and his sister. They were accompanied by Felix Hulme; and their advent completed the small party expected at Ragstaff Park.

"You late arrivals," said Lorian, "have only just time to dress, unless you want to miss everything but the nuts!"

"Oh, Harry!" said Mrs. Reynor, "you are as bad as your father!"

"Worse," said Lorian promptly. "I am altogether more rude and have a bigger appetite!"

With such seeming trivialities, then, opened the drama of Ragstaff, the drama in which Fate had cast four of us for leading rôles.

II

Following dinner, the men—or, as my friend has it, "the gunners"—drifted into the hall. The hall at Ragstaff Park is fitted as a smoking lounge. It dates back to Tudor days and affords some magnificent examples of mediæval panelling. At every point the eye meets the device of a man with a ragged staff—from which the place derives its name, and which is the crest of the Reynors.

A conversation took place to which, at the time, I attached small importance, but which, later, assumed a certain significance.

"Extraordinary business," said Felix Hulme—"that attempted burglary at Sir Julius's studio last night."

"Yes," replied Lorian. "Who told you?"

Hulme appeared to be confused by the abrupt question.

"Oh," he replied, "I heard of it from Baxter, who has the next studio, you know."

"When did you see Baxter?" asked Lorian casually.

"This morning."

"I suppose," said Colonel Reynor to my friend, "a number of your father's drawings are there?"

"Yes," answered Lorian slowly; "but the more valuable ones I have at my own studio, including those intended for use in his book."

Something in his tone caused me to glance hard at him.

"You don't think they were the burglar's objective?" I suggested.

"Hardly," was the reply. "They would be worthless to a thief."

"First I've heard of this attempt, Lorian," said Edie. "Anything missing?"

"No. The thing is an utter mystery. There were some odds and ends lying about which no ordinary burglar could very well have overlooked."

"If any loss had been sustained," said the Colonel, half jestingly, "I should have put it down to the Riddle!"

"Don't quite follow you. Colonel," remarked Edie. "What riddle?"

"The family Riddle of the Ragstaffs," explained Lorian. "You've seen it—over there by the staircase."

"Oh!" exclaimed the other, "you mean that inscription on the panel—which means nothing in particular? Yes, I have examined it several times. But why should it affect the fortunes of Sir Julius?"

"You see," was the Colonel's reply, "we have a tradition in the family, Edie, that the Riddle brings us luck, but brings misfortune to anyone else who has it in his possession. It's never been copied before; but I let Lorian—Sir Julius—make a drawing of it for his forthcoming book on Decorative Wood-carving. I don't know," he added smilingly, "if the mysterious influence follows the copy or only appertains to the original."

"Let us have another look at it," said Edie. "It has acquired a new interest!"

The whole party of us passed idly across the hall to the foot of the great staircase. From the direction of the drawing-room proceeded the softly played strains of the *Duetto* from *Cavalleria*. I knew Sybil Reynor was the player, and I saw Lorian glance impatiently in the direction of the door. Hulme detected the glance, too, and an expression rested momentarily upon his handsome face which I found myself at a loss to define.

"You see," said the Colonel, holding a candle close to the time-blackened panel, "it is a meaningless piece of mediæval doggerel roughly carved in the wood. The oak-leaf border is very fine, so your father tells me, Harry"—to Lorian—"but it is probably the work of another hand, as is the man and ragged staff which form the shield at the top."

"Has it ever occurred to you," asked Hulme, "that the writing might be of a very much later date—late Stuart, for instance?"

"No," replied the Colonel abruptly, and turned away. "I am sure it is earlier than that."

I was not the only member of the party who noticed the curt tone of his reply; and when we had all retired for the night I lingered in Lorian's room and reverted to the matter.

"Is the late Stuart period a sore point with the Colonel?" I asked.

Lorian, who was in an unusually thoughtful mood, lighted his pipe and nodded.

"It is said," he explained, "that a Reynor at about that time turned buccaneer and became the terror of the two Atlantics! I don't know what possessed Hulme to say such a thing. Probably he doesn't know about the piratical page in the family records, however. He's a strange chap."

"He is," I agreed. "Everybody seems to know him, yet nobody knows anything *about* him. I first met him at the Travellers' Club. I was unaware, until I came down here this time, that the Colonel was one of his friends."

"Edie brought him down first," replied Lorian. "But I think Hulme had met Sybil—Miss Reynor—in London, before. I may be a silly ass, but somehow I distrust the chap—always have. He seems to know altogether too much about other people's affairs."

I mentally added that he also took too great an interest in a certain young lady to suit Lorian's taste. We chatted upon various matters—principally upon the manners, customs, and manifold beauties of Sybil Reynor—until my friend's pipe went out. Then I bade him good night and went to my own room.

III

With that abruptness characteristic of the coast and season, a high wind had sprung up since the party had separated. Now a continuous booming filled the night, telling how the wrath of the North Atlantic spent itself upon the western rocks.

To a town-dweller, more used to the vaguely soothing hum of the metropolis, this grander music of the elements was a poor sedative. Sleep evaded me, tired though I was, and I presently found myself drifting into that uncomfortable frame of mind between dreaming and waking, wherein one's brain becomes a torturing parrot-house, filled with some meaningless reiteration.

"The riddle of the ragged staff—the riddle of the ragged staff," was the phrase that danced maddeningly through my brain. It got to that pass with me, familiar enough to victims of insomnia, when the words began to go to a sort of monotonous melody.

Thereupon, I determined to light a candle and read for a while, in the hope of inducing slumber.

The old clock down in the hall proclaimed the half-hour. I glanced at my watch. It was half-past one. The moaning of the wind and the wild song of the sea continued unceasingly.

Then I dropped my paper—and listened.

Amid the mighty sounds which raged about Ragstaff Park it was one slight enough which had attracted my attention. But in the elemental music there was a sameness which rendered it, after a time, negligible. Indeed, I think sleep was not far off when this new sound detached itself from the old—like the solo from its accompaniment.

Something had fallen, crashingly, within the house.

It might be some object insecurely fastened which had been detached in the breeze from an open window. And, realising this, I waited and listened.

For some minutes the wind and the waves alone represented sound. Then my ears, attuned to this stormy conflict, and sensitive to anything apart from it, detected a faint scratching and tapping.

My room was the first along the corridor leading to the west wing, and therefore the nearest to the landing immediately above the hall. I determined that this mysterious disturbance proceeded from downstairs. At another time, perhaps, I might have neglected it, but to-night, and so recently following upon Lorian's story of the attempt upon his father's studio, I found myself keenly alive to the burglarious possibilities of Ragstaff.

I got out of bed, put on my slippers, and, having extinguished the candle, was about to open the door when I observed a singular thing.

A strong light—which could not be that of the moon, for ordinarily the corridor beyond was dark—shone under the door!

Even as I looked in amazement it was gone.

Very softly I turned the knob.

Careful as I was, it slipped from my grasp with a faint *click*. To this, I think, I owed my failure to see more than I did see. But what I saw was sufficiently remarkable.

Cloud-banks raced across the sky tempestuously, and, as I peered over the oaken balustrade down into the hall, one of these impinged upon the moon's disc and, within the space of two seconds or less, had wholly obscured it. Upon where a long, rectangular patch of light, splashed with lozenge-shaped shadows spread from a mullioned window across the polished floor, crept a band of blackness—widened—claimed half—claimed the whole—and left the hall in darkness.

Yet, in the half-second before the coming of the cloud, and as I first looked down, I had seen something—something indefinable. All but immediately it was lost in the quick gliding shadow—yet I could be sure that I had seen—what?

A gleaming, metallic streak—almost I had said a sword—which leapt from my view into the bank of gloom!

Passing the cloud, and the moon anew cutting a line of light through the darkness of the hall, nothing, no one, remained to be seen. I might have imagined the presence of the shining blade, rod, or whatever had seemed to glitter in the moon-rays; and I should have felt assured that such was the case but for the suspicion (and it was nearly a certainty) that a part of the shadow which had enwrapped the mysterious appearance had been of greater depth than the rest—more tangible; in short, had been no shadow, but a substance—the form of one who lurked there.

Doubtful how to act, and unwilling to disturb the house without good reason, I stood hesitating at the head of the stairs.

A grating sound, like that of a rusty lock, and clearly distinguishable above the noise occasioned by the wind, came to my ears. I began slowly and silently to descend the stairs.

At the foot I paused, looking warily about me. There was no one in the hall.

A new cloud swept across the face of the moon, and utter darkness surrounded me again. I listened intently, but nothing stirred.

Briefly I searched all those odd nooks and corners in which the rambling place abounded, but without discovering anything to account for the phenomena which had brought me there at that hour of the night. The big doors were securely bolted, as were all the windows. Extremely puzzled, I returned to my room and to bed.

In the morning I said nothing to our host respecting the mysterious traffic of the night, since nothing appeared to be disturbed in any way.

"Did you hear it blowing?" asked Colonel Reynor during breakfast. "The booming of the waves sounded slap under the house. Good job the wind has dropped this morning."

It was, indeed, a warm and still morning, when on the moorland strip beyond the long cornfield, where the thick fir-tufts marked the warren honeycomb, partridges might be met with in many coveys, basking in the sandy patches.

There were tunnels through the dense bushes to the west, too, which led one with alarming suddenness to the very brink of the cliff. And here went scurrying many a hare before the armed intruder.

Lorian and I worked around by lunch-time to the spinneys east of the cornfield, and, nothing loath to partake of the substantial hospitalities of Ragstaff, made our way up to the house. There is a kind of rock-garden from which you must approach from that side. It affords an uninterrupted view of the lower part of the grounds from the lawn up to the terrace.

Only two figures were in sight; and they must have been invisible from any other point, as we, undoubtedly, were invisible to them.

They were those of a man and a girl. They stood upon the steps leading down from the lawn to the rose-garden. It was impossible to misunderstand the nature of the words which the man was speaking. But I saw the girl turn aside and shake her head. The man sought to take her hand and received a further and more decided rebuff.

We hurried on. Lorian, though I avoided looking directly at him, was biting his lip. He was very pale, too. And I knew that he had recognized, as I had recognized, Sybil Reynor and Felix Hulme.

IV

During lunch, a Mr. Findon, who had driven over with one of the Colonel's neighbours, asked Sybil Reynor whether the peculiar and far from beautiful ring which she invariably wore was Oriental. From his conversation I gathered that he was something of an expert.

"It is generally supposed to be Phœnician, Mr. Findon," she answered; and slipping it from her finger she passed it to him. "It is my lot in life to wear it always, hideous though it is!"

"Indeed! An heirloom, I suppose?"

"Yes," replied the girl; "and an ugly one."

In point of fact, the history of the ring was as curious as that of the Riddle. For generations it had been worn by the heir of Ragstaff from the day of his majority to that of his eldest son's. Colonel Reynor had no son. Hence, following the tradition as closely as circumstances allowed, he had invested Sybil with the ring upon the day that she came of age—some three months prior to the time of which I write.

As Mr. Findon was about to return the ring, Lorian said:

"Excuse me. May I examine it for a moment?"

"Of course," replied Sybil.

He took it in his hand and bent over it curiously. I cannot pretend to explain what impelled me to glance towards Hulme at that moment; but I did do so. And the expression which rested upon his dark and usually handsome face positively alarmed me.

I concluded that, beneath the cool surface, he was a man of hot passions, and I would have ascribed the fixed glare to the jealousy of a rejected suitor in presence of a more favoured rival, had it centred upon Lorian. But it appeared to be focused, particularly, upon the ring.

The incident impressed me very unfavourably. A sense of mystery was growing up around me—pervading the atmosphere of Ragstaff Park.

After lunch Lorian and I again set out in company, but my friend appeared to be in anything but sporting humour. We bore off at a sharp angle from the Colonel and some others who were set upon the rough shooting on the western rim of the moors and made for the honeycombed ground which led one upward to the cliff edge.

Abruptly, we found ourselves upon the sheer brink, with the floor of the ocean at our feet and all the great Atlantic before us.

"Let us relent of our murderous purpose," said Lorian, dropping comfortably on to a patch of velvety turf and producing his pipe. "I have dragged you up here with the malicious intention of talking to you."

I was not sorry to hear it. There was much that I wished to discuss with him.

"I should have stayed to say something to some one," he added, carefully stuffing his briar, "but first I wanted to say something to you." He paused, fumbling for matches. "What," he continued, finding some and striking one, "is Felix Hulme's little game?"

"He wants to marry Miss Reynor."

"I know; but he needn't get so infernally savage because she won't accept him. He looked at me in a positively murderous way at lunch to-day."

"So you noticed that?"

"Yes—and I saw that you noticed it, too."

"Listen," I said. "Leaving Hulme out of the question, there is an altogether more mysterious business afoot." And I told him of the episode of the previous night.

He smoked stolidly whilst I spoke, frowning the while; then:

"Old chap," he said, "I begin to have a sort of glimmering of intelligence. I believe I am threatened with an idea! But it's such an utterly fantastic hybrid that I dare not name it—yet."

He asked me several questions respecting what I had seen, and my replies appeared to confirm whatever suspicion was gathering in his mind. We saw little enough sport, but came in later than anyone.

During dinner there was an odd incident. Lorian said:

"Colonel, d'you mind my taking a picture of the Riddle?"

"Eh!" said the Colonel. "What for? Your father made a drawing of it."

"Yes, I know," replied Lorian. "I mean a photograph."

"Well," mused the Colonel, "I don't know that there can be much objection, since it has been copied once. But have you got a camera here?"

"Ah—no," said my friend thoughtfully, "I haven't. Can anybody lend me one?"

Apparently no one could.

"If you care to drive over to Dr. Mason's after dinner," said our host, "he will lend you one. He has several."

Lorian said he would, and I volunteered to accompany him. Accordingly the Colonel's high dogcart was prepared; and beneath a perfect moon, swimming in a fleckless sky which gave no hint of the storm to come, we set off for the doctor's.

My friend's manœuvres were a constant source of surprise to me. However, I allowed him to know his own business best, and employed my mind with speculations respecting this mystery, what time the Colonel's spirited grey whisked us along the dusty roads.

We had just wheeled around Dr. Mason's drive, when the fact broke in upon my musings that a Stygian darkness had descended upon the night, as though the moon had been snuffed, candle-wise.

"Devil of a storm brewing," said Lorian. "Funny how the weather changes at night."

Two minutes after entering the doctor's cosy study, down came the rain.

"Now we're in for it!" said Mason. "I'll send Wilkins to run the dogcart into the stable until it blows over."

The storm proved to be a severe one; and long past midnight, despite the doctor's hospitable attempts to detain us, we set off for Ragstaff Park.

"We can put up the grey ourselves," said Lorian. "I love grooming horses! And by going around into the yard and throwing gravel up at his window, we can awaken Peters without arousing the house. This plan almost startles me by its daring originality. I fear that I detect within myself the symptoms of genius."

So, with one of Dr. Mason's cameras under the seat, we started back through the sweet-smelling lanes; and, at about twenty minutes past one, swung past the gate lodge and up the long avenue, the wheels grinding crisply upon the newly wetted gravel. There was but little moon, now, and the house stood up, an irregular black mass, before us.

Then, from three of the windows, there suddenly leapt out a dazzling white light!

Lorian pulled up the grey with a jerk.

"Good God!" he said. "What's that! An explosion!"

But no sound reached us. Only, for some seconds, the hard, white glare streamed out upon the steps and down on to the drive. Suddenly as it had come—it was gone, and the whole of Ragstaff was in darkness as before!

The horse started nervously, but my friend held him with a firm hand, turning and looking at me queerly.

"That's what shone under your door last night!" he said. "That light was in the hall!"

V

Peters was awakened, the horse stabled and ourselves admitted without arousing another soul. As we came around from the back of the house (we had not entered by the main door), and, candles in hand, passed through the hall, nothing showed as having been disturbed.

"Don't breathe a word of our suspicions to anyone," counselled Lorian.

"What *are* our suspicions?" said I.

"At present," he replied, "indefinable."

To-night the distant murmur of the sea proved very soothing, and I slept soundly. I was early afoot, however, but not so early as Lorian. As I passed around the gallery above the hall, on my way to the bathroom, I saw him folding up the tripod of the camera which he had borrowed from Dr. Mason. The morning sun was streaming through the windows.

"Hullo!" Lorian called to me. "I've got a splendid negative, I think. Peters is rigging up a dark-room in the wine-cellar—delightful site for the purpose! Will you join me in developing?"

Although I was unable to conjecture what my friend hoped to gain by his photographic experiments, I agreed, prompted as much by curiosity as anything else. So, after my tub, I descended to the cellar and splashed about in Hypo., until Lorian declared himself satisfied.

"The second is the best," he pronounced critically, holding the negative up to the red lamp. "I made three exposures in all; but the reflection from the polished wood has rather spoiled the first and also the third."

"Whatever do you want with this photograph, anyway," I said, "when the original is available?"

"My dear chap," he replied, "one cannot squat in the hall fixedly regarding a section of panel like some fakir staring at a palm leaf!"

"Then you intend to study it?"

"Closely!"

As a matter of fact, he did not join us during the whole of the day; but since he spent the greater part of the time in his own room, I did not proffer my aid. From a remark dropped by the Colonel, I gathered that Sybil had volunteered to assist, during the afternoon, in preparing prints.

I was one of the first in to tea, and Lorian came racing out to meet me.

"Not a word yet," he said, "but if the Colonel is agreeable, I shall tell them all at dinner!"

"Tell them what?" I began——

Then I saw Sybil Reynor standing in the shadow of the porch, and, even from that distance, saw her rosy blushes.

I understood.

"Lucky man!" I cried, and wrung his hand warmly. "The very best of good wishes, old chap. I am delighted!"

"So am I!" replied Lorian. "But come and see the print."

We went into the house together; and Sybil blushed more furiously than ever when I told her how I envied Lorian—and added that he deserved the most beautiful girl in England, and had won her.

Lorian had a very clear print of the photograph pinned up to dry on the side of his window.

"We shall be busy to-night!" he said mysteriously.

He had planned to preserve his great secret until dinner-time; but, of course, it came out whilst we sat over tea on the balcony. The Colonel was unfeignedly delighted, and there is nothing secretive about Colonel Reynor. Consequently, five minutes after he had been informed how matters were between his daughter and Lorian, all the house knew.

I studied the face of Hulme, to see how he would take the news. But he retained a perfect mastery of himself, though his large dark eyes gleamed at discord with the smile which he wore.

Our photographic experiments were forgotten; and throughout dinner, whereat Sybil looked exquisitely lovely and very shy, and Lorian preserved an unruffled countenance, other topics ruled.

It was late before we found ourselves alone in Lorian's room, with the print spread upon the table beneath the light of the shaded lamp.

We bent over it.

"Now," said Lorian, "I assume that this is some kind of cipher!"

I stared at him surprisedly.

"And," he continued, "you and I are going to solve it if we sit up all night!"

"How do you propose to begin?"

"Well, as it appears to mean nothing in particular, as it stands, I thought of beginning by assuming that the letters have other values altogether. Therefore, upon the basis that *e* is the letter which most frequently occurs in English, with *a, o, i, d, h, n, r*, afterwards, I had thought of resolving it into its component letters."

"But would that rule apply to mediæval English?"

"Ah," said Lorian thoughtfully, "most sage counsellor! A wise and timely thought! I'm afraid it wouldn't."

"What now?"

Lorian scratched his head in perplexity.

"Suppose," he suggested, "we write down the words plainly, and see if, treating each one separately, we can find other meanings to them."

Accordingly, upon a sheet of paper, I wrote:

Wherso eer thee doome bee
Looke untoe ye strypped tree
Offe ragged staffe. Upon itte ley
Golde toe greene ande kay toe kay.

Our efforts in the proposed direction were rewarded with poor success. Some gibberish even less intelligible than the original was the only result of our labour.

Lorian threw down his pencil and began to reload his pipe.

"Let us consider possible meanings to the original words," he said. "Do you know of anything in the neighbourhood which might answer to the description of a 'strypped tree'?"

I shook my head.

"What has occasioned your sudden interest in the thing?" I asked wearily.

"It is a long story," he replied; "and I have an idea that there's no time to be lost in solving the Riddle!"

However, even Lorian's enthusiasm flagged at last. We were forced to admit ourselves hopelessly beaten by the Riddle. I went to my own room feeling thoroughly tired. But I was not destined to sleep long. A few minutes after closing my eyes (or so it seemed), came a clamouring at the door.

I stumbled sleepily out of bed, and, slipping on my dressing-gown, admitted Lorian. Colonel Reynor stood immediately behind him.

"Most extraordinary business!" began the latter breathlessly. "Sybil had—*you* tell him, Harry!"

"Well," said Lorian, "it is not unexpected! Listen: Sybil woke up a while ago, with the idea that she had forgotten something or lost something—you know the frame of mind! She went to her dressing-table and found the family ring missing!"

"*The* ring!" burst in the Colonel excitedly. "Amazing!"

"She remembered having taken it off, during the evening, to—er—to put another one on! But she was unable to recall having replaced it. She determined to run down and see if she had left it upon the seat in the corner of the library. Well, she went downstairs in her dressing-gown, and, carrying a candle, very quietly, in order to wake no one, crossed to the library and searched unavailingly. She heard a faint noise outside in the hall."

Lorian paused. Felix Hulme had joined the party.

"What's the disturbance?" he asked.

"Oh," said Lorian, turning to him, "it's about Sybil. She was down in the library a while ago to look for something, and heard a sort of grating sound out in the hall. She came out, and almost fell over an iron-bound chest, about a foot and a half long, which stood near the bottom of the staircase!"

"Good heavens, Lorian!" I cried, "how had it come there?"

"Sybil says," he resumed, "that she could not believe her eyes. She stooped to examine the thing ... and with a thrill of horror saw it to be roughly marked *with a skull and cross-bones*!"

"My dear Lorian," said Hulme, "are you certain that Miss Reynor was awake?"

"She woke *us* quickly enough!" interrupted the Colonel. "Poor girl, she was shaking dreadfully. Thought it was a supernatural appearance. She's with her mother now."

"But the box!" I cried. "Where is the box?"

"That's the mystery," answered Colonel Reynor. "I was downstairs two minutes later, and there was nothing of the kind to be seen! Has our Ragstaff ghost started walking again, I wonder? You ought to know, Hulme; you're in the Turret Room—that is the authentic haunted chamber!"

"I was aroused by the bell ringing," replied Hulme. "I am a very light sleeper. But I heard or saw nothing supernatural."

"By the way, Hulme," said my friend, "the Turret Room is directly above the hall. I have a theory. Might I come up with you for a moment?"

"Certainly," replied Hulme.

We all went up to the Turret Room. Having climbed the stairs to this apartment, you enter it by descending three steps. It is octagonal and panelled all around. My friend tapped the panels and sounded all the oaken floor-boards. Then, professing himself satisfied, he bade Hulme good night, and accompanied me to my room.

VI

Ragstaff Park slumbered once more. But Lorian sat upon the edge of my bed, smoking and thinking hard. He had been to his own room for the print of the Riddle, and it lay upon a chair before him.

"Listen to this," he said suddenly: "(*a*) Some one breaks into the governor's studio, and takes nothing. His drawings of the Ragstaff Riddle happen to be at my studio. (*b*) You hear a noise in the night, and see (1) a bright light; (2) a gleaming rod. (*c*) You and I see a bright light on the following night, and presumably proceeding from the same place; i.e., the hall. (*d*) Something I have not mentioned before—Hulme has a camera in his kit! And he doesn't want the fact known!"

"What do you mean?"

"I tested him the other night, by inquiring if anyone could lend me a camera. He did not volunteer! The morning following the mysterious business in the hall, observed by you, I saw a photographic printing frame in his window! He must have one of those portable developers with him."

"And to what does all this point?"

"To the fact that he has made at least three attempts to obtain a copy of the Riddle, and has at last succeeded!"

"Three!"

"I really think so. The evidence points to him as the person who broke into the studio. He made a bad slip. He referred to the matter, and cited Horace Baxter as his informant. Baxter is away!"

"But this is serious!"

"I should say so! He couldn't attempt to photograph the panel in daylight, so he employed magnesium ribbon at night! First time his tripod slipped. It is evidently one of the light, telescopic kind. His negative proved useless. It was one of the metal legs of the tripod which you saw shining! The second time he was more successful. That was the light of his magnesium ribbon you and I saw from the drive!"

"But, Lorian, I went down and searched the hall!"

"Now we come on to the, at present, conjectural part," explained Lorian. "My theory is that Hulme, somewhere or other, has come across some old documents which give the clue to those secret passages said to exist in Ragstaff, but which the Colonel has never been able to locate. I feel assured that there is some means of secret communication between the Turret Room and the hall. I further believe that Hulme has in some way got upon the track of another secret—that of the Riddle."

"But what *is* the secret of the Riddle?"

"In my opinion the Riddle is a clue to another hiding-place, evidently not connected with the maze of passages; possibly what is known as a Priest's Hole. As you know, Hulme asked Sybil to marry him. I believe the man to be in financial straits; so that we must further assume the Riddle to conceal the whereabouts of a treasure, since the Reynors are far from wealthy."

"The *chest*! Lorian! The chest!" I cried.

"Quite so. But what immediately preceded its appearance? The loss of the family ring! If I am not greatly in error, Hulme found that ring! And the ring is the key to the riddle! Do you recall the shape of the bezel? Simply *a square peg of gold*! Look at the photograph!"

He was excited, for once.

"What does it say?" he continued: "'Ye strypped tree!' That means the device of leaves, twigs, and acorns—stripped *from* a tree—see? Here, at the bottom of the panel, is such a group, and (this is where we have been so blind!) intertwined with the design is the word *CAEG*—Ancient Saxon for *key*! Look! 'Golde toe Greene and kay toe kay'! Amongst the *green* leaves is a square hole. The *gold* knob on the ring fits it!"

For a moment I was too greatly surprised for speech. Then:

"You think Hulme discovered this?"

"I do. And I think Sybil's mislaying her ring gave him his big chance. He had got the chest out whilst she was in the library. He must have been inside somewhere looking for it when she passed through the hall. Then, hearing her approach from the library, he was forced to abandon his heavy 'find' and hide in the secret passage which communicates with his room. Directly she ran upstairs he returned for the chest!"

I looked him hard in the face.

"We don't want a scene, Lorian," I began. "Besides, it's just possible you may be wrong."

"I agree," said Lorian. "Come up to his room, now."

Passing quietly upstairs, we paused before the door of the Turret Room. A faint light showed under it. Lorian glanced at me—then knocked.

"Who's there?" came sharply.

"Lorian," answered my friend. "I want a chat with you about the secret passage and the old treasure chest—*before speaking to the Colonel*!"

There was a long silence, then:

"Just a moment," came hoarsely. "Don't come in until I call."

We looked at one another doubtfully. A long minute passed. I could hear a faint sound within. At last came Hulme's voice:

"All right. Come in."

As Lorian threw the door open, a faint *click* sounded from somewhere.

The Turret Room was empty!

"By heaven! he's given us the slip!" cried my friend.

We glanced around the room. A candle burnt upon the table. And upon the bed stood an iron-barred chest, with a sheet of notepaper lying on its lid!

Lorian pounced upon the note. We read it together.

"Mr. Henry Lorian" (it went), "I realize that you have found me out. I will confess that I had no time to open the chest. But as matters stand I only ask you not to pursue me. I have taken nothing not my own. The ring, and an interesting document which I picked up some years ago, are on the table. Offer what explanation of my disappearance you please. I am in your hands."

We turned again to the table. Upon a piece of worn parchment lay the missing ring. Lorian spread out the parchment and bent over it.

"Why," I cried, "it is a plan of Ragstaff Park!"

"With a perfect network of secret passages!" added my friend, "and some instructions, apparently, as to how to enter them. It bears the initials 'R. R.' and, in brackets, 'Capt. S.' I begin to understand."

He raised the candle and stepped across to the ancient chest. It bore a roughly designed skull and cross-bones, and, in nearly defaced red characters, the words:

"CAPTAIN SATAN."

"Captain Satan!" I said. "He was one of the most bloodthirsty pirates who ever harried the Spanish Main!"

"He was," agreed Lorian; "and his real name was Roderick Reynor. He evidently solved the riddle some generations earlier than Hulme—and stored his bloodstained hoard in the ancient hiding-place. Also, you see, he knew about the passages."

"What shall we do?"

"Hulme has surrendered. You can see that the chest has not been opened. Therefore there is only one thing that we *can* do. We must keep what we know to ourselves, return the chest to its hiding-place, and proclaim that we have found the missing ring!"

Down to the hall we bore the heavy chest. The square knob on the ring fitted, as Lorian had predicted, into the hole half hidden among the oak leaves of the design. Without much difficulty we forced back the fastening (it proved to be of a very simple pattern), and slid the whole panel aside. A small, square chamber was revealed by the light of the candle—quite empty.

"As I had surmised," said my friend; "a Priest's Hole."

We carried the chest within, and reclosed the panel, which came to with a sharp *click*.

The story which we invented to account for Hulme's sudden departure passed muster; for one topic usurped the interests of all—the ghostly box, with its piratical emblem.

"My boy," Colonel Reynor said to Lorian, "I cannot pretend to explain what Sybil saw. But it bears curiously upon a certain black page in the family history. If the chest had been tangible, and had contained a fortune, I would not have opened it. Let all pertaining to that part of our records remain buried, say I."

"Which determines our course," explained Lorian to me. "The chest is not ours, and the Colonel evidently would rather not know about it. I regret that I lack the morals of a burglar."

THE MASTER OF HOLLOW GRANGE

I

Jack Dillon came to Hollow Grange on a thunderous black evening when an ebony cloud crested the hill-top above, and, catching the upflung rays of sunset, glowed redly like the pall of Avalon in the torchlight. Through the dense ranks of firs cloaking the slopes a breeze, presaging the coming storm, whispered evilly, and here in the hollow the birds were still.

The man who had driven him from the station glanced at him, with a curiosity thinly veiled.

"What about your things, sir?" he inquired.

Dillon stared rather blankly at the ivy-covered lodge, which, if appearances were to be trusted, was unoccupied.

"Wait a moment; I will ring," he said curtly; for this furtive curiosity, so ill concealed, had manifested itself in the manner of the taxi-driver from the moment that Dillon had directed him to drive to Hollow Grange.

He pushed open the gate and tugged at the iron ring which was suspended from the wall of the lodge. A discordant clangour rewarded his efforts, the cracked note of a bell that spoke from somewhere high up in the building, that seemed to be buffeted to and fro from fir to fir, until it died away, mournfully, in some place of shadows far up the slope. In the voice of the bell there was something furtive, something akin to the half-veiled curiosity in the eyes of the man who stood watching him; something fearful, too, in both, as though man and bell would whisper: "Return! Beware of disturbing the dwellers in this place."

But Dillon angrily recalled himself to the realities. He felt that these ghostly imaginings were born of the Boche-maltreated flesh, were products of lowered tone; that he would have perceived no query in the glance of the taxi-driver and heard no monkish whisper in the clang of the bell had he been fit, had he been fully recovered from the effects of his wound. Monkish whisper? Yes, that was it—his mind had supplied, automatically, an aptly descriptive term: the cracked bell spoke with the voice of ancient monasteries, had in it the hush of cloisters and the sigh of renunciation.

"Hang it all!" muttered Dillon. "This won't do."

A second time he awoke the ghostly bell-voice, but nothing responded to its call; man, bird, and beast had seemingly deserted Hollow Grange. He was conscious of a sudden nervous irritation, as he turned brusquely and met the inquiring glance of the taxi-man.

"I have arrived before I was expected," he said. "If you will put my things in the porch here I will go up to the house and get a servant to fetch them. They will be safe enough in the meantime."

His own words increased his irritability; for were they not in the nature of an apology on behalf of his silent and unseen host? Were they not a concession to that nameless query in the man's stare? Moreover, deep within his own consciousness, some vague thing was stirring; so that, the man dismissed and promptly departing, Dillon stood glancing from the little stack of baggage in the lodge porch up the gloomy, narrow, and over-arched drive, indignantly aware that he also carried a question in his eyes.

The throb of the motor mounting the steep, winding lane grew dim and more dim until it was borne away entirely upon the fitful breeze. Faintly he detected the lowing of cattle in some distant pasture; the ranks of firs whispered secretly one to another, and the pall above the hills grew blacker and began to extend over the valley.

Amid that ominous stillness of nature he began to ascend the cone-strewn path. Evidently enough, the extensive grounds had been neglected for years, and that few pedestrians, and fewer vehicles, ever sought Hollow Grange was demonstrated by the presence of luxuriant weeds in the carriage way. Having proceeded for some distance, until the sheer hillside seemed to loom over him like the wall of a tower, Dillon paused, peering about in the ever-growing darkness. He was aware of a physical chill; certainly no ray of sunlight ever penetrated to this tunnel through the firs. Could he have mistaken the path and be proceeding, not toward the house, but away from it and into the midnight of the woods mantling the hills?

There was something uncomfortable in that reflection; momentarily he knew a childish fear of the darkening woods, and walked forward rapidly, self-assertively. Ten paces brought him to one of the many bends in the winding road—and there, far ahead, as though out of some cavern in the very hillside, a yellow light shone.

He pressed on with greater assurance until the house became visible. Now he perceived that he had indeed strayed from the carriage-sweep in some way, for the path that he was following terminated at the foot of a short flight of moss-covered brick steps. He mounted the steps and found himself at the bottom of a terrace. The main entrance was far to his left and separated from the terrace by a neglected lawn. That portion of the place was Hanoverian and ugly, whilst the wing nearest to him was Tudor and picturesque. Excepting the yellow light shining out from a sunken window almost at his feet, no illuminations were visible about the house, although the brewing storm had already plunged the hollow into premature night.

Indeed, there was no sign of occupancy about the strange-looking mansion, which might have hidden forgotten for centuries in the horseshoe of the hills. He had sought for rest and quiet; here he should find them. The stillness of the place was of that sort which almost seems to be palpable; that can be seen and felt. A humid chill arose apparently from the terrace, with its stone pavings outlined in moss, crept up from the wilderness below and down from the fir-woods above.

A thought struggled to assume form in his mind. There was something reminiscent about this house of the woods, this silent house which struck no chord of human companionship, in which was no warmth of life or love. Suddenly, the thought leapt into complete being.

This was the palace of the sleeping beauty to which he had penetrated. It was the fairy-tale dear to childhood which had been struggling for expression in his mind ever since he had emerged from the trees on to the desolate terrace. With the departure of the station cab had gone the last link with to-day, and now he was translated to the goblin realm of fable.

He had crossed the terrace and the lawn, and stood looking through an open French window into a room that evidently adjoined the hall. A great still darkness had come, and on a little table in the room a reading-lamp was burning. It had a quaint, mosaic shade which shut in much of the light, but threw a luminous patch directly on a heap of cushions strewn upon the floor. Face downward in this silken nest, her chin resting upon her hands and her elfin curly brown hair tousled bewitchingly, lay a girl so audaciously pretty that Dillon hesitated to accept the evidence of his eyes.

The crunching of a piece of gravel beneath his foot led to the awakening of the sleeping beauty. She raised her head quickly and then started upright, a lithe, divinely petite figure in a green velvet dress, having short fur-trimmed sleeves that displayed her pretty arms. For an instant it was a startled nymph that confronted him; then a distracting dimple appeared in one fair cheek, and:

"Oh! how you frightened me!" said the girl, speaking with a slight French accent which the visitor found wholly entrancing. "You must be Jack Dillon? I am Phryné."

Dillon bowed.

"How I envy Hyperides!" he said.

A blush quickly stained the lovely face of Phryné, and the roguish eyes were lowered, whereby the penitent Dillon, who had jested in the not uncommon belief that a pretty girl is necessarily brainless, knew that the story of the wonder-woman of Thespiæ was familiar to her modern namesake.

"I am afraid," declared Phryné, with a return of her mischievous composure, "that you are very wicked."

Dillon, who counted himself a man of the world, was temporarily at a loss for a suitable rejoinder. The cause of his hesitancy was twofold. In the first place he had reached the age of disillusionment, whereat a man ceases to believe that a perfectly lovely woman exists in the flesh, and in the second place he had found such a fabulous being in a house of gloom and silence to which, a few moments ago, he had deeply regretted having come.

His father, who had accepted the invitation from an old college friend on his son's behalf, had made no mention of a Phryné, whereas Phryné clearly took herself for granted and evidently knew all about Jack Dillon. The latter experienced a volcanic change of sentiment; Hollow Grange was metamorphosed, and assumed magically the guise of a Golden House, an Emperor's pleasure palace, a fair, old-world casket holding this lovely jewel. But who was she?—and in what spirit should he receive her bewildering coquetries?

"I trust," he said, looking into the laughing eyes, "that you will learn to know me better."

Phryné curtsied mockingly.

"You have either too much confidence in your own character or not enough in my wisdom," she said.

Dillon stepped into the room, and, stooping, took up a book which lay open upon the floor. It was a French edition of *The Golden Ass* of Apuleius.

The hollow was illuminated by a blinding flash of lightning, and Phryné's musical laughter was drowned in the thunder that boomed and crashed in deepening peals over the hills. In a sudden tropical torrent the rain descended, as Dr. Kassimere entered the room.

II

Jack Dillon leant from his open window and looked out over the valley to where a dull red glow crowned the hill-top. There was a fire somewhere in the neighbourhood of the distant town; probably a building had been struck by lightning. The storm had passed, although thunder was still audible dimly, like the roll of muffled drums or a remote bombardment. Stillness had reclaimed Hollow Grange.

He was restless, uneasy; he sought to collate his impressions of the place and its master. Twelve years had elapsed since his one previous meeting with Dr. Kassimere, and little or no memory of the man had remained. So much had intervened; the war—and Phryné. Now that he was alone and could collect his ideas he knew of what Dr. Kassimere's gaunt, wide-eyed face had reminded him: it was of Thoth, the Ibis-headed god whose figure he had seen on the walls of the temples during his service in Egypt.

"Kassimere was always a queer fish, Jack," his father had said; "but most of his eccentricities were due to his passion for study. The Grange is the very place Sir Francis" (the specialist) "would have chosen for your convalescence, and you'll find nothing dangerously exciting in Kassimere's atmosphere!"

Yet there was that about Dr. Kassimere which he did not and could not like; his quietly cordial welcome, his courteous regret that his guest's arrival by an earlier train (a circumstance due to reduced service) had led to his not being met at the station; the charming simplicity with which he confessed to the smallness of his household, and to the pleasure which it afforded him to have the son of an old chum beneath his roof—all these kindly overtures had left the bird-like eyes cold, hard, watchful, calculating. The voice was the voice of a friend and a gentleman, but the face was the face of Thoth.

The mystery of Phryné was solved in a measure. She was Dr. Kassimere's adopted daughter and the orphaned child of Louis Devant, the famous Paris cartoonist, who had died penniless in 1911, at the height of his success. In his selection of a name for her, the brilliant and dissolute artist had exhibited a breadth of mind which Phryné inherited in an almost embarrassing degree.

Her mental equipment was bewildering: the erudition of an Oxford don spiced with more than a dash of Boul' Mich', which made for complexity. Her curious learning was doubtless due to the setting of a receptive mind amid such environment, but how she had retained her piquant vivacity in Hollow Grange was less comprehensible. The servants formed a small and saturnine company, only two—the housekeeper, Mrs. Harman, a black and forbidding figure, and Madame Charny, a French companion—sleeping in the house. Gawly, a surly creature who neglected the gardens and muttered savagely over other duties, together with his wife, who cooked, resided at the lodge. There were two maids, who lived in the village....

The glow from the distant fire seemed to be reflected upon the firs bordering the terrace below; then Dillon, watching the dull, red light, remembered that Dr. Kassimere's laboratory adjoined the tiny chapel, and that, though midnight drew near, the doctor was still at work there.

Owls and other night birds hooted and shrieked among the trees and many bats were in flight. He found himself thinking of the pyramid bats of Egypt, and of the ibis-headed Thoth who was the scribe of the under-world.

Dr. Kassimere had made himself medically responsible for his case, and had read attentively the letters which Dillon had brought from his own physician. He was to prescribe on the following day, and to-night the visitor found Morpheus a treacherous god. Furtive activities disturbed the house, or so it seemed to the sleepless man tossing on his bed; alert intelligences within Hollow Grange responded to the night-life of the owls without, and he seemed to lie in the shadow of a watchfulness that never slumbered.

III

"There's many a fine walk hereabouts," said the old man seated in the arm-chair in the corner of the *Threshers' Inn* bar-parlour.

Dillon nodded encouragingly.

"There's Ganton-on-the-Hill," continued the ancient. "You can see the sea from there in clear weather; and many's the time I've heard the guns in France from Upper Crobury of a still night. Then, four mile away, there's the haunted Grange, though nobody's allowed past the gate. Not as nobody wants to be," he added, reflectively.

"The haunted Grange?" questioned Dillon. "Where is that?"

"Hollow Grange?" said the old man. "Why, it lies——"

"Oh, Hollow Grange—yes! I know where Hollow Grange is, but I was unaware that it was reputed to be haunted."

"Ah," replied the other, pityingly, "you're new to these parts; I see that the minute I set eyes on you. Maybe you was wounded in France, and you're down here to get well, like?"

"Quite so. Your deductive reasoning is admirable."

"Ah," said the sage, chuckling with self-appreciation, "I ain't lived in these here parts for nigh on seventy-five years without learning to use my eyes, I ain't. For seventy-four years and seven months," he added proudly, "I ain't been outside this here county where I was born, and I can use my eyes, I can; I know a thing I do, when I see it. Maybe it was providence, as you might say, what brought you to the *Threshers* to-day."

"Quite possibly," Dillon admitted.

"He was just such another as you," continued the old man with apparent irrelevance. "You don't happen to be stopping at Hainingham Vicarage?"

"No," replied Dillon.

"Ah! he was stopping at Hainingham Vicarage and he'd been wounded in France. How he got to know Dr. Kassimere I can't tell you; not at parson's, anyway. Parson won't never speak to him. Only last Sunday week he preached agin him; not in so many words, but I could see his drift. He spoke about them heathen women livin' on an island—sort of female Robinson Crusoes, I make 'em out, I do—as saves poor shipwrecked sailors from the sea and strangles of 'em ashore."

Dillon glanced hard at the voluble old man.

"The sirens?" he suggested, conscious of a sudden hot surging about his heart.

"Ah, that's the women I mean."

"But where is the connection?"

"Ah, you're new to these parts, you are. That Dr. Kassimere he keeps a siren down in Hollow Grange. They see her—these here strangers (same as the shipwrecked sailors parson told about)—and it's all up with 'em."

Dillon stifled a laugh, in which anger would have mingled with contempt. To think that in the twentieth century a man of science was like to meet with the fate of Dr. Dee in the days of Elizabeth! Truly there were dark spots in England. But could he credit the statement of this benighted elder that a modern clergyman had actually drawn an analogy between Phryné Devant and the sirens? It was unbelievable.

"What was the unhappy fate," he asked, masking his intolerance, "of the young man staying at the Vicarage?"

"The same as them afore him," came the startling reply; "for he warn't the first, and maybe"—with a shrewd glance of the rheumy old eyes— "he won't be the last. Them sirens has the powers of darkness. I know, 'cause I've seen one—her at the Grange; and though I'm an old man, nigh on seventy-five, I'll never forget her face, I won't, and the way she smiled at me!"

"But," persisted Dillon, patiently, "what became of this particular young man, the one who was staying at the Vicarage?"

The ancient sage leant forward in his chair and tapped the speaker upon the knee with the stem of his clay pipe.

"Ask them as knows," he said, with impressive solemnity. "Nobody else can tell you!"

And, having permitted an indiscreet laugh to escape him, not another word on the subject could Dillon induce the old man to utter, he strictly confining himself, in his ruffled dignity, to the climatic conditions and the crops.

When Dillon, finally, set out upon the four-mile walk back to the Grange, he realised, with annoyance, that the senile imaginings of his bar-parlour acquaintance lingered in his mind. That Dr. Kassimere dwelt outside the social life of the county he had speedily learnt; but for this he had been prepared. That he might possibly be, not a recluse, but a pariah, was a new point of view. Trivial things, to which hitherto he had paid scant attention, began to marshal themselves as evidence. The two village "helpers," he knew, received extravagant wages, because, as Phryné had confessed, they had "found it almost impossible to get girls to stay." Why?

Of the earlier guest, or guests, who had succumbed to the siren lure of Phryné, he had heard no mention. Why? Save at meal-times he rarely saw his host, who frankly left him to the society of Phryné. Again—why? Dr. Kassimere, in his jealously locked laboratory, was at work day and night upon his experiments. What were these experiments? What was the nature of the doctor's studies?

He had now been for nearly three weeks at Hollow Grange, and never had Dr. Kassimere spoken of his work. And Phryné? The sudden, new thought of Phryné was so strange, so wonderful and overwhelming, that it reacted physically; and he pulled up short in the middle of a field-path, as though some palpable obstacle blocked the way.

Why had he set out alone that day, when all other days had been spent in the girl's company? He had deliberately sought solitude— because of Phryné; because he wanted to think calmly, judicially, to arraign himself before his own judgment, remote from the witchery of her presence. He had tried to render his mind a void, wherein should linger not one fragrant memory of her delicate beauty and charm, so that he might return unbiased to his judgment. He had returned; he was judged.

He loved Phryné madly, insanely. His future, his life, lay in the hollow of her hands.

IV

"Yes," admitted Phryné, "it is true. There were two of them."

"And"—Dillon hesitated—"were they in love with you?"

"Of course," said Phryné, naïvely.

"But you——"

Phryné shook her curly head.

"I rather liked the French boy, but I do not believe anything that a

Frenchman says to a girl; and Harry, the other, was handsome, but so silly...."

"So you did not love either of them?"

"Of course not."

"But," said Dillon, and impulsively he swept her into his arms, "you are going to love me."

One quick upward glance she gave, but instantly lowered her eyes and withheld her bewitching face from him.

"Am I?" she whispered. "You are so conceited."

But as she spoke the words he kissed her, and she surrendered sweetly, nestling her head against his shoulder for a moment. Then, leaping back, bright-eyed and blushing, she turned and ran like a startled fawn across the terrace and into the house.

He saw no more of her until dinner-time, and spent the interval in a kind of suspended consciousness that was new and perturbing. Within him life pulsed at delirious speed, but the universe seemed to have slowed upon its course so that each hour became as two. Throughout dinner, Phryné was deliciously shy to the point of embarrassment; and Dillon, who several times surprised the bird-eyes of Dr. Kassimere studying the girl's face, detained his host, and being a young man of orderly mind, formally asked his consent to an engagement.

The doctor's joy was seemingly so unfeigned that Dillon almost liked him for a moment. He placed no obstacle in the path of the suitor for his adopted daughter's hand, graciously expressing every confidence in the future. His joy was genuine enough, Dillon determined; but from what source did it actually spring? The Thoth-like eyes were exultant, and all the old mistrust poured back in a wave upon the younger man. Was this distrust becoming an obsession? Why should he eternally be seeking an ulterior motive for every act in this man's life?

He went to look for Phryné, and found her in the spot where he had first seen her, prone in a nest of cushions. She sprang up as he entered the room, and glanced at him in that new way which set his heart leaping....

And because of the magic of her presence, it was not until later, when he stood alone in his own room, that he could order the facts gleaned from her.

There was some grain of truth in the story of the ancient gossip at the *Threshers* after all. A young French lieutenant of artillery had received an invitation to spend a leave at Hollow Grange. His Gallic soul had been fired by Phryné's beauty, and although his advances had been met with rebuff, he had asked Dr. Kassimere's permission to pay his court to the girl. On the same evening he had departed hurriedly, and Phryné had supposed, since the doctor never referred to him again, that he had been sent about his business. Then came a strange letter, which Phryné had shown to Dillon. Its tone throughout was of passionate anger, and one passage recurred again and again to Dillon's mind. "I would give my life for you gladly," it read, "but my soul belongs to God...."

Phryné had counted him demented and Dr. Kassimere had agreed with her. But there was Harry Waynwright, the nephew of the vicar of St. Peter's at Hainingham. An accidental meeting with Phryné had led to a courtesy call—and the inevitable. It had all the seeming of a case of love-sickness, and the unhappy youth grew seriously ill. From pestering her daily he changed his tactics to studiously avoiding her, until, meeting her in the village one morning, he greeted her with, "I can't do it, Phryné! tell him I can't do it. He can rely upon my word; but I'm going away to try to forget!"

Dr. Kassimere had professed entire ignorance of the meaning of the words. A faint shadow had crossed Phryné's face as she spoke of these matters, but, as a result of her extraordinary beauty, she was somewhat callous where languishing admirers were concerned, and she had dismissed the gloomy twain with a shrug of her charming shoulders.

"Mad!" she had said. "It seems my fate always to meet mad-men!"

The night silence had descended again upon Hollow Grange, disturbed only by the mournful cry of the owl and the almost imperceptible note of the bat. But to the nervous alertness of Dillon, a deep unrest seemed to stir within the house; yet—an unrest not physical but spiritual; it was as the shadow of a sleepless watcher—a shadow creeping over his soul.

What was the explanation lying at the back of it all? Vainly he sought for a theory, however wild, however improbable, that should embrace all the facts known to him and serve either to banish his black doubts or to focus them. Upon one thing he had determined: There was some thing or some one in Hollow Grange that he *feared*, some centre from whence fear radiated.

Phryné, for one fleeting moment, had revealed to him that she, too, had known this formless dread, but only latterly; probably from lack of a more definite date, she had spoken of this fear as first visiting her at about the time of the Frenchman's advent.

"Slowly, he has changed towards me," she had whispered, referring to Dr. Kassimere. "He watches me, sometimes, in a strange way. Oh, he has been so good, so very kind and good, but—I shall be glad when—"

Could some part of the mystery be explained away by the doctor's increasing absorption in his studies, which led him to regard the charge of a ward, and a wayward one at that, as unduly onerous and disturbing? Might it not fairly be supposed that ignorant superstition and the ravings of unrequited passion accounted for the rest?

At the nature of Dr. Kassimere's studies he could not even guess. The greater number of the works in the library related to mysticism in one form or another, although there was a sprinkling of exact science to leaven the whole.

"He can rely upon my word," Waynwright had said. Regarding what, or regarding whom, had he given his word?

The cry of a night-hawk came, as if in answer; the hoot of an owl, as if in mockery. Out beyond the terrace a dull red light showed from Dr. Kassimere's laboratory.

V

Enlightenment came about in this fashion—seeking to quench a feverish thirst, Dillon discovered that no glass had been left in his room. He determined to fetch one from the buffet cupboard downstairs. Softly, in slippered feet, he descended the stairs and was crossing the hallway when he kicked something—a small book, he thought—that lay there upon the floor. Groping, he found it, slipped it into the pocket of his dressing-gown, and entered the dining-room. He found a tumbler without difficulty, in the dark, noted the presence of a heavy, oppressive odour, and returned upstairs. Now he made another discovery. He had forgotten the nightly draught of medicine prescribed by Dr. Kassimere; a new unopened phial stood upon the dressing-table.

He mixed himself a mild whisky and soda from the decanter and siphon which his host's hospitality caused nightly to be placed in his room, and then, seized by a sudden thought, took out the little book which he had found in the hall.

It was a faded manuscript, in monkish Latin; a copy of an unpublished work of Paracelsus. Many passages had been rendered into English, and the translations, in Dr. Kassimere's minute, cramped writing, were interposed between the bound pages. In these again were interpolated marginal notes, some in the shape of unintelligible symbols, others in that of chemical formulæ. Several passages were marked in red ink. And, having perused the first of these which he chanced upon, a clammy moisture broke out upon his skin, accompanied by so marked a nervous trembling that he was forced to seat himself upon the bed.

The secret of this man's ghastly life-work was in his hands; he knew, now, what bargain Dr. Kassimere had proposed to the Frenchman and to the other; he knew why he had adopted the lovely daughter of Louis Devant—and he knew why he, Jack Dillon, had been invited to Hollow Grange. That such a ghoul in human shape could live and have his being amid ordinary mankind was a stupendous improbability which, ten minutes earlier, he would have laughed to scorn.

"My God!" he whispered. "My God!"

His glance fell upon the unopened phial on his dressing-table, and from his soul a silent thanksgiving rose to heaven that he had left that potion untasted. He realised that his own case differed from those of his predecessors in two particulars: He was actually in residence under Dr. Kassimere's roof and receiving treatment from the man's hands. No option was to be offered to *him*; the great experiment, the *Magnum Opus*, was to be performed without his consent!

And Phryné!—Phryné, the other innocent victim of this fiend's lust for knowledge! The thought restored his courage. More than life itself depended upon his coolness and address; he must act, at once. The monstrous possibility hinted at by von Hohenheim—in his earliest published work, *Practica D. Theophrasti Paracelsi*, printed at Augsburg in 1529, was, in this hideous pamphlet, elaborated and brought within the bounds of practical experiment.

He crept to the door, opened it, and stood listening intently. That silence which seemed like a palpable cloud—a cloud masking the presence of one who watched—lay over the house. Slowly he descended to the hall and dropped the horror which the evil genius of von Hohenheim had conceived, upon the spot where it had lain when his foot had discovered it.

A creaking sound warned him of some one's approach, and he had barely time to slip behind some draperies ere a cowled figure bearing a lantern came out into the hall. It was Dr. Kassimere, wearing a loose gown having a monkish hood—and he was searching for something.

Nothing in his experience—not the blood-lust seen in the eyes of men in battle—had prepared him for that which transfigured the face of Dr. Kassimere. The strange semblance of Thoth was there no more; it had given place to another, more active malevolence, to a sort of Satanic *eagerness* indescribably terrifying; it was the face of one possessed.

Like some bird of prey he pounced upon the book, thrust it into the pocket of his gown, and began furtively to retrace his steps. As he entered the big dining-room, Dillon was close upon his heels.

Dr. Kassimere passed into the small room beyond and turned from thence into the library. Dillon, observing every precaution, followed. From the library the doctor entered the short, narrow passage leading to that quaint relic of bygone days and ways—the tiny chapel. At the entrance Dillon paused, watchful. Once, the man in the monkish robe turned, on the time-worn step of the altar, and looked back over his shoulder, revealing a face that might well have been that of Asmodeus himself.

On the left of the altar was the cupboard wherein, no doubt, in past ages, the priest had kept his vestments. The oppressive odour which Dillon had first observed in the dining-room was very perceptible in the chapel; and as Dr. Kassimere opened the door of the cupboard and stepped within, an explanation of the presence of this deathly smell in the house occurred to Dillon's mind. The laboratory adjoined the Grange on this side; here was a private entrance known to, and used by, Dr. Kassimere alone.

His surmise proved to be correct. Occasioning scarcely a sound, the secret door opened, and a fiery glow leapt out across the altar steps, accompanied by a wave of heated air laden with the nauseous, unnameable smell. Within the redly lighted doorway, Dr. Kassimere paused, and glanced at a watch which he wore upon his wrist. Then for a moment he disappeared, to reappear carrying a small squat bottle and a contrivance of wire and gauze the sight of which created in Dillon a sense of physical nausea. It was a chloroform-mask! Both he placed upon a vaguely seen table and again approached the door.

Weakly, Dillon fell back, pressing himself, closely against the chapel wall, as the doctor, this time leaving the secret entrance open—with a purpose in view which the watcher shudderingly recognized—recrossed the chapel and went off, softly treading, in the direction of the library.

All his courage, moral and physical, was called upon now, and knowing, by some intuition of love, what and whom he should find there, he stepped unsteadily into Dr. Kassimere's laboratory....

That there were horrors—monstrosities that may not be described, whose names may not be written—in the place, he realised, in some subconscious fashion; but—prone upon a low, metal couch of most curious workmanship lay Phryné, in her night-robe, still—white; perfect in her pale beauty as her namesake who posed for Praxiteles.

Dillon reeled, steadied himself, and sank upon his knees by the couch.

"Phryné!" he whispered, locking his arms about her—"my Phryné!..."

Then he remembered the gauze mask and even detected the sickly, sweet smell of the anaesthetic. Anger gave him new strength; he raised the girl in his arms and turned towards the door communicating with the chapel.

Framed in the opening was the hooded figure of Dr. Kassimere, confronting him. His face was immobile again, with the immobility of ibis-headed Thoth; his eyes were hard, his voice was cold.

"What is the meaning of this outrage?" he demanded sternly. "Phryné has been taken suddenly ill; an immediate operation may be necessary—"

"Out of my way!" said Dillon, advancing past a huge glass jar filled with reddish liquid that stood upon a pedestal between the couch and the door.

"Be careful, you fool!" shrieked Dr. Kassimere, frenziedly, his calm dropping from him like a cloak and a new and dreadful light coming into the staring eyes.

But he was too late. Dillon's foot had caught the pedestal. With a resounding crash the thing overturned; as Dr. Kassimere sprang forward, he slipped in the slimy stream that was pouring over the laboratory floor—and fell....

Laying Phryné upon the altar, her head resting against the age-worn communion rails, Dillon turned and closed the secret door dividing the house of God from the house of Satan. One glimpse, in the red furnace glow, he had of Dr. Kassimere, writhing upon the slimy floor, shrieking, blaspheming—and fighting, fighting madly, as a man fights for life and more than life....

He had not yet carried the unconscious girl beyond the dining-room, when, above that other smell, he detected the odour of burning wood. A fire had broken out in the laboratory.

Mrs. Jack Dillon mourns her guardian (no trace of whom was ever found in the charred remains of Hollow Grange) to this day; for she retains no memory of the night of the great fire, but believes that, overcome by the fumes, she was rescued and carried insensible from the house, by her lover. In the latter's bosom the grim secret is locked, with the memory of a demoniac figure, fighting, fighting....

THE CURSE OF A THOUSAND KISSES

Introductory

Saville Grainger will long be remembered by the public as a brilliant journalist and by his friends as a confirmed misogynist. His distaste for the society of women amounted to a mania, and to Grainger a pretty face was like a red rag to a bull. This was all the more extraordinary and, for Grainger, more painful, because he was one of the most handsome men I ever knew—very dark, with wonderful flashing eyes and the features of an early Roman—or, as I have since thought, of an aristocratic Oriental; aquiline, clean-cut, and swarthy. At any mixed gathering at which he appeared, women gravitated in his direction as though he possessed some magnetic attraction for the sex; and Grainger invariably bolted.

His extraordinary end—never explained to this day—will be remembered by some of those who read of it; but so much that affected whole continents has occurred in the interval that to the majority of the public the circumstances will no longer be familiar. It created a considerable stir in Cairo at the time, as was only natural, but when the missing man failed to return, the nine days' wonder of his disappearance was forgotten in the excitement of some new story or another.

Briefly, Grainger, who was recuperating at Mena House after a rather severe illness in London, went out one evening for a stroll, wearing a light dust-coat over his evening clothes and smoking a cigarette. He turned in the direction of the Great Pyramid—and never came back. That is the story in its bald entirety. No one has ever seen him since—or ever reported having seen him.

If the following story is an elaborate hoax—perpetrated by Grainger himself, for some obscure reason remaining in hiding, or by another well acquainted with his handwriting—I do not profess to say. As to how it came into my possession, that may be told very briefly. Two years after Grainger's disappearance I was in Cairo, and although I was not staying at Mena House I sometimes visited friends there. One night as I came out of the hotel to enter the car which was to drive me back to the Continental, a tall native, dressed in white and so muffled up that little more of his face than two gleaming eyes was visible, handed me a packet—a roll of paper, apparently—saluted me with extraordinary formality, and departed.

No one else seemed to have noticed the man, although the chauffeur, of course, was nearly as close to him as I was, and a servant from the hotel had followed me out and down the steps. I stood there in the dusk, staring at the packet in my hand and then after the tall figure— already swallowed up in the shadow of the road. Naturally I assumed that the man had made some mistake, and holding the package near the lamp of the car I examined it closely.

It was a roll of some kind of parchment, tied with a fragment of thin string, and upon the otherwise blank outside page my name was written very distinctly!

I entered the car, rather dazed by the occurrence, which presented several extraordinary features, and, unfastening the string, began to read. Then, in real earnest, I thought I must be dreaming. Since I append the whole of the manuscript I will make no further reference to the contents here, but will content myself with mentioning that it was written—with dark-brown ink—in Saville Grainger's unmistakable hand upon some kind of parchment or papyrus which has defied three different experts to whom I have shown it, but which, in short, is of unknown manufacture. The twine with which it was tied proved to be of finely plaited reed.

That part of Grainger's narrative, if the following amazing statement is really the work of Grainger, which deals with events up to the time that he left Mena House—and the world—I have been able to check. The dragoman, Hassan Abd-el-Kebîr, was still practising his profession at Mena House at the time of my visit, and he confirmed the truth of Grainger's story in regard to the heart of lapis-lazuli, which he had seen, and the meeting with the old woman in the Mûski—of which Grainger had spoken to him.

For the rest, the manuscript shall tell Grainger's story.

The Manuscript

I

Two years have elapsed since I quitted the world, and the presence in Egypt of a one-time colleague, of which I have been advised, prompts me to put on record these particulars of the strangest, most wonderful, and most beautiful experience which has ever befallen any man. I do not expect my story to be believed. The scepticism of the material world of Fleet Street will consume my statement with its devouring fires. But I do not care. The old itching to make a "story" is upon me. As a "story" let this paper be regarded.

Where the experience actually began I must leave to each reader to judge for himself. I, personally, do not profess to know, even now. But the curtain first arose upon that part of the story which it is my present purpose to chronicle one afternoon near the corner of the Street of the Silversmiths in Cairo. I was wandering in those wonderful narrow, winding lanes, unaccompanied, for I am by habit a solitary being; and despite my ignorance of the language and customs of the natives I awakened to the fact that a link of sympathy—of silent understanding— seemed to bind me to these busy brown men.

I had for many years cherished a secret ambition to pay a protracted visit to Egypt, but the ties of an arduous profession hitherto had rendered its realisation impossible. Now, a stranger in a strange land, I found myself *at home*. I cannot hope to make evident to my readers the completeness of this recognition. From Shepheard's, with its throngs of cosmopolitan travellers and its hosts of pretty women, I had early fled in dismay to the comparative quiet of Mena House. But the only real happiness I ever knew—indeed, as I soon began to realise, had ever known—I found among the discordant cries and mingled smells of perfume and decay in the native city. The desert called to me sweetly, but it was the people, the shops, the shuttered houses, the noise and the smells of the Eastern streets which gripped my heart.

Delightedly I watched the passage of those commercial vehicles, narrow and set high upon monstrous wheels, which convey loads of indescribable variety along streets no wider than the "hall" of a small suburban residence. The Parsees in the Khân Khalîl with their carpets and shining silk-ware, the Arab dealers, fierce swarthy tradesmen from the desert, and the smooth-tongued Cairenes upholding embroidered cloths and gauzy *yashmaks* to allure the eye—all these I watched with a kind of gladness that was almost tender, that was unlike any sentiment I had ever experienced toward my fellow-creatures before.

Mendicants crying the eternal *"Bakshîsh!"*, *Sakhas* with their skins of Nile water, and the other hundred and one familiar figures of the quarter filled me with a great and glad contentment.

I purposely haunted the Mûski during the heat of the day because at that hour it was comparatively free from the presence of Europeans and Americans. Thus, on the occasion of which I write, coming to the end of the street in which the shops of the principal silversmiths are situated, I found myself to be the only white man (if I except the Greeks) in the immediate neighbourhood.

A group of men hurrying out of the street as I approached it first attracted my attention. They were glancing behind them apprehensively as though at a rabid dog. Then came a white-bearded man riding a tiny donkey and also glancing back apprehensively over his shoulder. He all but collided with me in his blind haste; and, stepping quickly aside to avoid him, I knocked down an old woman who was coming out of the street.

The man who had been the real cause of the accident rode off at headlong speed and I found myself left with the poor victim of my clumsiness in a spot which seemed miraculously to have become deserted. If the shopkeepers remained in their shops, they were invisible, and must have retreated into the darkest corners of the caves in the wall which constitute native emporiums. Pedestrians there were none.

I stooped to the old woman, who lay moaning at my feet ... and as I did so, I shrank. How can I describe the loathing, the repulsion which I experienced? Never in the whole of my career had I seen such a hideous face. A ragged black veil which she wore had been torn from its brass fastenings as she fell, and her countenance was revealed in all its appalling ugliness. Yellow, shrivelled, toothless, it was scarcely human; but, above all, it repelled because of its aspect of *extreme age*. I do not mean that it was like the face of a woman of eighty; it was like that of a woman who had miraculously survived decease for several centuries! It was a witch-face, a deathly face.

And as I shrank, she opened her eyes, moaning feebly, and groping with claw-like hands as if darkness surrounded her. Furthermore I saw a new pain, and a keener pain, light up those aged eyes. She had detected my involuntary movement of loathing.

Those who knew me will bear testimony to the fact that I was not an emotional man or one readily impressionable by any kind of human appeal. Therefore they will wonder the more to learn that this pathetic light in the old woman's eyes changed my revulsion to a poignant sorrow. I had roughly knocked her from her feet and now hesitated to assist her to rise again! Truly, she was scorned and rejected by all. A wave of tenderness, that cannot be described, that could not be resisted, swept over me. My eyes grew misty and a great remorse claimed me.

"Poor old soul!" I whispered.

Stooping, I gently raised the shrivelled, ape-like head, resting it against my knee; and, bending down, I kissed the old woman on the brow!

I record the fact, but even now, looking back upon its happening, and seeking to recapture the cold, solitary Saville Grainger who has left the world, I realise the wonder of it. That *I* should have given rein to such an impulse! That such an impulse should have stirred me! Which phenomenon was the more remarkable?

The result of my act—regretted as soon as performed—was singular. The aged, hideous creature sighed in a manner I can never forget, and an expression that almost lent comeliness to her features momentarily crept over her face. Then she rose to her feet with difficulty, raised her hands as if blessing me, and muttering something in Arabic went shuffling along the deserted street, stooping as she walked.

Apparently the episode had passed unnoticed. Certainly if anyone witnessed it he was well concealed. But, conscious of a strange embarrassment, with which were mingled other tumultuous emotions, I turned out of the Street of the Silversmiths and found myself amid the normal activities of the quarter again. The memory of the Kiss was repugnant, I wanted to wipe my lips—but something seemed to forbid the act; a lingering compassion that was almost a yearning.

For once in my life I desired to find myself among normal, healthy, moderately brainless Europeans. I longed for the smell of cigar-smoke, for the rattle of the cocktail-maker and the sight of a pretty face. I hurried to Shepheard's.

II

The same night, after dinner, I walked out of Mena House to look for Hassan Abd-el-Kebîr, the dragoman with whom I had contracted for a journey, by camel, to Sakhâra on the following day. He had promised to attend at half-past eight in order to arrange the time of starting in the morning, together with some other details.

I failed to find him, however, among the dragomans and other natives seated outside the hotel, and to kill time I strolled leisurely down the road toward the electric-tram terminus. I had taken no more than ten paces, I suppose, when a tall native, muffled to the tip of his nose in white and wearing a white turban, appeared out of the darkness beside me, thrust a small package into my hand, and, touching his brow, his lips and his breast with both hands, bowed and departed. I saw him no more!

Standing there in the road, I stared at the little package stupidly. It consisted of a piece of fine white silk fastened about some small, hard object. Evidently, I thought, there had been a mistake. The package could not have been intended for me.

Returning to the hotel, I stood near a lamp and unfastened the silk, which was delicately perfumed. It contained a piece of lapis-lazuli carved in the form of a heart, beautifully mounted in gold and bearing three Arabic letters, inlaid in some way, also in gold!

At this singular ornament I stared harder than ever. Certainly the muffled native had made a strange mistake. This was a love-token—and emphatically not for *me*!

I was standing there lost in wonderment, the heart of lapis-lazuli in my palm, when the voice of Hassan disturbed my stupor.

"Ah, my gentleman, I am sorry to be late but——"

The voice ceased. I looked up.

"Well?" I said.

Then I, too, said no more. Hassan Abd-el-Kebîr was glaring at the ornament in my hand as though I had held, not a very choice example of native jewellery, but an adder or a scorpion!

"What's the matter?" I asked, recovering from my surprise. "Do you know to whom this amulet belongs?"

He muttered something in guttural Arabic ere replying to my question. Then:

"It is the heart of lapis," he said, in a strange voice. "It is the heart of lapis!"

"So much is evident," I cried, laughing. "But does it alarm you?"

"Please," he said softly, and held out a brown hand—"I will see."

I placed the thing in his open palm and he gazed at it as one might imagine an orchid hunter would gaze at a new species of *Odontoglossum*.

"What do the figures mean?" I asked.

"They form the word *alf*," he replied.

"*Alf*? Somebody's name!" I said, still laughing.

"In Arab it mean ten hundred," he whispered.

"A thousand?"

"Yes—one thousand."

"Well?"

Hassan returned the ornament to me, and his expression was so strange that I began to grow really annoyed. He was looking at me with a mingling of envy and compassion which I found to be quite insufferable.

"Hassan," I said sternly, "you will tell me all you know about this matter. One would imagine that you suspected me of stealing the thing!"

"Ah, no, my gentleman!" he protested earnestly. "But I will tell you, yes, only you will not believe me."

"Never mind. Tell me."

Thereupon Hassan Abd-el-Kebîr told me the most improbable story to which I had ever listened. Since to reproduce it in his imperfect

English, with my own frequent interjections, would be tedious, I will give it in brief. Some of the historical details, imperfectly related by Hassan as I learned later, I have corrected.

In the reign of the Khalîf El-Mamûn—a son of Hárûn er-Rashîd and brother of the prototype of Beckford's *Vathek*—one Shâwar was Governor of Egypt, and the daughter of the Governor, Scheherazade, was famed throughout the domains of the Khalîf as the most beautiful maiden in the land. Wazîrs and princes sought her hand in vain. Her heart was given to a handsome young merchant of Cairo, Ahmad er-Mâdi, who was also the wealthiest man in the city. Shâwar, although an indulgent father, would not hear of such a union, however, but he hesitated to destroy his daughter's happiness by forcing her into an unwelcome marriage. Finally, passion conquered reason in the breasts of the lovers and they fled, Scheherazade escaping from the palace of her father by means of a rope-ladder smuggled into the *harêm* apartments by a slave whom Ahmad's gold had tempted, and meeting Ahmad outside the gardens where he waited with a fleet horse.

Even the guard at the city gate had been bought by the wealthy merchant, and the pair succeeded in escaping from Cairo.

The extensive possessions of Ahmad were confiscated by the enraged father and a sentence of death was passed upon the absent man—to be instantly put into execution in the event of his arrest anywhere within the domain of the Khalîf.

Exiled in a distant oasis, the Sheikh of which was bound to Ahmad by ties of ancient friendship, the prospect which had seemed so alluring to Scheherazade became clouded. Recognising this change in her attitude, Ahmad er-Mâdi racked his brains for some scheme whereby he might recover his lost wealth and surround his beautiful wife with the luxury to which she had been accustomed. In this extremity he had recourse to a certain recluse who resided in a solitary spot in the desert far from the haunts of men and who was widely credited with magical powers.

It was a whole week's journey to the abode of the wizard, and, unknown to Ahmad, during his absence a son of the Khalîf, visiting Egypt, chanced to lose his way on a hunting expedition, and came upon the secret oasis in which Scheherazade was hiding. This prince had been one of her most persistent suitors.

The ancient magician consented to receive Ahmad, and the first boon which the enamoured young man craved of him was that he might grant him a sight of Scheherazade. The student of dark arts consented. Bidding Ahmad to look into a mirror, he burned the secret perfumes and uttered the prescribed incantation. At first mistily, and then quite clearly, Ahmad saw Scheherazade, standing in the moonlight beneath a tall palm tree—her lips raised to those of her former suitor!

At that the world grew black before the eyes of Ahmad. And he, who had come a long and arduous journey at the behest of love, now experienced an equally passionate hatred. Acquainting the magician with what he had seen, he demanded that he should exercise his art in visiting upon the false Scheherazade the most terrible curse that it lay within his power to invoke!

The learned man refused; whereupon Ahmad, insane with sorrow and anger, drew his sword and gave the magician choice of compliance or instant death. The threat sufficed. The wizard performed a ghastly conjuration, calling down upon Scheherazade the curse of an ugliness beyond that of humanity, and which should remain with her not for the ordinary span of a lifetime but for incalculable years, during which she should continue to live in the flesh, loathed, despised, and shunned of all!

"Until one thousand compassionate men, unasked and of their own free will, shall each have bestowed a kiss upon thee," was the exact text of the curse. "Then thou shalt regain thy beauty, thy love—and death."

Ahmad er-Mâdi staggered out from the cavern, blinded by a hundred emotions—already sick with remorse; and one night's stage on his return journey dropped dead from his saddle ... stricken by the malignant will of the awful being whose power he had invoked! I will conclude this wild romance in the words of Hassan, the dragoman, as nearly as I can recall them.

"And so," he said, his voice lowered in awe, "Scheherazade, who was stricken with age and ugliness in the very hour that the curse was spoken, went out into the world, my gentleman. She begged her way from place to place, and as the years passed by accumulated much wealth in that manner. Finally, it is said, she returned to Cairo, her native city, and there remained. To each man who bestowed a kiss upon her—and such men were rare—she caused a heart of lapis to be sent, and upon the heart was engraved in gold the number of the kiss! It is said that these gifts ensured to those upon whom they were bestowed the certain possession of their beloved! Once before, when I was a small child, I saw such an amulet, and the number upon it was nine hundred and ninety-nine."

The thing was utterly incredible, of course; merely a picturesque example of Eastern imagination; but just to see what effect it would have upon him, I told Hassan about the old woman in the Mûski. I had to do so. Frankly, the coincidence was so extraordinary that it worried me. When I had finished:

"It was she—Scheherazade," he said fearfully. "And it was the *last* kiss!"

"What then?" I asked.

"Nothing, my gentleman. I do not know!"

III

Throughout the expedition to Sakhâra on the following day I could not fail to note that Hassan was covertly watching me—and his expression annoyed me intensely. It was that compound of compassion and resignation which one might bestow upon a condemned man.

I charged him with it, but of course he denied any such sentiment. Nevertheless, I knew that he entertained it, and, what was worse, I began, in an uncomfortable degree, to share it with him! I cannot make myself clearer. But I simply felt the normal world to be slipping from under my feet, and, no longer experiencing a desire to clutch at modernity as I had done after my meeting with the old woman, I found myself to be reconciled to my fate!

To my fate? ... to what fate? I did not know; but I realised, beyond any shade of doubt, that something tremendous, inevitable, and ultimate was about to happen to me. I caught myself unconsciously raising the heart of lapis-lazuli to my lips! Why I did so I had no idea; I seemed to have lost identity. I no longer knew myself.

When Hassan parted from me at Mena House that evening he could not disguise the fact that he regarded the parting as final; yet my plans were made for several weeks ahead. Nor did I quarrel with the man's curious attitude. *I* regarded the parting as final, also!

In a word I was becoming reconciled—to something. It is difficult, all but impossible, to render such a frame of mind comprehensible, and I shall not even attempt the task, but leave the events of the night to speak for themselves.

After dinner I lighted a cigarette, and avoiding a particularly persistent and very pretty widow who was waiting to waylay me in the lounge, I came out of the hotel and strolled along in the direction of the Pyramid. Once I looked back—bidding a silent farewell to Mena House! Then I took out the heart of lapis-lazuli from my pocket and kissed it rapturously—kissed it as I had never kissed any object or any person in the whole course of my life!

And why I did so I had no idea.

All who read my story will be prepared to learn that in this placid and apparently feeble frame of mind I slipped from life, from the world.

It was not so. The modern man, the Saville Grainger once known in Fleet Street, came to life again for one terrible, strenuous moment ... and then passed out of life for ever.

Just before I reached the Pyramid, and at a lonely spot in the path— for this was not a "Sphinx and Pyramid night"—that is to say, the moon was not at the full—a tall, muffled native appeared at my elbow. He was the same man who had brought me the heart of lapis-lazuli, or his double. I started.

He touched me lightly on the arm.

"Follow," he said—and pointed ahead into the darkness below the plateau.

I moved off obediently. Then—suddenly, swiftly, came revolt. The modern man within me flared into angry life. I stopped dead, and

"Who are you? Where are you leading me?" I cried.

I received no reply.

A silk scarf was slipped over my head by some one who, silently, must have been following me, and drawn tight enough to prevent any loud outcry but not so as to endanger my breathing. I fought like a madman. I knew, and the knowledge appalled me, that I was fighting for life. Arms like bands of steel grasped me; I was lifted, bound and carried—I knew not where....

Placed in some kind of softly padded saddle, or, as I have since learned, into a *shibrîyeh* or covered litter on a camel's back, I felt the animal rise to its ungainly height and move off swiftly. As suddenly as revolt had flamed up, resignation returned. I was contented. My bonds were unnecessary; my rebellion was ended. I yearned, wildly, for the end of the desert journey! Some one was calling me and all my soul replied.

For hours, as it seemed, the camel raced ceaselessly on. Absolute silence reigned about me. Then, in the distance I heard voices, and the gait of the camel changed. Finally the animal stood still. Came a word of guttural command, and the camel dropped to its knees. Pillowed among a pile of scented cushions, I experienced no discomfort from this usually painful operation.

I was lifted out of my perfumed couch and set upon my feet. Having been allowed to stand for a while until the effects of remaining so long in a constrained position had worn off, I was led forward into some extensive building. Marble pavements were beneath my feet, fountains played, and the air was heavy with burning ambergris.

I was placed with my back to a pillar and bound there, but not harshly. The bandage about my head was removed. I stared around me.

A magnificent Eastern apartment met my gaze—a great hall open on one side to the desert. Out upon the sands I could see a group of men who had evidently been my captors and my guards. The one who had unfastened the silk scarf I could not see, but I heard him moving away behind the pillar to which I was bound.

Stretched upon a luxurious couch before me was a woman.

If I were to seek to describe her I should inevitably fail, for her loveliness surpassed everything which I had ever beheld—of which I had ever dreamed. I found myself looking into her eyes, and in their depths I found all that I had missed in life, and lost all that I had found.

She smiled, rose, and taking a jewelled dagger from a little table beside her, approached me. My heart beat until I felt almost suffocated as she came near. And when she bent and cut the silken lashing which bound me, I knew such rapture as I had hitherto counted an invention of Arabian poets. I was raised above the joys of common humanity and tasted the joy of the gods. She placed the dagger in my hand.

"My life is thine," she said. "Take it."

And clutching at the silken raiment draping her beautiful bosom, she invited me to plunge the blade into her heart!

The knife dropped, clattering upon the marble pavement. For one instant I hesitated, watching her, devouring her with my eyes; then I swept her to me and pressed upon her sweet lips the thousand and first kiss....

(NOTE.—The manuscript of Saville Grainger finishes here.)

THE TURQUOISE NECKLACE

I

"He is the lord of the desert, Effendi," declared Mohammed the dragoman. "From the Valley of Zered to Damascus he is known and loved, but feared. They say"—he lowered his voice—"that he is a great *welee*, and that he is often seen in the street of the attars, having the appearance of a simple old man; but in the desert he is like a bitter apple, a viper and a calamity! Overlord is he of the Bedouins, and all the sons of the desert bow to Ben Azreem, Sheikh of the Ibn-Rawallah."

"What is a *welee*, exactly?" asked Graham.

"A man of God, Effendi, favoured beyond other men."

"And this Arab Sheikh is a *welee*?"

"So it is said. He goes about secretly aiding the poor and afflicted, when he may be known by his white beard——"

"There are many white beards in Egypt," said Graham.

But the other continued, ignoring the interruption:

"And in the desert, Ben Azreem, a horseman unrivalled, may be known by the snow-white horse which he rides, or if he is not so mounted, by his white camel, swifter than the glance of envy, more surefooted than the eager lover who climbs to his enslaver's window."

"Indeed!" said Graham dryly. "Well, I hope I may have the pleasure of meeting this mysterious notability before I leave the country."

"Unless you journey across the sands for many days, it is unlikely. For when he comes into Egypt he reveals himself to none but the supremely good,"—Graham stared—"and the supremely wicked!" added Mohammed.

The poetic dragoman having departed, Graham leaned over to his wife, who had sat spellbound, her big blue eyes turned to the face of Mohammed throughout his romantic narrative.

"These wild native legends appeal to you, don't they?" he said, smiling and patting her hand affectionately. "You superstitious little colleen!"

Eileen Graham blushed, and the blush of a pretty Irish bride is a very beautiful thing.

"Don't you believe it at all, then?" she asked softly.

"I believe there may be such a person as Ben Azreem, and possibly he's a very imposing individual. He may even indulge in visits, incognito, to Cairo, in the manner of the late lamented Hárûn er-Rashîd of

Arabian Nights memory, but I can't say that I believe in *welees* as a class!"

His wife shrugged her pretty shoulders.

"There is something that *I* have to tell you, which I suppose you will also refuse to believe," she said, with mock indignation. "You remember the Arabs whom we saw at the exhibition in London?"

Graham started.

"The gentlemen who were advertised as 'chiefs from the Arabian Desert'? I remember *one* in particular."

"That is the one I mean," said Eileen.

Her husband looked at her curiously.

"Your explanation is delightfully lucid, dear!" he said jocularly. "My memories of the gentleman known as El-Suleym, I believe, are not pleasant; his memories of me must be equally unfavourable. He illustrated the fact that savages should never be introduced into civilised society, however fascinating they may be personally. Mrs. Marstham was silly enough to take the man up, and because of the way he looked at you, I was wise enough to knock him down! What then?"

"Only this—I saw him, to-day!"

"Eileen!" There was alarm in Graham's voice. "Where? Here, or in Cairo?"

"As we were driving away from the mosque of the Whirling Dervishes. He was one of a group who stood by the bridge."

"You are certain?"

"Quite certain."

"Did he see you?"

"I couldn't say. He gave no sign to show that he had seen me."

John Graham lighted a cigarette with much care.

"It doesn't matter, anyway," he said, carelessly. "You are as safe here as at the *Ritz*."

But there was unrest in the glance which he cast out across the prospect touched by moon-magic into supernatural beauty.

In the distance gleamed a fairy city of silvern minarets, born, it seemed, from the silvern stream. Beyond lay the night mystery of the desert, into whose vastness marched the ghostly acacias. The discordant chattering and chanting from the river-bank merged into a humming song, not unmusical. The howling of the dogs, even, found a place in the orchestral scheme.

Behind him, in the hotel, was European and American life—modernity; before him was that other life, endless and unchanging. There was something cold, sombre, and bleak in the wonderful prospect, something shocking in the presence of those sight-seeing, careless folk, the luxurious hotel, *all* that was Western and new, upon that threshold of the ancient, changeless desert.

A menace, too, substantial yet cloaked with the mystery of the motherland of mysteries, had arisen now. Although he had assured Eileen that Gizeh was as safe as Piccadilly, he had too much imagination to be unaware that from the Egypt of Cook's to the Egypt of secrets is but a step.

None but the very young or very sanguine traveller looks for adventure nowadays in the neighbourhood of Mena House. When the intrepid George Sandys visited and explored the Great Pyramid, it was at peril of his life, but Graham reflected humorously that the most nervous old ladies now performed the feat almost daily. Yet out here in the moonlight where the silence was, out beyond the radius of "sights," lay a land unknown to Europe, as every desert is unknown.

It was a thought that had often come to him, but it came to-night with a force and wearing a significance which changed the aspect of the sands, the aspect of all Egypt.

He glanced at the charming girl beside him. Eileen, too, was looking into the distance with far-away gaze. The pose of her head was delightful, and he sat watching her in silence. Within the hotel the orchestra had commenced softly to play; but Graham did not notice the fact. He was thinking how easily one could be lost out upon that grey ocean, with its islands of priestly ruins.

"It is growing rather chilly, dear," he said suddenly; "even for fur wraps. Suppose we go in?"

II

The crowd in the bazaar was excessive, and the bent old figure which laboured beneath a nondescript burden, wrapped up in a blue cloth, passed from the noisiness out into the narrow street which ran at right-angles with the lane of many shops.

Perhaps the old Arab was deaf, perhaps wearied to the point of exhaustion; but, from whatever cause, he ignored, or was unaware of, the oncoming *arabeeyeh*, whose driver had lost control of his horse. Even the shrill scream of the corpulent, white-veiled German lady, who was one of its passengers, failed to arouse him. Out into the narrow roadway he staggered, bent almost double.

Graham, accompanied by Mohammed, was some distance away, haggling with a Greek thief who held the view that a return of three hundred and fifty per cent. spelled black ruination.

Eileen, finding the air stifling, had walked on in the direction of the less crowded street above. Thus it happened that she, and the poor old porter, alone, were in the path of the onward-whirling carriage.

Many women so placed would have stood, frozen with horror, have been struck down by the frantic animal; some would have had sufficient presence of mind to gain the only shelter attainable in time—that of a deep-set doorway. Few would have acted as Eileen acted.

It was under the stimulus of that Celtic impetuosity—that generous madness which seems to proceed, not from the mind, but from the heart—that she leapt, not back, but forward.

She never knew exactly what took place, nor how she escaped destruction; but there was a roaring in her ears, above it rising the Teutonic screams of the lady in the *arabeeyeh*; there was a confused chorus of voices, a consciousness of effort; and she found herself, with wildly beating heart, crouching back into the recess which once had held a *mastabah*.

From some place invisible, around a bend in the tortuous street, came sounds of shouting and that of lashing hoofs. The runaway was stopped. At her feet lay a shapeless bundle wrapped in a blue cloth, and beside her, leaning back against the whitewashed wall, and breathing with short, sobbing breaths, was the old porter.

Now, her husband had his arms about her, and Mohammed, with frightened eyes, hovered in the background. Without undue haste, all the bazaar gradually was coming upon the scene.

"My darling, are you hurt?"

John Graham's voice shook. He was deathly pale.

Eileen smiled reassuringly.

"Not a bit, dear," she said breathlessly. "But I am afraid the poor old man is."

"You are quite sure you are not hurt?"

"I was not so much as touched, though honestly I don't know how either of us escaped. But do see if the old man is injured."

Graham turned to the rescued porter, who now had recovered his composure.

"Mohammed, ask him if he is hurt," he directed.

Mohammed put the question. A curious group surrounded the party. But the old man, ignoring all, knelt and bowed his bare head to the dust at Eileen's feet.

"Oh, John," cried the girl, "ask him to stand up! I feel ashamed to see such a venerable old man kneeling before me!"

"Tell him it is—nothing," said Graham hastily to Mohammed, "and—er—"—he fumbled in his pocket—"give him this."

But Mohammed, looking ill at ease, thrust aside the proffered *bakshîsh*—a novel action which made Graham stare widely.

"He would not take it, Effendi," he whispered. "See, his turban lies there; he is a *hadj*. He is praying for the eternal happiness of his preserver, and he is interceding with the Prophet (*Salla—'lláhu 'aleyhi wasellum*), that she may enjoy the delights of Paradise equally with all true Believers!"

"Very good of him," said Graham, who, finding the danger passed and his wife safe, was beginning to feel embarrassed. "Thank him, and tell him that she is greatly indebted!"

He took Eileen's arm, and turned to force a way through the strangely silent group about. But the aged porter seized the hem of the girl's white skirt, gently detaining her. As he rose upon his knees, Mohammed, with marks of unusual deference, handed him his green turban. The old man, still clutching Eileen's dress, signed that his dirty bundle should likewise be passed to him. This was done.

Graham was impatient to get away. But——

"Humour him for a moment, dear," said Eileen softly. "We don't want to hurt the poor old fellow's feelings."

Into the bundle the old man plunged his hand, and drew out a thin gold chain upon which hung a queerly cut turquoise. He stood upright, raised the piece of jewellery to his forehead and to his lips, and held it out, the chain stretched across his open palms, to Eileen.

"He must be some kind of pedlar," said Graham.

Eileen shook her head, smiling.

"Mohammed, tell him that I cannot possibly take his chain," she directed. "But thank him all the same, of course."

Mohammed, his face averted from the statuesque old figure, bent to her ear.

"Take it!" he whispered. "Take it! Do not refuse!"

There was a sort of frightened urgency in his tones, so that both Graham and his wife looked at him curiously.

"Take it, then, Eileen," said Graham quickly. "And, Mohammed, you must find out who he is, and we will make it up to him in some way."

"Yes, yes, Effendi," agreed the man readily.

Eileen accordingly accepted the present, glancing aside at her husband to intimate that they must not fail to pay for it. As she took the chain in her hands, the donor said something in a low voice.

"Hang it round your neck," translated Mohammed.

Eileen did so, whispering:

"You must not lose sight of him, Mohammed."

Mohammed nodded; and the old man, replacing his turban and

making a low obeisance, spoke rapidly a few words, took up his bundle, and departed. The silent bystanders made way for him.

"Come on," said Graham; "I am anxious to get out of this. Find a carriage, Mohammed. We'll lunch at Shepheard's."

A carriage was obtained, and they soon left far behind them the scene of this odd adventure. With Mohammed perched up on the box, Graham and his wife could discuss the episode without restraint. Graham, however, did most of the talking, for Eileen was strangely silent.

"It is quite a fine stone," he said, examining the necklace so curiously acquired. "We must find some way of repaying the old chap which will not offend his susceptibilities."

Eileen nodded absently; and her husband, with his eyes upon the dainty white figure, found gratitude for her safety welling up like a hot spring in his heart. The action had been characteristic; and he longed to reprove her for risking her life, yet burned to take her in his arms for the noble impulse that had prompted her to do so.

He wondered anxiously if her silence could be due to the after-effects of that moment of intense excitement.

"You don't feel unwell, darling?" he whispered.

She smiled at him radiantly, and gave his hand a quick little squeeze. "Of course not," she said.

But she remained silent to the end of the short drive. This was not due to that which her husband feared, however, but to the fact that she had caught a glimpse, amongst the throng at the corner of the bazaar, of the handsome, sinister face of El-Suleym, the Bedouin.

III

The moon poured radiance on the desert. At the entrance to a camel-hair tent stood a tall, handsome man, arrayed in the picturesque costume of the Bedouin. The tent behind him was upheld by six poles. The ends and one side were pegged to the ground, and the whole of that side before which he stood was quite open, with the exception of a portion before which hung a goat-hair curtain.

This was the "house of hair" of the Sheikh El-Suleym, of the Masr-Bishareen—El-Suleym, "the Regicide" outcast of the great tribe of the Bishareen. At some distance from the Sheikh's tent were some half a dozen other and smaller tents, housing the rascally following of this desert outcast.

Little did those who had engaged the picturesque El-Suleym, to display his marvellous horsemanship in London, know that he and those that came with him were a scorn among true sons of the desert, pariahs of that brotherhood which extends from Zered to the Nile, from Tanta to the Red Sea; little did those who had opened their doors in hospitality to the dashing horseman dream that they entertained a petty brigand, sought for by the Egyptian authorities, driven out into ostracism by his own people.

And now before his tent he stood statuesque in the Egyptian moonlight, and looked towards Gizeh, less than thirty miles to the north-east.

As El-Suleym looked towards Gizeh, Graham and his wife were seated before Mena House looking out across the desert. The adventure of the morning had left its impression upon both of them, and Eileen wore the gold chain with its turquoise pendant. Graham was smoking in silence, and thinking, not of the old porter and his odd Eastern gratitude, but of another figure, and one which often came between his mental eye and the beauties of that old, beautiful land. Eileen, too, was thinking of El-Suleym; for the Bedouin now was associated in her mind with the old pedlar, since she had last seen the handsome, sinister face amid the throng at the entrance to the bazaar.

Telepathy is a curious fact. Were Graham's reflections *en rapport* with his wife's, or were they both influenced by the passionate thoughts of that other mind, that subtle, cunning mind of the man who at that moment was standing before his house of hair and seeking with his eagle glance to defy distance and the night?

"Have you seen—him, again?" asked Graham abruptly. "Since the other day at the bridge?"

Eileen started. Although he had endeavoured to hide it from her, she was perfectly well aware of her husband's intense anxiety on her behalf. She knew, although he prided himself upon having masked his feelings, that the presence of the Bedouin in Egypt had cast a cloud upon his happiness. Therefore she had not wished to tell him of her second encounter with El-Suleym. But to this direct question there could be only one reply.

"I saw him again—this morning," she said, toying nervously with the pendant at her neck.

Graham clasped her hand tensely.

"Where?"

"Outside the bazaar, in the crowd."

"You did not—tell me."

"I did not want to worry you."

He laughed dryly.

"It doesn't worry me, Eileen," he said carelessly. "If I were in Damascus or Aleppo, it certainly might worry me to know that a man, no doubt actively malignant towards us, was near, perhaps watching; but Cairo is really a prosaically safe and law-abiding spot. We are as secure here as we should be at—Shepherd's Bush, say!"

He laughed shortly. Voices floated out to them, nasal, guttural, strident; voices American, Teutonic, Gallic, and Anglo-Saxon. The orchestra played a Viennese waltz. Confused chattering, creaking, and bumping sounded from the river. Out upon the mud walls dogs bayed the moon.

But beyond the native village, beyond the howling dogs, beyond the acacia ranks out in the silver-grey mystery of the sands hard by, an outpost of the Pharaohs, where a ruined shrine of Horus bared its secret places to the peeping moon, the Sheikh of the Masr-Bishareen smiled.

Graham felt strangely uneasy, and sought by light conversation to shake off the gloom which threatened to claim him.

"That thief, Mohammed," he said tersely, "has no more idea than Adam, I believe, who your old porter friend really is."

"Why do you think so?" asked Eileen.

"Because he's up in Cairo to-night, searching for him!"

"How do you know?"

"I cornered him about it this afternoon, and although I couldn't force an admission from him—I don't think anybody short of an accomplished K.C. could—he was suspiciously evasive! I gave him four hours to procure the name and address of the old gentleman to whom we owe the price of a turquoise necklace. He has not turned up yet!"

Eileen made no reply. Her Celtic imagination had invested the morning's incident with a mystic significance which she could not hope to impart to her hard-headed husband.

A dirty and ragged Egyptian boy made his way on to the verandah, furtively glancing about him, as if anticipating the cuff of an unseen hand. He sidled up to Graham, thrusting a scrap of paper on to the little table beside him.

"For me?" said Graham.

The boy nodded; and whilst Eileen watched him interestedly, Graham, tilting the communication so as to catch the light from the hotel windows, read the following:

"He is come to here but cannot any farther. I have him waiting the boy will bring you.

"Your obedient Effendi,

MOHAMMED."

Graham laughed grimly, glancing at his watch.

"Only half an hour late," he said, standing up, "Wait here, Eileen; I shall not be many minutes."

"But I should like to see him, too. He might accept the price from me where you would fail to induce him to take it."

"Never fear," said her husband; "he wouldn't have come if he meant to refuse. What shall I offer him?"

"Whatever you think," said Eileen, smiling; "be generous with the poor old man."

Graham nodded and signed to the boy that he was ready to start.

The night swallowed them up; and Eileen sat waiting, whilst the band played softly and voices chatted incessantly around her.

Some five minutes elapsed; ten; fifteen. It grew to half an hour, and she became uneasy. She stood up and began to pace up and down the verandah. Then the slinking figure of the Egyptian youth reappeared.

"Graham Effendi," he said, showing his gleaming teeth, "says you come too."

Eileen drew her wrap more closely about her and smiled to the boy to lead the way.

They passed out from the hotel, turned sharply to the left, made in the direction of the river, then bore off to the right in the direction of the sand-dunes. The murmuring life of Mena House died into remoteness; the discordance of the Arab village momentarily took precedence; then this, in turn, was lost, and they were making out desert-ward to the hollow which harbours the Sphinx. Great events in our lives rarely leave a clear-cut impression; often the turning-point in one's career is a confused memory, a mere clash of conflicting ideas. Trivial episodes are sharp silhouettes; unforgettable; great happenings but grey, vague things in life's panorama. Thus, Eileen never afterwards could quite recall what happened that night. The thing that was like to have wrecked her life had no sharp outlines to etch themselves upon the plate of memory. Vaguely she wondered to what meeting-place the boy was leading her. Faintly she was conscious of a fear of the growing silence, of a warning instinct whispering her to beware of the loneliness of the desert.

Then the boy was gone; the silence was gone; harsh voices were in her ears—a cloth was whipped about her face and strong arms lifted her. She was not of a stock that swoon or passively accept violence. She strove to cry out, but the band was too cunningly fastened to allow of it; she struck out with clenched fists and not unshrewdly, for twice her knuckles encountered a bearded face and a suppressed exclamation told that the blows were not those of a weakling. She kicked furiously and drew forth a howl of pain from her captor. Her hands flew up to the bandage, but were roughly seized, thrust down and behind her, and tied securely.

She was thrown across a saddle, and with a thrill of horror knew herself a captive. Out into the desert she was borne, into that unknown land which borders so closely upon the sight-seeing track of Cook's. And her helplessness, her inability to fight, broke her spirit, born fighter that she was; and the jarring of the saddle of the galloping horse, the dull thud of the hoofs on the sand, the iron grip which held her, fear, anger, all melted into a blank.

IV

Mohammed the dragoman, with two hotel servants, came upon Graham some time later, gagged and bound behind a sand hillock less than five hundred yards from Mena House. They had him on his feet in an instant, unbound; and his face was ghastly—for he knew too well what the outrage portended.

"Quick!" he said hoarsely. "How long is she gone?"

Mohammed was trembling wildly.

"Nearly an hour, Effendi—nearly an hour. Allah preserve us, what shall we do? I heard it in Cairo to-night—it is all over the bazaars— the Sheikh El-Suleym with the Masr-Bishareen is out. They travel like the wind, Effendi. It is not four days since they stopped a caravan ten miles beyond Bir-Amber, now they are in Lower Egypt. Allah preserve her!" he ran on volubly—"who can overtake the horsemen of the Bishareen?"

So he ran on, wildly, panting as they raced back to the hotel. The place was in an uproar. It was an event which furnished the guests with such a piece of local colour as none but the most inexperienced tourist could have anticipated.

An Arab raid in these days of electric tramways! A captive snatched from the very doors of Mena House! One would as little expect an Arab raid upon the *Ritz*!

The authorities at headquarters, advised of the occurrence, found themselves at a loss how to cope with this stupendous actuality. The desert had extended its lean arm and snatched a captive to its bosom. Cairo had never before entirely realised the potentialities of that all-embracing desert. There are a thousand ways, ten thousand routes, across that ruin-dotted wilderness. Justly did the ancient people worship in the moon the queenly Isis; for when the silver emblem of the goddess claims the sands for her own, to all save the desert-born they become a place of secrets. Here is a theatre for great dramas, wanting only the tragedian. The outlawed Sheikh of the Bishareen knew this full well, but, unlike others who know it, he had acted upon his convictions and revealed to wondering Egypt what Bedouin craft and a band of intrepid horsemen can do, aided by a belt of sand, and cloaked by night.

Graham was distracted. For he was helpless, and realised it. Already the news was in Cairo, and the machinery of the Government at work. But what machinery, save that of the Omniscient, could avail him now?

A crowd of visitors flocked around him, offering frightened consolation. He broke away from them violently—swearing—a primitive man who wanted to be alone with his grief. The idea uppermost in his mind was that of leaping upon a horse and setting out in pursuit. But in which direction should he pursue? One declared that the Arabs must have rode this way, another that, and yet another a third.

Some one shouted—the words came to him as if through a thick curtain—that the soldiers were coming.

"What the hell's the good of it!" he said, and turned away, biting his lips.

When a spruce young officer came racing up the steps to gather particulars, Graham stared at him dully, said, "The Arabs have got her—my wife," and walked away.

The hoof-clatter and accompanying martial disturbance were faint in the distance when Mohammed ran in to where Graham was pacing up and down in an agony of indecision—veritably on the verge of insanity. The dragoman held a broken gold chain in his hand, from which depended a big turquoise that seemed to blink in the shaded light.

"Effendi," he whispered, and held it out upon trembling fingers, "it is her necklet! I found it yonder,"—pointing eastward. "*Sallee 'a-nebee!* it is her necklet!"

Graham turned, gave one wild glance at the thing, and grasped the man by the throat, glaring madly upon him.

"You dog!" he shouted. "You were in the conspiracy! It was you who sent the false messages!"

A moment he held him so, then dropped his hands. Mohammed fell back, choking; but no malice was in the velvet eyes. The Eastern understands and respects a great passion.

"Effendi," he gasped—"I am your faithful servant, and—I cannot write! *Wa-llah!* and by His mercy, this will save her if anything can!"

He turned and ran fleetly out, Graham staring after him.

It may seem singular that John Graham remained thus inert—inactive. But upon further consideration his attitude becomes explainable. He knew the futility of a blind search, and dreaded being absent if any definite clue should reach the hotel. Meanwhile, he felt that madness was not far off.

"They say that they have struck out across the Arabian Desert, Mr. Graham—probably in the direction of the old caravan route."

Graham did not turn; did not know nor care who spoke.

"It's four hundred miles across to the caravan route," he said slowly; "four hundred miles of sand—of sand."

V

The most simple Oriental character is full of complexity. Mohammed the dragoman, by birth and education a thief, by nature a sluggard, spared no effort to reach Cairo in the shortest space of time humanly possible. The source of his devotion is obscure. Perhaps it was due to a humble admiration which John Graham's attempt to strangle him could not alter, or perhaps to a motive wholly unconnected with mundane matters. Certain it is that a sort of religious fervour latterly had possessed the man. From being something of a scoffer (for Islam, like other creeds, daily loses adherents), he was become a most devout Believer. To what this should be ascribed I shall leave you to judge.

Exhausted, tottering with his giant exertions, he made his way through the tortuous streets of Old Cairo—streets where ancient palaces and mansions of wealthy Turks displayed their latticed windows, and, at that hour, barred doors to the solitary, panting wayfarer.

Upon one of these barred doors he beat. It was that of an old palace which seemed to be partially in ruins. After some delay, the door was opened and Mohammed admitted. The door was reclosed. And, following upon the brief clamour, silence claimed the street again.

Much precious time had elapsed since Eileen Graham's disappearance from the hotel by the Pyramids, when a belated and not too sober Greek, walking in the direction of Cairo, encountered what his muddled senses proclaimed to be an apparition—that of a white-robed figure upon a snow-white camel, which sped, silent, and with arrow-like swiftness, past him towards Gizeh. About this vision of the racing camel (a more beautiful creature than any he had seen since the last to carry the Mahmal), about the rider, spectral in the moonlight, white-bearded, there was that which suggested a vision of the Moslem Prophet. Ere the frightened Greek could gather courage to turn and look after the phantom rider, man and camel were lost across the sands.

Mena House was in an uproar. No one beneath its roof had thought of sleep that night. Futile searches were being conducted in every direction, north, south, east, and west. Graham, feeling that another hour of inactivity would spell madness, had succumbed to the fever to be up and doing, and had outdistanced all, had left the boy far behind and was mercilessly urging his poor little mount out into the desert, well knowing that in all probability he was riding further and further away from the one he sought, yet madly pressing on. He felt that to stop was to court certain insanity; he must press on and on; he must search—search.

His mood had changed, and from cursing fate, heaven, everything and every one, he was come to prayer.

He, then, was the next to see the man on the white camel, and, like the Greek, he scarcely doubted that it was a wraith of his tortured imagination. Indeed, he took it for an omen. The Prophet had appeared to him to proclaim that the desert, the home of Islam, had taken Eileen from him. The white-robed figure gave no sign, looked neither to the right nor to the left, but straight ahead, with eagle eyes.

Graham pulled up his donkey, and sat like a shape of stone, until the silver-grey distance swallowed up the phantom.

Out towards the oasis called the Well of Seven Palms, the straggling military company proceeded in growing weariness. The officer in charge had secured fairly reliable evidence to show that the Arabs had struck out straight for the Red Sea. Since he was not omniscient, he could not know that they had performed a wide detour which would lead them back an hour before dawn to the camp by the Nile beside the Temple of Horus, where El-Suleym waited for his captive.

It was at the point in their march when, to have intercepted the raiders, they should have turned due south instead of proceeding toward the oasis, that one of them pulled up, rubbed his eyes, looked again and gave the alarm.

In another moment they all saw it—a white camel; not such a camel as tourists are familiar with, the poor hacks of the species, but a swan-like creature, white as milk, bearing a white-robed rider who ignored utterly the presence of the soldiers, who answered by no word or sign to their challenge, but who passed them like a cloud borne along by a breeze and melted vaporously into the steely distances of the desert. The captain was hopelessly puzzled.

"Too late to bring him down," he muttered, "and no horse that was ever born could run down a racing camel. Most mysterious."

Twenty miles south of their position, and exactly at right-angles to their route, rode the Bishareen horsemen, the foremost with Eileen

Graham across his saddle. And now, eighteen miles behind the Bishareen, a white camel, of the pure breed which yearly furnishes the stately bearer of the Mahmal, spurned the sand and like a creature of air gained upon the Arabs, wild riders though they were, mile upon mile, league upon league.

Within rifle-shot of the camp, and with the desert dawn but an hour ahead, only a long sand-ridge concealed from the eyes of the Bishareen troupe that fleet shape which had struck wonder to the hearts of all beholders. Despite their start of close upon two hours, despite the fact that the soldiers were now miles, and hopeless miles, in their rear, the racer of the desert had passed them!

Eileen Graham had returned to full and agonizing consciousness. For hours, it seemed, her captives had rode and rode in silence. Now a certain coolness borne upon the breeze told her that they were nearing the river again. Clamour sounded ahead. They were come to the Arab camp. But ere they reached it they entered some lofty building which echoed hollowly to the horses' tread. She was lifted from her painful position, tied fast against a stone pillar, and the bandage was unfastened from about her head.

She saw that she was lashed to one of the ruined pillars which once had upheld the great hall of a temple. About her were the crumbling evidences of the sacerdotal splendour that was Ancient Egypt. The moon painted massive shadows upon the debris, and carpeted the outer place with the black image of a towering propylæum. Upon the mound which once had been the stone avenue of approach was the Bedouin camp. It was filled with a vague disturbance. She was quite alone; for those who had brought her there were leading their spent horses out to the camp.

Eileen could not know what the hushed sounds portended; but actually they were due to the fact that the outlaw chief, wearied with that most exhausting passion—the passion of anticipation—had sought his tent, issuing orders that none should disturb him. Many hours before he knew they could return, he had stood looking out across the sands, but at last had decided to fit himself, by repose, for the reception of his beautiful captive.

A sheikh's tent has two apartments—one sacred to the lord and master, the other sheltering his harem. To the former El-Suleym had withdrawn; and now his emissaries stood at the entrance, where the symbolic spear was stuck, blade upward, in the sand. Those who had thrown in their lot with El-Suleym, called the Regicide, had learnt that a robber chief whose ambitions have been whetted by a sojourn in Europe is a hard master, though one profitable to serve. They hesitated to arouse him, even though their delicate task was well accomplished.

And whilst they debated before the tent, which stood alone, as is usual, at some little distance from the others, amid which moved busy figures engaged in striking camp, Eileen, within the temple, heard a movement behind the pillar to which she was bound.

She was in no doubt respecting the identity of her captor, and the author of the ruse by which she had been lured from the hotel, and now, unable to turn, it came to her that this was *he*, creeping to her through the moon-patched shadows. With eyes closed, and her teeth clenched convulsively, she pictured the sinister, approaching figure. Then, from close beside her, came a voice:

"Only I can save you from him. Do not hesitate, do not speak. Do as I tell you."

Eileen opened her eyes. She could not see the speaker, but the voice was oddly familiar. Her fevered brain told her that she had heard it before, but speaking Arabic. It was the voice of an old man, but a strong, vibrant voice.

"It is the will of Allah, whose name be exalted, that I repay!"

A lean hand held before her eyes a broken gold chain, upon which depended a turquoise. She knew the voice, now: it was that of the old pedlar! But his English, except for the hoarse Eastern accent, was flawless, and this was the tone of no broken old man, but of one to be feared and respected.

Her reason, she thought, must be tricking her. How could the old pedlar, however strong in his queer gratitude, save her now? Then the hand came again before her eyes, and it held a tiny green phial.

"Be brave. Drink, quickly. They are coming to take you to him. It is the only escape!"

"Oh, God!" she whispered, and turned icily cold.

This was the boon he brought her. This was the road of escape, escape from El-Suleym—the road of death! It was cruel, unspeakably horrible, with a bright world just opening out to her, with youth, beauty, and— — She could not think of her husband.

"God be merciful to him!" she murmured. "But he would prefer me dead to——"

"Quick! They are here!"

She placed her lips to the phial, and drank.

It seemed that fire ran through every vein in her body. Then came chill. It grew, creeping from her hands and her feet inward and upward to her heart.

"Good-bye ... dear...." she whispered, and sobbed once, dryly.

The ropes held her rigidly upright.

VI

"Wa-llah! she is dead, and we have slain her!"

El-Suleym's Bedouins stood before the pillar in the temple, and fear was in their eyes. They unbound the girl, beautiful yet in her marble pallor, and lowered her rigid body to the ground. They looked one at another, and many a glance was turned toward the Nile.

Then the leader of the party extended a brown hand, pointing to the tethered horses. They passed from the temple, muttering. No one among them dared to brave the wrath of the terrible sheikh. As they came out into the paling moonlight, the camp seemed to have melted magically; for ere dawn they began their long march to the lonely oasis in the Arabian Desert which was the secret base of the Masr-Bishareen's depredatory operations.

Stealthily circling the camp, which buzzed with subdued activity— even the dogs seemed to be silent when the sheikh slept—they came to the horses. Solitary, a square silhouette against the paling blue, stood the sheikh's tent, on top of the mound, which alone was still untouched.

The first horseman had actually leapt into the saddle, and the others, with furtive glances at the ominous hillock, were about to do likewise, when a low wail, weird, eerie, rose above the muffled stirring of the camp.

"Allah el-'Azeen!" groaned one of the party—"what is that?"

Again the wail sounded—and again. Other woman voices took it up. It electrified the whole camp. Escape, undetected, was no longer possible. Men, women, and children were abandoning their tasks and standing, petrified with the awe of it, and looking towards the sheikh's tent.

As they looked, as the frightened fugitives hesitated, looking also, from the tent issued forth a melancholy procession. It was composed of the women of El-Suleym's household. They beat their bared breasts and cast dust upon their heads.

For within his own sacred apartment lay the sheikh in his blood—a headless corpse.

And now those who had trembled before him were hot to avenge him. Riders plunged out in directions as diverse as the spokes of a wheel. Four of them rode madly through the temple where they had left the body of their captive, leaping the debris, and circling about the towering pillars, as only Arab horsemen can. Out into the sands they swept; and before them, from out of a hollow, rose an apparition that brought all four up short, their steeds upreared upon their haunches.

It was the figure of a white-bearded man, white-robed and wearing the green turban, mounted upon a camel which, to the eyes of the four, looked in its spotless whiteness a creature of another world. Before the eagle-eyed stranger lay the still form of Eileen Graham, and as the camel rose to its feet, its rider turned, swung something high above him, and hurled it back at the panic-stricken pursuers. Right amongst their horses' feet it rolled, and up at them in the moonlight from out a mass of blood-clotted beard, stared the glassy eyes of El-Suleym!

The sun was high in the heavens when the grey-faced and haggard-eyed searchers came straggling back to Mena House. Two of them, who had come upon Graham ten miles to the east, brought him in. He was quite passive, and offered no protest, spoke no word, but stared straight in front of him with a set smile that was dreadful to see.

No news had come from the company of soldiers; no news had come from anywhere. It was ghastly, inconceivable; people looked at one another and asked if it could really be possible that one of their number had been snatched out from their midst in such fashion.

Officials, military and civil, literally in crowds, besieged the hotel. Amid that scene of confusion no one missed Mohammed; but when all the rest had given up in despair, he, a solitary, patient figure, stood out upon a distant mound watching the desert road to the east. He alone saw the return of the white camel with its double burden, from a distance of a hundred yards or more; for he dared approach no closer, but stood with bowed head pronouncing the *fáthah* over and over again. He saw it kneel, saw its rider descend and lift a girl from its back. He saw him force something between her lips, saw him turn and make a deep obeisance toward Mecca. At that he, too, knelt and did likewise. When he arose, camel and rider were gone.

He raced across the sands as Eileen Graham opened her eyes, and supported her as she struggled to her feet, pale and trembling.

"I don't understand it at all," said Graham.

Eileen smiled up at him from the long cane chair. She was not yet recovered from her dreadful experience. "Perhaps," she said softly, "you will not laugh in future at my Irish stories of the 'good people'!"

Graham shook his head and turned to Mohammed.

"What does it all mean, Mohammed?" he said. "Thank God it means that I have got her back, but how was it done? She returned wearing the turquoise necklace, which I last saw in your hand."

Mohammed looked aside.

"I took it to him, Effendi. It was the token by which he knew her need."

"The pedlar?"

"The pedlar, Effendi."

"You knew where to find him, then?"

"I knew where to find him, but I feared to tell you; feared that you might ridicule him."

He ceased. He was become oddly reticent. Graham shrugged his shoulders, helplessly.

"I only hope the authorities will succeed in capturing the Bishareen brigands," he said grimly.

"The authorities will never capture them," replied the dragoman with conviction. "For five years they have lived by plunder, and laughed at the Government. But before another moon is risen"—he was warming to his usual eloquence now—"no Masr-Bishareen will remain in the land, they will be exterminated—purged from the desert!"

"Indeed," said Graham; "by whom?"

"By the Rawallah, Effendi."

"Are they a Bedouin tribe?"

"The greatest of them all."

"Then why should they undertake the duty?"

"Because it is the will of the one who saved her for you, Effendi! I am blessed that I have set eyes upon him, spoken with him. Paradise is assured to me because my hand returned to him his turban when it lay in the dust!"

Graham stared, looking from his wife, who lay back smiling dreamily, to Mohammed, whose dark eyes burnt with a strange fervour—the fervour of one mysteriously converted to an almost fanatic faith.

"Are you speaking of our old friend, the pedlar?"

"I am almost afraid to speak of him, Effendi, for he is the chosen of heaven, a cleanser of uncleanliness; the scourge of God, who holds His flail in his hand—the broom of the desert!"

Graham, who had been pacing up and down the room, paused in front of Mohammed.

"Who is he, then?" he asked quietly. "I owe him a debt I can never hope to repay, so I should at least like to know his real name."

"I almost fear to speak it, Effendi." Mohammed's voice sank to a whisper, and he raised the turquoise hanging by the thin chain about Eileen's throat, and reverently touched it with his lips. "He is the *welee*—Ben Azreem, Sheikh of the Ibn-Rawallah!"

THE END

TALES OF SECRET EGYPT

— — —

SAX ROHMER

PART I

TALES OF ABÛ TABÂH

I

THE YASHMAK OF PEARLS

The *duhr*, or noonday call to prayer, had just sounded from the minarets of the Mosques of Kalaûn and En-Nasîr, and I was idly noting the negligible effect of the *adan* upon the occupants of the neighboring shops—coppersmiths for the most part—when suddenly my errant attention became arrested.

A mendicant of unwholesome aspect crouched in the shadow of the narrow gateway at the entrance to the Sûk es-Saîgh, or gold and silver bazaar, having his one serviceable eye fixed in a malevolent stare upon something or someone immediately behind me.

It is part and parcel of my difficult profession to subdue all impulses and to think before acting. I sipped my coffee and selected a fresh cigarette from the silver box upon the rug beside me. In this interval I had decided that the one-eyed mendicant cherished in his bosom an implacable and murderous hatred for my genial friend, Ali Mohammed, the dealer in antiques; that he was unaware of my having divined his bloody secret; and that if I would profit by my accidental discovery, I must continue to feign complete ignorance of it.

Turning casually to Ali Mohammed, I was startled to observe the expression upon his usually immobile face: he was positively gray, and I thought I detected a faint rattling sound, apparently produced by his teeth; his eyes were set as if by hypnosis upon the uncleanly figure huddled in the shadow of the low gate.

"You are unwell, my friend," I said.

Ali Mohammed shook his head feebly, removed his eyes by a palpable effort from the watcher in the gateway, but almost instantly reverted again to that fixed and terrified scrutiny.

"Not at all, Kernaby Pasha," he chattered; "not in the least."

He passed a hand rapidly over a brow wet with perspiration, and moistened his lips, which were correspondingly dry. I determined upon a diplomatic *tour de force*; I looked him squarely in the face.

"For some reason," I said distinctly, "you are in deadly fear of the wall-eyed mendicant who is sitting by the gate of the Sûk es-Saîgh, O Ali Mohammed, my friend."

I turned with assumed carelessness. The beggar of murderous appearance had vanished, and Ali Mohammed was slowly recovering his composure. I knew that I must act quickly, or he would deny with the urbane mendacity of the Egyptian all knowledge of the one-eyed one; therefore—

"Acquaint me with the reason of your apprehensions," I said, at the same time offering him one of his own cigarettes; "it may be that I can assist you."

A moment he hesitated, glancing doubtfully in the direction of the gate and back to my face; then—

"It is one of the people of Tîr," he whispered, bending close to my ear; "of the evil *ginn* who are the creatures of Abû Tabâh."

I was puzzled and expressed my doubt in words.

"Alas," replied Ali Mohammed, "the Imám Abû Tabâh is neither a man nor an official; he is a magician."

"Indeed! then you speak of one bearing the curious name of Abû Tabâh, who is at once the holder of a holy office and also one who has dealings with the *ginn* and the *Efreets*. This is strange, Ali Mohammed, my friend."

"It is strange and terrible," he whispered, "and I fear that my path is beset with pitfalls and slopeth down to desolation." He pronounced the *Takbîr*, "*Alláhu akbar!*" and uttered the words "*Hadeed! yá mashûm!*" (Iron! thou unlucky!), a potent invocation, as the *ginn's* dread of that metal is well known. "There are things of which one may not speak," he declared; "and this is one of them."

Sorely puzzled as I was by this most mysterious happening, yet, because of the pious words of my friend, I knew that the incident was closed so far as confidences were concerned; and I presently took my departure, my mind filled with all sorts of odd conjectures by which I sought to explain the matter. I was used to the superstitions of that quarter where almost every gate and every second street has its guardian *ginnee*, but who and what was Abû Tabâh? An Imám, apparently, though to what mosque attached Ali Mohammed had not mentioned. And why did Ali Mohammed fear Abû Tabâh?

So my thoughts ran, more or less ungoverned, whilst I made my way through streets narrow and tortuous in the direction of the Rondpoint du Mûski. I saw no more of the wall-eyed mendicant; but in a court hard by the Mosque of el-Ashraf I found myself in the midst of a squabbling crowd of natives surrounding someone whom I gathered, from the direction of their downward glances, to be prone upon the ground. Since the byways of the Sûk el-Attârin are little frequented by Europeans, at midday, I thrust my way into the heart of the throng, thinking that some stray patron of Messrs. Cook and Son (Egypt, Ltd.) might possibly have got into trouble or have been overcome by the heat.

Who or what lay at the heart of that gathering I never learned. I was still some distance from the centre of the disturbance when an evil-smelling sack was whipped over my head and shoulders from behind, a hand clapped upon my mouth and jaws; and, lifted in muscular arms, I found myself being borne inarticulate down stone steps, as I gathered from the sound, into some cool cellar-like place.

II

In my capacity as Egyptian representative of Messrs. Moses, Murphy & Co., of Birmingham, I have sometimes found myself in awkward corners; but in Cairo, whether the native or European quarter, I had hitherto counted myself as safe as in London and safer than in Paris. The unexpectedness of the present outrage would have been sufficient to take my breath away without the agency of the filthy sack, which had apparently contained garlic at some time and now contained my head.

I was deposited upon a stone-paved floor and my wrists were neatly pinioned behind me by one of my captors, whilst another hung on to my ankles. The sack was raised from my body but not from my face; and whilst a hand was kept firmly pressed over the region of my mouth, nimble fingers turned my pockets inside out. I assumed at first that I had fallen into the clutches of some modern brethren of the famous Forty, but when my purse, note-case, pocket-book, and other belongings were returned to me, I realized that something more underlay this attempt than the mere activity of a gang of footpads.

At this conclusion I had just arrived when the stinking sack was pulled off entirely and I found myself sitting on the floor of a small and very dark cellar. Beside me, holding the sack in his huge hands, stood a pock-marked negro of most repulsive appearance, and before me, his slim, ivory-colored hands crossed and resting upon the head of an ebony cane, was a man, apparently an Egyptian, whose appearance had something so strange about it that the angry words which I had been prepared to utter died upon my tongue and I sat staring mutely into the face of my captor; for I could not doubt that the outrage had been dictated by this man's will.

He was, then, a young man, probably under thirty, with perfectly chiseled features and a slight black moustache. He wore a black *gibbeh*, and a white turban, and brown shoes upon his small feet. His face was that of an ascetic, nor had I ever seen more wonderful and liquid eyes; in them reposed a world of melancholy; yet his red lips were parted in a smile tender as that of a mother. Inclining his head in a gesture of gentle dignity, this man—whom I hated at sight—addressed me in Arabic.

"I am desolated," he said, "and there is no comfort in my heart because of that which has happened to you by my orders. If it is possible for me to recompense you by any means within my power, command and you shall find a slave."

He was poisonously suave. Beneath the placid exterior, beneath the sugar-lipped utterances, in the deeps of the gazelle-like eyes, was hid a cold and remorseless spirit for which the man's silken demeanor was but a cloak. I hated him more and more. But my trade—for I do not blush to own myself a tradesman—has taught me caution. My ankles were free, it is true, but my hands were still tied behind me and over me towered the hideous bulk of the negro. This might be modern Cairo, and no doubt there were British troops quartered at the Citadel and at the Kasr en-Nîl; probably there was a native policeman, a representative of twentieth-century law and order, somewhere in the maze of streets surrounding me: but, in the first place, I was at a physical disadvantage, in the second place I had reasons for not desiring unduly to intrude my affairs upon official notice, and in the third place some hazy idea of what might be behind all this business had begun to creep into my mind.

"Have I the pleasure," I said, and electing to speak, not in Arabic but in English, "of addressing the *Imám Abû Tabâh?*"

I could have sworn that despite his amazing self-control the man started slightly; but the lapse, if lapse it were, was but momentary. He repeated the dignified obeisance of the head—and answered me in English as pure as my own.

"I am called Abû Tabâh," he said; "and if I assure you that my discourteous treatment was dictated by a mistaken idea of duty, and if I offer you this explanation as the only apology possible, will you permit me to untie your hands and call an *arabîyeh* to drive you to your hotel?"

"No apology is necessary," I assured him. "Had I returned direct to Shepheard's I should have arrived too early for luncheon; and the odor of garlic, which informed the sack that your zeal for duty caused to be clapped upon my head, is one for which I have a certain penchant if it does not amount to a passion."

Abû Tabâh smiled, inclined his head again, and slightly raising the ebony cane indicated my pinioned wrists, at the same time glancing at the negro. In a trice I was unbound and once more upon my feet. I looked at the dilapidated door which gave access to the cellar, and I made a rapid mental calculation of the approximate weight in pounds of the large negro; then I looked hard at Abû Tabâh—who smilingly met my glance.

"Any one of my servants," he said urbanely, "who wait in the adjoining room, will order you an *arabîyeh*."

III

When the card of Ali Mohammed was brought to me that evening, my thoughts instantly flew to the wall-eyed mendicant of the Sûk en-Nahhasîn, and to Abû Tabâh, the sugar-lipped. I left the pleasant company of the two charming American ladies with whom I had been chatting on the terrace and joined Ali Mohammed in the lounge.

Without undue preamble he poured his tale of woe into my sympathetic ears. He had been lured away from his shop later that afternoon, and, in his absence, someone had ransacked the place from floor to roof. That night on his way to his abode, somewhere out Shubra direction I understood, he had been attacked and searched, finally to reach his house and to find there a home in wild disorder.

"I fear for my life," he whispered and glanced about the lounge in blackest apprehension; "yet where in all Cairo may I find an intermediary whom I can trust? Suppose," he pursued, and dropped his voice yet lower, "that a commission of ten per cent—say, one hundred pounds, English—were to be earned, should you care, Kernaby Pasha, to earn it?"

I assured him that I should regard such a proposal with the utmost affection.

"It would be necessary," he continued, "for you to disguise yourself as an aged woman and to visit the *harêm* of a certain wealthy Bey. I have a ring which must be shown to the *bowwab* at the gate of the *harêm* gardens upon which you would knock three times slowly and then twice rapidly. You would collect the thousand *ginêh* agreed upon and would deliver to a certain lady a sandalwood box, the possession of which endangers my life and has brought about me the hosts of Abû Tabâh the magician."

So the head of the cat was out of the bag at last. But there was more to come and it was not a proposition to plunge at, as I immediately perceived; and I parted from Ali Mohammed upon the prudent understanding that I should acquaint him with my decision on the morrow.

The terrace of Shepheard's was deserted, when, having escorted my visitor to the door, he made his way down into the Shâria Kâmel Pasha. Two white-robed figures who looked like hotel servants, and a little nondescript group of natives, stood at the foot of the steps. At the instant that doubt entered my mind and too late to warn the worthy Ali Mohammed, the group parted to give him passage; then ... a terrific scuffle was in progress and one of the wealthiest merchants of the Mûski was being badly hustled.

I ran down the steps, the carriage-despatcher and some other officials, whom the disturbance had aroused from their secret lairs, appearing almost simultaneously. As I reached the street, out from the feet of the wrestling throng, like a football from a scrum, rolled a neat *tarbûsh*.

Automatically I stooped and picked it up. Its weight surprised me. Then, glancing inside the *tarbûsh*, I perceived that a little oblong box, together with a quaint signet ring, were ingeniously attached to the crown by means of silk threads tied around the knot of the tassel. I glanced rapidly about me. I, alone, had seen the cap roll out upon the pavement.

A hard jerk, and I had the box and the ring free in my hand. The tall carriage-despatcher, his ferocious efforts now seconded by a native policeman who freely employed his cane upon the thinly-clad persons of the group, had terminated the scuffle.

Right and left active figures darted, pursued for some little distance by the policeman and the two men from the hotel. There were no captures.

A very dusty and bemused Ali Mohammed, his shaven skull robbing him of much of the dignity which belonged to his *tarbûsh*, confronted me, ruefully dusting his garments.

"Your *tarbûsh*, my friend," I said, restoring his property to him with a bow.

One piercing glance he cast into the interior, then—

"O Allah!" he wailed—"O Allah! I am robbed! Yet——"

A sort of martyred resignation, a beatific peace, crept over his features.

"To war against Abû Tabâh is the act of a fool," he declared. "To have obtained the Bey's money would have been good, but to have obtained peace is better!"

IV

I awoke that night from a troubled sleep and from a dream wherein magnetic fingers caressed my forehead hypnotically. For a moment I could not believe that I was truly awake; the long ivory hand of my dreams was still moving close before me with a sort of slow fanning movement—and other, nimble, fingers crept beneath my pillow!

Of my distaste for impulse I have already spoken, and even now, with my mind not wholly under control, I profited by those years of self-imposed discipline. Without fully opening my eyes, cautiously, inch by inch, I moved my hand to that side of the bed nearer to the wall, where there reposed a leather holster containing my pistol.

My fingers closed over the butt of the weapon; and in a flash I became wide awake ... and had the ring of the barrel within an inch of the smiling face of Abû Tabâh!

I sat up.

"Be good enough, my friend," I said, "to turn on the center lamp. The switch, as you have probably noted, is immediately to the left of the door."

Abû Tabâh, straightening his figure and withdrawing his hand from beneath my pillow, inclined his picturesque head in grave salute and moved stately in the direction indicated. The room was flooded with yellow light. Its disorder was appalling; apparently no item of my gear had escaped attention.

"Pray take a seat," I said; "this one close beside me."

Abû Tabâh gravely accepted the invitation.

"This is the second occasion," I continued, "upon which you have unwarrantably submitted me to a peculiar form of outrage——"

"Not unwarrantably," replied Abû Tabâh, his speech suave and gentle; "but I fear I am too late!"

His words came as a beam of enlightenment. At last I had the game in my hands did I but play my cards with moderate cunning.

"You must pursue your inquiries in the *harêm* of the Bey," I said.

Abû Tabâh shrugged his shoulders.

"The house of Yûssuf Bey has been watched," he replied; "therefore my agents have failed me and must be punished."

"They are guiltless. It was humanly impossible to perceive my entrance to the house," I declared truthfully.

Abû Tabâh smiled into my face.

"So it was *you* who carried the sacred *burko* of the Seyyîdeh Nefîseh," he said; "and to-night Ali Mohammed brought you the reward for your perilous journey."

"Your reasoning is sound," I replied, "and the accuracy of your information remarkable."

I had scored the first point in the game; for I had learned that the wonderful silken *yashmak*, pearl embroidered, which I had found in the sandalwood box, was no less a curiosity than the face-veil of the Seyyîdeh Nefiseh and must therefore be of truly astounding antiquity and unique of its kind.

"The woman Sháhmarâh," continued my midnight visitor, the eerie light of fanaticism dawning in his eyes, "who was once a dancing girl, and who will ruin Yûssuf Bey as she ruined Ghûri Pasha before him, must be for ever accursed and meet with the fate of courtesans if she dare to wear the *burko* of Nefiseh."

I had scored my second point; I had learned that the lady to whom Ali Mohammed would have had me deliver the *yashmak* was named Sháhmarâh and was evidently the favorite of the notorious Yûssuf Bey. The complacent self-satisfaction of Abû Tabâh amused me vastly, for he clearly entertained no doubts respecting his efficiency as a searcher.

He was watching me now with his strange hypnotic eyes, which had softened again, and his fixed stare caused me a certain uneasiness. For a captured thief, sitting covered by the pistol of his captor, he was ridiculously composed.

"You have performed an immoral deed," he said sweetly, "and have pandered to the base desires of a woman of poor repute. I offer you an opportunity of performing a good deed—and of trebling your profit."

This was as I would have it, and I nodded encouragingly.

"Unfold to me the thing that is in your mind," I directed him.

"I am a Moslem," he said; "and although Yûssuf Bey is a dog of dogs, he is nevertheless a True Believer—and I may not force my way into his *harêm*."

"He might return the veil if he knew that Sháhmarâh had it," I suggested ingenuously.

Abû Tabâh shook his head.

"There are difficulties," he replied, "and if the theft is not to be proclaimed to the world, there is no time to be lost. This is my proposal: Return to the woman Sháhmarâh, and acquaint her with the fact that the sacred veil has been traced to her abode and her death decided upon by the Grand Mufti if it be not given up. Force the merchant Ali Mohammed to return the money received by him, using the same threat—which will prove a talisman of power. Return to the infidel woman the full amount; I will make good your commission, to which, if you be successful, I will add two hundred pounds."

I performed some rapid thinking.

"You must give me a little time to consider this matter," I said.

Abû Tabâh graciously inclined his head.

"On Tuesday next a company of holy men who have journeyed hither from Ispahân, go to view this relic; you have therefore five days to act."

"And if I decline?"

Abû Tabâh shrugged his shoulders.

"The loss must be made known—it would be a great scandal; the merchant Ali Mohammed, and the woman, Sháhmarâh, must be arrested—very undesirable; *you* must be arrested—most undesirable; and your banking account will be poorer by three hundred pounds."

"Frightfully undesirable," I declared. "But suppose I strike the first blow and give you in charge of the police here and now?"

"You may try the experiment," he said.

I waved my hand in the direction of the door (I had reasons for remaining in bed). "*Ma'salâma!* (Good-bye)," I said. "Don't stay to restore the room to order. I shall expect you early in the morning. You will find the door of the hotel open any time after eight and I can highly recommend it as a mode of entrance."

Having saluted me with both hands, Abû Tabâh made his stately departure, leaving me much exercised in mind as to how he proposed to account to the *bowwab* for his sudden appearance in the building. This, however, was no affair of mine, and, first reclosing the window, I unfastened from around my left ankle the sandalwood box and the ring which I had bound there by a piece of tape—a device to which I owed their preservation from the subtle fingers of Abû Tabâh. Furthermore, to their presence there I owed my having awakened when I did. I am persuaded that the mysterious Egyptian's passes would have continued to keep me in a profound sleep had it not been for the pain occasioned by the pressure of the tape.

Opening the sandalwood box, and then the silver one which it enclosed, I re-examined the really wonderful specimen of embroidery whereof they formed the reliquary. The *burko* was of Tussur silk, its texture so fine that the whole veil, which was some four feet long by two wide, might have been passed through the finger ring and would readily be concealed in the palm of the hand.

It was of unusual form, having no forehead band, more nearly resembling a *yashmak* than a true *burko*, and was heavily embroidered with pearls of varying sizes and purity, although none of them were large. Its intrinsic value was considerable, but in view of its history such a valuation must have fallen far below the true one. When its loss became known, I estimated that Messrs. Moses, Murphy & Co. could readily dispose of three duplicates through various channels to wealthy collectors whose enthusiasms were greater than their morality. The sale to a museum, or to the lawful owners, of the original (known technically as "the model") would crown a sound commercial transaction.

Cock-crow that morning discovered me at the private residence, in the Boulevard Clot-Bey, of one Suleyman Levi, with whom I had had minor dealings in the past.

V

At nine o'clock on the following Monday night, an old Egyptian woman, enveloped from head to foot in a black *tôb* and wearing a black crêpe face-veil boasting a hideous brass nose-piece, halted before a doorway set in the wall guarding the great gardens of the palace of Yûssuf Bey. I was the impersonator of this decrepit female. Abû Tabâh, who thus far had accompanied me, stepped into the dense shadow of the opposite wall and was thereby swallowed up.

I rapped three times slowly upon the doorway, then twice rapidly. Almost at once a little wicket therein flew open, and a bloated negro face showed framed in the square aperture.

"The messenger from Ali Mohammed of the Sûk en-Nahhasîn," I said, in a croaky voice. "Conduct me to the Lady Sháhmarâh."

"Show her seal," answered the eunuch, extending through the opening a large, fat hand.

I gave him the ring so fortunately discovered in the *tarbûsh* of my friend the merchant and the hand was withdrawn. Within a colloquy took place in which a female voice took part. Then the door was partly opened for my admittance—and I found myself in the gardens of the Bey.

In the moonlight it was a place of wonder, an enchanted demesne; but more like an Edmond Dulac water-color than a real garden. The palace with its magnificent *mushrabîyeh* windows, so poetically symbolical of veiled women, guarded by several fine, straight-limbed palm trees, spoke of the Old Cairo which saw the birth of *The Arabian Nights* and which so many of us imagine to have vanished with the *khalîfate*.

A girl completely muffled up in many-hued shawls and scarves, so that her red-slippered feet and two bright eyes heavily darkened with *kohl* were the only two portions of her person visible, stood before me, her figure seeming childish beside that of the gross negro—whom I hated at sight because he reminded me of the one whom I had encountered in Abû Tabâh's cellar.

"Follow me, quickly, mother," said the girl. "You"—pointing imperiously at the black man—"remain here."

I followed her in silence, noting that she pursued a path which ran parallel with the wall and lay wholly in its shadow. The gardens were fragrant with the perfume of roses, and in the center was a huge marble fountain surrounded by kiosks projecting into the water, tall acacias overshadowing them. We skirted two sides of the palace, its *mushrabîyeh* windows mysteriously lighted by the moon but showing no illumination from within. There we came to the entrance to a kind of trellis-covered walk, mosaic paved and patched delightfully with mystic light. It terminated before a small but heavy and nail-studded door, of which my guide held the key.

Entering, whilst she held the door ajar, I found myself in utter darkness, to be almost immediately dispelled by the yellow gleam of a lamp which the girl took from some niche, wherein, already lighted, it had been concealed. Up a flight of bare wooden stairs she conducted me, and opened a second prison-like door at their head. Leaving the lamp upon the top step, she pushed me gently forward into a small, octagonal room, paneled in dark wood inlaid with mother-o'-pearl and reminding me of the interior of a magnified *kursee* or coffee table.

Rugs and carpets strewed the floor and the air was heavy with the smell of musk, a perfume which I detest, it having characterized the personality of a certain Arab lady who sold me so marvelous a Damascus scimitar that I was utterly deceived by it until too late.

Raising a heavy curtain draped in a door shaped like an old-fashioned keyhole, and embellished with an intricate mass of fretwork carving, my guide went out, leaving me alone with my reflections. This interval was very brief, however, and was terminated by the reappearance of the girl, who this time made her entrance through a second doorway masked by the paneling. A faint musical splashing sound greeted me through the opening; and when my guide beckoned me to enter and I obeyed, I found myself in a chamber of barbaric beauty and in the presence of the celebrated Sháhmarâh.

The apartment, save for one end being wholly occupied by a magnificent *mushrabîyeh* screen, was walled with what looked like Verde Antico marble or green serpentine. An ebony couch having feet shaped as those of a leopard and enriched with gleaming bronze, having the skins of leopards cast across it, and, upon the skins, silken soft cushions wrought in patterns of green and gold, stood upon the mosaic floor at the head of three shallow steps which descended to a pool where a fountain played, softly musical; wherein lurked gleaming shapes of silver and gold. Bright mats were strewn around, and at one corner of the pool a huge silver *mibkharah* sent up its pencilings of aromatic smoke.

Upon this couch Sháhmaráh reclined, and I perceived immediately that her reputation for beauty was richly deserved. There was something leopardine in her pliant shape, which seemed to harmonize with the fierce black and gold of the skins upon which she was stretched; she had the limbs of a Naiad and the eyes of an Egyptian Circe. Upon her head she wore a *rabtah,* or turban, of pure white, secured and decorated in front by a brooch of ancient Egyptian enamel-work probably fourteenth dynasty, and for which I would gladly have given her one hundred pounds. If I have forgotten what else she wore it may be because my senses were in somewhat of a turmoil as I stood before her in that opulent apartment—which I suddenly recognized, and not without discomfiture, to be the *meslakh* of the *hammám.* I can only relate, then, that the image left upon my mind was one of jewels and dusky peach-like loveliness. Jewels there were in abundance, clasped about the warm curves of her arms and overloading her fingers; she wore gold bands thickly encrusted with gems about her ankles (the slim ankles of a dancing girl); and a fiery ruby of the true pigeon's-blood color gleamed upon the first toe of her left foot, the nails of which were highly manicured and stained with henna.

Fixing her wonderful eyes upon me—

"You have brought the veil?" she said.

"The merchant Ali Mohammed ordered me to convey to him the price agreed upon, O jewel of Egypt," I mumbled, "ere I yielded up this a poor man's only treasure."

Sháhmaráh sat upright upon the couch. Her delicate brows were drawn together in a frown, and her eyes, rendered doubly luminous by the pigment with which they were surrounded, glared fiercely at me, whilst she stamped one bare foot upon a cushion lying on the mosaic floor.

"The veil!" she cried imperiously. "I will send the merchant Ali Mohammed an order on the treasury of the Bey."

"O moon of the Orient," I replied, "O ravisher of souls, I am but a poor ugly old woman basking in the radiance of beauty and loveliness. Would you ruin one so old and feeble and helpless? I must have the price agreed upon; let it be counted into this bag"—and concealing my tell-tale hands as much as possible, I bent humbly and placed a leather wallet upon a little table beside her which bore fruits, sweetmeats, and a long-necked gold flagon. "When it is done, the *yashmak* of pearls, which only thy dazzling perfection might dare to wear, shall be yielded up to thee, O daughter of musk and ambergris."

There fell a short silence, wherein the fountain musically plashed and Sháhmaráh shot little inquiring glances laden with venom into the mists of my black veil, and others which held a query over my shoulder at her confidant.

"I might have you cast into a dungeon beneath this palace," she hissed at me, bending lithely forward and extending a jeweled forefinger. "No one would miss thee, O mother of afflictions."

"In that event," I crooned quaveringly, "O tree of pearls, the veil could never be thine; for the merchant Ali Mohammed, who awaits me at the gate, refuses to deliver it up until the price agreed upon has been placed in his hands."

"He is a Jew, and a son of Jews, who eats without washing! a devourer of pork, and an unclean insect," she cried.

She extended the jeweled hand towards the girl who stood behind me and who, having loosened her wraps, proved to be a comely but shrewd-looking Assyrian. "Let the money be counted into the bag," she ordered, "that we may be rid of the presence of this garrulous and hideous old hag."

"O fountain of justice," I exclaimed; "O peerless *houri*, to behold whom is to swoon with delight and rapture."

From a locked closet the Assyrian girl took a wooden coffer, and before my gratified eyes began to count out upon the little table notes and gold until a pile lay there to have choked a miser with emotion. (The ready-money transactions of the East have always delighted me.) But, with the chinking of the last piece of gold upon the pile—

"There is no more," said the girl. "It is one hundred pounds short."

"It is more than enough!" cried Sháhmaráh. "I am ruined. Give me the veil and go."

"O vision of paradise," I exclaimed in anguish, "the merchant Ali Mohammed would never consent. In lieu of the remainder"—I pointed to the antique enamel in her turban—"give me the brooch from thy *rabtah*."

"O sink of corruption!" was her response, her whole body positively quivering with rage, "it is not for thy filthy claws. Here!"—she pulled a ring containing a fair-sized emerald from one of her fingers and tossed it contemptuously upon the pile of money—"thou art more than repaid. The veil! the veil!"

I turned to the girl who had counted out the gold.

"O minor moon, whom even the glory of paradise cannot dim," I said, "put the money in the wallet, for my hands are old and infirm, and give it to me."

The Assyrian scooped the gold and notes into the leather bag with the utmost unconcern, and as though she had been shelling peas into a basket. The profound disregard for wealth exhibited in the *harêm* of Yûssuf Bey was extraordinary; and I mentally endorsed the opinion expressed by Abû Tabâh that the ruin of the Bey was imminent.

Securing the heavy wallet to the girdle which I wore beneath my veilings, I placed upon the table where the money had lain a small silken packet.

"Here is the veil," I said; "for my story of the merchant, Ali Mohammed, who had refused to yield it up, was but a stratagem to test the generosity of thy soul, as thy refusal to give me the price agreed upon was but a subterfuge to test my honesty."

Heedless of the words, Sháhmarâh snatched up the packet, tore off the wrappings, and in a trice was standing upright before me wearing the *yashmak* of pearls.

I think I had never seen a figure more barbarically lovely than that of this soulless Egyptian so adorned.

"My mirror, Sáfiyeh! my mirror!" she cried.

And the girl placing a big silver mirror in her hand, she stood there looking into its surface, her wonderful eyes swimming with ecstasy and her slim body swaying in a perfect rapture of admiration for her own beauty.

Suddenly she dropped the mirror upon the cushions and threw wide her arms.

"Am I not the fairest woman in Egypt?" she exclaimed. "I tread upon the hearts of men and my power is above the power of kings!"

Then a subtle change crept over her features; and ere I could utter the first of the honeyed compliments ready upon my tongue—

"Send Amineh to warn Mahmûd that the old woman is about to depart," she directed her attendant; and, turning to me: "Wait in the outer room. Thy presence is loathsome to me, O mother of calamities."

"I hear and obey," I replied, "O pomegranate blossom"—and, following the direction of her rigidly extended finger, I shuffled back to the little octagonal apartment and the masked door was slammed almost upon my heels.

This room, which possessed no windows, was solely illuminated by a silken-shaded lantern, but I had not long to wait in that weird half-light ere my conductress, again closely muffled in her shawls, opened the door at the head of the steps and signed to me to descend.

"Lead the way, my beautiful daughter," I said; for I had no intention of submitting myself to the risk of a dagger in the back.

She consented without demur, which served to allay my suspicions somewhat, and in silence we went down the uncarpeted stairs and out into the trellis-covered walk. The shadow beneath the high wall had deepened and widened since we had last skirted the gardens, and I felt my way along with my hand cautiously outstretched.

At a point within sight of the flower-grown arbor beneath which I knew the gate to be concealed, my guide halted.

"I must return, mother," she said quickly. "There is the gate, and Mahmûd will open it for you."

"Farewell, O daughter of the willow branch," I replied. "May Allah, the Great, the Compassionate, be with thee, and may thou marry a prince of Persia."

Light of foot she sped away, and, my forebodings coming to a sudden climax, I crept forward with excessive caution, holding my clenched hand immediately in front of my face—a device which experience of the hospitable manners of the East had taught me.

It was well that I did so. Within three spaces of the gate a noose fell accurately over my head and was drawn tight with a strangling jerk!

But that it also encircled my upraised arm, its clasp must have terminated my worldly affairs.

My assailant had sprung upon me from behind; and, in the fleeting instant between the fall of the noose and its tightening, I turned about ... and thrust the nose of my Colt repeater (which I grasped in that protective upraised hand) fully into the grinning mouth of the negro gate-keeper!

There was a rattle and gleam of falling ivory, for several of the *bowwab's* teeth had been dislodged by the steel barrel. Keeping the weapon firmly thrust into the man's distended jaws, I circled around him, whilst his hands relaxed their hold upon the strangling-cord, and pushed him backward in the direction of the door.

"Open thou black son of offal!" I said, "or I will blow thee a cavity as wide as thy blubber mouth through the back of that fat and greasy neck! This was, no doubt, a stratagem of thy mistress to test my fitness to be entrusted with large sums of money?"

When, a few moments later, I stood in the lane outside the gardens of Yûssuf Bey, and felt with my hand the fat wallet at my waist, I experienced a thrill of professional satisfaction, for had I not successfully negotiated a duplicate veil, embroidered with imitation pearls which the excellent Suleyman Levi by dint of four days of almost ceaseless toil had made for me?...

From the shadows of the opposite wall Abû Tabâh stepped forth, stately.

"Quick!" I said. "I fear pursuit at any moment! Is the *arabîyeh* waiting?"

"You have it?" he demanded, some faint sign of human animation creeping over his impassive face.

"I have!" I replied. "I will give it to you in the *arabîyeh*."

Side by side we passed down the deserted thoroughfare to where, beside a solitary palm, a pair-horse carriage was waiting. Appreciating something of my companion's natural impatience, I pressed into his hand the famous sandalwood box which once had reposed in the *tarbûsh* of Ali Mohammed. The carriage rolled around a corner and out into the lighted Shâria Mobâdayân. Abû Tabâh opened the sandalwood box, and then, reverently, the inner box of silver. Within shimmered the pearls of the sacred *burko*. He did not touch the relic with his hands, but reclosed the boxes and concealed the reliquary beneath his black robe. I heard the crackle of notes; and a little packet surrounded by a band of elastic was pressed into my hand.

"Three hundred pounds, English," said Abû Tabâh. "One hundred pounds in recompense for the commission you returned, and two hundred pounds for the recovery of the relic."

I thrust the wad into the bag beneath my robe containing the other spoils of the evening. A second and even more grateful glow of professional joy warmed my heart. For in the reliquary which I had handed to Abû Tabâh reposed the second product of Suleyman Levi's scientific toils; his four days' labor having resulted in the production of two quite passable duplicates; although neither were by any means up to the standard of Messrs. Moses, Murphy & Co.

Coming to the house wherein I had endued my disguise, Abû Tabâh left me to metamorphose myself into a decently dressed Englishman suitable for admission to an hotel of international repute.

"*Lîltâk sa'îda*, Abû Tabâh," I said.

In the open doorway he turned.

"*Lîltâk sa'îda*, Kernaby Pasha," he replied, and smiled upon me very sweetly.

VI

It was after midnight when I returned to Shepheard's, but I went straight to my room, and switching on the table-lamp, wrote a long letter to my principals. Something seemed to have gone wrong with the lock of my attaché-case, and my good humor was badly out of joint by the time that I succeeded in opening it. From underneath a mass of business correspondence I took out a large, sealed envelope, which I enclosed with a letter in one yet larger, to be registered to Messrs. Moses, Murphy & Co., Birmingham, in the morning. I turned in utterly tired but happy, to dream complacently of the smile of Abû Tabâh and of the party of holy men who had journeyed from Ispahân.

Exactly a fortnight later the following registered letter was handed to me as I was about to sit down to lunch—

The Hon. Neville Kernaby.
Shepheard's Hotel,
Cairo, Egypt.

DEAR MR. NEVILLE KERNABY—
We are returning herewith the silken veil which you describe as "the authentic *burko* of the Seyyîdeh Nefîseh, stolen from her shrine in the Tombs of the Khalîfs." Your statement that you can arrange for its purchase at the cost of one thousand pounds does not interest us, nor do we expect so high-salaried an expert as yourself to send us palpable and very inferior forgeries. We are manufacturers of duplicates, not buyers of same.

> Yours truly,
> LLOYD LLEWELLYN.
> (For Messrs. Moses, Murphy & Co.).

I was positively aghast. Tearing open the enclosed package, I glared like a madman at the *yashmak* which it contained. The silk, in comparison with that of which the real veil was compared, was coarse as cocoanut matting; the embroidery was crude; the pearls shrieked "imitation" aloud! At a glance I knew the thing for one of the pair made by Suleyman Levi!

The truth crashed in upon my mind. Following my visit to the *harêm* of Yûssuf Bey, I had bestowed no more than a glance upon the envelope wherein, early on the morning of the same day, I had lovingly sealed the authentic veil; and a full hour had elapsed between the time of parting with the sugar-lipped one and my return to my rooms at the hotel.

I understood, now, why the lock of my attaché-case had been out of order on that occasion ... and I comprehended the sweet smile of Abû Tabâh!

II

THE DEATH-RING OF SNEFERU

I

The orchestra had just ceased playing; and, taking advantage of the lull in the music, my companion leaned confidentially forward, shooting suspicious glances all around him, although there was nothing about the well-dressed after-dinner throng filling Shepheard's that night to have aroused misgiving in the mind of a cinema anarchist.

"I have a very big thing in view," he said, speaking in a husky whisper. "I shall be one up on you, Kernaby, if I pull it off."

He glanced sideways, in the manner of a pantomime brigand, at a party of New York tourists, our immediate neighbors, and from them to an elderly peer with whom I was slightly acquainted and who, in addition to his being stone deaf, had never noticed anything in his life, much less attempted so fatiguing an operation as intrigue.

"Indeed," I commented; and rang the bell with the purpose in view of ordering another cooling beverage.

True, I might be the Egyptian representative of a Birmingham commercial enterprise, but I did not gladly suffer the society of this individual, whose only claim to my acquaintance lay in the fact that he was in the employ of a rival house. My lack of interest palpably disappointed him; but I thought little of the man's qualities as a connoisseur and less of his company. His name was Theo Bishop and I fancy that his family was associated with the tanning industry. I have since thought more kindly of poor Bishop, but at the time of which I write nothing could have pleased me better than his sudden dissolution.

Perhaps unconsciously I had allowed my boredom to become rudely apparent; for Bishop slightly turned his head aside, and—

"Right-o, Kernaby," he said; "I know you think I am an ass, so we will say no more about it. Another cocktail?"

And now I became conscience-stricken; for mingled with the disappointment in Bishop's tone and manner was another note. Vaguely it occurred to me that the man was yearning for sympathy of some kind, that he was bursting to unbosom himself, and that the vanity of a successful rival was by no means wholly responsible. I have since placed that ambiguous note and recognized it for a note of tragedy.

But at the time I was deaf to its pleading.

We chatted then for some while longer on indifferent topics, Bishop being, as I have indicated, a man difficult to offend; when, having correspondence to deal with, I retired to my own room. I suppose I had been writing for about an hour, when a servant came to announce a caller. Taking an ordinary visiting-card from the brass salver, I read—

Abû Tabâh.

No title preceded the name, no address followed, but I became aware of something very like a nervous thrill as I stared at the name of my visitor. Personality is one of the profoundest mysteries of our being. Of the person whose card I held in my hand I knew little, practically nothing; his actions, if at times irregular, had never been wantonly violent; his manner was gentle as that of a mother to a baby and his singular reputation among the natives I thought I could afford to ignore; for the Egyptian, like the Celt, with all his natural endowments, is yet a child at heart. Therefore I cannot explain why, sitting there in my room in Shepheard's Hotel, I knew and recognized, at the name of Abû Tabâh, the touch of fear.

"I will see him downstairs," I said.

Then, as the servant was about to depart, recognizing that I had made a concession to that strange sentiment which the Imám Abû Tabâh had somehow inspired in me—

"No," I added; "show him up here to my room."

A few moments later the man returned again, carrying the brass salver, upon which lay a sealed envelope. I took it up in surprise, noting that it was one belonging to the hotel, and, ere opening it—

"Where is my visitor?" I said in Arabic.

"He regrets that he cannot stay," replied the man; "but he sends you this letter."

Greatly mystified, I dismissed the servant and tore open the envelope. Inside, upon a sheet of hotel notepaper I found this remarkable message—

Kernaby Pasha—

There are reasons why I cannot stay to see you personally, but I would have you believe that this warning is dictated by nothing but friendship. Grave peril threatens. It is associated with the hieroglyphic—

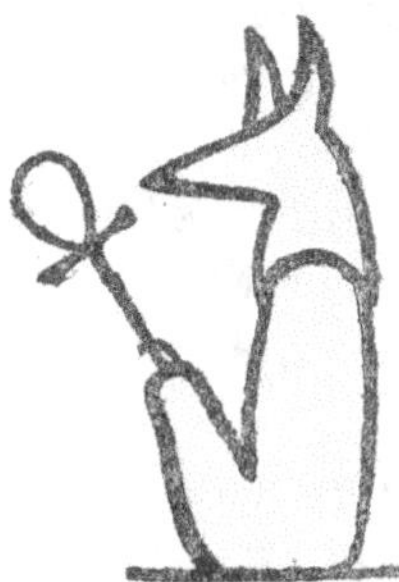

If you would avert it, and if you value your life, avoid all contact with anything bearing this figure.

ABÛ TABÂH.

The mystery deepened. There had been something incongruous about the modern European visiting-card used by this representative of Islam, this living illustration of the *Arabian Nights*; now, his incomprehensible "warning" plunged me back again into the mediæval Orient to which he properly belonged. Yet I knew Abû Tabâh, for all his romantic aspect, to be eminently practical, and I could not credit him with descending to the methods of melodrama.

As I studied the precise wording of the note, I seemed to see the slim figure of its author before me, black-robed, white-turbaned, and urbane, his delicate ivory hands crossed and resting upon the head of the ebony cane without which I had never seen him. Almost, I succumbed to a sort of subjective hallucination; Abû Tabâh became a veritable presence, and the poetic beauty of his face struck me anew, as, fixing upon me his eyes, which were like the eyes of a gazelle, he spoke the strange words cited above, in the pure and polished English which he held at command, and described in the air, with a long nervous forefinger, the queer device which symbolized the Ancient Egyptian god, Set, the Destroyer.

Of course, it was the aura of a powerful personality, clinging even to the written message; but there was something about the impression made upon me which argued for the writer's sincerity.

That Abû Tabâh was some kind of agent, recognized—at any rate unofficially—by the authorities, I knew or shrewdly surmised; but the exact nature of his activities, and how he reconciled them with his religious duties, remained profoundly mysterious. The episode had rendered further work impossible, and I descended to the terrace, with no more definite object in view than that of finding a quiet corner where I might meditate in the congenial society of my briar, and at the same time seek inspiration from the ever-changing throng in the Shâria Kâmel Pasha.

I had scarcely set my foot upon the terrace, however, ere a hand was laid upon my arm. Turning quickly I recognized, in the dusk, Hassan es-Sugra, for many years a trusted employee of the British Archæological Society.

His demeanor was at once excited and furtive, and I recognized with something akin to amazement that he, also, had a story to unfold. I mentally catalogued this eventful evening "the night of strange confidences."

Seated at a little table on the deserted balcony (for the evening was very chilly) and directly facing the shop of Philip, the dealer in Arab woodwork, Hassan es-Sugra told his wonder tale; and as he told it I knew that Fate had cast me, willy-nilly, for a part in some comedy upon which the curtain had already risen here in Cairo, and whereof the second act should be played in perhaps the most ancient setting which the hand of man has builded. As the narrative unrolled itself before me, I perceived wheels within wheels; I was wholly absorbed, yet half incredulous.

"... When the professor abandoned work on the pyramid, Kernaby Pasha," he said, bending eagerly forward and laying his muscular brown hand upon my sleeve, "it was not because there was no more to learn there."

"I am aware of this, O Hassan," I interrupted, "it was in order that they might carry on the work at the Pyramid of Illahûn, which resulted in a find of jewelery almost unique in the annals of Egyptology."

"Do I not know all this!" exclaimed Hassan impatiently; "and was not mine the hand that uncovered the golden uræus? But the work projected at the Pyramid of Méydûm was never completed, and I can tell you why."

I stared at him through the gloom; for I had already some idea respecting the truth of this matter.

"It was that the men, over two hundred of them, refused to enter the passage again," he whispered dramatically, "it was because misfortune and disaster visited more than one who had penetrated to a certain place therein." He bent further forward. "The Pyramid of Méydûm is the home of a powerful *Efreet*, Kernaby Pasha! But I who was the last to leave it, know what is concealed there. In a certain place, low down in the corner of the King's Chamber, is a ring of gold, bearing a cartouche. It is the royal ring of the Pharaoh who built the pyramid."

He ceased, watching me intently. I did not doubt Hassan's word, for I had always counted him a man of integrity; but there was much that was obscure and much that was mysterious in his story.

"Why did you not bring it away?" I asked.

"I feared to touch it, Kernaby Pasha; it is an evil talisman. Until to-day I have feared to speak of it."

"And to-day!"

Hassan extended his hands, palms upward.

"I am threatened with the loss of my house," he said simply, "if I do not find a certain sum of money within a period of twelve days."

I sat resting my chin on my hand and staring into the face of Hassan es-Sugra. Could it be that from superstitious motives such a treasure had indeed been abandoned? Could it be that Fate had delivered into my hands a relic so priceless as the signet-ring of Sneferu, one of the earliest Memphite Pharaohs? Since I had recently incurred the displeasure of my principals, Messrs. Moses, Murphy & Co., of Birmingham, the mere anticipation of such a "find" was sufficient to raise my professional enthusiasm to white heat, and in those few moments of silence I had decided upon instant action.

"Meet me at Rikka Station, to-morrow morning at nine o'clock," I said, "and arrange for donkeys to carry us to the pyramid."

II

On my arrival at Rikka, and therefore at the very outset of my inquiry, I met with what one slightly prone to superstition might have regarded as an unfortunate omen. A native funeral was passing out of the town amid the wailing of women and the chanting by the *Yemeneeyeh*, of the Profession of the Faith, with its queer monotonous cadences, a performance which despite its familiarity in the Near East never failed to affect me unpleasantly. By the token of the *tarbûsh* upon the bier, I knew that this was a man who was being hurried to his lonely resting-place on the fringe of the desert.

As the procession wound its way out across the sands, I saw to the removal of my baggage and joined Hassan es-Sugra, who awaited me by the wooden barrier. I perceived immediately that something was wrong with the man; he was palpably laboring under the influence of some strong excitement, and his dark eyes regarded me almost fearfully. He was muttering to himself like one suffering from an over-indulgence in *Hashish*, and I detected the words "*Allahu akbar!*" (God is most great) several times repeated.

"What ails you, Hassan, my friend?" I said; and noting how his gaze persistently returned to the melancholy procession wending its way towards the little Moslem cemetery:—"Was the dead man some relation of yours?"

"No, no, Kernaby Pasha," he muttered gutturally, and moistened his lips with his tongue; "I was but slightly acquainted with him."

"Yet you are much disturbed."

"Not at all, Kernaby Pasha," he assured me; "not in the slightest."

By which familiar formula I knew that Hassan es-Sugra would conceal from me the cause of his distress, and therefore, since I had no appetite for further mysteries, I determined to learn it from another source.

"See to the loading of the donkey," I directed him—for three sleek little animals were standing beside him, patiently awaiting the toil of the day.

Hassan setting about the task with a cheerful alacrity obviously artificial, I approached the native station master, with whom I was acquainted, and put to him a number of questions respecting his important functions—in which I was not even mildly interested. But to the Oriental mind a direct inquiry is an affront, almost an insult; and to have inquired bluntly the name of the deceased and the manner of his death would have been the best way to have learned nothing whatever about the matter. Therefore having discussed in detail the slothful incompetence of Arab ticket collectors and the lazy condition and innate viciousness of Egyptian porters as a class, I mentioned incidentally that I had observed a funeral leaving Rikka.

The station master (who was bursting to talk about this very matter, but who would have declined on principle to do so had I definitely questioned him) now unfolded to me the strange particulars respecting the death of one, Ahmed Abdulla, who had been a retired dragoman though some time employed as an excavator.

"He rode out one night upon his white donkey," said my informant, "and no man knows whither he went. But it is believed, Kernaby Pasha, that it was to the Haram el-Kaddâb" (the False Pyramid)—extending his hand to where, beyond the belt of fertility, the tomb of Sneferu up-reared its three platforms from the fringe of the desert. "To enter the pyramid even in day time is to court misfortune; to enter at night is to fall into the hands of the powerful *Efreet* who dwells there. His donkey returned without him, and therefore search was made for Ahmed Abdulla. He was found the next day"—again the long arm shot out towards the desert—"dead upon the sands, near the foot of the pyramid."

I looked into the face of the speaker; beyond doubt he was in deadly earnest.

"Why should Ahmed Abdulla have wanted to visit such a place at night?" I asked.

My acquaintance lowered his voice, muttered "*Sahâm Allah fee 'adoo ed—dîn!*" (May God transfix the enemies of the religion) and touched his forehead, his mouth, and his breast with the iron ring which he wore.

"There is a great treasure concealed there, Kernaby Pasha," he replied; "a treasure hidden from the world in the days of Suleyman the Great, sealed with his seal, and guarded by the servants of Gánn Ibn-Gánn."

"So you think the guardian *ginn* killed Ahmed Abdulla?"

The station master muttered invocations, and—

"There are things which may not be spoken of," he said; "but those who saw him dead say that he was terrible to look upon. A great *Welee*, a man of wisdom famed throughout Egypt, has been summoned to avert the evil; for if the anger of the *ginn* is aroused they may visit the most painful and unfortunate penalties upon all Rikka...."

Half an hour later I set out, having confidentially informed the station master that I sought to obtain a fine turquoise necklet which I knew to be in the possession of the Sheikh of Méydûm. Little did I suspect how it was written that I should indeed visit the house of the venerable Sheikh. Out through the fields of young green corn, the palm groves and the sycamore orchards I rode, Hassan plodding silently behind me and leading the donkey who bore the baggage. Curious eyes watched our passage, from field, doorway, and *shadûf*; but nothing of note marked our journey save the tremendous heat of the sun at noon, beneath which I knew myself a fool to travel.

I camped on the western side of the pyramid, but well clear of the marshes, which are the home of countless wild-fowl. I had no idea how long it would take me to extract the coveted ring from its hiding-place (which Hassan had closely described to me); and, remembering the speculative glances of the villagers, I had no intention of exposing myself against the face of the pyramid until dusk should have come to cloak my operations.

Hassan es-Sugra, whose new taciturnity was remarkable and whose behavior was distinguished by an odd disquiet, set out with his gun to procure our dinner, and I mounted the sandy slope on the southwest of the pyramid, where from my cover behind a mound of rubbish, I studied through my field-glasses the belt of vegetation marking the course of the Nile. I could detect no sign of surveillance, but in view of the fact that the smuggling of relics out of Egypt is a punishable offence my caution was dictated by wisdom.

We dined excellently, Hassan the Silent and I, upon quail, tinned tomatoes, fresh dates, bread, and Vichy-water (to which in my own case was added a stiff three fingers of whisky).

When the newly risen moon cast an ebon shadow of the Pyramid of Sneferu upon the carpet of the sands, I made my way around the angle of the ancient building towards the mound on the northern side whereby one approaches the entrance. Three paces from the shadow's edge, I paused, transfixed, because of that which confronted me.

Outlined against the moon-bright sky upon a ridge of the desert behind and to the north of the great structure, stood the motionless figure of a man!

For a moment I thought that my mind had conjured up this phantasmal watcher, that he was a thing of moon-magic and not of flesh and blood. But as I stood regarding him, he moved, seemed to raise his head, then turned and disappeared beyond the crest.

How long I remained staring at the spot where he had been I know not; but I was aroused from my useless contemplation by the jingling of camel bells. The sound came from behind me, stealing sweetly through the stillness from a great distance. I turned in a flash, whipped out my glasses and searched the remote fringe of the Fáyûm. Stately across the jeweled curtain of the night moved a caravan, blackly marked against that wondrous background. Three walking figures I counted, three laden donkeys, and two camels. Upon the first of the camels a man was mounted, upon the second was a *shibreeyeh*, a sort of covered litter, which I knew must conceal a woman. The caravan passed out of sight into the palm grove which conceals the village of Méydûm.

I returned my glasses to their case, and stood for some moments deep in reflection; then I descended the slope, to the tiny encampment where I had left Hassan es-Sugra. He was nowhere to be seen; and having waited some ten minutes I grew impatient, and raising my voice:

"Hassan!" I cried; "Hassan es-Sugra!"

No answer greeted me, although in the desert stillness the call must have been audible for miles. A second and a third time I called his name ... and the only reply was the shrill note of a pyramid bat that swooped low above my head; the vast solitude of the sands swallowed up my voice and the walls of the Tomb of Sneferu mocked me with their echo, crying eerily:

"Hassan! Hassan es-Sugra.... Hassan!..."

III

This mysterious episode affected me unpleasantly, but did not divert me from my purpose: I succeeded in casting out certain demons of superstition who had sought to lay hold upon me; and a prolonged scrutiny of the surrounding desert somewhat allayed my fears of human surveillance. For my visit to the chamber in the heart of the ancient building I had arrayed myself in rubber-soled shoes, an old pair of drill trousers, and a pyjama jacket. A Colt repeater was in my hip pocket, and, in addition to several instruments which I thought might be useful in extracting the ring from its setting, I carried a powerful electric torch.

Seated on the threshold of the entrance, fifty feet above the desert level, I cast a final glance backward towards the Nile valley, then, the lighted torch carried in my jacket pocket, I commenced the descent of the narrow, sloping passage. Periodically, when some cranny between the blocks offered a foothold, I checked my progress, and inspected the steep path below for snake tracks.

Some two hundred and forty feet of labored, descent discovered me in a sort of shallow cavern little more than a yard high and partly hewn out of the living rock which formed the foundation of the pyramid. In this place I found the heat to be almost insufferable, and the smell of remote mortality which assailed my nostrils from the sand-strewn floor threatened to choke me. For five minutes or more I lay there, bathed in perspiration, my nerves at high tension, listening for the slightest sound within or without. I cannot pretend that I was entirely master of myself. The stuff that fear is made of seemed to rise from the ancient dust; and I had little relish for the second part of my journey, which lay through a long horizontal passage rarely exceeding fourteen inches in height. The mere memory of that final crawl of forty feet or so is sufficient to cause me to perspire profusely; therefore let it suffice that I reached the end of the second passage, and breathing with difficulty the deathful, poisonous atmosphere of the place, found myself at the foot of the rugged shaft which gives access to the King's Chamber. Resting my torch upon a convenient ledge, I climbed up, and knew myself to be in one of the oldest chambers fashioned by human handiwork.

The journey had been most exhausting, but, allowing myself only a few moments' rest, I crossed to the eastern corner of the place and directed a ray of light upon the crevice which, from Hassan's description, I believed to conceal the ring. His account having been detailed, I experienced little difficulty in finding the cavity; but in the very moment of success the light of the torch grew dim ... and I recognized with a mingling of chagrin and fear that it was burnt out and that I had no means of recharging it.

Ere the light expired, I had time to realize two things: that the cavity was empty ... and that someone or something was approaching the foot of the shaft along the horizontal passage below!

Strictly though I have schooled my emotions, my heart was beating in a most uncomfortable fashion, as, crouching near the edge of the shaft, I watched the red glow fade from the delicate filament of the lamp. Retreat was impossible; there is but one entrance to the pyramid; and the darkness which now descended upon me was indescribable; it possessed horrific qualities; it seemed palpably to enfold me like the wings of some monstrous bat. The air of the King's Chamber I found to be almost unbearable, and it was no steady hand with which I gripped my pistol.

The sounds of approach continued. The suspense was becoming intolerable—when, into the Memphian gloom below me, there suddenly intruded a faint but ever-growing light. Between excitement and insufficient air, I regarded suffocation as imminent. Then, out into view beneath me, was thrust a slim ivory hand which held an electric pocket lamp. Fascinatedly I watched it, saw it joined by its fellow, then observed a white-turbaned head and a pair of black-robed shoulders follow. In my surprise I almost dropped the weapon which I held. The new arrival now standing upright and raising his head, I found myself looking into the face of *Abû Tabâh!*

"To Allah, the Great, the Compassionate, be all praise that I have found you alive," he said simply.

He exhibited little evidence of the journey which I had found so fatiguing, but an expression strongly like that of real anxiety rested upon his ascetic face.

"If life is dear to you," he continued, "answer me this, Kernaby Pasha; have you found the ring?"

"I have not," I replied; "my lamp failed me; but I think the ring is gone."

And now, as I spoke the words, the strangeness of his question came home to me, bringing with it an acute suspicion.

"What do you know of this ring, O my friend?" I asked.

Abû Tabâh shrugged his shoulders.

"I know much that is evil," he replied; "and because you doubt the purity of my motives, all that I have learned you shall learn also; for Allah the Great, the Merciful, this night has protected you from danger and spared you a frightful death. Follow me, Kernaby Pasha, in order that these things may be made manifest to you."

IV

A pair of fleet camels were kneeling at the foot of the slope below the entrance to the pyramid, and having recovered somewhat from the effect of the fatiguing climb out from the King's Chamber—

"It might be desirable," I said, "that I adopt a more suitable raiment for camel riding?"

Abû Tabâh slowly shook his head in that dignified manner which never deserted him. He had again taken up his ebony walking-stick and was now resting his crossed hands upon it and regarding me with his strange, melancholy eyes.

"To delay would be unwise," he replied. "You have mercifully been spared a painful and unfortunate end (all praise to Him who averted the peril); but the ring, which bears an ancient curse, is gone: for me there is no rest until I have found and destroyed it."

He spoke with a solemn conviction which bore the seal of verity.

"Your destructive theory may be perfectly sound," I said; "but as one professionally interested in relics of the past, I feel called upon to protest. Perhaps before we proceed any further you will enlighten me respecting this most obscure matter. Can you inform me, for example, what became of Hassan es-Sugra?"

"He observed my approach from a distance, and fled, being a man of little virtue. Respecting the other matters you shall be fully enlightened, to-night. The white camel is for you."

There was a gentle finality in his manner to which I succumbed. My feelings towards this mysterious being had undergone a slight change; and whilst I cannot truthfully say that I loved him as a brother, a certain respect for Abû Tabâh was taking possession of my mind. I began to understand his reputation with the natives; beyond doubt his uncanny wisdom was impressive; his lofty dignity awed. And no man is at his best arrayed in canvas shoes, very dirty drill trousers, and a pyjama jacket.

As I had anticipated, the village of Méydûm proved to be our destination, and the gait of the magnificent creatures upon which we were mounted was exhausting. I shall always remember that moonlight ride across the desert to the palm groves of Méydûm. I entered the house of the Sheikh with misgivings; for my attire fell short of the ideal to which every representative of protective Britain looks up, but often fails to realize.

In a *mandarah*, part of it inlaid with fine mosaic and boasting a pretty fountain, I was presented to the imposing old man who was evidently the host of Abû Tabâh. Ere taking my seat upon the *dîwan*, I shed my canvas shoes, in accordance with custom, accepted a pipe and a cup of excellent coffee, and awaited with much curiosity the next development. A brief colloquy between Abû Tabâh and the Sheikh, at the further end of the apartment resulted in the disappearance of the Sheikh and the approach of my mysterious friend.

"Because, although you are not a Moslem, you are a man of culture and understanding," said Abû Tabâh, "I have ordered that my sister shall be brought into your presence."

"That is exceedingly good of you," I said, but indeed I knew it to be an honor which spoke volumes at once for Abû Tabâh's enlightenment and good opinion of myself.

"She is a virgin of great beauty," he continued; "and the excellence of her mind exceeds the perfection of her person."

"I congratulate you," I answered politely, "upon the possession of a sister in every way so desirable."

Abû Tabâh inclined his head in a characteristic gesture of gentle courtesy.

"Allah has indeed blessed my house," he admitted; "and because your mind is filled with conjectures respecting the source of certain information which you know me to possess, I desire that the matter shall be made clear to you."

How I should have answered this singular man I know not; but as he spoke the words, into the *mandarah* came the Sheikh, followed by a girl robed and veiled entirely in white. With gait slow and graceful she approached the *dîwan*. She wore a white *yelek* so closely wrapped about her that it concealed the rest of her attire, and a white *tarbar*, or head-veil, decorated with gold embroidery, almost entirely concealed her hair, save for one jet-black plait in which little gold ornaments were entwined and which hung down on the left of her forehead. A white *yashmak* reached nearly to her feet, which were clad in little red leather slippers.

As she approached me I was impressed, not so much with the details of her white attire, nor with the fine lines of a graceful figure which the gossamer robe quite failed to conceal, but with her wonderful gazelle-like eyes, which wore uncannily like those of her brother, save that their bordering of *kohl* lent them an appearance of being larger and more luminous.

No form of introduction was observed; with modestly lowered eyes the girl saluted me and took her seat upon a heap of cushions before a small coffee table set at one end of the *dîwan*. The Sheikh, seated himself beside me, and Abû Tabâh, with a reed pen, wrote something rapidly on a narrow strip of paper. The Sheikh clapped his hands, a man entered bearing a brazier containing live charcoal, and, having placed it upon the floor, immediately withdrew. The *dîwan* was lighted by a lantern swung from the ceiling, and its light, pouring fully down upon the white figure of the girl, and leaving the other persons and objects in comparative shadow, produced a picture which I am unlikely to forget.

Amid a tense silence, Abû Tabâh took from a box upon the table some resinous substance. This he sprinkled upon the fire in the brazier; and the girl extending a small hand and round soft arm across the table, he again dipped his pen in the ink and drew upon the upturned palm a rough square which he divided into nine parts, writing in each an Arabic figure. Finally, in the centre he poured a small drop of ink, upon which, in response to words rapidly spoken, the girl fixed an intent gaze.

Into the brazier Abû Tabâh dropped one by one fragments of the paper upon which he had written what I presumed to be a form of invocation. Immediately, standing between the smoking brazier and the girl, he commenced a subdued muttering. I recognized that I was about to be treated to an exhibition of *darb el-mendel*, Abû Tabâh being evidently a *sahhar*, or adept in the art called *er-roohânee*. Save for this indistinct muttering, no other sound disturbed the silence of the apartment, until suddenly the girl began to speak Arabic and in a sweet but monotonous voice.

"Again I see the ring," she said, "a hand is holding it before me. The ring bears a green scarab, upon which is written the name of a king of Egypt.... The ring is gone. I can see it no more."

"Seek it," directed Abû Tabâh in a low voice, and threw more incense upon the fire. "Are you seeking it?"

"Yes," replied the girl, who now began to tremble violently, "I am in a low passage which slopes downwards so steeply that I am afraid."

"Fear nothing," said Abû Tabâh; "follow the passage."

With marvelous fidelity the girl described the passage and the shaft leading to the King's Chamber in the Pyramid of Méydûm. She described the cavity in the wall where once (if Hassan es-Sugra was worthy of credence) the ring had been concealed.

"There is a freshly made hole in the stonework," she said. "The picture has gone; I am standing in some dark place and the same hand again holds the ring before me."

"Is it the hand of an Oriental," asked Abû Tabâh, "or of a European?"

"It is the hand of a European. It has disappeared; I see a funeral procession winding out from Rikka into the desert."

"Follow the ring," directed Abû Tabâh, a queer, compelling note in his voice.

Again he sprinkled perfume upon the fire and—

"I see a Pharaoh upon his throne," continued the monotonous voice, "upon the first finger of his left hand he wears the ring with the green scarab. A prisoner stands before him in chains; a woman pleads with the king, but he is deaf to her. He draws the ring from his finger and hands it to one standing behind the throne—one who has a very evil face. Ah!..."

The girl's voice died away in a low wail of fear or horror. But—

"What do you see?" demanded Abû Tabâh.

"The death-ring of Pharaoh!" whispered the soft voice tremulously; "it is the death-ring!"

"Return from the past to the present," ordered Abû Tabâh. "Where is the ring now?"

He continued his weird muttering, whilst the girl, who still shuddered violently, peered again into the pool of ink. Suddenly—

"I see a long line of dead men," she whispered, speaking in a kind of chant; "they are of all the races of the East, and some are swathed in mummy wrappings; the wrappings are sealed with the death-ring of Pharaoh. They are passing me slowly, on their way across the desert from the Pyramid of Méydûm to a narrow ravine where a tent is erected. They go to summon one who is about to join their company...."

I suppose the suffocating perfume of the burning incense was chiefly responsible, but at this point I realized that I was becoming dizzy and that immediate departure into a cooler atmosphere was imperative. Quietly, in order to avoid disturbing the séance, I left the *mandarah*. So absorbed were the three in their weird performance that my departure was apparently unnoticed. Out in the coolness of the palm grove I soon recovered. I doubt if I possess the temperament which enables one to contemplate with equanimity a number of dead men promenading in their shrouds.

V

"The truth is now wholly made manifest," said Abû Tabâh; "the revelation is complete."

Once more I was mounted upon the white camel and the mysterious *imâm* rode beside me upon its fellow, which was of less remarkable color.

"I hear your words," I replied.

"The poor Ahmed Abdulla," he continued, "who was of little wisdom, knew, as Hassan es-Sugra knew, of the hidden ring; for he was one of those who fled from the pyramid refusing to enter it again. Greed spoke to him, however, and he revealed the secret to a certain Englishman, called Bishop, contracting to aid him in recovering the ring."

At last enlightenment was mine ... and it brought in its train a dreadful premonition.

"Something I knew of the peril," said Abû Tabâh, "but not, at first, all. The Englishman I warned, but he neglected my warning. Already Ahmed Abdulla was dead, having been despatched by his employer to the pyramid; and the people of Rikka had sent for me. Now, by means known to you, I learned that evil powers threatened your life also, in what form I knew not at that time save that the sign of Set had been revealed to me in conjunction with your death."

I shuddered.

"That the secret of the pyramid was a Pharaoh's ring I did not learn until later; but now it is made manifest that the thing of power is the death-ring of Sneferu...."

The huge bulk of the Pyramid of Méydûm loomed above us as he spoke the words, for we were nearly come to our destination; and its proximity occasioned within me a physical chill. I do not think an open check for a thousand pounds would have tempted me to enter the place again. The death-ring of Sneferu possessed uncomfortable and supernatural properties. So far as I was aware, no example of such a ring (the *lettre de cachet* of the period) was included in any known collection. One dating much after Sneferu, and bearing the cartouche of Apepi II (one of the Hyksos, or Shepherd Kings) came to light late in the nineteenth century; it was reported to be the ring which, traditionally, Joseph wore as emblematical of the power vested in him by Pharaoh. Sir Gaston Maspero and other authorities considered it to be a forgery and it vanished from the ken of connoisseurs. I never learned by what firm it was manufactured.

A mile to the west of the pyramid we found Theo Bishop's encampment. I thought it to be deserted—until I entered the little tent....

An oil-lamp stood upon a wooden box; and its rays made yellow the face of the man stretched upon the camp-bed. My premonition was realized; Bishop must have entered the pyramid less than an hour ahead of me; he it was who had stood upon the mound, silhouetted against the sky, when I had first approached the slope. He had met with the fate of Ahmed Abdulla.

He had been dead for at least two hours, and by the token of certain hideous glandular swellings, I knew that he had met his end by the bite of an Egyptian viper.

"Abû Tabâh!" I cried, my voice hoarsely unnatural—"the *recess* in the King's Chamber is a viper's nest!"

"You speak wisdom, Kernaby Pasha; the viper is the servant of the *ginn*."

Upon the third finger of his swollen right hand Bishop wore the ring of ghastly history; and the mysterious significance of the Sign of Set became apparent. For added to the usual cartouche of the Pharaoh was the symbol of the god of destruction, thus:

We buried him deeply, piling stones upon the grave, that the jackals of the desert might never disturb the last holder of the death-ring of Sneferu.

III

THE LADY OF THE LATTICE

I

The interior of the room was very dark, but with the aid of the electric torch which I carried I was enabled to form a fairly good impression of its general character, and having now surveyed the entire house I had concluded that it might possibly serve my purpose. The real ownership of many native houses in Cairo is difficult to establish, and the unveracious Egyptian from whom I had procured the keys may or may not have been entitled to let the premises. However, he had the keys; and that in the Near East is a sufficient evidence of ownership. My viewing the place at night was dictated by motives of prudence; for I did not propose unduly to impress my personality upon the inhabitants of the Darb el-Ahmar.

Curiosity respecting the outlook at the rear now led me to enter the deep recess at one end of the room, which boasted an imperfect but not unpicturesque *mushrabîyeh* window. Moonlight slanted down into the narrow lane which the window overhung and cast a quaint fretwork shadow upon the dusty floor at my feet. Idly I opened one of the little square lattices and peered down into the shadowy gully beneath. The lane was silent and empty, and I next directed my attention to a similar window which protruded from the adjoining house.

A panel corresponding to mine stood open also in the neighboring window; and by means of a soft light in the room I detected the head and shoulders of a woman, who, her arm resting upon the ledge, surveyed the vacant night.

By reason of her position, whilst her hand and arm lay fully in the moonlight, her face and figure were indistinct. I, on the contrary, was clearly visible to her, and although I knew that she must have seen me she made no effort to withdraw. On the contrary, she leaned artlessly forward as if to gaze upon the stars, permitting me a sight of her unveiled face and of a portion of her shapely neck.

Her eyes, as is usual with Egyptian women, were large and fine, and as is usual with all women, she was aware of the fact, casting glances upward and to the right and left calculated to exhibit their beauty.

The coquetry of her movements was unmistakable; and when, lifting a pretty arm, she brushed aside a lock of hair which overhung her brow and uttered a tremulous sigh, I perceived that I had found favor in her sight.

And indeed the graceful gesture had inclined my heart towards her; for it had served to reveal not only the symmetry of her shape but the presence upon her arm, immediately above the elbow, of a magnificent bangle in gold and lapis-lazuli which, if I might trust my judgment, was fashioned no later than the XIXth dynasty! Clearly the house next door, and its occupant, were the property of some man of wealth and taste.

There is a maxim in the East—"Avoid the veil"; and to this hitherto I had paid the strictest attention. Soft glances from *harêm* windows usually leave me cold. But the presence of an armlet finer than anything in the Treasure of Zagazig placed a new complexion upon this affair, and the connoisseur within me took the matter out of my hands.

Across the intervening patch of darkness our glances met; the girl's dark lashes were lowered demurely, then raised again, and the boldness of my unfaltering gaze was rewarded by a smile. Thus encouraged:—

"O daughter of the moon," I whispered fancifully in Arabic, "condescend to speak to one whom the sight of thy beauty hath enslaved."

"I fear to be discovered, Inglîsi," came the soft reply; "or willingly would I converse with thee, for I am lonely and wretched."

She sighed again and directed upon me a glance that was less wretched than roguish. Evidently the adventure was much to her liking.

"Let me solace your loneliness," I replied; "for assuredly we can conceive some plan of meeting."

She lowered her eyes at that, and seemed to hesitate; then—

"In the roof of your house," she whispered, often glancing over her shoulder into the room beyond, "is a trap—which is bolted...."

Footsteps sounded in the lane beneath—whereat the vision at the window vanished and the lattice was closed; but not before the girl had intimated by a gesture that I was to remain.

Discreetly withdrawing into my dusty apartment, I endeavored to make out the form of the intruder who now was passing underneath the window; but the density of the shadows in the lane rendered it impossible for me to do so. He seemed to pause for a time and I imagined that I could see him staring upward; then he passed on and silence again claimed that deserted quarter of Cairo.

For fully half an hour I waited, and was preparing to depart when a part of the shadows overlying the projecting window seemed to grow blacker, and I realized with joy that at last the lattice was reopening, but that the room within was now in darkness. Whilst I watched, remaining scrupulously invisible, a small parcel deftly thrown dropped upon the floor at my feet—and my neighbor's window was reclosed.

Closing my own, I picked up the parcel. It proved to be a small ivory box, which at some time had evidently contained *kohl*, wrapped in a piece of silk and containing a note. Returning to the lower floor I directed the light of my electric torch upon this charmingly romantic billet. It was conceived in English and characterized by the rather alarming *naiveté* of the Oriental woman. I give it in its entirety.

"To-morrow night, nine o'clock."

II

My cautious inquiries respecting the house in the Darb el-Ahmar led only to the discovery that it belonged to a mysterious personage whose real identity was unknown even to his servants; but this did not particularly intrigue me; for in the East the maintenance of two entirely self-contained establishments is not more uncommon than in countries less generously provided in the matter of marriage laws. After all the taking of a second wife does not so much depend on a man's religious convictions as upon his first wife.

Reflecting upon the probable history of the armlet of lapis-lazuli, I returned to Shepheard's in time to keep my appointment with Joseph Malaglou—a professed Christian who claimed to be of Greek parentage. I may explain here that it was necessary to provide for the safe conduct through the customs and elsewhere of those cases of "Sheffield cutlery" which actually contained the scarabs, necklaces, and other "antiques," the sale of which formed a part of the business of my firm. Joseph Malaglou had hitherto successfully conducted this matter for me, receiving the goods and storing them at his own warehouse; but for various reasons I had decided in future to lease an establishment of my own for this purpose.

He was waiting in the lounge as I entered, and had he been less useful to me I think I should have had him thrown out; for if ever a swarthy villain stepped forth from the pages of an illustrated "penny dreadful," that swarthy villain was Joseph Malaglou. He approached me with outstretched hand; he was perniciously polite; his ingratiating smile fired my soul with a lust of blood. Fortunately, our business was brief.

"The latest consignment is in the hands of my agent at Alexandria," he said, "and if you are still determined that the ten cases shall be despatched to you direct, I will instruct him; but you cannot very well have them sent *here*."

He shrugged and smiled, glancing all about the lounge.

"I have no intention of converting Shepheard's Hotel into a cutlery warehouse," I replied. "I will advise you in the morning of the address to which the cases should be despatched."

Joseph Malaglou was palpably disturbed—a mysterious circumstance, since, whilst I had made no mention of reducing his fees, under the new arrangement he would be saved trouble and storage.

"As delay in these matters is unwise," he urged, "why not have the goods despatched immediately, and consigned to you at my address?"

There was reason on the man's side, for I had not yet actually leased the house in the Darb el-Ahmar; therefore—

"I will sleep on the problem," I said, "and communicate my decision in the morning."

I stood on the steps watching him depart, a man palpably disturbed in mind; indeed his behavior was altogether singular, and could only portend one thing—knavery. I think it highly probable that the Ottoman Empire had a certain claim upon Joseph Malaglou. He was one of those nondescript brutes whose mere existence is a menace to our rule in the Near East. He openly applauded British methods, and was the worst possible advertisement for the cause he claimed to have espoused. Altogether he left me in an uneasy mood; so that shortly after the third, or daybreak, call to prayer had sounded from Cairo's minarets on the morrow, I had arranged to lease the house in the Darb el-Ahmar for a period of three months, in the name of one Ahmed Ben Tawwab, a mythical friend, and had instructed Joseph Malaglou accordingly.

Other affairs claimed my attention throughout the day; but dusk discovered me at my newly acquired house in the quaint street adjoining the Bâb ez-Zuwêla. I procured the keys from the venerable old thief who had leased me the premises and learned from him that a representative of Joseph Malaglou had been admitted to the house earlier in the evening, in accordance with my instructions, and had delivered a load of boxes there.

Thus, on opening the door, I was not surprised to find the ten cases from Alexandria lying within, neatly labelled:

To Ahmed Ben Tawwab,
Darb el-Ahmar,
Sukkarîya,
Cairo.

Ascending to the top floor, I mounted the rickety ladder and unbolted and opened the trap. A cautious glance to the right revealed the fact that little difficulty existed in passing from roof to roof; for in Egyptian houses these are flat and are used for various domestic purposes. I consulted my watch: the hour of the tryst was come.

And even as I learned the fact, from my neighbor's roof sounded the faint creaking of hinges ... and out into the moonlight stepped an odd figure—that of the lady of the lattice, dressed in a "European" blue serge costume which had obviously been purchased, ready made, in the bazaars! She wore high-heeled French shoes upon her pretty feet and her picturesque hair was concealed beneath a large Panama hat, from the brim of which floated one of those voluminous green veils dear to the heart of touring woman and so arranged as to hide her face. Only the gleam of her eyes and teeth was visible through the gauze.

I assisted her to step across, wondering since she was thus attired, to what crazy expedition I was committed.

"Please do not kiss me," she whispered, speaking in moderately good English, "Fatimah is listening!"

Such ingenuousness was rather alarming.

"But," I replied, "you have left the trap open."

"It is all right. Fatimah has locked the door of my room and will admit no one, because I have a headache and am sleeping!"

Resting her hand confidingly in mine, she descended the ladder into the adjoining house, and, removing the veil from her face, looked up at me.

"You will be kind to me, will you not?" she asked.

I suppose a lengthy essay upon the mentality of Oriental womanhood would serve no purpose here, therefore I refrain from inserting it. Seated upon the chests in the room below, Mizmûna—for this was her name—confided her troubles with perturbing frankness. She had conceived a characteristically Eastern and sudden infatuation for my society; nor am I prepared to maintain that she would have remained obdurate to anyone else who had been in a position to unbolt the door which offered the only chance of escape from her prison. The house of mystery, she informed me, belonged to a person styling himself Yûssuf of Rosetta (a name that sounded factitious) and she hated him. For two months, I gathered, she had been in Cairo, during which time she had never passed beyond the walls of the neighboring courtyard. And the object of her nocturnal adventure was innocent enough; she wanted to see the European shops and the tourists passing in and out of the big hotels in the Shâria Kâmel Pasha!

III

It was as we passed along the Shâria el-Maghribi, where I had pointed out the St. James's Restaurant, better known as "Jimmy's," I remember, that Mizmûna uttered a little, suppressed cry, and clutched my arm sharply.

"Oh!" she whispered fearfully, "it is Hanna! and he has seen me!"

With frightened, fascinated eyes she was staring across the street, apparently at a group of curiously muffled natives—and her whole body was trembling.

"Quick!" she said, pulling me urgently, "take me back! if they find me they will kill me!"

"But if they have already seen you——"

"Oh! take me back," she entreated piteously. "Hanna must not find out where I live."

Here was mystery; but evidently my first dreadful theory that Hanna was Mizmûna's husband had been incorrect. Apparently he was not even acquainted with Yûssuf of Rosetta. But whoever or whatever he might be, I silently cursed the lapis armlet which had led me to involve myself in his affairs, as I hurried my companion across the Place de l'Opera and homeward....

We were come indeed unmolested but breathless, as near our destination as that nameless street beside the Mosque of Muayyâd, when Mizmûna suddenly stopped, uttered a stifled shriek, and—

"Oh, save me!" she panted, winding her arms about my neck. "Look! Look! in the shadow of the mosque door!"

Panic threatened me for one fleeting moment; for this part of Cairo is utterly deserted at night and the mystery of the thing was taking toll of my nerves; then firmly unclasping the trembling arms, I pushed Mizmûna behind me and snatched out my Colt automatic ... as a group of muffled figures became magically detached from the shadows that had hidden them; and began silently to advance.

I raised the pistol.

"*Usbur!*" I cried "*âuz eh?*" (Stop! what do you want?)

They halted at once; but no answering voice broke the uncanny silence in which they regarded me. Mizmûna plucked at my arm.

"Quick! Quick!" she whispered tremulously, "the keys! the keys!"

I was swift to grasp her meaning.

"My right pocket!" I whispered in answer.

The girl's shaking hand groped for the keys, found them; and, uttering no parting word, Mizmûna darted off along the Sukkarîya, which here bisects the Darb el-Ahmar. An angry muttering arose from the little knot of oddly muffled figures, but not one of them had the courage to attempt a pursuit of the fugitive. Keeping my back to the wall of the mosque and feeling along it with one hand outstretched, I began to back away from the attacking party; intending to take to my heels along the first lane I came to.

This plan was sound enough; its weakness lay in the fact that I could make no proper survey of that which lay immediately behind me. The result was that I backed into someone who must have been stealthily approaching from the rear.

I knew nothing of his presence until he suddenly threw himself upon from behind, and I was down on my face in the dust! My pistol was jerked out of my hand, and, still preserving that unbroken disconcerting silence, the muffled group bore down upon me.

I gave myself up for lost. My unseen assailant, who seemingly possessed wrists of steel, jerked my right hand up into the region of my shoulder-blades and pinioned my left arm so as to render me helpless as an infant. Then two of the muffled Nubians—for Nubians the moonlight now showed them to be—raised me to my feet, and the grip from behind was removed.

That I had unwittingly intruded upon the amours of some wealthy and unscrupulous pasha I no longer doubted; and knowing somewhat of the ways of outraged lovers of the East, the mental vision which arose before me was unpleasing to contemplate. Yet even the extravagant picture which my imagination had painted fell short of the ferocious reality. For even as I was lifted upright, in the grasp of my huge guards, a door in the side of the neighboring mosque burst open, and there sprang into view an excessively tall, excessively lean and hawk-faced old man carrying a naked scimitar in his hand.

He possessed eyes like the eyes of an eagle, and a thin, hooked nose having dilated, quivering nostrils. In three huge strides he reached me, towered over me like some evil *ginnee* of Arabian lore, and raised his gleaming scimitar with the unmistakable intention of severing my head from my trunk at a single blow!

I think I have never experienced an identical sensation in my life; my tongue clave to the roof of my mouth; my heart suspended its functions; and I felt my eyes start forward in their sockets. I had not thought my constitution capable of such profound and helpless fear, nor had I hitherto paid proper respect to the memory of Charles I. I would gladly have closed my eyes in order that I might not witness the downward sweep of the fatal blade, but the lids seemed to be paralysed. Never whilst memory serves me can I forget one detail of the appearance of that frightful old devil; and never can I forget my gratitude to that unseen captor, the man who had seized me from behind, and who now, alone, averted the blade from my neck.

Over my head he lunged—with an ebony stick—and skilfully; so that the pointed ferrule came well and truly into contact with the knuckles of my would-be executioner. The weapon fell, jingling, at my feet … and a slim, black-robed figure was suddenly interposed between myself and the furious old Arab.

It was Abû Tabâh!

Dignified, unruffled, his classically beautiful face composed and resembling, in the moonlight, beneath the snowy turban, that of some young prophet, he stood, one protective hand resting upon my shoulder, and confronted my assailant. His eyes were aglow with the eerie light of fanaticism.

"It is written that the wrath of fools is the joy of Iblees,"* he declared.

Their glances met in conflict, the eagle eyes of my aged but formidable enemy glaring insanely into the fine, dark eyes of Abû Tabâh. The Arab was by no means quelled; yet presently his glance fell before the hypnotic stare of the mysterious *imám*.

"The Prophet (may God be kind to him) spared not the despoiler!" he said heavily. "With these, my two hands"—he extended the twitching, sinewy members before Abû Tabâh—"will I choke the life from the throat of the dog who wronged me."

Abû Tabâh raised his hand sternly.

"This matter has been entrusted to *me*," he said, staring down the enraged old man. "If you would have me abandon it, say so; if you would have me pursue it, be silent."

For five seconds the other sustained the strange gaze of those big, mysterious eyes, then folded his arms upon his breast, audibly gnashing his large and strong-looking teeth and averting his head from my direction in order that spleen might not consume him. Abû Tabâh turned and confronted me.

"Explain the cause of your presence here," he demanded, continuing to speak in Arabic, "and unfold to me the whole truth respecting your case."

"My friend," I replied, steadily regarding him, "I am eternally your debtor; but I decline to utter one word for explanation until these fellows unhand me and until I am offered some suitable excuse for the outrageous attack upon my person."

Abû Tabâh performed his curiously Gallic shrug of the shoulders—

---

*Satan.

and pointed, with his ebony cane, to my pinioned arms. In a trice the Nubians fell back, and I was free. The infuriated old man directed upon me a glance that was bloodily ferocious, but—

"O persons of little piety," I said, "is it thus that a true Moslem rewards the generous impulse and the meritorious deed? To-night a damsel in distress, flying from a brutal captor, solicited my aid. I was treacherously assaulted ere I could escort her to a place of safety, and all but murdered by the man who would appear to be that damsel's natural protector. Alas, I fear to contemplate what may have befallen her as a result of such vile and foolish conduct."

Abû Tabâh slightly inclined his body resting his slim, ivory hands upon his cane; his face remained perfectly tranquil as he listened to this correct, though misleading statement; but—

"Ah!" cried the old man of the scimitar, adopting an unpleasant, crouching attitude, "perjured liar that thou art! Did I not see with mine own eyes how she embraced thee? O, son of a mange, that I should have lived to have witnessed so obscene a spectacle. Not content with despoiling me of this jewel of my *harêm*, thou dost parade her abandonment and my shame in the public highways of Cairo!..."

In vain Abû Tabâh strove to check this tirade. Step by step the Sheikh approached closer; syllable by syllable his voice rose higher.

"What!" he shrieked, "is it for this that I have offered five thousand English pounds to whomsoever shall restore her to me! Faugh! I spit upon her memory!—and though I pursue thee to the Mountains of the Moon, across the Bridge Es-Sîrat, and through the valley of Gahennam, lo! my hour will come to slay thee, noisome offal!"

He ceased from lack of breath, and stood quivering before me. But at last I had grasped the clue to this imbroglio into which fate had thrust me.

"O misguided man," I replied, "grief hath upset thine intelligence. Again I tell thee that I sought to deliver the damsel from her persecutor, and, perceiving an ambush, she clung to me as her only protector. Thou are demented. Let another earn the paltry reward; I will have none of it."

I turned to Abû Tabâh, addressing him in English.

"Relieve me of the society of this infatuated old ruffian," I said, "and accompany me to some place where I can quietly explain what I know of the matter."

"Assuredly I will accompany you to such a spot," he answered suavely; "for whilst, knowing your character, I do not believe you to be the abductor of the damsel Mizmûna, a warrant to search your house was issued an hour ago, on a charge of *hashish* smuggling!"

IV

There are certain shocks that numb the brain. This was one of them. My recollection of the period immediately following those words of Abû Tabâh is hazy and indistinct. My narrow escape from decapitation at the hands of the ferocious Arab assassin and the tangled love-affairs of that aged Othello became insignificant memories. (I seem to recollect that we left him in tears.)

My next clear-cut memory is that of walking beside the mysterious *imâm* along the Darb el-Ahmar and of stopping before the closed door of my newly acquired premises!

The street was quite deserted again. Those muffled Nubians who seemed to constitute a bodyguard for my inscrutable companion had disappeared in company with the bereaved Sheikh.

"This is your house?" said Abû Tabâh sweetly.

My habit of thinking before I speak or act asserted itself automatically.

"I recently leased it on another's behalf," I replied.

"In that event," continued the *imâm*, "unless the information lodged with me to-night prove to be inaccurate, that other must speedily proclaim himself."

He tested the cumbersome lock, and, as I knew would be the case, since Mizmûna had recently entered, found it to be unfastened, opened the door and stepped in.

"Have you a pocket lamp?" he asked.

I pressed the button of my electric torch and directed its rays fully upon the stack of boxes. It was the great sage, Apollonius of Tyana, who said "loquacity has many pitfalls, but silence none"; therefore I silently watched Abû Tabâh consulting the label on the topmost chest. Presently—

"Ahmed Ben Tawwab," he read aloud; "is that the name of the friend on whose behalf you secured a lease of this house?"

"It is," I answered.

"If you will rest the light upon this box and assist me to open one of the others, I shall be obliged to you," said Abû Tabâh.

Knowing, as I did, that this strange man was in some way connected with the native police and with the guardianship of Egyptian morals, I recognized refusal to be impolitic if not impossible. But, as we set to work to raise the lid of the chest, my mind was more feverishly busy than my fingers.

Ere long our task was successful, and the contents of the chest lay exposed. These were: two hundred Osiris statuettes, twelve one-pound tins of mummy heads ... *and fifty packets of hashish.*

Silence was no effort to me now; I was dumbfounded. The musical voice of my companion broke in upon my painful reverie.

"The information upon which I now am acting," he said, "reached me to-night in the form of a letter, bearing no address and no signature. The suppression of this vile *hashish* traffic is so near to my heart that I immediately secured the necessary powers to search the premises named, and was on my way hither when I observed you (although I did not at once recognize you) in the act of escaping from a group of my servants who had been detailed, some weeks ago, to trace a missing damsel known to be in Cairo. Concerning your share in that affair I await a full statement from your own lips; concerning your share in this I can only say that unless Ahmed Ben Tawwab comes forward by to-morrow and admits his guilt, I must apply to the British agent for a formal inquiry. Is there anything that you would wish to say, or any action you desire that I should take?"

I turned to him in the dim light. Habitually I am undemonstrative, especially with natives. But there was a nobility and an implacable sense of justice about this singular *religieux* which conquered me completely.

"Abû Tabâh," I said, "I thank you for your friendship. I have committed a grave folly; but I am neither an abductor nor a *hashish* dealer. This is the work of an unknown enemy, and already I have a theory respecting his identity."

"Can I aid you—or do you prefer that I leave you to pursue this clue in your own way?" he asked tactfully.

"I prefer to work alone."

"The affair is truly mysterious," he admitted, "and I purpose to spend the night in meditation respecting it. After the hour of morning prayer, therefore, I will visit you. *Lîltâk sa'îda*, Kernaby Pasha."

"*Lîltâk sa'îda*, Abû Tabâh," I said, as he stepped out of the door.

Slowly and stately the *imám* passed down the street; and the *ginnee* of solitude reclaimed that deserted spot. A night watchman, *nebbut*on shoulder, passed along the distant Sukkarîya. A dog howled.

I re-entered the doorway conscious of a sudden mental excitement; for an explanation of the anonymous letter had just presented itself to my mind. The owner of the neighboring house must have detected my rendezvous with his lady-love, have investigated the contents of the cases, and denounced me from motives of revenge! That the villainous Joseph Malaglou had been in the habit of smuggling *hashish* into Egypt in my cases of "cutlery" was evident enough and accounted for his reluctance to fall in with the new arrangement; but my bemused brain utterly failed to grapple with the problem of why, knowing their damning contents, he had permitted these ten cases to be delivered at *my* address. Moreover, how my worthy neighbor—who had evidently abducted Mizmûna from the old man of the scimitar—had learned my real name was another mystery which I found no leisure to examine. For I had but just set foot again within the ill-omened place when there came a patter of swift, light footsteps—and out from behind the fatal stack of boxes ran Mizmûna, and threw herself into my arms!

"Oh, my friend, my protector!" she cried distractedly, "what shall I do? Yûssuf has discovered our plot! Fatimah, that mother of calamities, has betrayed me, and I dare not return! I am an outcast; for although I was stolen from the Sheikh Ismail without my consent, how can I hope for his forgiveness?"

Such a flood of sorrows and confidences overwhelmed me, and I placed a silent but deathless curse upon the lapis armlet which had brought me to this pass. Mizmûna sobbed upon my shoulder.

"Yûssuf has planned your ruin as well as mine," she said brokenly. "For it was he who denounced you to the Magician." (As "the Magician" Abû Tabâh was known and feared throughout Lower Egypt.) "Oh that I might return to the house of Ismail where I lived in luxury in a marble pavilion, guarded by Hanna and a hundred negroes, where I possessed the robes of a princess and was laden with costly jewels!"

So very human and natural an ambition met with my hearty approval, and, upon consideration of the word-picture of his domestic state, the old man of the scimitar rose immensely in my esteem. How my malevolent neighbor had succeeded in abducting Mizmûna from such a fortress I failed to imagine. But I began to see my way more clearly and hope was reborn in my bosom.

"Fear nothing, child," I said to the weeping girl. "You shall return to your marble pavilion and to the care of that worthy, if somewhat hasty man, from whose arms you were torn. And now inform me—where is Yûssuf?"

Mizmûna raised her face and looked up at me, her long lashes wet with tears, but the slow, childish smile of the Eastern woman already curving her red lips.

"He is in his own room destroying papers," she said.

"Who told you this?"

"Ali, the *bowwab*, who is faithful to me—and who hates Fatimah."

"Is the trap rebolted?"

"I know not."

"Remain here until I return," I said, seating her upon one of the boxes. "Where are my keys?"

"I hid them upon the ledge of the window, beside the door yonder."

Taking them from this simple "hiding-place," I locked the door to give Mizmûna courage, and, taking the lamp with me, began to mount the stairs, first assuring myself of the presence in my pocket of my Colt automatic, which Abû Tabâh had restored to me.

The ray of my lamp shining out ahead, I came to the crazy ladder giving access to the trap. I climbed up, raising the trap, and gazed upon the jeweled dome of midnight Egypt. Dire necessity spurred me, and I walked across to the adjoining trap, carefully inserted two fingers in the iron ring and pulled.

It was not fastened below! Inch by inch I raised it, and, finding the room beneath it to be in darkness, opened the trap fully and descended the ladder.

I flashed the light quickly about the place; then stood staring at what it revealed. My heart began to beat rapidly, for in that dirty attic I had found salvation ... and a further clue to the mystery of all my misfortunes.

It was a *hashish* warehouse!

Taking off my shoes, I thrust one into either pocket of my jacket, and, perceiving that the house was constructed on a plan identical with that adjoining it, I crept downstairs to the apartment of the *mushrabîyeh* window. A heavy curtain was draped in the doorway, but I could see that the room within was illuminated.

I drew the curtains slowly aside and peeped in. I saw an apartment that had evidently been furnished very luxuriantly, but which now was partially dismantled. In the recess formed by the window a low table was placed, bearing a shaded lamp. The table was littered with papers, account books and ledgers; and, seated thereat, his back towards the door, was a man who figured feverishly. I stepped into the room.

"Good evening, Yûssuf of Rosetta," I said; "you do well to set your affairs in order."

V

Swiftly as though a serpent had touched him, the man in the recess leaped to his feet and twisted about to confront me.

I found myself looking into a hideous, swarthy face—blanched now to the lips, so that the cunning black eyes glared out as from a mask— into the hideous swarthy face of *Joseph Malaglou!*

The store of *hashish* in the upper room had somewhat prepared me for this discovery; yet, momentarily, the consummate villainy of the Greek had me bereft of speech. As I stood there glaring at him, he began furtively to grope with one hand along the edge of the *dîwan* behind him. Then, suddenly, he became aware of the pistol which I carried—and abandoned the quest of whatever weapon he had sought, swallowing audibly.

"So, my good Malaglou," I said, "you sought to make me responsible for your sins, my friend? I perceive now how the Fates have played with me. My very first conversation with your charming protégée——"

He bit savagely at his black moustache, advanced upon me; then, his gaze set upon the Colt, he stood still again.

"... was reported to you by the traitorous Fatimah," I continued evenly; "and, when, on the morrow, I advised you of my new address, the identity of the hitherto unknown Romeo who had raised his eyes to your Juliet became apparent. You doubtless had designed to unpack my boxes for me as you have been in the habit of doing; but green-eyed jealousy suggested how, by the sacrifice of only one consignment of *hashish*, you might wreak my ruin. I disapprove of your morals, Malaglou. My own code may be peculiar, but it does not embrace *hashish* dealing; therefore, Malaglou, you are about to take a sheet of note-paper—bearing your office heading—and write from my dictation...."

"And suppose I refuse? You dare not shoot me!"

"You little know my true character, Malaglou. But I should not shoot you, as you say; I should introduce you to a gentleman who is very anxious to make your acquaintance—the venerable Sheikh Ismail."

The effect of this remark greatly exceeded my most sanguine expectations. I think I have never seen a man so pitiably frightened.

"The Sheikh ... Ismail!" gasped Joseph Malaglou. "He is in Cairo?"

"He has generously offered me five thousand pounds for your name and address."

"Ah, my God!" whispered Malaglou. "Kernaby, you will not betray me to that fiend? You are an Englishman and you will not soil your hands with such a deed!"

To my dismay—for it was a disgusting sight—Malaglou fell trembling upon his knees before me. The threat of shooting had had no such effect as the mere name of the Sheikh Ismail. My respect for that really remarkable old ruffian rose by leaps and bounds.

"Get up," I said harshly, "and, if you can, write."

He obeyed me; the man was almost hysterical. And, very shakily, this is what he wrote:

"I, Joseph Malaglou, also known as *Ahmed Ben Tawwab*, confess that I am a dealer in *hashish* and spurious antiques, which I have been in the habit of storing at my warehouse in Cairo, and also in my private residence in the Darb el Ahmar. Finding it desirable to enlarge the facilities of the latter, I induced the Hon. Neville Kernaby, who is ignorant of my real business, to lease for me a house which adjoins my own, as I did not desire it to be known that I was the lessee. Subsequently, learning that the suspicions of the authorities had been aroused, I anonymously denounced Kernaby, thus hoping to avert suspicion from myself and cause his arrest as the consignee of the cases which had been delivered at the new premises."

"Very good," I said, when this precious document had been completed. "You understand that you will now accompany me to the central police station in the Place Bâb el-Khalk and sign this confession in the presence of suitable witnesses? You will doubtless be detained; therefore in the interests of your safety, we must arrange that Mizmûna be hidden securely until the case is settled. Oh! set your evil mind at rest! I shall not betray you to the Sheikh; unless—" I looked him squarely in the eyes—"any whisper of my name appears in this matter!"

"But where is she?" he said hoarsely.

"She is hiding in the adjoining house."

"I have a small place at Shubra where I can conceal her."

"Very well. I will bring her here and permit you to make suitable arrangements, but let them be complete; for if Ismail should find the girl and thus discover your identity, nothing could save you—and you will be unable to leave Cairo (I shall see to that) until the case is settled."

VI

It was on the following evening, as I sat smoking upon the terrace of the hotel and reflecting upon the execrably bad luck which pursued me, that I observed Abû Tabâh mounting the carpeted steps with slow and stately carriage. He saluted me gravely and accepted the seat which I offered him.

My plan had run smoothly; Malaglou had given himself up to the authorities, but had been released upon payment of a substantial bail. Mizmûna was concealed at Shubra, and I was flogging my brain in a vain endeavor to conjure up a plan whereby, without betraying the villainous Greek and thus causing him to betray *me*, I might secure the Sheikh's reward—or, at least, the lapis armlet.

"Alas," said Abû Tabâh, "that the wicked should prosper."

"To whose prosperity," I inquired, "do you more especially refer?"

He regarded me with his fine melancholy eyes.

"You have an English adage," he continued, "which says, 'set a thief to catch a thief.'"

"Quite so. But might I inquire what bearing this crystallized wisdom has upon our present conversation?"

"The man, Joseph Malaglou," he replied, "learning of the hue-and-cry after a certain missing damsel——"

I remember I was about to light a cigar as he uttered those words, but a dawning perception of the iniquitous truth crept poisonously into my mind, and I threw both cigar and matches over the rail into the Shâra Kâmel and clutched fiercely at the little table between us.

"And of the reward offered for her recovery," pursued the *imám*, "denounced to us, one Yûssuf of Rosetta, a man owning a small house at Shubra. Yûssuf had fled, and the only occupant of the place was the missing damsel Mizmûna. Alas that fortune should so favor the sinful. The abductor, the despoiler, escapes retribution; and the traitor, the informer, the dealer in *hashish* is rewarded."

The Turk has signally failed to rule Egypt; but there are certain Ottoman institutions which are not without claims, as I realized at that moment in regard to Joseph Malaglou: I was thinking, particularly, of the bow-string.

"Already," said Abû Tabâh, with his sweet but melancholy smile, "the heart of the Sheikh Ismail inclined toward the damsel, for whom his soul yearned; and has not it been written that he who heals the breach betwixt man and wife shall himself be blessed? Behold the reward of the peace-maker—which I design as a gift to my sister."

I was unable to speak, but I became aware of a bitter taste upon my palate as, from beneath his robe, the smiling *imám* took out the armlet of gold and lapis-lazuli!

IV

OMAR OF ISPÂHAN

I

"I hear that the Harêm Suite is occupied," said Sir Bertram Collis, bustling up to me as I sat smoking in the gardens of a certain Cairo hotel, which I shall not name because of the matters that befell there. "Daphne is full of curiosity respecting the romantic occupant."

"Don't let Lady Collis be too sure," put in Chundermeyer, "that there is anything romantic about the occupant."

"Your definition of romance, Chundermeyer," I interrupted, "would probably be 'a diamond the size of a Spanish onion.'"

Chundermeyer smiled, but it was a smile in which his dark eyes, twinkling through the pebbles of horn-rimmed spectacles, played no part. I must confess that the society of this unctuous partner in the well-known Madras firm of Isaacs and Chundermeyer palled somewhat at times. He, on the other hand, was eternally dropping into a chair beside me, and proffering huge and costly cigars from a huge and costly case. This sort of parvenu persecution is one of the penalties of being recognized by Debrett.

"As a matter of fact," I continued, "the occupant of the Harêm Suite is no less romantic a personage than the daughter of the Mudîr (Governor) of the Fayûm."

"Really!" said Chundermeyer, with that sudden interest which mention of a title always aroused in him. "Surely it is most unusual for so highly placed a Moslem lady to reside at an hotel?"

"Most unusual," I replied. "Of course such a thing would be inconceivable in India; but the management of this establishment, who cater almost exclusively to tourists, find, I am told, that a 'harêm suite' is quite a good advertisement. The reason of the presence of this lady in the hotel is a diplomatic one. She is visiting Cairo in order to witness the procession of Ashûra, peculiarly sacred to Egyptian women, and it appears that, having no blood relations here, she could not accept the hospitality of any one of the big families without alienating the others."

"By Jove!" said Sir Bertram, "I must tell Daphne this yarn. She'll be delighted! Come along, Kernaby; if we're to have tea at Mena House, it is high time we were off."

I left Chundermeyer to his opulent cigar without regret. That he was an astute man of affairs and an expert lapidary I did not doubt, for he had offered to buy my Hatshepsu scarab ring at a price exactly ten per cent below its trade value; but to my mind there is something almost as unnatural about a Hindu-Hebrew as about a Græco-Welshman or a griffin.

Of course, Daphne Collis was not ready; and, Sir Bertram going up to their apartments to induce her to hurry, I strolled out again into the gardens for a quiet cigarette and a cocktail. As I approached a suitable seat in a sort of charming little arbor festooned with purple blossom, a man who had been waiting there rose to greet me.

With a certain quickening of the pulse, I recognized Abû Tabâh, arrayed, as was his custom, in black, only relieved by a small snowy turban, which served to enhance the ascetic beauty of his face and the mystery of the wonderful, liquid eyes.

He inclined his head in that gesture of gentle dignity which I knew; and:

"I have been awaiting an opportunity of speech with you, Kernaby Pasha," he said, in his flawless, musical English, "upon a matter in which I hope you will consent to aid me."

Since this mysterious man, variously known as "the *imám*" and "the Magician," but whom I knew to be some kind of secret agent of the Egyptian Government, had recently saved me from assassination, to decline to aid him was out of the question. We seated ourselves in the arbor.

"I should welcome an opportunity of serving you, my friend," I assured him, "since your services to me can never be repaid."

His lips moved slightly in the curiously tender smile which a poor physiognomist might have mistaken for evidence of effeminacy, bending towards me with a cautious glance about.

"You are staying at this hotel throughout the Christmas festivities?" he asked.

"Yes; I have temporarily deserted Shepheard's in order to accept the hospitality of Sir Bertram Collis, a very old friend. I shall probably return on the Tuesday following Christmas Day."

"There is to be a carnival and masquerade ball here to-morrow. You shall be present?"

"I hope so," I replied in surprise. "To what does all this tend?"

Abû Tabâh bent yet closer.

"Many of your friends and acquaintances possess valuable jewels?"

"They do."

"Then warn them—individually, in order to occasion no general alarm—to guard these with the utmost care."

My surprise increased. "You alarm me," I said. "Are there rogues in our midst?"

"No," answered the *imám*, fixing his melancholy gaze upon my face; "so far as my knowledge bears me, there is but one, yet that one is worse than a host of others."

"Do you mean that he is here—in the hotel?"

Abû Tabâh shrugged his slim shoulders.

"If I knew his exact whereabouts," he replied, "there would be no occasion to fear him. All that I know is that he is in Cairo; and since many richly attired women of Europe and America will be here to-morrow night, of a surety Omar Ali Khân will be here also!"

I shook my head in perplexity.

"Omar Ali Khân?"——I began.

"Ah," continued Abû Tabâh, "to you that name conveys nothing, but to me it signifies Omar of Ispahân, 'the Father of Thieves.' Do you remember," fixing his strange eyes hypnotically upon me, "the theft of the sacred *burko* of Nefîseh?"

"Quite well," I replied hastily; since the incident represented an unpleasant memory.

"It was Omar of Ispahân who stole it from the shrine. It was Omar of Ispahân who stole the blue diamond of the Rajah of Bagore from the treasure-room at Jullapore, and Omar of Ispahân"—lowering his voice almost to a whisper—"who stole the Holy Carpet ere it reached Mecca!"

"What!" I cried. "When did that happen? I never heard of such an episode!"

Abû Tabâh raised his long, slim hand warningly.

"Be cautious!" he whispered; "the flowers of the garden, the palms in the grove, the very sands of the desert have ears! The lightest word spoken in the *harêm* of the Khedive, or breathed from a minaret of the Citadel, is heard by Omar of Ispahân! The holy covering for the Kaaba was restored, on payment of a ruinous ransom by the Sherîf of Mecca, and none save the few ever knew of its loss."

For a time I was silent; words failed me; for the veil of the Kaaba, miscalled "the Carpet," is about the size of a bowling-green; then—

"In what manner does this affair concern you, Abû Tabâh?" I asked.

"In this way: the daughter of the Mudîr el-Fáyûm is here, in order that she may be present on the Night of Ashûra in the Mûski. For a Moslem lady to stay in such a place as this"—there was a faint note of contempt in the speaker's voice—"is without precedent, but the circumstances are peculiar. The *khân* near the Mosque of Hosein is full, and it is not seemly that the Mudîr's daughter should live at any lesser establishment. Therefore, as she brings her two servants, it has been possible for her to remain here. But"—his voice sank again—"her ornaments are famed throughout Islâm."

I nodded comprehendingly.

"To me," Abû Tabâh whispered, "has been entrusted the task of guarding them; to you, I entrust that of guarding the possessions of the other guests!"

I started.

"But, my friend," I said, "this is a dreadful responsibility which you impose upon me."

"Other precautions are being taken," he replied calmly; "but you, observing great circumspection, can speak to the guests, and, being forewarned of his presence, can even watch for the coming of Omar of Ispahân."

II

The effect of my news upon Lady Collis was truly dramatic.

"Oh," she cried, "my rope of pearls. Mr. Chundermeyer only told me last week that it was worth at least two hundred pound more than I gave for it."

Mr. Chundermeyer had made himself popular with many of the ladies in the hotel by similar diplomatic means, but I think that if he had been compelled to purchase at his own flattering valuations Messrs. Isaacs and Chundermeyer would have been ruined.

"You need not wear it, my dear," said her husband tactlessly.

"Don't be so ridiculous!" she retorted. "You know I have brought my Queen of Sheba costume for to-morrow night."

That, of course, settled the matter, so that beyond making one pretty woman extremely nervous, my campaign against the dreaded Omar of Ispahân had opened—blankly. Later in the day I circulated my warning right and left, and everywhere sowed consternation without reaping any appreciable result.

"One naturally expects thieves on these occasions," said a little Chicago millionairess, "and if I only wore my diamonds when no rogues were about, I might as well have none. There are crooks in America I'd back against your Persian thief any day."

On the whole, I think, the best audience for my dramatic recitation was provided by Mr. Chundermeyer, whom I found in the American bar, just before the dinner hour. His yellow skin perceptibly blanched at my first mention of Omar Ali Khân, and one hand clutched at a bulging breast pocket of the dinner-jacket he wore.

"Good heavens, Mr. Kernaby," he said, "you alarm me—you alarm me, sir!"

"The reputation of Omar is not unknown to you?"

"By no means unknown to me," he responded in the thick, unctuous voice which betrayed the Semitic strain in his pedigree. "It was this man who stole the pair of blue diamonds from the Rajah of Bagore."

"So I am told."

"But have you been told that it was my firm who bought those diamonds for the Rajah?"

"No; that is news to me."

"It was my firm, Mr. Kernaby, who negotiated the sale of the blue diamonds to the Rajah; therefore the particulars of their loss, under most extraordinary circumstances, are well known to me. You have made me very nervous. Who is your informant?"

"A member of the native police with whom I am acquainted."

Mr. Chundermeyer shook his head lugubriously.

"I am conveying a parcel of rough stones to Amsterdam," he confessed, glancing warily about him over the rims of his spectacles, "and I feel very much disposed to ask for more reliable protection than is offered by your Egyptian friend."

"Why not lodge the stones in a bank, or in the manager's safe?"

He shook his head again, and proffered an enormous cigar.

"I distrust all safes but my own," he replied. "I prefer to carry such valuables upon my person, foolish though the plan may seem to you. But do you observe that squarely built, military looking person standing at the bar, in conversation with M. Balabas, the manager?"

"Yes; an officer, I should judge."

"Precisely; a *police* officer. That is Chief Inspector Carlisle of New Scotland Yard."

"But he is a guest here."

"Certainly. The management sustained a severe loss last Christmas during the progress of a ball at which all Cairo was present, and as the inspector chanced to be on his way home from India, where official business had taken him, M. Balabas induced him to break his journey and remain until after the carnival."

"Wait a moment," I said; "I will bring him over."

Crossing to the bar, I greeted Balabas, with whom I was acquainted, and—

"Mr. Chundermeyer and I have been discussing the notorious Omar of Ispahân, who is said to be in Cairo," I remarked.

Inspector Carlisle, being introduced, smiled broadly.

"Mr. Balabas is very nervous about this Omar man," he replied, with a slight Scottish accent; "but, considering that everybody has been warned, I don't see myself that he can do much damage."

"Perhaps you would be good enough to reassure Mr. Chundermeyer," I suggested, "who is carrying valuables."

Chief Inspector Carlisle walked over to the table at which Chundermeyer was seated.

"I have met your partner, sir," he said, "and I gathered that you were on your way to Amsterdam with a parcel of rough stones; in fact, I supposed that you had arrived there by now."

"I am fond of Cairo during the Christmas season," explained the other, "and I broke my journey. But now I sincerely wish I were elsewhere."

"Oh, I shouldn't worry!" said the detective cheerily. "There are enough of us on the look-out."

But Mr. Chundermeyer remained palpably uneasy.

III

The gardens of the hotel on the following night presented a fairy-like spectacle. Lights concealed among the flower-beds, the bloom-covered arbors, and the feathery leafage of the acacias, suffused a sort of weird glow, suggesting the presence of a million fire-flies. Up beneath the crowns of the lofty palms little colored electric lamps were set, producing an illusion of supernatural fruit, whilst the fountain had been magically converted into a cascade of fire.

In the ball-room, where the orchestra played, and a hundred mosque lamps bathed the apartment in soft illumination, a cosmopolitan throng danced around a giant Christmas tree, their costumes a clash of color to have filled a theatrical producer with horror, outraging history and linking the ages in startling fashion. Thus, St. Antony of the Thebäid danced with Salome, the luresome daughter of Herodias; Nero's arm was about the waist of Good Queen Bess; Charles II cantered through a two-step with a red-haired Vestal Virgin; and the Queen of Sheba (Daphne Collis) had no less appropriate a partner than Sherlock Holmes.

Doubtless it was all very amusing, but, personally, I stand by my commonplace dress-suit, having, perhaps, rather a ridiculous sense of dignity. Inspector Carlisle also was soberly arrayed, and we had several chats during the evening; he struck me as being a man of considerable culture and great shrewdness.

For Abû Tabâh I looked in vain. Following our conservation on the previous afternoon, he had vanished like a figment of a dream. I several times saw Chundermeyer, who had elected to disguise himself as Al-Mokanna, the Veiled Prophet of Khorassan. He seemed to be an enthusiastic dancer, and there was no lack of partners.

But of these mandarins, pierrots, Dutch girls, monks, and court ladies I speedily tired, and sought refuge in the gardens, whose enchanted aspect was completed by that wondrous inverted bowl, jewel-studded, which is the nightly glory of Egypt. In the floral, dim-lighted arbors many romantic couples shrank from the peeping moon; but quiet and a hushful sense of peace ruled there beneath the stars more in harmony with my mood.

One corner of the gardens, in particular, seemed to be quite deserted, and it was the most picturesque spot of all. For here a graceful palm upstood before an outjutting *mushrabîyeh* window, dimly lighted, over which trailed a wealth of bougainvillea blossom, whilst beneath it lay a floral carpet, sharply bisected by the shadow of the palm trunk. It was like some gorgeous illustration to a poem by Hafiz, only lacking the figure at the window.

And as I stood, enchanted, before the picture, the central panels of the window were thrown open, and, as if conjured up by my imagination, a woman appeared, looking out into the gardens—an Oriental woman, robed in shimmering, moon-kissed white, and wearing a white *yashmak*. Her arms and fingers were laden with glittering jewels.

I almost held my breath, drawing back into the sheltering shadow, for I had not hitherto suspected myself of being a sorcerer. For perhaps a minute, or less, she stood looking out, then the window closed, and the white phantom disappeared. I recovered myself, recognizing that I stood before the isolated wing of the hotel known as the Harêm Suite, and that Fate had granted me a glimpse of the daughter of the Mudîr of the Fáyûm.

Recollecting, in the nick of time, an engagement to dance with Lady Collis, I hurried back to the ball-room. On its very threshold I encountered Chundermeyer. I could see his spectacles glittering through the veil of his ridiculous costume, and even before he spoke I detected about him an aura of tragedy.

"Mr. Kernaby," he gasped, "for Heaven's sake help me to find Inspector Carlisle! I have been robbed!"

"What?"

"My diamonds!"

"You don't mean——"

"Find the inspector, and come to my rooms. I am nearly mad!"

Daphne Collis, who had seen me enter, joined us at this moment, and, overhearing the latter part of Chundermeyer's speech:

"Oh, whatever is the matter?" she whispered.

As for Chundermeyer the effect upon him of her sudden appearance was positively magical. He stared through his veil as though her charming figure had been that of some hideous phantom. Then slowly, as if he dreaded to find her intangible, he extended one hand and touched her rope of pearls.

"Ah, heavens!" he gasped. "I am really going mad, or is there a magician amongst us?"

Daphne Collis's blue eyes opened very widely, and the color slowly faded from her cheeks.

"Mr. Chundermeyer," she began. But—

"Let us go into this little recess, where there is a good light," mumbled Chundermeyer shakily, "and I will make sure."

The three of us entered the palm-screened alcove, Chundermeyer leading. He stood immediately under a lamp suspended by brass chains from the roof.

"Permit me to examine your pearls for one moment," he said.

Her hands trembling, Daphne Collis took off the costly ornament and placed it in the hands of the greatly perturbed expert. Chundermeyer ran the pearls through his fingers, then lifted the largest of the set towards the light and scrutinized it closely. Suddenly he dropped his arms, and extended the necklace upon one open palm.

"Look for yourself," he said slowly. "It does not require the eyes of an expert."

Daphne Collis snatched the pearls and stared at them dazedly. Her pretty face was now quite colorless.

"This is not my rope of pearls," she said, in a monotonous voice; "it is a very poor imitation!"

Ere I could frame any kind of speech—

"Look at this," groaned Chundermeyer, "as you talk of a poor imitation!"

He was holding out a leather-covered box, plush-lined, and bearing within the words, "Isaacs and Chundermeyer, Madras." Nestling grotesquely amid the blue velvet were six small pieces of coal!

Chundermeyer sank upon the cushions of the settee, tossing the casket upon a little coffee table.

"I am afraid I feel unwell," he said feebly. "Mr. Kernaby, I wonder if you would be so kind as to find Inspector Carlisle, and ask a waiter to bring me some cognac."

"Oh, what shall I do, what shall I do?" whispered poor Daphne Collis.

"Just remain here," I said soothingly, "with Mr. Chundermeyer." And I induced her to sit in a big cane rest-chair. "I will return in a moment with Bertram and the inspector."

Desiring to avoid a panic, I walked quietly into the ball-room and took stock of the dancers, for a waltz was in progress. The inspector I could not see, but Sir Bertram I observed at the further end of the floor, dancing with Mrs. Van Heysten, the Chicago lady whom I had warned to keep a close watch upon her diamonds.

I managed to attract Collis's attention, and the pair, quitting the floor, joined me where I stood. A few words sufficed in which to inform them of the catastrophe, and, pointing out the alcove wherein I had left Chundermeyer and Lady Collis, I set off in search of Inspector Carlisle.

Ten minutes later, having visited every likely spot, I came to the conclusion that he was not in the hotel, and with M. Balabas I returned to the alcove adjoining the ball-room. Dancing was in full swing, and I thought as we passed along the edge of the floor how easily I could have checked the festivities by announcing that Omar of Ispahân was present.

The first sight to greet me upon entering the little palm-shaded alcove was that of Mrs. Van Heysten in tears. She had discovered herself to be wearing a very indifferent duplicate of her famous diamond tiara.

I think it was my action of soothingly patting her upon the shoulder that drew Chundermeyer's attention to my Hatshepsu scarab.

"Mr. Kernaby!" he cried—"Mr. Kernaby!" And pointed to my finger.

I had had the scarab set in a revolving bezel, and habitually wore it with its beetle uppermost and the cartouche concealed. As I glanced down at the ring, Chundermeyer stretched out his hand and detached it from my finger. Approaching the light, he turned the bezel.

The flat part of the scarab was quite blank, bearing no inscription whatever. Like Lady Collis's rope of pearls, Mrs. Van Heysten's tiara, and Chundermeyer's diamonds, it was a worthless and very indifferent duplicate!

IV

Never can I forget the scene in that crowded little room—poor M. Balabas all anxiety respecting the reputation of his establishment, and vainly endeavoring to reason with the victims of the amazing Omar Khân. Finally—

"I will search for Inspector Carlisle myself," said Mr. Chundermeyer; "and if I cannot find him, I shall be compelled to communicate with the local police authorities."

M. Balabas still volubly protesting, the unfortunate Veiled Prophet made his way from the alcove. I cannot say if the inspiration came as the result of a sort of auto-hypnosis induced by staring at the worthless ring in my hand—the stone was not even real lapis-lazuli—but a theory regarding the manner in which these ingenious substitutions had been effected suddenly entered my mind.

Three minutes later I was knocking at the door of Chundermeyer's room. I received no invitation to enter, and the door was locked. I sought M. Balabas; and, without confiding to him the theory upon which I was acting, I urged the desirability of gaining access to the apartment. As a result, a master key was procured, and we entered.

At the first glance the room seemed to be empty, though it showed evidence of having recently been occupied, for it was in the utmost disorder. Perhaps we should have quitted it unenlightened, if I had not detected the sound of a faint groan proceeding from the closed wardrobe. Stepping across the room, I opened the double doors, and out into my arms fell a limp figure, bound hand and foot, and having a bath-towel secured tightly around the head to act as a gag. It was Mr. Chundermeyer!

I think, as I helped to unfasten him, I was the most surprised man in the land of Egypt. He was arrayed only in a bath-robe and slippers, and his bare wrists and ankles were cruelly galled by the cords which had bound him. For some minutes he was unable to utter a word, and when at last he achieved speech, his first utterance constituted a verbal thunderbolt.

"I have been robbed!" he cried huskily. "I was sand-bagged as I came from my bath, and look—everyone of my cases is gone!"

It was M. Balabas who answered him.

"As you returned from your *bath*, Mr. Chundermeyer?" he said. "At what time was that?"

"About a quarter-past seven," was the amazing reply.

"But, good Heaven!" cried M. Balabas, "I was speaking to you less than ten minutes ago!"

"You are mad!" groaned Chundermeyer, rubbing his bruised wrists. "Have I not been locked in the wardrobe all night!"

"Ah, merciful saints," cried M. Balabas, dramatically raising his clenched fists to heaven, "I see it all! You understand, Mr. Kernaby. It is *not* Mr. Chundermeyer with whom we have been conversing, in whose hands you have been placing your valuables, it is that devil incarnate who three years ago impersonated the Emîr al-Hadj, in order to steal the Holy Carpet; who can impersonate anyone; who, it is said, can transform himself at will into an old woman, a camel, or a fig tree; it is the conjuror, the wizard—Omar of Ispahân!"

My own ideas were almost equally chaotic; for although, as I now recalled, I had never throughout the evening obtained a thoroughly good view of the features of the Veiled Prophet, I could have sworn to the voice, to the carriage, to the manner of Mr. Chundermeyer.

The puzzling absence of Chief Inspector Carlisle now engaged everybody's attention; and, acting upon the precedent afforded by the finding of Mr. Chundermeyer, we paid a visit to the detective's room.

Inspector Carlisle, fully dressed, and still wearing a soft felt hat, as though he had but just come in, lay on the floor, unconscious, with the greater part of a cigar, which examination showed to be drugged, close beside him.

As I entered my room that night and switched on the light, in through the open window from the balcony stepped Abû Tabâh.

His frequent and mysterious appearances in my private apartments did not surprise me in the least, and I had even ceased to wonder how he accomplished them; but—

"You are too late, my friend," I said. "Omar of Ispahân has outwitted you."

"Omar of Ispahân has outwitted men wiser than I," he replied gravely; "but covetousness is a treacherous master, and I am not without hope that we may yet circumvent the father of thieves."

"You are surely jesting," I replied. "In all probability he is now far from Cairo."

"I, on the contrary, have reason to believe," replied Abû Tabâh calmly, "that he is neither far from Cairo, far from the hotel, nor far from this very apartment."

His manner was strange and I discovered excitement to be growing within me.

"Accompany me on the balcony," he said; "but first extinguish the light."

A moment later I stood looking down upon the moon-bathed gardens, and Abû Tabâh, beside me, stretched out his hand.

"You see the projecting portion of the building yonder?"

"Yes," I replied; "the Harêm Suite."

"Immediately before the window there is a palm tree."

"I have observed it."

"And upon the opposite side of the path there is an acacia."

"Yes; I see it."

"The moon is high, and whilst all the side of the hotel is in shadow the acacia is in the moonlight. Its branches would afford concealment, however; and one watching there could see what would be hidden from one on this balcony. I request you, Kernaby Pasha, to approach that *lebbekh* tree from the further side of the fountain, in order to remain invisible from the hotel. Climb to one of the lower branches, and closely watch four windows."

I stared at him in the darkness.

"Which are the four windows that I am to watch?"

"They are—one, that immediately below your own; two, that to the right of it; three, the window above the Harêm Suite; and, four, the extreme east window of this wing, on the first floor."

Now, my state of mystification grew even denser. For the windows specified were, in the order of mention, that of Inspector Carlisle, who had not yet recovered consciousness; of Mr. Chundermeyer; of Major Redpath, a retired Anglo-Indian who had been confined to his room for some time with an attack of malaria; and of M. Balabas, the manager.

"For what," I inquired, "am I to watch?"

"For a man to descend."

"And then?"

"You will hold your open watch case where it is clearly visible from this spot. Instant upon the man's appearance you will cover it up, and then uncover it, either once, twice, thrice, or four times."

"After which?"

"Remain scrupulously concealed. Have the collar of your dinner jacket turned up in order to betray as little whiteness as possible. Do not interfere with the man who descends; but if he enters the Harêm Suite, see that he does not come out again! There is no time for further explanation, Kernaby Pasha; it is Omar of Ispahân with whom we have to deal!"

V

Perched up amid the foliage of the acacia, I commenced that singular guard imposed upon me by Abû Tabâh. Did he suspect one of these four persons of being the notorious Omar? Or had his mysterious instructions some other significance? The problem defied me; and, recognizing that I was hopelessly at sea, I abandoned useless conjecture and merely watched.

Nor was my vigil a long one. I doubt if I had been at my post for ten minutes ere a vague figure appeared upon the shadow-veiled balcony of one of the suspected windows—that of Major Redpath, above the Harêm Suite!

Scarcely daring to credit my eyes, I saw the figure throw down on to the projecting top of the *mushrabîyeh* window below a slender rope ladder. I covered the gleaming gold of my watch-case with my hand, and gave the signal—*three*.

The spirit of phantasy embraced me; and, unmoved to further surprise, I watched the unknown swarm down the ladder with the agility of an ape. He seemed to wear a robe, surely that of the *Veiled Prophet*! He silently manipulated one of the side-panels of the window, opened it, and vanished within the Harêm Suite.

Raising my eyes, I beheld a second figure—that of Abû Tabâh—descending a similar ladder to the balcony of Inspector Carlisle's room. He gained the balcony and entered the room. Four seconds elapsed; he reappeared, unfurled a greater length of ladder, and came down to the flower-beds. Lithely as a cat he came to the projecting *mushrabîyeh*, swung himself aloft, and as I watched breathlessly, expecting him to enter in pursuit of the intruder, climbed to the top and began to mount the ladder descending from Major Redpath's room!

He had just reached the major's balcony, and was stepping through the open window, when a most alarming din arose in the Harêm Suite; evidently a fierce struggle was proceeding in the apartments of the Mudîr's daughter!

I scrambled down from the acacia and ran to the spot immediately below the window, arriving at the very moment that the central lattice was thrown open, and a white-veiled figure appeared there and prepared to spring down! Perceiving my approach:

"Oh, help me, in the name of Allah!" cried the woman, in a voice shrill with fear. "Quick—catch me!"

Ere I could frame any reply, she clutched at the palm tree and dropped down right into my extended arms, as a crashing of overturned furniture came from the room above.

"Help them!" she entreated. "You are armed, and my women are being murdered."

"Help, Kernaby Pasha!" now reached my ears, in the unmistakable voice of Abû Tabâh, from somewhere within. "See that he does not escape from the window!"

"Coming!" I cried.

And, by means of the palm trunk, I began to mount towards the open lattice.

Gaining my objective, I stumbled into a room which presented a scene of the wildest disorder. It was a large apartment, well but sparsely furnished in the Eastern manner, and lighted by three hanging lamps. Directly under one of these, beside an overturned cabinet of richly carven wood inlaid with mother-o'-pearl, lay a Nubian, insensible, and arrayed only in shirt and trousers. There was no one else in the room, and, not pausing to explore those which opened out of it, I ran and unbolted the heavy door upon which Abû Tabâh was clamoring for admittance.

The *imám* leaped into the room, rebolted the door, and glanced to the right and left; then he ran into the adjoining apartments, and finally, observing the insensible Nubian upon the floor, he stared into my face, and I read anger in the eyes that were wont to be so gentle.

"Did I not enjoin you to prevent his escape from the window?" he cried.

"No one escaped from the window, my friend," I retorted, "except the lady who was occupying the suite."

Abû Tabâh fixed his weird eyes upon me in a hypnotic stare of such uncanny power that I was angrily conscious of much difficulty in sustaining it; but gradually the quelling look grew less harsh, and finally his whole expression softened, and that sweet smile, which could so transform his face, disturbed the severity of the set lips.

"No man is infallible," he said. "And wiser than you or I have shown themselves the veriest fools in contest with Omar Ali Khân. But know, O Kernaby Pasha, that the lady who occupied this suite secretly left it at sunset to-night, bearing her jewels with her, and he"—pointing to the insensible Nubian on the floor—"took her place and wore her raiment——"

"Then the Mudîr's daughter——"

"Is my sister Ayesha!"

I looked at him reproachfully, but he met my gaze with calm pride.

"Subterfuge was permitted by the Prophet, (on whom be peace)," he continued; "but not lying! My sister *is* the daughter of the Mudîr el-Fáyûm."

It was a rebuke, perhaps a merited one; and I accepted it in silence. Although, from the moment that I had first set eyes on him, I had never doubted Abû Tabâh to be a man of good family, this modest avowal was something of a revelation.

"Her presence here, which was permitted by my father," he said, "was a trap; for it is well known throughout the Moslem world that she is the possessor of costly ornaments. The trap succeeded. Omar of Ispahân, at great risk of discovery, remained to steal her jewels, although he had already amassed a choice collection."

Someone had begun to bang upon the bolted door, and there was an excited crowd beneath the window.

"You supposed, no doubt," the *imám* resumed calmly, "that I suspected

Major Redpath and M. Balabas, as well as Mr. Chundermeyer and the English detective? It was not so. But I regarded the room of M. Balabas as excellently situated for Omar's purpose, and I knew that M. Balabas rarely retired earlier than one o'clock. Even more suitable was that of Major Redpath, whose illness I believe to have been due to some secret art of Omar's."

"But he is down with chronic malaria!"

"It may even be so; yet I believe the attack to have been induced by Omar of Ispahân."

"But why?"

"Because, as I learned to-night, Major Redpath is the only person in Cairo who has ever met Mr. Chundermeyer! I will confess that until less than an hour ago I did not know if Inspector Carlisle was *really* an inspector! Oh, it is a seeming absurdity; but Omar of Ispahân is a wizard! Therefore I entered the inspector's room, and found him to be still unconscious. Major Redpath was in deep slumber, and Omar had entered and quitted his room without disturbing him. I did likewise, and visited Mr. Chundermeyer's—the door was ajar—on my way downstairs."

"But, my friend," I said amazedly, "with my own eyes I beheld Mr. Chungermeyer gagged and bound in his wardrobe! I saw his bruised wrists!"

"He gagged, bound, and bruised himself!" replied Abû Tabâh calmly. "With my own eyes I once beheld a blind mendicant hanging by the neck from a fig tree, a bloody froth upon his lips. I cut him down and left him for dead. Yet was he neither dead nor a blind mendicant; he was Omar Ali Khân! Oblige me by opening the door, Kernaby Pasha."

I obeyed, and an excited throng burst in, headed by M. Balabas and Inspector Carlisle, the latter looking very pale and haggard!

"Where is the man posing as Chundermeyer?" began the detective hoarsely. "By sheer sleight-of-hand, and under ye're very noses"—excitement rendered him weirdly Caledonian—"he has robbed ye! I cabled Madras to-day, and the real Chundermeyer arrived at Amsterdam last Friday! As I returned with the reply cable in my pocket to-night I became so dizzy I was only just able to get to my room. He'd doctored every smoke in my case! Where is he?"

"I assisted him to escape, disguised as a woman, some ten minutes ago," I replied feebly. "I should be sincerely indebted to you if you would kick me."

"Escaped!" roared Inspector Carlisle. "Then what are ye doing here? Pursue him, somebody! Are ye all mad?"

"We should be," said Abû Tabâh, "to attempt pursuit. As well pursue the shadow of a cloud, the first spear of sunrise, or the phantom heifer of Pepi-Ankh, as pursue Omar of Ispahân! He is gone—but empty-handed. Behold what I recovered from 'Mr. Chundermeyer's' room."

From beneath his black *gibbeh* he took out a leather bag, opened it, and displayed to our startled eyes the tiara of Mrs. Van Heysten, the rope of pearls, and—my Hatshepsu scarab!

Ere anyone could utter a word, Abû Tabâh inclined his head in dignified salutation, turned, and walked stately from the room.

V

BREATH OF ALLAH

I

For close upon a week I had been haunting the purlieus of the Mûski, attired as a respectable dragoman, my face and hands reduced to a deeper shade of brown by means of a water-color paint (I had to use something that could be washed off and grease-paint is useless for purposes of actual disguise) and a neat black moustache fixed to my lip with spirit-gum. In his story *Beyond the Pale*, Rudyard Kipling has trounced the man who inquires too deeply into native life; but if everybody thought with Kipling we should never have had a Lane or a Burton and I should have continued in unbroken scepticism regarding the reality of magic. Whereas, because of the matters which I am about to set forth, for ten minutes of my life I found myself a trembling slave of the unknown.

Let me explain at once that my undignified masquerade was not prompted by mere curiosity or the quest of the pomegranate, it was undertaken as the natural sequel to a letter received from Messrs. Moses, Murphy and Co., the firm which I represented in Egypt, containing curious matters affording much food for reflection. "We would ask you," ran the communication, "to renew your inquiries into the particular composition of the perfume 'Breath of Allah,' of which you obtained us a sample at a cost which we regarded as excessive. It appears to consist in the blending of certain obscure essential oils and gum-resins; and the nature of some of these has defied analysis to date. Over a hundred experiments have been made to discover substitutes for the missing essences, but without success; and as we are now in a position to arrange for the manufacture of Oriental perfume on an extensive scale we should be prepared to make it *well worth your while* (the last four words characteristically underlined in red ink) if you could obtain for us a correct copy of the original prescription."

The letter went on to say that it was proposed to establish a separate company for the exploitation of the new perfume, with a registered address in Cairo and a "manufactory" in some suitably inaccessible spot in the Near East.

I pondered deeply over these matters. The scheme was a good one and could not fail to reap considerable profits; for, given extensive advertising, there is always a large and monied public for a new smell. The particular blend of liquid fragrance to which the letter referred was assured of a good sale at a high price, not alone in Egypt, but throughout the capitals of the world, provided it could be put upon the market; but the proposition of manufacture was beset with extraordinary difficulties.

The tiny vial which I had despatched to Birmingham nearly twelve months before had cost me close upon £100 to procure, for the reason that "Breath of Allah" was the secret property of an old and aristocratic Egyptian family whose great wealth and exclusiveness rendered them unapproachable. By dint of diligent inquiry I had discovered the *attár* to whom was entrusted certain final processes in the preparation of the perfume—only to learn that he was ignorant of its exact composition. But although he had assured me (and I did not doubt his word) that not one grain had hitherto passed out of the possession of the family, I had succeeded in procuring a small quantity of the precious fluid.

Messrs. Moses, Murphy and Co. had made all the necessary arrangements for placing it upon the market, only to learn, as this eventful letter advised me, that the most skilled chemists whose services were obtainable had failed to analyse it.

One morning, then, in my assumed character, I was proceeding along the Shâria el-Hamzâwi seeking for some scheme whereby I might win the confidence of Mohammed er-Rahmân the *attár*, or perfumer. I had quitted the house in the Darb el-Ahmar which was my base of operations but a few minutes earlier, and as I approached the corner of the street a voice called from a window directly above my head: "Saïd! Saïd!"

Without supposing that the call referred to myself, I glanced up, and met the gaze of an old Egyptian of respectable appearance who was regarding me from above. Shading his eyes with a gnarled hand—

"Surely," he cried, "it is none other than Saïd the nephew of Yûssuf Khalig! *Es-selâm 'aleykûm, Saïd!*"

"*Aleykûm, es-selâm,*" I replied, and stood there looking up at him.

"Would you perform a little service for me, Saïd?" he continued. "It will occupy you but an hour and you may earn five piastres."

"Willingly," I replied, not knowing to what the mistake of this evidently half-blind old man might lead me.

I entered the door and mounted the stairs to the room in which he was, to find that he lay upon a scantily covered *dîwan* by the open window.

"Praise be to Allah (whose name be exalted)!" he exclaimed, "that I am thus fortunately enabled to fulfil my obligations. I sometimes suffer from an old serpent bite, my son, and this morning it has obliged me to abstain from all movement. I am called Abdûl the Porter, of whom you will have heard your uncle speak; and although I have long retired from active labor myself, I contract for the supply of porters and carriers of all descriptions and for all purposes; conveying fair ladies to the *hammám*, youth to the bridal, and death to the grave. Now, it was written that you should arrive at this timely hour."

I considered it highly probable that it was also written how I should shortly depart if this garrulous old man continued to inflict upon me details of his absurd career. However—

"I have a contract with the merchant, Mohammed er-Rahmân of the Sûk el-Attârin," he continued, "which it has always been my custom personally to carry out."

The words almost caused me to catch my breath; and my opinion of Abdul the Porter changed extraordinary. Truly my lucky star had guided my footsteps that morning!

"Do not misunderstand me," he added. "I refer not to the transport of his wares to Suez, to Zagazig, to Mecca, to Aleppo, to Baghdad, Damascus, Kandahar, and Pekin; although the whole of these vast enterprises is entrusted to none other than the only son of my father: I speak, now, of the bearing of a small though heavy box from the great magazine and manufactory of Mohammed er-Rahmân at Shubra, to his shop in the Sûk el-Attârin, a matter which I have arranged for him on the eve of the Molid en-Nebi (birthday of the Prophet) for the past five-and-thirty years. Every one of my porters to whom I might entrust this special charge is otherwise employed; hence my observation that it was written how none other than yourself should pass beneath this window at a certain fortunate hour."

Fortunate indeed had that hour been for me, and my pulse beat far from normally as I put the question: "Why, O Father Abdul, do you attach so much importance to this seemingly trivial matter?"

The face of Abdul the Porter, which resembled that of an intelligent mule, assumed an expression of low cunning.

"The question is well conceived," he said, raising a long forefinger and wagging it at me. "And who in all Cairo knows so much of the secrets of the great as Abdul the Know-all, Abdul the Taciturn! Ask me of the fabled wealth of Karafa Bey and I will name you every one of his possessions and entertain you with a calculation of his income, which I have worked out in *nûss-faddah*!* Ask me of the amber mole upon

---

* A *nûss-faddah* equals a quarter of a farthing.

the shoulder of the Princess Azîza and I will describe it to you in such a manner as to ravish your soul! Whisper, my son"—he bent towards me confidentially—"once a year the merchant Mohammed er-Rahmân prepares for the Lady Zuleyka a quantity of the perfume which impious tradition has called 'Breath of Allah.' The father of Mohammed er-Rahmân prepared it for the mother of the Lady Zuleyka and his father before him for the lady of that day who held the secret—the secret which has belonged to the women of this family since the reign of the Khalîf el-Hakîm from whose favorite wife they are descended. To her, the wife of the Khalîf, the first *dirhem* (drachm) ever distilled of the perfume was presented in a gold vase, together with the manner of its preparation, by the great wizard and physician Ibn Sina of Bokhara" (Avicenna).

"You are well called Abdul the Know-all!" I cried in admiration. "Then the secret is held by Mohammed er-Rahmân?"

"Not so, my son," replied Abdul. "Certain of the essences employed are brought, in sealed vessels, from the house of the Lady Zuleyka, as is also the brass coffer containing the writing of Ibn Sina; and throughout the measuring of the quantities, the secret writing never leaves her hand."

"What, the Lady Zuelyka attends in person?"

Abdul the Porter inclined his head serenely.

"On the eve of the birthday of the Prophet, the Lady Zuelyka visits the shop of Mohammed er-Rahmân, accompanied by an *imám* from one of the great mosques."

"Why by an *imám*, Father Abdul?"

"There is a magical ritual which must be observed in the distillation of the perfume, and each essence is blessed in the name of one of the four archangels; and the whole operation must commence at the hour of midnight on the eve of the Molid en-Nebi."

He peered at me triumphantly.

"Surely," I protested, "an experienced *attár* such as Mohammed er-Rahmân would readily recognize these secret ingredients by their smell?"

"A great pan of burning charcoal," whispered Abdul dramatically, "is placed upon the floor of the room, and throughout the operation the attendant *imám* casts pungent spices upon it, whereby the nature of the secret essences is rendered unrecognizable. It is time you depart, my son, to the shop of Mohammed, and I will give you a writing making you known to him. Your task will be to carry the materials necessary for the secret operation (which takes place to-night) from the magazine of Mohammed er-Rahmân at Shubra, to his shop in the Sûk el-Attârin.

My eyesight is far from good, Saïd. Do you write as I direct and I will place my name to the letter."

II

The words "well worth your while" had kept time to my steps, or I doubt if I should have survived the odious journey from Shubra. Never can I forget the shape, color, and especially the weight, of the locked chest which was my burden. Old Mohammed er-Rahmân had accepted my service on the strength of the letter signed by Abdul, and of course, had failed to recognize in "Saïd" that Hon. Neville Kernaby who had certain confidential dealings with him a year before. But exactly how I was to profit by the fortunate accident which had led Abdul to mistake me for someone called "Saïd" became more and more obscure as the box grew more and more heavy. So that by the time that I actually arrived with my burden at the entrance to the Street of the Perfumers, my heart had hardened towards Abdul the Know-all; and, setting my box upon the ground, I seated myself upon it to rest and to imprecate at leisure that silent cause of my present exhaustion.

After a time my troubled spirit grew calmer, as I sat there inhaling the insidious breath of Tonquin musk, the fragrance of attár of roses, the sweetness of Indian spikenard and the stinging pungency of myrrh, opoponax, and ihlang-ylang. Faintly I could detect the perfume which I have always counted the most exquisite of all save one—that delightful preparation of Jasmine peculiarly Egyptian. But the mystic breath of frankincense and erotic fumes of ambergris alike left me unmoved; for amid these odors, through which it has always seemed to me that that of cedar runs thematically, I sought in vain for any hint of "Breath of Allah."

Fashionable Europe and America were well represented as usual in the Sûk el-Attârin, but the little shop of Mohammed er-Rahmân was quite deserted, although he dealt in the most rare essences of all. Mohammed, however, did not seek Western patronage, nor was there in the heart of the little white-bearded merchant any envy of his seemingly more prosperous neighbors in whose shops New York, London, and Paris smoked amber-scented cigarettes, and whose wares were carried to the uttermost corners of the earth. There is nothing more illusory than the outward seeming of the Eastern merchant. The wealthiest man with whom I was acquainted in the Muski had the aspect of a mendicant; and whilst Mohammed's neighbors sold phials of essence and tiny boxes of pastilles to the patrons of Messrs. Cook, were not the silent caravans following the ancient desert routes laden with great crates of sweet merchandise from the manufactory at Shubra? To the city of Mecca alone Mohammed sent annually perfumes to the value of two thousand pounds sterling; he manufactured three kinds of incense exclusively for the royal house of Persia; and his wares were known from Alexandria to Kashmîr, and prized alike in Stambûl and Tartary. Well might he watch with tolerant smile the more showy activities of his less fortunate competitors.

The shop of Mohammed er-Rahmân was at the end of the street remote from the Hamzâwi (Cloth Bazaar), and as I stood up to resume my labors my mood of gloomy abstraction was changed as much by a certain atmosphere of expectancy—I cannot otherwise describe it—as by the familiar smells of the place. I had taken no more than three paces onward into the Sûk ere it seemed to me that all business had suddenly become suspended; only the Western element of the throng remained outside whatever influence had claimed the Orientals. Then presently the visitors, also becoming aware of this expectant hush as I had become aware of it, turned almost with one accord, and following the direction of the merchants' glances, gazed up the narrow street towards the Mosque of el-Ashraf.

And here I must chronicle a curious circumstance. Of the Imám Abû Tabâh I had seen nothing for several weeks, but at this moment I suddenly found myself thinking of that remarkable man. Whilst any mention of his name, or nickname—for I could not believe "Tabâh" to be patronymic—amongst the natives led only to pious ejaculations indicative of respectful fear, by the official world he was tacitly disowned. Yet I had indisputable evidence to show that few doors in Cairo, or indeed in all Egypt, were closed to him; he came and went like a phantom. I should never have been surprised, on entering my private apartments at Shepheard's, to have found him seated therein, nor did I question the veracity of a native acquaintance who assured me that he had met the mysterious *imám* in Aleppo on the same morning that a letter from his partner in Cairo had arrived mentioning a visit by Abû Tabâh to el-Azhar. But throughout the native city he was known as the Magician and was very generally regarded as a master of the *ginn*. Once more depositing my burden upon the ground, then, I gazed with the rest in the direction of the mosque.

It was curious, that moment of perfumed silence, and my imagination, doubtless inspired by the memory of Abû Tabâh, was carried back to the days of the great *khalîfs*, which never seem far removed from one in those mediæval streets. I was transported to the Cairo of Harûn al Raschîd, and I thought that the Grand Wazîr on some mission from Baghdad was visiting the Sûk el-Attârin.

Then, stately through the silent group, came a black-robed, white-turbaned figure outwardly similar to many others in the bazaar, but followed by two tall muffled negroes. So still was the place that I could hear the tap of his ebony stick as he strode along the centre of the street.

At the shop of Mohammed er-Rahmân he paused, exchanging a few words with the merchant, then resumed his way, coming down the Sûk towards me. His glance met mine, as I stood there beside the box; and, to my amazement, he saluted me with smiling dignity and passed on. Had he, too, mistaken me for Saïd—or had his all-seeing gaze detected beneath my disguise the features of Neville Kernaby?

As he turned out of the narrow street into the Hamzâwi, the commercial uproar was resumed instantly, so that save for this horrible doubt which had set my heart beating with uncomfortable rapidity, by all the evidences now about me his coming might have been a dream.

III

Filled with misgivings, I carried the box along to the shop; but Mohammed er-Rahmân's greeting held no hint of suspicion.

"By fleetness of foot thou shalt never win Paradise," he said.

"Nor by unseemly haste shall I thrust others from the path," I retorted.

"It is idle to bandy words with any acquaintance of Abdul the Porter's," sighed Mohammed; "well do I know it. Take up the box and follow me."

With a key which he carried attached to a chain about his waist, he unlocked the ancient door which alone divided his shop from the outjutting wall marking a bend in the street. A native shop is usually nothing more than a double cell; but descending three stone steps, I found myself in one of those cellar-like apartments which are not uncommon in this part of Cairo. Windows there were none, if I except a small square opening, high up in one of the walls, which evidently communicated with the narrow courtyard separating Mohammed's establishment from that of his neighbor, but which admitted scanty light and less ventilation. Through this opening I could see what looked like the uplifted shafts of a cart. From one of the rough beams of the rather lofty ceiling a brass lamp hung by chains, and a quantity of primitive chemical paraphernalia littered the place; old-fashioned alembics, mysterious looking jars, and a sort of portable furnace, together with several tripods and a number of large, flat brass pans gave the place the appearance of some old alchemist's den. A rather handsome ebony table, intricately carved and inlaid with mother-o'-pearl and ivory, stood before a cushioned *dîwan* which occupied that side of the room in which was the square window.

"Set the box upon the floor," directed Mohammed, "but not with such undue dispatch as to cause thyself to sustain an injury."

That he had been eagerly awaiting the arrival of the box and was now burningly anxious to witness my departure, grew more and more apparent with every word. Therefore—

"There are asses who are fleet of foot," I said, leisurely depositing my load at his feet; "but the wise man regulateth his pace in accordance with three things: the heat of the sun; the welfare of others; and the nature of his burden."

"That thou hast frequently paused on the way from Shubra to reflect upon these three things," replied Mohammed, "I cannot doubt; depart, therefore, and ponder them at leisure, for I perceive that thou art a great philosopher."

"Philosophy," I continued, seating myself upon the box, "sustaineth the mind, but the activity of the mind being dependent upon the welfare of the stomach, even the philosopher cannot afford to labor without hire."

At that, Mohammed er-Rahmân unloosed upon me a long pent-up torrent of invective—and furnished me with the information which I was seeking.

"O son of a wall-eyed mule!" he cried, shaking his fists over me, "no longer will I suffer thy idiotic chatter! Return to Abdul the Porter, who employed thee, for not one *faddah* will I give thee, calamitous mongrel that thou art! Depart! for I was but this moment informed that a lady of high station is about to visit me. Depart! lest she mistake my shop for a pigsty."

But even as he spoke the words, I became aware of a vague disturbance in the street, and—

"Ah!" cried Mohammed, running to the foot of the steps and gazing upwards, "now am I utterly undone! Shame of thy parents that thou art, it is now unavoidable that the Lady Zuleyka shall find thee in my shop. Listen, offensive insect—thou art Saïd, my assistant. Utter not one word; or with this"—to my great alarm he produced a dangerous-looking pistol from beneath his robe—"will I blow a hole through thy vacuous skull!"

Hastily concealing the pistol, he went hurrying up the steps, in time to perform a low salutation before a veiled woman who was accompanied by a Sûdanese servant-girl and a negro. Exchanging some words with her which I was unable to detect, Mohammed er-Rahmân led the way down into the apartment wherein I stood, followed by the lady, who in turn was followed by her servant. The negro remained above. Perceiving me as she entered, the lady, who was attired with extraordinary elegance, paused, glancing at Mohammed.

"My lady," he began immediately, bowing before her, "it is Saïd my assistant, the slothfulness of whose habits is only exceeded by the impudence of his conversation."

She hesitated, bestowing upon me a glance of her beautiful eyes. Despite the gloom of the place and the *yashmak* which she wore, it was manifest that she was good to look upon. A faint but exquisite perfume stole to my nostrils, whereby I knew that Mohammed's charming visitor was none other than, the Lady Zuleyka.

"Yet," she said softly, "he hath the look of an active young man."

"His activity," replied the scent merchant, "resideth entirely in his tongue."

The Lady Zuleyka seated herself upon the *dîwan*, looking all about the apartment.

"Everything is in readiness, Mohammed?" she asked.

"Everything, my lady."

Again the beautiful eyes were turned in my direction, and, as their inscrutable gaze rested upon me, a scheme—which, since it was never carried out, need not be described—presented itself to my mind. Following a brief but eloquent silence—for my answering glances were laden with significance:—

"O Mohammed," said the Lady Zuleyka indolently, "in what manner doth a merchant, such as thyself, chastise his servants when their conduct displeaseth him?"

Mohammed er-Rahmân seemed somewhat at a loss for a reply, and stood there staring foolishly.

"I have whips for mine," murmured the soft voice. "It is an old custom of my family."

Slowly she cast her eyes in my direction once more.

"It seemed to me, O Saïd," she continued, gracefully resting one jeweled hand upon the ebony table, "that thou hadst presumed to cast love-glances upon me. There is one waiting above whose duty it is to protect me from such insults. Miska!"—to the servant girl—"summon El-Kimri (The Dove)."

Whilst I stood there dumbfounded and abashed the girl called up the steps:

"El-Kimri! Come hither!"

Instantly there burst into the room the form of that hideous negro whom I had glimpsed above; and—

"O Kimri," directed the Lady Zuleyka, and languidly extended her hand in my direction, "throw this presumptuous clown into the street!"

My discomfiture had proceeded far enough, and I recognized that, at whatever risk of discovery, I must act instantly. Therefore, at the moment that El-Kimri reached the foot of the steps, I dashed my left fist into his grinning face, putting all my weight behind the blow, which I followed up with a short right, utterly outraging the pugilistic proprieties, since it was well below the belt. El-Kimri bit the dust to the accompaniment of a human discord composed of three notes—and I leaped up the steps, turned to the left, and ran off around the Mosque of el-Ashraf, where I speedily lost myself in the crowded Ghurîya.

Beneath their factitious duskiness my cheeks were burning hotly: I was ashamed of my execrable artistry. For a druggist's assistant does not lightly make love to a duchess!

IV

I spent the remainder of the forenoon at my house in the Darb el-Ahmar heaping curses upon my own fatuity and upon the venerable head of Abdul the Know-all. At one moment it seemed to me that I had wantonly destroyed a golden opportunity, at the next that the seeming opportunity had been a mere mirage. With the passing of noon and the approach of evening I sought desperately for a plan, knowing that if I failed to conceive one by midnight, another chance of seeing the famous prescription would probably not present itself for twelve months.

At about four o'clock in the afternoon came the dawn of a hazy idea, and since it necessitated a visit to my rooms at Shepheard's, I washed the paint off my face and hands, changed, hurried to the hotel, ate a hasty meal, and returned to the Darb el-Ahmar, where I resumed my disguise.

There are some who have criticized me harshly in regard to my commercial activities at this time, and none of my affairs has provoked greater acerbitude than that of the perfume called "Breath of Allah." Yet I am at a loss to perceive wherein my perfidy lay; for my outlook is sufficiently socialistic to cause me to regard with displeasure the conserving by an individual of something which, without loss to himself, might reasonably be shared by the community. For this reason I have always resented the way in which the Moslem veils the faces of the pearls of his *harêm*. And whilst the success of my present enterprise would not render the Lady Zuleyka the poorer, it would enrich and beautify the world by delighting the senses of men with a perfume more exquisite than any hitherto known.

Such were my reflections as I made my way through the dark and deserted bazaar quarter, following the Shâria el-Akkadi to the Mosque of el-Ashraf. There I turned to the left in the direction of the Hamzâwi, until, coming to the narrow alley opening from it into the Sûk el-Attârin, I plunged into its darkness, which was like that of a tunnel, although the upper parts of the houses above were silvered by the moon.

I was making for that cramped little courtyard adjoining the shop of Mohammed er-Rahmân in which I had observed the presence of one of those narrow high-wheeled carts peculiar to the district, and as the entrance thereto from the Sûk was closed by a rough wooden fence I anticipated little difficult in gaining access. Yet there was one difficulty which I had not foreseen, and which I had not met with had I arrived, as I might easily have arranged to do, a little earlier. Coming to the corner of the Street of the Perfumers, I cautiously protruded my head in order to survey the prospect.

Abû Tabâh was standing immediately outside the shop of Mohammed er-Rahmân!

My heart gave a great leap as I drew back into the shadow, for I counted his presence of evil omen to the success of my enterprise. Then, a swift revelation, the truth burst in upon my mind. He was there in the capacity of *imám* and attendant magician at the mystical "Blessing of the perfumes"! With cautious tread I retraced my steps, circled round the Mosque and made for the narrow street which runs parallel with that of the Perfumers and into which I knew the courtyard beside Mohammed's shop must open. What I did not know was how I was going to enter it from that end.

I experienced unexpected difficulty in locating the place, for the height of the buildings about me rendered it impossible to pick up any familiar landmark. Finally, having twice retraced my steps, I determined that a door of old but strong workmanship set in a high, thick wall must communicate with the courtyard; for I could see no other opening to the right, or left through which it would have been possible for a vehicle to pass.

Mechanically I tried the door, but, as I had anticipated, found it to be securely locked. A profound silence reigned all about me and there was no window in sight from which my operations could be observed. Therefore, having planned out my route, I determined to scale the wall. My first foothold was offered by the heavy wooden lock which projected fully six inches from the door. Above it was a crossbeam and then a gap of several inches between the top of the gate and the arch into which it was built. Above the arch projected an iron rod from which depended a hook; and if I could reach the bar it would be possible to get astride the wall.

I reached the bar successfully, and although it proved to be none too firmly fastened, I took the chance and without making very much noise found myself perched aloft and looking down into the little court. A sigh of relief escaped me; for the narrow cart with its disproportionate wheels stood there as I had seen it in the morning, its shafts pointing gauntly upward to where the moon of the Prophet's nativity swam in a cloudless sky. A dim light shone out from the square window of Mohammed er-Rahmân's cellar.

Having studied the situation very carefully, I presently perceived to my great satisfaction that whilst the tail of the cart was wedged under a crossbar, which retained it in its position, one of the shafts was in reach of my hand. Thereupon I entrusted my weight to the shaft, swinging out over the well of the courtyard. So successful was I that only a faint creaking sound resulted; and I descended into the vehicle almost silently.

Having assured myself that my presence was undiscovered by Abû Tabâh, I stood up cautiously, my hands resting upon the wall, and peered through the little window into the room. Its appearance had changed somewhat. The lamp was lighted and shed a weird and subdued illumination upon a rough table placed almost beneath it. Upon this table were scales, measures, curiously shaped flasks, and odd-looking chemical apparatus which might have been made in the days of Avicenna himself. At one end of the table stood an alembic over a little pan in which burnt a spirituous flame. Mohammed er-Rahmân was placing cushions upon the *dîwan* immediately beneath me, but there was no one else in the room. Glancing upward, I noted that the height of the neighboring building prevented the moonlight from penetrating into the courtyard, so that my presence could not be detected by means of any light from without; and, since the whole of the upper part of the room was shadowed, I saw little cause for apprehension within.

At this moment came the sound of a car approaching along the Shâria esh-Sharawâni. I heard it stop, near the Mosque of el-Ashraf, and in the almost perfect stillness of those tortuous streets from which by day arises a very babel of tongues I heard approaching footsteps. I crouched down in the cart, as the footsteps came nearer, passed the end of the courtyard abutting on the Street of the Perfumers, and paused before the shop of Mohammed er-Rahmân. The musical voice of Abû Tabâh spoke and that of the Lady Zuleyka answered. Came a loud rapping, and the creak of an opening door: then—

"Descend the steps, place the coffer on the table, and then remain immediately outside the door," continued the imperious voice of the lady. "Make sure that there are no eavesdroppers."

Faintly through the little window there reached my ears a sound as of some heavy object being placed upon a wooden surface, then a muffled disturbance as of several persons entering the room; finally, the muffled bang of a door closed and barred ... and soft footsteps in the adjoining street!

Crouching down in the cart and almost holding my breath, I watched through a hole in the side of the ramshackle vehicle that fence to which I have already referred as closing the end of the courtyard which adjoined the Sûk el-Attârin. A spear of moonlight, penetrating through some gap in the surrounding buildings, silvered its extreme edge. To an accompaniment of much kicking and heavy breathing, into this natural limelight arose the black countenance of "The Dove." To my unbounded joy I perceived that his nose was lavishly decorated with sticking-plaster and that his right eye was temporarily off duty. Eight fat fingers clutching at the top of the woodwork, the bloated negro regarded the apparently empty yard for a space of some three seconds, ere lowering his ungainly bulk to the level of the street again. Followed a faint "pop" and a gurgling quite unmistakable. I heard him walking back to the door, as I cautiously stood up and again surveyed the interior of the room.

V

Egypt, as the earliest historical records show, has always been a land of magic, and according to native belief it is to-day the theater of many super-natural dramas. For my own part, prior to the episode which I am about to relate, my personal experiences of the kind had been limited and unconvincing. That Abû Tabâh possessed a sort of uncanny power akin to second sight I knew, but I regarded it merely as a form of telepathy. His presence at the preparation of the secret perfume did not surprise me, for a belief in the efficacy of magical operations prevailed, as I was aware, even among the more cultured Moslems. My scepticism, however, was about to be rudely shaken.

As I raised my head above the ledge of the window and looked into the room, I perceived the Lady Zuleyka seated on the cushioned *dîwan*, her hands resting upon an open roll of parchment which lay upon the table beside a massive brass chest of antique native workmanship. The lid of the chest was raised, and the interior seemed to be empty, but near it upon the table I observed a number of gold-stoppered vessels of Venetian glass and each of which was of a different color.

Beside a brazier wherein glowed a charcoal fire, Abû Tabâh stood;

and into the fire he cast alternately strips of paper bearing writing of some sort and little dark brown pastilles which he took from a sandalwood box set upon a sort of tripod beside him. They were composed of some kind of aromatic gum in which benzoin seemed to predominate, and the fumes from the brazier filled the room with a blue mist.

The *imám*, in his soft, musical voice, was reciting that chapter of the Korân called "The Angel." The weird ceremony had begun. In order to achieve my purpose I perceived that I should have to draw myself right up to the narrow embrasure and rest my weight entirely upon the ledge of the window. There was little danger in the maneuver, provided I made no noise; for the hanging lamp, by reason of its form, cast no light into the upper part of the room. As I achieved the desired position I became painfully aware of the pungency of the perfume with which the apartment was filled.

Lying there upon the ledge in a most painful attitude, I wriggled forward inch by inch further into the room, until I was in a position to use my right arm more or less freely. The preliminary prayer concluded, the measuring of the perfumes had now actually commenced, and I readily perceived that without recourse to the parchment, from which the Lady Zuleyka never once removed her hands, it would indeed be impossible to discover the secret. For, consulting the ancient prescription, she would select one of the gold-stoppered bottles, unscrew it, direct that so many grains should be taken from it, and never removing her gaze from Mohammed er-Rahmân whilst he measured out the correct quantity, would restopper the vessel and so proceed. As each was placed in a wide-mouthed glass jar by the perfumer, Abû Tabâh, extending his hands over the jar, pronounced the names:

"Gabraîl Mikaîl, Israfîl, Israîl."

Cautiously I raised to my eyes the small but powerful opera-glasses to procure which I had gone to my rooms at Shepheard's. Focussing them upon the ancient scroll lying on the table beneath me, I discovered, to my joy, that I could read the lettering quite well. Whilst Abû Tabâh began to recite some kind of incantation in the course of which the names of the Companions of the Prophet frequently occurred, I commenced to read the writing of Avicenna.

"In the name of God, the Compassionate, the Merciful, the High, the Great...."

So far had I proceeded and no further when I became aware of a curious change in the form of the Arabic letters. They seemed to be moving, to be cunningly changing places one with another as if to trick me out of grasping their meaning!

The illusion persisting, I determined that it was due to the unnatural strain imposed upon my vision, and although I recognized that time was precious I found myself compelled temporarily to desist, since nothing was to be gained by watching these letters which danced from side to side of the parchment, sometimes in groups and sometimes singly, so that I found myself pursuing one slim Arab A (*'Alif*) entirely up the page from the bottom to the top where it finally disappeared under the thumb of the Lady Zuleyka!

Lowering the glasses I stared down in stupefaction at Abû Tabâh. He had just cast fresh incense upon the flames, and it came home to me, with a childish and unreasoning sense of terror, that the Egyptians who called this man the Magician were wiser than I. For whilst I could no longer hear his voice, I now could *see* the words issuing from his mouth! They formed slowly and gracefully in the blue clouds of vapour some four feet above his head, revealed their meaning to me in letters of gold, and then faded away towards the ceiling!

Old-established beliefs began to totter about me as I became aware of a number of small murmuring voices within the room. They were the voices of the perfumes burning in the brazier. Said one, in a guttural tone:

"I am Myrrh. My voice is the voice of the Tomb."

And another softly: "I am Ambergris. I lure the hearts of men."

And a third huskily: "I am Patchouli. My promises are lies."

My sense of smell seemed to have deserted me and to have been replaced by a sense of hearing. And now this room of magic began to expand before my eyes. The walls receded and receded, until the apartment grew larger than the interior of the Citadel Mosque; the roof shot up so high that I knew there was no cathedral in the world half so lofty. Abû Tabâh, his hands extended above the brazier, shrank to minute dimensions, and the Lady Zuleyka, seated beneath me, became almost invisible.

The project which had led me to thrust myself into the midst of this feast of sorcery vanished from my mind. I desired but one thing: to depart, ere reason utterly deserted me. But, to my horror, I discovered that my muscles were become rigid bands of iron! The figure of Abû Tabâh was drawing nearer; his slowly moving arms had grown serpentine and his eyes had changed to pools of flame which seemed to summon me. At the time when this new phenomenon added itself to the other horrors, I seemed to be impelled by an irresistible force to jerk my head downwards: I heard my neck muscles snap metallically: I *saw* a scream of agony spurt forth from my lips ... and I saw upon a little ledge immediately below the square window a little *mibkharah*, or incense burner, which hitherto I had not observed. A thick, oily brown stream of vapor was issuing from its perforated lid and bathing my face clammily. Sense of smell I had none; but a chuckling, demoniacal voice spoke from the *mibkharah*, saying—

"I am *Hashish*! I drive men mad! Whilst thou hast lain up there like a very fool, I have sent my vapors to thy brain and stolen thy senses from thee. It was for this purpose that I was set here beneath the window where thou couldst not fail to enjoy the full benefit of my poisonous perfume...."

Slipping off the ledge, I fell ... and darkness closed about me.

VI

My awakening constitutes one of the most painful recollections of a not uneventful career; for, with aching head and tortured limbs, I sat upright upon the floor of a tiny, stuffy, and uncleanly cell! The only light was that which entered by way of a little grating in the door. I was a prisoner; and, in the same instant that I realized the fact of my incarceration, I realized also that I had been duped. The weird happenings in the apartment of Mohammed er-Rahmân had been hallucinations due to my having inhaled the fumes of some preparation of *hashish*, or Indian hemp. The characteristic sickly odor of the drug had been concealed by the pungency of the other and more odoriferous perfumes; and because of the position of the censer containing the burning *hashish*, no one else in the room had been affected by its vapor. Could it have been that Abû Tabâh had known of my presence from the first?

I rose, unsteadily, and looked out through the grating into a narrow passage. A native constable stood at one end of it, and beyond him I obtained a glimpse of the entrance hall. Instantly I recognized that I was under arrest at the Bâb el-Khalk police station!

A great rage consumed me. Raising my fists I banged furiously upon the door, and the Egyptian policeman came running along the passage.

"What does this mean, *shawêsh*?" I demanded. "Why am I detained here? I am an Englishman. Send the superintendent to me instantly."

The policeman's face expressed alternately anger, surprise, and stupefaction.

"You were brought here last night, most disgustingly and speechlessly drunk, in a cart!" he replied.

"I demand to see the superintendent."

"Certainly, certainly, *effendim*!" cried the man, now thoroughly alarmed. "In an instant, *effendim*!"

Such is the magical power of the word "Inglîsi" (Englishman).

A painfully perturbed and apologetic native official appeared almost immediately, to whom I explained that I had been to a fancy dress ball at the Gezira Palace Hotel, and, injudiciously walking homeward at a late hour, had been attacked and struck senseless. He was anxiously courteous, sending a man to Shepheard's with my written instructions to bring back a change of apparel and offering me every facility for removing my disguise and making myself presentable. The fact that he palpably disbelieved my story did not render his concern one whit the less.

I discovered the hour to be close upon noon, and, once more my outward self, I was about to depart from the Place Bâb el-Khalk, when, into the superintendent's room came Abû Tabâh! His handsome ascetic face exhibited grave concern as he saluted me.

"How can I express my sorrow, Kernaby Pasha," he said in his soft faultless English, "that so unfortunate and unseemly an accident should have befallen you? I learned of your presence here but a few moments ago, and I hastened to convey to you an assurance of my deepest regret and sympathy."

"More than good of you," I replied. "I am much indebted."

"It grieves me," he continued suavely, "to learn that there are footpads infesting the Cairo streets, and that an English gentleman may not walk home from a ball safely. I trust that you will provide the police with a detailed account of any valuables which you may have lost. I have here"—thrusting his hand into his robe—"the only item of your property thus far recovered. No doubt you are somewhat short-sighted, Kernaby Pasha, as I am, and experience a certain difficulty in discerning the names of your partners upon your dance programme."

And with one of those sweet smiles which could so transfigure his face, Abû Tabâh handed me my opera-glasses!

VI

THE WHISPERING MUMMY

I

Felix Bréton and I were the only occupants of the raised platform at the end of the hall; and the inartistic performance of the bulky dancer who occupied the stage promised to be interminable. From motives of sheer boredom I studied the details of her dress—a white dress, fitting like a vest from shoulder to hip, and having short, full sleeves under which was a sort of blue gauze. Her hair, wrists, and ankles glittered with barbaric jewelery and strings of little coins.

A deafening orchestra consisting of tambourines, shrieking Arab viols, and the inevitable *daràbukeh*, surrounded the performer in a half-circle; and three other large-sized *ghawâzi* mingled their shrill voices with the barbaric discords of the musicians. I yawned.

"As a quest of local color, Bréton," I said, "this evening's expedition can only be voted a dismal failure."

Felix Bréton turned to me, with a smile, resting his elbows upon the dirty little marble-topped table. He looked sufficiently like an artist to have been merely a painter; yet his gruesome picture "Le Roi S'Amuse" had proved the salvation of the previous Salon.

"Have patience," he said; "it is Shejeret ed-Durr (Tree of Pearls) that we have come to see, and she has not yet appeared."

"Unless she appears shortly," I replied, stifling another yawn, "I shall disappear."

But even as I spoke, there arose a hum of excitement throughout the crowded room; the fat dancer, breathless from her unpleasing exertions, resumed her seat; and all the performers turned their heads towards a door at the side of the stage. A veiled figure entered, with slow, lithe step; and her appearance was acclaimed excitedly. Coming to the centre of the stage, she threw off her veil with a swift movement, and confronted the audience, a slim, barbaric figure. I glanced at Felix Bréton. His eyes were glittering with excitement. Here at last was the *ghazîyeh* of romance, the *ghazîyeh* of the Egyptian monuments; a true daughter of that mysterious tribe who, in the remote past of the Nile-land, wove spells of subtle moon-magic before the golden Pharaoh.

A monstrous crash from the musicians opened the music of the dance—the famous Gazelle dance—which commenced to a measure of long, monotonous cadences. Shejeret ed-Durr began slowly to move her arms and body in that indescribable manner which, like the stirring of palm fronds, speaks the veritable language of the voluptuous Orient. The attendant dancers clashing their miniature cymbals, the measure quickened, and swift passion informed the languorous body, which magically became transformed into that of a leaping nymph, a bacchante, a living illustration of Keats' wonder-words:

> "Like to a moving vintage, down they came,
> Crown'd with green leaves, and faces all aflame;
> All madly dancing through the pleasant valley,
> To scare thee, Melancholy!"

At the conclusion of her dance, Shejeret ed-Durr, resuming her veil, descended to the floor of the hall and passed from table to table, exchanging light badinage with those patrons known to her.

"Do you think you could induce her to come up here, Kernaby?" said Bréton excitedly; "she is simply the ideal model for my 'Danse Funébre.'"

"Any inducement other than our presence in this select part of the establishment," I replied, offering him a cigarette, "is unnecessary. She will present herself with all reasonable despatch."

Indeed, I had seen the dark eyes glance many times towards us, as we sat there in distinguished isolation; and, even as I spoke, the girl was ascending the steps, from whence she approached our table, smiling in friendly fashion. Bréton's surprise was rather amusing when she confidently seated herself, giving an order to the cross-eyed waiter in close attendance. It would be our privilege, of course, to pay the bill. Of its being a privilege, no one could doubt who had observed the envious glances cast in our direction by less favored patrons.

As Bréton spoke no Arabic, the task of interpreter devolved upon me; and I was carrying on quite mechanically when my attention was drawn to a peculiarly sinister-looking person seated alone at a table close beside the corner of the stage. I remembered having observed him address some remark to Shejeret ed-Durr, and having noted that she seemed to avoid him. Now, he was directing upon us a glare so electrically baleful that when I first detected it I was conscious of a sort of shock. The man was rather oddly dressed, wearing a black turban and a sort of loose robe not unlike the *burnûs* of the desert Arabs. I concluded that he belonged to some religious order, and that his bosom was inflamed with a hatred of a most murderous character towards myself, Felix Bréton, and the dancer.

I endeavored, without attracting the girl's notice to indicate to Bréton the presence of the Man of the Glare; but the artist was so engrossed in contemplation of Shejeret ed-Durr and kept me so busy interpreting, that I abandoned the attempt in despair. Having made his wishes evident to her, the girl readily consented to pose for him; and when next I glanced at the table near the stage, the Man of the Glare had disappeared.

What induced me to look towards the rear of the platform upon which we were seated I know not, unless I did so in obedience to a species of hypnotic suggestion; but something prompted me to glance over my shoulder. And, for the second time that night, I encountered the gaze of mysterious eyes. From a little square window these compelling eyes regarded me fixedly, and presently I distinguished the outline of a head surmounted by a white turban.

The second watcher was Abû Tabâh!

What business could have brought the mysterious *imám* to such a place was a problem beyond my powers of conjecture, but that he was silently directing me to depart with all speed I presently made out. Having signified, by a gesture, that I had grasped the purport of his message, I turned again to Bréton, who was struggling to carry on a conversation with Shejeret ed-Durr in his native French.

I experienced some difficulty in inducing him to leave, but my arguments finally prevailed, and we passed out into the dimly lighted street. About us in the darkness pipes wailed, and there was the dim throbbing of the eternal *darábukeh*. We were in that part of El-Wasr adjoining the notorious Square of the Fountain. Discordant woman voices filled the night, and strange figures flitted from the shadows into the light streaming from the open doorways. It was the centre of secret Cairo, the midnight city; and three paces from the door of the dance hall, a slim, black-robed figure suddenly appeared at my elbow, and the musical voice of Abû Tabâh spoke close to my ear:

"Be on the terrace of Shepheard's in half an hour."

The mysterious figure melted again into the shadows about us.

II

On the deserted hotel balcony, Abû Tabâh awaited me.

"It was indeed fortunate, Kernaby Pasha," he said, "that I observed you this evening."

"I am greatly obliged to you," I replied, "for watching over me with such paternal solicitude. May I inquire what danger I have incurred?"

I was angrily conscious of feeling like a schoolboy suffering reproof.

"A very great danger," Abû Tabâh assured me, his gentle, musical voice expressing real concern. "Ahmad es-Kebîr is the lover of the dancer called Shejeret ed-Durr, although she who is of the *ghawâzi*, of Keneh does not return his affections."

"Ahmad es-Kebîr?—do you refer to a malignant looking person in a black turban?" I inquired.

Abû Tabâh gravely inclined his head.

"He is one of the *Rifa'îyeh*, the Black *Darwîshes*. They practise strange rites and are by some accredited with supernatural powers. For you the danger is not so great as for your friend, who seemed to be speaking words of love to the *ghazîyeh*."

I laughed shortly.

"You are mistaken, Abû Tabâh," I replied; "his interest was not of the character which you suppose. He is an artist and merely desired the girl to pose for him."

Abû Tabâh shrugged his shoulders.

"She is an unveiled woman," he said contemptuously, "but love in the heart of such a one as Ahmad is a terrible passion, consuming the vitals and rendering whom it afflicts either a partaker of Paradise or as one of the evil *ginn*."

"In the particular case under consideration," I said, "it would seem distinctly to have produced the latter and less agreeable symptoms."

"Let your friend step warily," advised Abû Tabâh; "for some who have aroused the enmity of the Black *Darwîshes* have met with strange ends, nor has it been possible to fix responsibility upon any member of the order."

"You think my poor friend, Felix Bréton, may be discovered some morning in an unpleasantly messy condition?"

"The Black *Darwîshes* do not employ the knife," answered Abû Tabâh; "they employ strange and more subtle weapons."

I stared hard at him in the darkness. I thought I knew my Cairo, but this sounded unpleasantly mysterious. However—

"I am indebted to you, Abû Tabâh," I said, "for your timely warning. As you know, I always personally avoid any possibility of misunderstanding in regard to my relations with Egyptian womenfolk."

"With some rare exceptions," agreed Abû Tabâh, "particulars of which escape my memory at the moment, you have always been a model of discretion, Kernaby Pasha."

"I will warn my friend," I said hastily, "of the view of his conduct mistakenly taken by the gentleman in the black turban."

"It is well," replied Abû Tabâh; "we shall meet again ere long."

With that and the customary dignified salutations he departed, leaving me wondering what hidden significance lay in his words, "we shall meet again ere long."

Experience had taught me that Abû Tabâh's warnings were not to be lightly dismissed, and I knew enough of the fanaticism of those strange Eastern sects whereof the *Rifa'îyeh*, or Black *Darwîshes*, was one, to realize that it would prove an unhealthy amusement to interfere with their domestic affairs. Felix Bréton, who possessed the rare gift of capturing and transferring to canvas the atmosphere of the East with the opulent colorings and vivid contrasts which constitute its charm, had nevertheless but little practical experience of the manners and customs of the golden Orient. He had leased a large studio situated on the roof of a fine old Cairene palace hidden away behind the Street of the Booksellers and almost in the shadow of the Mosque of el-Azhar. His romantic spirit had prompted him after a time to give up his rooms at the Continental and to take up his abode in the apartment adjoining the studio; that is to say, completely to cut himself off from European life and to become an inhabitant of the Oriental city. With his imperfect knowledge of the practical side of native life in the East, I did not envy him; but I was fully alive to his danger, isolated as he was from the European community, indeed from modernity; for out of the boulevards of modern Cairo into the streets of the *Arabian Nights* is but a step, yet a step that bridges the gulf of centuries.

As I entered his studio on the following morning, I discovered him at work upon the extraordinary picture "Danse Funébre." Shejeret ed-Durr was posing in the dress of an ancient priestess of Isis. Bréton briefly greeted me, waving his hand towards a cushioned *dîwan* before which stood a little coffee-table bearing decanters, siphons, cigarettes, and other companionable paraphernalia. Making myself comfortable, I studied the picture and the model.

"Danse Funébre" was an extraordinary conception, representing an elaborately furnished modern room, apparently that of an antiquary or Egyptologist; for a multitude of queer relics decorated the walls, cabinets, and the large table at which a man was seated. Boldly represented immediately to the left of his chair stood a mummy in an ornate sarcophagus, and forth from the swathed figure into the light cast downwards from an antique lamp, floated a beautiful spirit shape—that of an Egyptian priestess. Upon her face was an expression of intense anger, as, her fingers crooked in sinister fashion, she bent over the man at the table.

The mummy and sarcophagus depicted on the canvas stood before me against the wall of the studio, the lid resting beside the case. It was moulded, as is sometimes seen, to represent the face and figure of the occupant and was as fine an example of the kind as I had met with.

The mummy was that of a priestess and dancer of the Great Temple at Philæ, and it had been lent by the museum authorities for the purpose of Bréton's picture.

His enthusiasm at first seeing Shejeret ed-Durr was explainable by the really uncanny resemblance which the girl bore to the modeled figure. Studying her, from my seat on the *dîwan*, as she posed in that gauzy raiment depicted upon the lid of the sarcophagus, it seemed indeed that the ancient priestess was reborn in the form of Shejeret ed-Durr the *ghazîyeh*. Bréton had evidently tabooed make-up, with the exception of the characteristic black bordering to the eyes (which appeared in the presentment of the servant of Isis); and seen now in its natural coloring the face of the dancing-girl had undoubted beauty.

Presently, whilst the model rested, I informed Bréton of my conversation with Abû Tabâh; but, as I had anticipated, he was sceptical to the point of derision.

"My dear Kernaby," he said, "is it likely that I am going to interrupt my work now that I have found such an inspiring model, because some ridiculous *darwîsh* disapproves?"

"It is highly unlikely," I admitted; "but do not make the mistake of treating the matter lightly. You are right off the map here, and Cairo is not Paris."

"It is a great deal safer!" he cried in his boisterous fashion, "and infinitely more interesting."

But my mind was far from easy; for in the dark eyes of the model, when their glance rested upon Felix Bréton, there was that to have aroused poisonous sentiments in the bosom of the Man of the Glare.

III

During the course of the following month I saw Felix Bréton two or three times, and he was enthusiastic about the progress of his picture and the beauty of his model. The first hint that I received of the strange idea which was to lead to stranger happenings came one afternoon when he had called upon me at Shepheard's.

"Do you believe in reincarnation, Kernaby?" he asked suddenly.

I stared at him in surprise.

"Regardless of my personal views on the matter," I replied, "in what way does the subject interest you?"

Momentarily he hesitated; then—

"The resemblance between Yâsmîna" (this was the real name of Shejeret ed-Durr) "and the priestess of Isis," he said, "appears to me too marked to be explainable by mere coincidence. If the mummy were my personal property I should unwrap it——"

"Do you seriously desire me to believe that you regard Yâsmîna as a reincarnation of the elder lady?"

"That or a lineal descendant," he answered. "The tribe of the *Ghawâzi* is of unknown antiquity and may very well be descended from those temple dancers of the days of the Pharaohs. If you have studied the ancient wall paintings, you cannot have failed to observe that the dancing girls represented have entirely different forms from those of any other women depicted and from those of the ordinary Egyptian women of to-day."

His enthusiasm was tremendous; he was one of those uncomfortable fanatics who will ride a theory to the death.

"I cannot say that I have noticed it," I replied. "Your knowledge of the female form divine is doubtless more extensive than mine."

"My dear Kernaby," he cried excitedly, "to the trained eye the difference is extraordinary. Until I saw Yâsmîna I had believed the peculiar form to which I refer to be extinct like the blue enamel and the sacred lotus. If it is not reincarnation it is heredity."

I could not help thinking that it more closely resembled insanity than either; but since Bréton had made no reference to the wearer of the black turban, I experienced less anxiety respecting his physical than his mental welfare.

Three days later there was a dramatic development. Drifting idly into Bréton's studio one morning I found him pacing the place in despair and glaring at his unfinished canvas like a man distraught.

"Where is Shejeret ed-Durr?" I inquired.

"Gone!" he replied. "She disappeared yesterday and I can find no trace of her."

"Surely the excellent Suleyman, proprietor of the dancing establishment, can assist you?"

"I tell you," cried Bréton savagely, "that she has disappeared. No one knows what has become of her."

I looked at him in dismay. He presented a mournful spectacle. He was unshaven and his dark hair was wildly disordered. His despair was more acute than I should have supposed possible in the circumstances; and I concluded that his interest in Yâsmîna was deeper than I had assumed or that I was incapable of comprehending the artistic temperament. I suppose the Gallic blood in him had something to do with it, but I was unspeakably distressed to observe that the man was on the verge of tears.

Consolation was impossible, and I left him pacing his empty studio distractedly. That night at an unearthly hour, long after I had retired to my own apartments, he came to Shepheard's. Being shown into my room, and the servant having departed—

"Yâsmîna is dead!" he burst out, standing there, a disheveled figure, just within the doorway.

"What!" I exclaimed, standing up from the table at which I had been writing and confronting him. "Dead? Do you mean——"

"He has murdered her!" said Bréton, in a dull monotonous voice—"that fiend of whom you warned me."

I was appalled; for I had been utterly unprepared for such a tragedy. "Who discovered her?"

"No one discovered her; she will never be discovered! He has buried her body in some secret spot in the desert."

My amazement grew with every word that he uttered, and presently—

"Then how in Heaven's name did you learn of her murder?" I asked.

Felix Bréton, who had begun to pace up and down the room, a truly pitiable figure, paused and looked at me wildly.

"You will think that I am mad, Kernaby," he said; "but I must tell you—I must tell someone. I could see that you were incredulous when I spoke to you of reincarnation, but I was right, Kernaby, I was right! Either that or my reason is deserting me."

My opinion inclined distinctly in the direction of the latter theory, but I remained silent, watching Bréton's haggard face.

"To-night," he continued, "as I sat looking at my unfinished picture and trying to imagine what could have become of Yâsmîna, the mummy—the mummy of the priestess—*spoke to me!*"

I slowly sank back into my chair. I was now assured that Felix Bréton had formed a sudden and intense infatuation for Yâsmîna and that her mysterious disappearance had deranged his sensitive mind. Words failed me; I could think of nothing to say; and bending towards me his haggard face—

"It whispered to me," he said, "in *her* voice—in my own language, French, as I have taught it to her; just a few imperfect words, but sufficient to convey to me the story of the tragedy. Kernaby, what does it mean? Is it possible that her spirit, released from the body of Yâsmîna, has returned to that which I firmly believe it formerly inhabited?..."

I had had the misfortune to be a party to some distressing scenes, but few had affected me so unpleasantly as this. That poor Felix Bréton was raving I could not doubt, but having persuaded him to spend the night at Shepheard's and having seen him safely to bed, I returned to my own room to endeavor to work out the problem of what steps I should take regarding him on the morrow.

In the morning, however, he seemed more composed, having shaved and generally rendered himself more presentable; but the wild look still lingered in his eyes and I could see that the strange obsession had secured a firm hold upon him. He discussed the matter quite calmly during breakfast, and invited me to visit the scene of this supernatural happening. I assented, and hailing *arabîyeh* we drove together to the studio.

There was nothing abnormal in the appearance of the place, but I examined the mummy and the mummy case with a new curiosity; for if Felix Bréton was not mad (and this was a point upon which I recognized my incompetence to decide) the phantom voice was clearly the product of some trick. However, I was unable to discover anything to account for it. The sarcophagus stood against the outer wall of the studio and near to a large lattice window before which was draped a heavy tapestry curtain for the purpose of excluding undesirable light upon that side of the model's throne. There was no balcony outside the window, which was fully, thirty feet from the street below; therefore unless someone had been hiding in the window recess beside the sarcophagus, trickery appeared to be out of the question. Turning to Bréton, who was watching me haggardly—

"You searched the recess last night?" I said.

"I did—immediately. There was no one there. There was no one anywhere in the studio; and when I looked out of the open window, the street below was deserted from end to end."

Naturally, I took it for granted that he would avoid the place, at any rate by night; and I said as much, as we passed along the Mûski together. I can never forget the wildness in his eyes as he turned to me.

"I *must* go back, Kernaby," he said. "It seems like desertion, base and cowardly."

IV

Bréton did not join me at dinner that evening as we had arranged that he should do, and towards the hour of ten o'clock, growing more and more uneasy on his behalf, I set out for the studio, half hoping that I should meet him. I saw nothing of him, however, as I crossed the Ezbekîyeh Gardens and the Atabet el-Khadrâ into the Mûski. From thence onward to the Rondpoint the dark and narrow streets were almost deserted, and from the corner of the Shâria el-Khordâgîya to the Street of the Bookbinders I met with no living thing save a lean and furtive cat.

My footsteps echoed hollowly from wall to wall of the overhanging buildings, as I approached the door giving access to the courtyard from which a stair communicated with the studio above. The moonlight, slanting down into the ancient place, left more than half of it in densest shadow, but just touched the railing of the balcony and the lower part of the *mushrabîyeh* screen masking what once had been the *harêm* apartments from the view of one entering the courtyard. Far above me, through an open lattice, a dim light shone out, though vaguely. This part of the house was bathed in the radiance of the moon, which dimmed that of the studio lamp; for the open window was the window of Bréton's studio.

The door at the foot of the stairs was partly open, and I ascended slowly, since the place was quite dark and I was forced to feel my way around the eccentric turnings introduced by an Arab architect to whom simplicity had evidently been an abomination.

A modern door had been fitted to the studio; and although this door was also unfastened, I rapped loudly, but, receiving no answer, entered the studio. It was empty. The lamp was lighted, as I had observed from below, and a faint aroma of Turkish tobacco smoke hung in the air. Clearly, Bréton had left but a few moments earlier; and I judged it probable that he would be returning very shortly, for had he set out for Shepheard's he would not have left his door unlocked, and in any event I should have met him on the way. Therefore, having glanced into the inner room, which, latterly, Bréton had been using as a bedroom, I sat down on the *dîwan* and prepared to await his return.

The lamp whose light I had seen shining through the window was that which hung before the model's throne, and the curtain which usually draped the window recess had been partially pulled aside, so that from where I sat I could see part of the centre lattice, which was open. My mind at this time was entirely occupied with uneasy speculations regarding Bréton, and although I had glanced more than once at the large unfinished picture on the easel, from which the face of Shejeret ed-Durr peered out across the shoulder of the seated man, and several times had looked at the mummy set upright in its painted sarcophagus, no sense of the uncanny had touched me or in any way prepared me for the amazing manifestation which I was about to witness.

How long I had sat there I cannot say exactly; possibly for ten minutes or a quarter of an hour: when, suddenly, an eerie whisper crept through the stillness of the big room!

Since I had more than once been temporarily tricked into belief in the supernatural, by means of certain ingenious devices, I did not readily fall a victim to the mysterious nature of the present occurrence.

Yet I must confess that my heart gave a great leap and I was forced to exert all my will to control my nerves. I sat quite still, listening intently for a repetition of that evil whisper. Then, in the stillness, it came again.

"Felix," it breathed, "because of you I lie dead in a grave in the desert.... I died for you, Felix, and now I am so lonely...."

The whispering voice offered no clue to the age or the sex of the speaker; for a true whisper is toneless. But the words, as Bréton had declared, were uttered in broken French and spoken with a curious accent.

It ceased, that ghostly whispering; and I realized that my nerves could stand no more of it; for that it came or seemed to come from the mummy of the priestess was a fact as undeniable as it was horrible.

Resorting to action, I sprang up and leaped across the room, grasping first at the curtain draped in the window on the right of the sarcophagus. I jerked it fully aside. The recess was empty. All three lattices were open, on the right, left, and in the centre of the window; but, craning out from the latter, I saw the street below to be vacant from end to end.

Stepping back into the room, and metaphorically clutching my courage with both hands, I approached the sarcophagus, peered behind it, all around it, and, finally, into the swathed face of the mummy itself. Nothing rewarded my search. But the studio of Felix Bréton seemed to have become icily cold; at any rate I found myself to be shivering; and walking deliberately, although it cost me a monstrous effort to do so, I descended the dark winding stairway into the courtyard, and, on regaining the street, discovered to my intense annoyance that my brow was wet with cold perspiration.

I had taken no more than ten paces in the direction of the Sûk es-Sûdan when I heard the sound of approaching footsteps, and for some reason (I can only suppose as a result of my highly strung condition) I stepped into the shelter of a narrow gateway, where I could see without being seen, and there awaited the appearance of the one who approached.

It was Felix Bréton, his face showing ghastly in the moonlight as he turned the corner. I could not be certain if a mere echo had deceived me, but I thought I could detect faintly the softer footfalls of someone who was following him. From my cover I had an uninterrupted view of the entrance to the house which I had just left; and without showing myself I watched Bréton approach the door. At its threshold he seemed to hesitate; and in that brief hesitancy were illustrated the conflicting emotions driving the man. I recalled the words he had spoken to me that morning. "I must go back, Kernaby; it seems like desertion, base and cowardly." He opened the door and disappeared.

As he did so, a second figure crossed from the shadows on the opposite side of the street—that is, the side upon which I was concealed; and in turn advanced towards the door. As he passed my hiding-place I acted. Without an instant's hesitation I hurled myself upon him.

How he avoided that furious attack—if he did avoid it—or whether in the darkness I miscalculated my spring, I do not know to this day: I only know that I missed my objective, stumbled, recovered myself ... and turned with clenched fists to find *Abû Tabâh* confronting me!

"Kernaby Pasha!" he cried.

"Abû Tabâh!" said I dazedly.

"I perceive that I am not alone in my anxiety for the welfare of M. Felix Bréton."

"But why were you following him? I narrowly missed assaulting you."

"Very narrowly," he agreed in his gentle manner; "but you ask me why I was following M. Bréton. I was following him because I have seen so many of those who have crossed the path of the Black *Darwîshes* meet with violent and inexplicable deaths."

"Murder?" I whispered.

"Not murder—suicide. Therefore, observing, as I had anticipated, a strangeness in your friend's behavior, I have watched him."

"The strangeness of his behavior is easily accounted for," I said. And excitedly, for the horror of the episode in the studio was still strongly upon me, I told him of the whispering mummy.

"These are very dreadful things of which you speak, Kernaby Pasha," he admitted, "but I warned you that it was ill to incur the enmity of the Black *Darwîshes*. That there is a scheme afoot to compass the self-destruction or insanity of your friend is now evident to me; and he has brought this calamity upon himself; for the words which he believed to be spoken by the spirit of the girl Yâsmîna would not have affected him so unpleasantly if his attitude towards her had been marked by proper restraint and the affair confined within suitable limitations."

"Quite so. But although the Black *Darwîshes* may be both malignant and clever, that uncanny whispering is beyond the control of natural forces."

"Such is not my opinion," replied Abû Tabâh. "A spirit does not mistake one person for another; and the whispering voice addressed itself to 'Felix' when Felix was not present. I believe, Kernaby Pasha, that you are the possessor of a pair of excellent opera-glasses? May I suggest that you return to Shepheard's and procure them."

V

The platform of the minaret seemed very cold to the touch of my stockinged feet; for I had left my shoes at the entrance to the mosque below in accordance with custom; and now, from the wooden balcony, I overlooked the neighboring roofs of Cairo, and Abû Tabâh, beside me, pointed to where a vague patch of light broke the darkness beneath us to the left.

"The window of M. Felix Bréton's studio," he said.

Raising the glasses to his eyes, he gazed in that direction, whilst I also peered thither and succeeded in making out the well of the courtyard and the roofs of the buildings to right and left of it. It was not evident to me for what Abû Tabâh was looking, and when presently he lowered the glasses and turned to me I expressed my doubts in words.

"It is surely evident," I said, speaking, as I now almost invariably did to the *imám*, in English, of which he had a perfect mastery, "that we have little chance of discovering anything from here, since nothing was visible from the studio window. Furthermore, who save Yâsmîna could have spoken in the manner which I have related and in broken French?"

"An eavesdropper," he replied, "might have profited by the lessons which Yâsmîna received from M. Bréton; and all vocal characteristics are lost in a whisper. In the second place, Yâsmîna is not dead."

"What!" I cried.

Although, when Bréton had informed me of her death, I myself had doubted him, for some reason the ghostly whisper had convinced me as it had convinced him.

"She has been kept a prisoner during the past week in a house belonging to one of the Black *Darwîshes*," continued Abû Tabâh; "but my agents succeeded in tracing her this morning. By my orders, however, she has not been allowed to return to her home."

"And what was the object of those orders?"

"That I might learn for what purpose she had been made to disappear," replied Abû Tabâh; "and I have learned it to-night."

"Then you think that the whispering mummy——"

He suddenly clutched my arm.

"Quick! raise your glasses!" he said softly. "On the roof of the house to the left of the light. There is the whispering mummy!"

Strung up to a high pitch of excitement, I gazed through the glasses in the direction indicated by my companion. Without difficulty I discerned him—a man wearing a black turban—who crept like some ungainly cat along the flat roof, carrying in his hand what looked like one of those sugar canes which pass for a delicacy among the natives, but which to European eyes appear more suitable for curtain-poles than sweetmeats. Springing perilously across a yawning gulf, the wearer of the black turban gained the roof of the studio, crept along for some little distance further, and then, lying prone, began slowly to lower the bamboo rod in the direction of the lighted window.

I found that unconsciously I had suspended my respiration, and now, breathlessly, as the truth came home to me—

"It is a speaking-tube!" I cried, "I cannot see the end of it, but no doubt it is curved so as to protrude through the side of the lattice window. Do you look, Abû Tabâh: *I* propose to act."

Thrusting the glasses into the *imám's* hand, I took my Colt repeater from my pocket, and, having peered for some seconds steadily in the direction of the dimly visible *Darwîsh*, I opened fire! I had fired five shots in the heat of my anger at that sinister crouching figure, ere Abû Tabâh seized my wrist.

"Stop!" he cried; "do you forget where you stand?"

Truly I had forgotten in my indignation, or I should not have outraged his feelings by firing from the minaret of a mosque. But sufficient of my wrath remained to occasion me a thrill of satisfaction, when, peering through the dusk, I saw the *Darwîsh* throw up his arms and disappear from view.

"There is blood in the courtyard," said Abû Tabâh; "but Ahmad es-Kebîr has fled. Therefore he still lives, and his anger will be not the less but the greater. Depart from Cairo, M. Bréton: it is my counsel to you."

"But," cried Felix Bréton, glaring wildly at the big canvas on the easel, "I must finish my picture. As Yâsmîna is alive, she must return, and I must finish my picture!"

"Yâsmîna cannot return," replied Abû Tabâh, fixing his weird eyes upon the speaker. "I have caused her to be banished from Cairo." He raised his hand, checking Bréton's hot words ere they were uttered. "Recriminations are unavailing. Her presence disturbs the peace of the city, and the peace of the city it is my duty to maintain."

PART II
OTHER TALES

I
LORD OF THE JACKALS

In those days, of course (said the French agent, looking out across the sea of Yûssuf Effendis which billowed up against the balcony to where, in the moonlight, the minarets of Cairo pointed the way to God), I did not occupy the position which I occupy to-day. No, I was younger, and more ambitious; I thought to carve in the annals of Egypt a name for myself such as that of De Lesseps.

I had a scheme—and there were those who believed in it—for extending the borders of Egypt. Ah! my friends, Egypt after all is but a double belt of mud following the Nile, and terminated east and west by the desert. The desert! It was the dream of my life to exterminate that desert, that hungry gray desert; it was my plan—a foolish plan as I know now—to link the fertile Fáyûm to the Oases! How was this to be done? Ah!

Why should I dig up those buried skeletons? It was not done; it never could be done; therefore, let me not bore you with how I had proposed to do it. Suffice it that my ambitions took me far off the beaten tracks, far, even, from the caravan roads—far into the gray heart of the desert.

But I was ambitious, and only nineteen—or scarcely twenty. At nineteen, a man who comes from St. Rémy fears no obstacle which Fate can place in his way, and looks upon the world as a grape-fruit to be sweetened with endeavor and sucked empty.

It was in those days, then, that I learned as your Rudyard Kipling has also learned that "East is East"; it was in those days that I came face to face with that "mystery of Egypt" about which so much is written, has always been written, and always will be written, but concerning which so few people, so very few people, know anything whatever.

Yes, I, René de Flassans, saw with my own eyes a thing that I knew to be magic, a thing whereat my reason rebelled—a thing which my poor European intelligence could not grapple, could not begin to explain.

It was this which you asked me to tell you, was it not? I will do so with pleasure, because I know that I speak to men of honor, and because it is good for me, now that I cannot count the gray hairs in my beard, to confess how poor a thing I was when I could count every hair upon my chin—and how grand a thing I thought myself.

One evening, at the end of a dreadful day in the saddle—beneath a sky which seemed to reflect all the fires of hell, a day passed upon sands simply smoking in that merciless sun—I and my native companions came to an encampment of Arabs.

They were Bedouins* the tribe does not matter at the moment—and, as you may know, the Bedouin is the most hospitable creature whom God has yet created. The tent of the Sheikh is open to any traveller who cares to rest his weary limbs therein. Freely he may partake of all that the tribe has to offer, food and drink and entertainment; and to seek to press payment upon the host would be to insult a gentleman.

That is desert hospitality. A spear that stands thrust upright in the sand before the tent door signifies that whosoever would raise his hand against the guest has first to reckon with the Sheikh. Equally it would be an insult to erect one's own tent in the neighborhood of a Bedouin encampment.

Well, my friends, I knew this well, for I was no stranger to the nomadic life, and accordingly, without fear of the fierce-eyed throng who came forth to meet us, I made my respects to the Sheikh Saïd Mohammed, and was reckoned by him as a friend and a brother. His tent was placed at my disposal and provisions were made for the suitable entertainment of those who were with me.

You know how dusk falls in Egypt? At one moment the sky is a brilliant canvas, glorious with every color known to art, at the next the curtain—the wonderful veil of deepest violet—has fallen; the stars break through it like diamonds through the finest gauze; it is night, velvet, violet night. You see it here in this noisy modern Cairo. In the lonely desert it is ten thousand times grander, ten thousand times more impressive; it speaks to the soul with the voice of the silence. Ah, those desert nights!

So was the night of which I speak; and having partaken of the fare which the Sheikh caused to be set before me—and Bedouin fare is not for the squeamish stomach—I sipped that delicious coffee which, though an acquired taste, is the true nectar, and looked out beyond the four or five palm trees of this little oasis to where the gray carpet of the desert grew black as ebony and met the violet sweep of the sky.

....

* This incorrect but familiar spelling is retained throughout.

Perhaps I was the first to see him; I cannot say; but certainly he was not perceived by the Bedouins, although one stood on guard at the entrance to the camp.

How can I describe him? At the time, as he approached in the moonlight with a shambling, stooping gait, I felt that I had never seen his like before. Now I know the reason of my wonder, and the reason of my doubt. I know what it was about him which inspired a kind of horror and a revulsion—a dread.

Elfin locks he had, gray and matted, falling about his angular face, shading his strange, yellow eyes. His was dressed in rags, in tatters; he was furtive, and he staggered as one who is very weak, slowly approaching out of the vastness.

Then it appeared as though every dog in the camp knew of his coming. Out from the shadows of the tents they poured, those yapping mongrels. Never have I seen such a thing. In the midst of the yellowish, snarling things, at the very entrance to the camp, the wretched old man fell, uttering a low cry.

But now, snatching up a heavy club which lay close to my hand, I rushed out of the tent. Others were thronging out too, but, first of them all, I burst in among the dogs, striking, kicking, and shouting. I stooped and raised the head of the stranger.

Mutely he thanked me, with half-closed eyes. A choking sound issued from his throat, and he clutched with his hands and pointed to his mouth.

An earthenware jar, containing cool water, stood beside a tent but a few yards away. Hurling my club at the most furious of the dogs, which, with bared fangs, still threatened to attack the recumbent man, I ran and seized the *dorak*, regained his side, and poured water between his parched lips.

The throng about me was strangely silent, until, as the poor old man staggered again to his feet, supported by my arm, a chorus arose about me—one long, vowelled word, wholly unfamiliar, although my Arabic was good. But I noted that all kept a respectful distance from myself and the man whom I had succored.

Then, pressing his way through the throng came the Sheikh Saïd Mohammed. Saluting the ragged stranger with a sort of grim respect, he asked him if he desired entertainment for the night.

The other shook his head, mumbling, pointed to the water jar, and by dint of gnashing his yellow and pointed teeth, intimated that he required food.

Food was brought to him hurriedly. He tied it up in a dirty cloth, grasped the water jar, and, with never a glance at the Arabs, turned to me. With his hand he touched his brow, his lips, and his breast in salute; then, although tottering with weakness, he made off again with that queer, loping gait.

The camp dogs began to howl, and a strange silence fell upon the Arabs about me. All stood watching the departing figure until it was lost in a dip of the desert, when the watchers began to return again to their tents.

Saïd Mohammed took my hand, and in a few direct and impressive words thanked me for having spared him and his tribe from a grave dishonor. Need I say that I was flattered? Had you met him, my friends, that fine Bedouin gentleman, polished as any noble of old France, fearless as a lion, yet gentle as a woman, you would know that I rejoiced in being able to serve him even so slightly.

Two of the dogs, unperceived by us, had followed the weird old man from the camp; for suddenly in the distance I heard their savage growls. Then, these growls were drowned in such a chorus of howling—the howling of jackals—as I had never before heard in all my desert wanderings. The howling suddenly subsided ... but the dogs did not return.

I glanced around, meaning to address the Sheikh, but the Sheikh was gone.

Filled with wonder, then, respecting this singular incident, I entered the tent—it was at the farther end of the camp—which had been placed at my disposal, and lay down, rather to reflect than to sleep. With my mind confused in thoughts of yellow-eyed wanderers, of dogs, and of jackals, sleep came.

How long I slept I cannot say; but I was awakened as the cool fingers of dawn were touching the crests of the sand billows. A gray and dismal light filled the tent, and something was scratching at the flap.

I sat up immediately, quite wide awake, and taking my revolver, ran to the entrance and looked out.

A slinking shape melted into the shadows of the tent adjoining mine, and I concluded that a camp dog had aroused me. Then, in the early morning silence, I heard a faint call, and peering through the gloom to the east saw, in black silhouette, a solitary figure standing near the extremity of the camp.

In those days, my friends, I was a brave fellow—we are all brave at nineteen—and throwing a cloak over my shoulders I strode intrepidly towards this figure. I was within ten paces when a hand was raised to beckon me.

It was the mysterious stranger! Again he beckoned to me, and I approached yet nearer, asking him if it was he who had aroused me.

He nodded, and by means of a grotesque kind of pantomime ultimately made me understand that he had caused me to be aroused in order to communicate something to me. He turned, and indicated that we were to walk away from the camp. I accompanied him without hesitation.

Although the camp was never left unguarded, no one had challenged us; and, a hundred yards beyond the outermost tent, this strange old man stopped and turned to me.

First, he pointed back to the camp, then to myself, then out along the caravan road towards the Nile.

"Do you mean," I asked him—for I perceived that he was dumb or vowed to silence—"that I am to leave the camp?"

He nodded rapidly, his strange yellow eyes gleaming.

"Immediately?" I demanded.

Again he nodded.

"Why?"

Pantomimically he made me understand that death threatened me if I remained—that I must leave the Bedouins before sunrise.

I cannot convey to you any idea of the mad earnestness of the man. But, alas! youth regards the counsels of age with nothing but contempt; moreover, I thought this man mad, and I was unable to choke down a sort of loathing which he inspired in me.

I shook my head then, but not unkindly; and, waving my hand, prepared to leave him. At that, with a sorrow in his strange eyes which did not fail to impress me, he saluted me with gravity, turned, and passed out of sight.

Although I did not know it at the time, I had chosen of two paths the one that led through fire.

I slept little after this interview—if it was a real interview and not a dream—and feeling tired and unrefreshed, I saw the sun rise purple and angry over the distant hills.

You know what *khamsîn* is like, my friends? But you cannot know what *simoom* is like—*simoom* in the heart of the desert! It came that morning—a wall of sand so high as to shut out the sunlight, so dense as to turn the day into night, so suffocating that I thought I should never live through it!

It was apparent to me that the Bedouins were prepared for the storm. The horses, the camels and the asses were tethered in an enclosure specially strengthened to exclude the choking dust, and with their cloaks about their heads the men prepared for the oncoming of this terror of the desert.

My God! it was a demon which sought to blind me, to suffocate me, and which clutched at my throat with strangling fingers of sand! This,

I told myself, was the danger which I might have avoided by quitting the camp before sunrise.

Indeed, it was apparent to me that if I had taken the advice so strangely offered, I might now have been safe in the village of the Great Oasis for which I was bound. But I have since seen that the *simoom* was a minor danger, and not the real one to which this weird being had referred.

The storm passed, and every man in the encampment praised the merciful God who had spared us all. It was in the disturbance attendant upon putting the camp in order once more that I saw her.

She came out from the tent of Saïd Mohammed, to shake the sand from a carpet; the newly come sunlight twinkled upon the bracelets which clasped her smooth brown arms as she shook the gaily colored mat at the tent door. The sunlight shone upon her braided hair, upon her slight robe, upon her silver anklets, and upon her tiny feet. Transfixed I stood watching—indeed, my friends, almost holding my breath. Then the sunlight shone upon her eyes, two pools of mysterious darkness into which I found myself suddenly looking.

The face of this lovely Arab maiden flushed, and drawing the corner of her robe across those bewitching eyes, she turned and ran back into the tent.

One glance—just one glance, my friends! But never had Ulysses' bow propelled an arrow more sure, more deadly. I was nineteen, remember, and of Provence. What do you foresee! You who have been through the world, you who once were nineteen.

I feigned a sickness, a sickness brought about by the sandstorm, and taking base advantage of that desert hospitality which is unbounded, which knows no suspicion, and takes no count of cost, I remained in the tent which had been vacated for me.

In this voluntary confinement I learned little of the doings of the camp. All day I lay dreaming of two dark eyes, and at night when the jackals howled I thought of the wanderer who had counseled me to leave. One day, I lay so; a second; a third again; and the women of Saïd Mohammed's household tended me, closely veiled of course. But in vain I waited for that attendant whose absence was rendering my feigned fever a real one—whose eyes burned like torches in my dreams and for the coming of whose little bare feet across the sand to my tent door I listened hour by hour, day by day, in vain—always in vain.

But at nineteen there is no such thing as despair, and hope has strength to defy death itself. It was in the violet dusk of the fourth day, as I lay there with a sort of shame of my deception struggling for birth in my heart, that she came.

She came through the tent door bearing a bowl of soup, and the rays of the setting sun outlined her fairy shape through the gossamer robe as she entered.

At that my poor weak little conscience troubled me no more. How my heart leaped, leaped so that it threatened to choke me, who had come safe through a great sandstorm.

There is fire in the Southern blood at nineteen, my friends, which leaps into flame beneath the glances of bright eyes.

With her face modestly veiled, the Bedouin maid knelt beside me, placing the wooden bowl upon the ground. My eager gaze pierced the *yashmak*, but her black lashes were laid upon her cheek, her glorious eyes averted. My heart—or was it my vanity?—told me that she regarded me at least with interest, that she was not at ease in my company; and as, having spoken no word, having ventured no glance, she rose again to depart, I was emboldened to touch her hand.

Like a startled gazelle she gave me one rapid glance, and was gone!

She was gone—and my very soul gone with her! For hours I lay, not so much as thinking of the food beside me—dreaming of her eyes. What were my plans? Faith! Does one have plans at nineteen where two bright eyes are concerned?

Alas, my friends, I dare not tell you of my hopes, yet upon those hopes I lived. Oh, it is glorious to be nineteen and of Provence; it is glorious when all the world is young, when the fruit is ripe upon the trees and the plucking seems no sin. Yet, as we look back, we perceive that at nineteen we were scoundrels.

The Bedouin girl is a woman when a European woman is but a child, and Sakîna, whose eyes could search a man's soul, was but twelve years of age—twelve! Can you picture that child of twelve squeezing a lover's heart between her tiny hands, entwining his imagination in the coils of her hair?

You, my friend, may perhaps be able to conceive this thing, for you know the East, and the women of the East. At ten or eleven years of age many of them are adorable; at twenty-one most of them are *passé*; at twenty-six all of them—with rare exceptions—are shrieking hags.

But to you, my other friends, who are strangers to our Oriental ways, who know not that the peach only attains to perfect ripeness for one short hour, it may be strange, it may be horrifying, that I loved, with all the ardor which was mine, this little Arab maiden, who, had she been born in France, would not yet have escaped from the nursery. But I digress.

The Arabs were encamped, of course, in the neighborhood of a spring. It lay in a slight depression amid the tiny palm-grove. Here, at sunset, came the women with their pitchers on their heads, graceful of carriage, veiled, mysterious.

Many peaches have ripened and have rotted since those days of which I speak, but now—even now—I am still enslaved by the mystery of Egypt's veiled women. Untidy, bedraggled, dirty, she may be, but the real Egyptian woman when she bears her pitcher upon her head and glides, stately, sinuously, through the dusk to the well, is a figure to enchain the imagination.

Very soon, then, the barrier of reserve which, like the screen of the *harêm*, stands between Eastern women and love, was broken. My trivial scruples I had cast to the winds, and feigning weakness, I would sally forth to take the air in the cool of the evening; this two days later.

My steps, be assured, led me to the spring; and you who are men of the world will know that Sakîna, braving the reproaches of the Sheikh's household, neglectful of her duties, was last of all the women who came to the well for water.

I taught her to say my name—René! How sweet it sounded from her lips, as she strove in vain to roll the 'R' in our Provençal fashion. Some *ginnee* most certainly presided over this enchanted fountain, for despite the nearness of the camp our rendezvous was never discovered, our meetings were never detected.

With her pitcher upon the ground beside her, she would sit with those wistful, wonderful eyes upraised to mine, and sway before the ardor of my impassioned words as a young and tender reed sways in the Nile breeze. Her budding soul was a love lute upon which I played in ecstasy; and when she raised her red lips to mine…. Ah! those nights in the boundless desert! God is good to youth, and harsh to old age!

Next to Saïd Mohammed, her father, Sakîna's brother was the finest horseman of the tribe, and his white mare their fleetest steed. I had cast covetous eyes upon this glorious creature, my friends, and secretly had made such overtures as were calculated to win her confidence.

Within two weeks, then, my plans were complete—up to a point. Since they were doomed to failure, like my great scheme, I shall not trouble you with their details, but an hour before dawn on a certain night I cut the camel-hair tethering of the white mare, and, undetected, led the beautiful creature over the silent sands to a cup-like depression, a thousand yards distant from the camp.

The Bedouin who was upon guard that night had with him a gourd of *'erksoos*. This was customary, and I had chosen an occasion when the duty of filling the sentinel's gourd had fallen upon Sakîna; to his *'erksoos* I had added four drops of dark brown fluid from my medicine chest.

It was an hour before dawn, then, when I stood beside the white mare, watching and listening; it was an hour before dawn when she for whom my great scheme was forgotten, for whom I was about to risk the anger, the just anger, of men amongst the most fierce in the known world, came running fleetly over the hillocks down into the little valley, and threw herself into my arms....

When dawn burst in gloomy splendor over the desert, we were still five hours' ride from the spot where I had proposed temporarily to conceal myself, with perhaps an hour's start of the Arabs. I knew the desert ways well enough, but the ghostly and desolate place in which I now found myself nevertheless filled me with foreboding.

A seam of black volcanic rock split the sands for a great distance, forming a kind of natural wall of forbidding aspect. In places this wall was pierced by tunnel-like openings; I think they may have been prehistoric tombs. There was no scrap of verdure visible, north, south, east or west; only desolation, sand, grayness, and this place, ghostly and wan with that ancient sorrow, that odor of remote mortality which is called "the dust of Egypt."

Seated before me in the saddle, Sakîna looked up into my face with a never-changing confidence, having her little brown fingers interlocked about my neck. But her strength was failing. A short rest was imperative.

Thus far I had detected no evidence of pursuit and, descending from the saddle, I placed my weary companion upon a rock over which I had laid a rug, and poured out for her a draught of cool water.

Bread and dates were our breakfast fare; but bread and dates and water are nectar and ambrosia when they are sweetened with kisses. Oh! the glorious madness of youth! Sometimes, my friends, I am almost tempted to believe that the man who has never been wicked has never been happy!

Picture us, then, if you can, set amid that desolation, which for us was a rose-garden, eating of that unpalatable food—which for us was the food of the gods!

So we remained awhile, deliriously happy, though death might terminate our joys ere we again saw the sun, when something ... *something* spoke to me....

Understand me, I did not say that *someone* spoke, I did not say that anything *audible* spoke. But I know that, unlocking those velvet arms which clung to me, I stood up slowly—and, still slowly, turned and looked back at the frowning black rocks.

Merciful God! My heart beats wildly now when I recall that moment.

Motionless as a statue, but in a crouching attitude, as if about to leap down, he who had warned me so truly stood upon the highest point of the rocks watching us!

How long did I remain thus?

I cannot pretend to say; but when I turned to Sakîna—she lay trembling on the ground, with her face hidden in her hands.

Then, down over the piled-up rocks, this mysterious and ominous being came leaping. Old man though he was, he descended with the agility of a mountain goat—and sometimes, in the difficult places, *he went on all fours.*

Crossing the intervening strip of sand, he stood before me. You have seen the reproach in the eyes of a faithful dog whose master has struck him unjustly? Such a reproach shone out from the yellow eyes of this desert wanderer. I cannot account for it; I can say no more....

It was impossible for me to speak; I trembled violently; such a fear and such a madness of sorrow possessed me that I would have welcomed any death—to have freed me from that intolerable reproach.

He suddenly pointed towards the horizon where against the curtain of the dawn black figures appeared.

I fell upon my knees beside Sakîna. I was a poor, pitiable thing; the madness of my passion had left me, and already I was within the great Shadow; I could not even weep; I knew that I had brought Sakîna out into that desolate place—to die.

And now the man whose ways were unlike human ways began to babble insanely, gesticulating and plucking at me. I cannot hope to make you feel one little part of the emotion with which those instants were laden. Sakîna clung to me trembling in a way I can never forget— never, never forget. And the look in her eyes! even now I cannot bear to think of it, I cannot bear——

Those almost colorless lizards which dart about in the desert places with incredible swiftness were now coming forth from their nests; and all the while the black figures, unheard as yet, were approaching along the path of the sun.

My mad folly grew more apparent to me every moment. I realized that this which so rapidly was overtaking me had been inevitable from the first. The strange wild man stood watching me with that intolerable glare, so that my trembling companion shrank from him in horror.

But evidently he was seeking to convey some idea to me. He gesticulated constantly, pointing to the approaching Arabs and then over his shoulder to the frowning rock behind. Since it was too late for flight—for I knew that the white mare with a double burden could never outpace our pursuers—it occurred to me at the moment when the muffled beat of hoofs first became audible, that this hermit of the rocks was endeavoring to induce me to seek some hiding-place with which no doubt he was acquainted.

How I cursed the delay which had enabled the Arabs to come up with us! I know, now, of course, that even had I not delayed, our ultimate capture was certain. But at the moment, in my despair, I thought otherwise.

And now I cursed the stupidity which had prevented me from following this weird guide; I even thought wrathfully of the poor frightened child, whose weakness had necessitated the delay and whose fears had contributed considerably to this later misunderstanding.

The pursuing party, numbering four, and led by Saïd Mohammed, was no more than five hundred yards away when I came to my senses. The hermit now was tugging at my arm with frightful insistence; his eyes were glaring insanely, and he chattered in an almost pitiable manner.

"Quick!" I cried, throwing my arm about Sakîna, "up to the rocks. This man can hide us!"

"No, no!" she whispered, "I dare not——"

But I lifted her, and signing to the singular being to lead the way, staggered forward despairingly.

The distance was greater than it appeared, the climb incredibly difficult. My guide held out his hand to me to assist me to mount the slippery rocks; but I had much ado to proceed and also to support Sakîna.

Her terror of the man and of the place to which he was leading us momentarily increased. Indeed, it seemed that she was becoming mad with fear. When the man paused before an opening in the rocks not more than fifteen or sixteen inches in height, and wildly waving his arms in the air, his elfin locks flying about his shoulder, his eyes glassy, intimated that we were to crawl in—Sakîna writhed free of my grasp and bounded back some three or four paces down the slope.

"Not in there!" she cried, holding out her little hands to me pitifully. "I dare not! He would devour us!"

At the foot of the slope, Saïd Mohammed, who had dismounted from his horse, and who, far ahead of the others, was advancing towards us, at that moment raised his gun and fired....

Can I go on?

It is more years ago than I care to count, but it is fresher in my mind than the things of yesterday. A lonely old age is before me, my friends— for I have been a solitary man since that shot was fired. For me it changed the face of the world, for me it ended youth, revealing me to myself for what I was.

Something more nearly resembling human speech than any sound he had yet uttered burst from the lips of the wild man as the report of Saïd Mohammed's shot whispered in echoes through the mysterious labyrinths beneath us.

Fate had stood at the Sheikh's elbow as he pulled the trigger.

With a little soft cry—I hear it now, gentle, but having in it a world of agony—Sakîna sank at my feet ... and her blood began to trickle over the black rocks on which she lay.

The man who professes to describe to you his emotions at such a frightful moment is an impostor. The world grew black before my eyes; every emotion of which my being was capable became paralysed.

I heard nothing, I saw nothing but the little huddled figure, that red stream upon the black rock, and the agonized love in the blazing eyes of Sakîna. Groaning, I threw myself down beside her, and as she sighed out her life upon my breast, I knew—God help me—that what had been but a youthful amour, was now a life's tragedy; that for me the light of the world had gone out, that I should never again know the warmth of the sun and the gladness of the morning....

The cave man, with a dog-like fidelity, sought now to drag me from my dead love, to drag me into that gloomy lair which she had shrunk from entering. His incoherent mutterings broke in upon my semi-coma; but I shook him off, I shrieked curses at him....

Now the Bedouins were mounting the slope, not less than a hundred yards below me. In the growing light I could see the face of Saïd Mohammed....

The man beside me exerted all his strength to drag me back into the gallery or cave—I know not what it was; but with my arms locked about Sakîna I lay watching the pursuers coming closer and closer.

Then, those persistent efforts suddenly ceased, and dully I told myself that this weird being, having done his best to save me, had fled in order to save himself.

I was wrong.

You have asked me for a story of the magic of Egypt, and although, as you see, it has cost me tears—oh! I am not ashamed of those tears, my friends!—I have recounted this story to you. You say, where is the magic? and I might reply: the magic was in the changing of my false love to a true. But there was another magic as well, and it grew up around me now at this moment when I lay inert, waiting for death.

From behind me, from above me, arose a cry—a cry. You may have heard of the Bedouin song, the 'Mizmûne':

> "Ya men melek ana dêri waat sa jebb,
> Id el' ish hoos' a beb hatsa azât ta lebb."

You may have heard how when it is sung in a certain fashion, flowers drop from their stalks? Also, you may have doubted this, never having heard a magical cry.

I do not doubt it, my friends! For I *have* heard a magical cry—this cry which arose from behind me! It started some chord in my dulled consciousness which had never spoken before. I turned my head—and there upon the highest point of the rocks stood the cave man. He suddenly stretched forth his hands.

Again he uttered that uncanny, that indescribable cry. It was not human. It was not animal. Yet it was nearer to the cry of an animal than to any sound made by the human species. His eyes gleamed with an awful light, his spare body had assumed a strange significance; he was transfigured.

A third time he uttered the cry, and out from one of those openings in the rock which I have mentioned, crept a jackal. You know how a jackal avoids the day, how furtive, how nocturnal a creature it is? but there in the golden glory which proclaimed the coming of the sun, black silhouettes moved.

A great wonder possessed me, as the first jackal was followed by a second, by a third, by a fourth, by a fifth. Did I say a fifth?... By five hundred—by five thousand!

From every visible hole in the rocks, jackals poured forth in packs. Wonder left me, fear left me; I forgot my sorrow, I became a numbed intelligence amid a desert of jackals. Over a sea of moving furry backs, I saw that upstanding crag and the weird crouching figure upon it. Right and left, above and below, jackals moved ... and all turned their heads towards the approaching Bedouins!

Again—again I heard that dreadful cry. The jackals, in a pack, thousands strong, began to advance upon the Bedouins!...

Not east or west, north or south, could you hope to find a braver man than was the Sheikh Saïd Mohammed; but—he fled!

I saw the four horsemen riding like furies into the morning sun. The white mare, riderless, galloped with them—and the desert behind was yellow with jackals! For the last time I heard the cry.

The jackals began to return!

Forgive me, dear friends, if I seem an emotional fool. But when I recovered from the swoon which blotted out that unnatural spectacle, the wizard—for now I knew him for nothing less—had dug a deep trench—and had left me, alone.

Not a jackal was in sight; the sun blazed cruelly upon the desert. With my own hands I laid my love to rest in the sands. No cross, no crescent marks her resting-place; but I left my youth upon her grave, as a last offering.

You may say that, since I had sinned so grievously, since I had betrayed the noble confidence of Saïd Mohammed, my host, I escaped lightly.

Ah! you do not know!

And what of the strange being whose gratitude I had done so little to merit but yet which knew no bounds? It is of him that I will tell you.

Years later—how many it does not matter, but I was a man with no illusions—my restless wanderings (I being still a desert bird-of-passage) brought me one night to a certain well but rarely visited. It lay in a depression, like another well that I am fated often to see in my dreams, and, as one approached, the crowns of the palm trees which grew there appeared above the mounds of sand.

I was alone and tired out; the next possible camping-place—for I had no water—was many miles away. Yet it was written that I should press on to that other distant well, weary though I was.

First, then, as I came up, I perceived numbers of vultures in the air; and I began to fear that someone near to his end lay at the well. But when, from the top of a mound, I obtained a closer view, I saw a sight that, after one quick glance, caused me to spur up my tired horse and to fly—fly, with panic in my heart.

The brilliant moon bathed the hollow in light and cast dense shadows of the palm stems upon the slope beyond. By the spring, his fallen face ghastly in the moonlight, in a clear space twenty feet across, lay a dead man.

Even from where I sat I knew him; but, had I doubted, other evidence was there of his identity. As I mounted the slope, thousands of fiery eyes were turned upon me.

God! that arena all about was alive with jackals—jackals, my friends, eaters of carrion—which, silent, watchful, guarded the wizard dead, who, living, had been their lord!

II

LURE OF SOULS

I

This is the story which Bernard Fane told me one afternoon as we sat sipping China tea in the Heliopolis Palace Hotel, following a round upon the neighboring links.

The life of a master at the training college (said Fane) is beastly uneventful, taken all around; not even *your* keen sense of the romantic could long survive it. The duties are not very exacting, certainly, and in our own way I suppose we are Empire builders of a sort; but when you ask me for a true story of Egyptian life, I find myself floored at once.

We all come out with the idea of the mystic East strong upon us, but it is an idea that rarely survives one summer in Cairo. Personally, I made a more promising start than the average; an adventure came my way on the very day I landed in Port Said, in fact it began on the way out. But alas! it was not only the first, but the last adventure which Egypt has offered me.

I have not related the story more than five hundred times, so that you will excuse me if I foozle it in places. I will leave you to do the polishing.

On my first trip out, then, I joined the ship at Marseilles, and saw my cabin trunk placed in a nice deck berth, with the liveliest satisfaction. Walking along the white promenade deck, I felt no end of a man of the world. Every Anglo-Indian that I met seemed a figure from the pages of Kipling, and when I accidentally blundered into the *ayahs'* quarters, I could almost hear the jangle of the temple bells, so primed was I with traditions of the Orient—the traditions one gathers from books of the lighter sort, I mean.

You will see that in those days I was not a bit *blasé*; the glamour of the East was very real to me. For that matter, it is more real than ever, now; Near or Far, the East has a call which, once heard, can never be forgotten, and never be unheeded. But the call it makes to those who have never been there is out of tune, I have learned; or rather, it is not in the right key.

Well, I had a most glorious bath—I am sybarite enough to love the luxuriance of your modern liner—got into blue serge, and felt no end of an adventurer. There was a notice on the gangway that the steamer would not leave Marseilles until ten o'clock at night, but I was far too young a traveller to risk missing the boat by going ashore again. You know the feeling? Consequently I took my place in the saloon for dinner, and vaguely wondered why nobody else had dressed for the function. I was a proper Johnny Raw, no end of a Johnny Raw, but I enjoyed it all immensely, nevertheless. I personally superintended the departure of the ship, and believed that every deck-hand took me for a hardened globe-trotter; and when at last I sought my cosy cabin, all spotlessly white, with my trunk tucked under the bunk, and, drawing the little red curtain, I sat down to sum up the sensations of the day, I was thoroughly satisfied with it all.

Gad! novelty is the keynote of life, don't you think? When one is young, one envies older and more experienced men, but what has the world left of novelty to offer them? The simple matter of joining a steamboat, and taking possession of my berth, had afforded me thrills which some of my fellow-passengers—those whom I envied the most for the stories of life written upon their tanned features—could only hope to taste by means of big-game hunting, now, or other far-fetched methods of thrill-giving.

It wore off a bit the next day, of course, and I found that once one has settled down to it, ocean traveling is merely floating hotel life. But many of my fellow-passengers (the boat was fairly full) still appealed to me as books of romance which I longed to open. And before the end of that second day, I became possessed of the idea that there was some deep mystery aboard. Since this was my first voyage, something of that sort was to be expected of me; but it happened that I stood by no means alone in this belief.

In the smoking-room, after dinner, I got into conversation with a chap of about my own age who was bound for Colombo—tea-planting. We chatted on different topics for half an hour, and discovered that we had mutual friends, or rather, the other fellow discovered it.

"Have you noticed," he said, "a distinguished-looking Indian personage, who, with three native friends, sits at the small corner table on our left?"

Hamilton—that was my acquaintance's name—was my right-hand neighbor at the chief officer's table, and I recollected the group to which he referred immediately.

"Yes," I replied; "who are they?"

"I don't know," answered Hamilton, "but I have a suspicion that they are mysterious."

"Mysterious?"

"Well, they joined at Marseilles, just before yourself. They were received by the skipper in person, and two of them were closeted in his cabin for twenty minutes or more."

"What do you make of that?"

"Can't make anything of it, but their whole behavior strikes me as peculiar, somehow. I cannot quite explain myself, but you say that you have noticed something of the sort, yourself?"

"They certainly keep very much to themselves," I said. Hamilton glanced at me quickly.

"Naturally," he replied.

Not desiring to appear stupid, I did not ask him to elucidate this remark, although at the time it meant nothing to me. Of course I have learned since, as everyone learns whose lines are cast among Orientals, that iron barriers divide the races. But at the time I knew nothing of this—as will shortly appear.

During breakfast on the following morning, I glanced several times at the mysterious quartette. They had been placed at a separate table and were served with different courses from the rest of the passengers. I was not the only member of the company who found them interesting, but the Anglo-Indians on board, to a man, left the native party severely alone. You know the icy aloofness of the Anglo-Indians?

My second day at sea wore on, uneventfully enough; the bugle had already announced the hour for dressing, and the boat-deck outside my berth, where I had had my chair placed, was practically deserted, when something occurred to turn my thoughts from the four Indians. It was a glorious evening, with the sun setting out across the Mediterranean in such a red blaze of glory that I sat watching it fascinatedly, my book lying unheeded on the deck beside me. Right and left of me men occupying the other deck cabins had lighted up, and were busily dressing. Right aft was a corner cabin, larger than the others, and suddenly I observed the door of this to open.

A slim figure glided out on to the deck, and began to advance toward me. It proved to be that of a woman or girl dressed in clinging black silk, and wearing a *yashmak*! She had a richly embroidered shawl thrown over her head and shoulders, and in that coy half-light she presented a dazzlingly beautiful picture.

It was my first sight of a *yashmak*, and, because it was worn by a marvelously pretty woman, the thousands seen since have never entirely lost their charm for me. I could detect the lines of an exquisitely chiseled nose, and the long dark eyes of the apparition were entirely unforgettable. The hand with which she held her shawl about her was of ivory smoothness, and, like a little red lamp, a great ruby blazed upon the index finger.

With her high-heeled shoes tapping daintily upon the deck she advanced; then, suddenly perceiving that the promenade was not entirely deserted, she turned, but not hastily or rudely, and glided back to her cabin.

I have endeavored to outline for your benefit the state of my mind at this period, hinting how keenly alive I was to romance of any sort, provided it wore the guise of the Orient; so that it will be unnecessary for me to explain how strong an impression this episode made upon me. The Indian party was forgotten, and as I hastily dressed and descended to dinner, I scarcely listened to Hamilton when he bent toward me and whispered something about the "Strong Room."

My gaze was roaming about the spacious saloon. Even in those days I might have known better; I might have known that no Mohammedan woman would take her meals in a public saloon. But I was too dazzled by my memories to summon to my aid such fragments of knowledge respecting Eastern customs as were mine.

Well, some little time elapsed before I saw or heard anything further of the houri. I began to settle down to the routine of the trip, and (you know how news circulates through a ship?) it was not very long before I knew as much as any of the other passengers knew.

Hamilton was a sort of filter through which it all came to me, and of course it was not undiluted, but colored with his own views. The lady of the *yashmak*, he informed me, was a member of the household of a wealthy Moslem in the neighborhood of Damascus. She was travelling via Port Said, and taking a Khedivial boat from there to Beyrût. He was a perfect mine of information, but his real interest was centered all the time on the party of four Indians.

"They are emissaries of the Rajah of Bhotana," he informed me confidentially. "The mystery begins to clear up. You must have read about a month ago that Lola de l'Iris was selling some of her jewelery and devoting the proceeds to the founding of an orphanage or something of the kind; quite a unique advertisement. Well, the famous Indian diamond presented to her by one of the crowned heads of Europe was amongst the bunch which she sold; and after staying in the West for over fifty years, it is again on its way back to the East where it came from."

I began to recollect the circumstances, now; the historic Indian diamond—I do not know Hindustanî, but its name translated means "Lure of Souls"—had been in the possession of the dancer for many years, and its sale for such a purpose had turned the limelight upon her most enviably. It was a new idea in advertising, and had proved an admirable success.

So the four reticent gentlemen were the guardians of the diamond. Under normal circumstances this might have been interesting, but, as I have tried to make clear, another matter engrossed my attention. In fact, I was living in a dream-world.

Of course, my opportunity came, in due course. One evening, as I mooned on the shadowy deck—which was quite deserted, because an extempore dance was taking place on the deck below—*she* came gliding along towards me. I could see her eyes sparkling in the moonlight.

At first I feared that she was going to turn back. She hesitated, in a wildly alluring manner, when first she saw me sitting there watching her. Then, turning her head aside, she came on, and passed me. I never took my eyes off that graceful figure for a moment.

Coming to the rail, she leaned and looked out toward the coast of Crete, where silver tracings in the blue marked the mountain peaks; then, shivering slightly, and wrapping her embroidered shawl more closely about her shoulders, she retraced her steps.

Not a yard from where I sat, she dropped a little silk handkerchief on the deck!

How my heart leapt at that! the rest was a magical whirl; and ten seconds later I was chatting with her.

She spoke fluent French, but little English.

She appealed to me in a way that was new and almost irresistible; it was an appeal quite Oriental, sensuous—indescribable. I just wanted to take her in my arms and kiss those tantalizing lips; talking seemed a waste of time. Of course, I cannot hope to make you understand; but it was extraordinary. I felt that I was losing my head; the glances of those long dark eyes were setting me on fire.

Suddenly, she terminated this, our first *tête-à-tête*. She raised her finger to her veiled lips and glided away into the shadows like a phantom. A sentence died, unfinished, on my tongue. I turned, and looked over my shoulder.

Gad! I got a fright! A most hideous Oriental of some kind, having only one eye but that afire with malignancy, was watching me from where he stood half concealed by a boat.

My lily of Damascus was guarded!

Humming, with an assumption of unconcern, I strolled away and joined the dancers below.

II

That was the beginning, then. I cursed to think how short a time was at my disposal; but since, the very next morning, I found myself enjoying a second delicious little stolen interview, I perceived that my company was not unacceptable.

What? oh, I had lost my head entirely; I admit it.

It was an effort to speak of matters ordinary, topics of the ship; my impulse was to whisper delicious nonsense into those tiny ears. However, I forced myself to talk about things in general, and told her that the famous diamond, Lure of Souls, was aboard.

This was news to her, and she seemed to be tremendously interested. Her interest was of such a childish sort, so naïve, that the project grew up in my mind at that very moment—the project that was to terminate so disastrously. It was hardly a matter of so many words; there was nothing definite about the thing at all, and this, our second interview, was cut short in much the same manner as the first.

"Ssh! Mustapha!"

With those whispered words, and a dazzling smile, this jewel of Damascus who interested me so much more deeply than the Rajah's diamond, departed hurriedly—and I turned to meet again the malignant gaze of the wall-eyed guardian.

The sort of romance in which I was steeped at that time flourishes and grows fat upon incidents of this kind. I have searched my memory many a time since then, for some word or hint to prove that the conversation about the diamond was opened and guided in a desired direction by the lady of the *yashmak*; but excluding transmission of thought, I could never find any evidence of the kind—have never been able to do so.

Certainly my memories of that period are hazy except in regard to Nahèmah. If I were an artist, I could paint her portrait from memory without the slightest error, I think. She occupied my thoughts to the exclusion of all else. But the project was formed and carried out. Hamilton was one of those popular men who seem born to occupy the chair at any kind of meeting at which they may be present; he organized almost every entertainment that took place on board. At first he was not at all keen on the idea.

"There are all sorts of difficulties," he said; "and one doesn't care to ask a favor of a native. At any rate one doesn't care to be refused."

But I had set my heart upon gratifying Nahèmah's curiosity, and, with the aid of Hamilton, it was all arranged satisfactorily. The native guardians of the diamond were rather flattered than otherwise, and a select little party of the "best" people on board met in the chief officer's cabin to view Lure of Souls.

The difficulty in regard to Nahèmah was readily overcome by Hamilton the energetic, and Dr. Patterson's wife "took her up" for the occasion in a delightfully patronizing manner. The four swarthy, polite Orientals were there, of course; several other ladies in addition to Mrs. Patterson and Nahèmah, the chief officer, myself, Hamilton, and a sepulchral Scotch curate, the Rev. Mr. Rawlingson, whom I had scarcely noticed hitherto, and whose presence at this "select" gathering rather surprised me.

The sea was like a sheet of glass, and this was the hottest day which I had yet experienced. It was about an hour before lunch-time when we gathered to view the diamond; and Mr. Brodie, the chief officer, exercised his pawky humor in a series of elaborate pantomimic precautions, locking the door with labored care, and treating the ladies of the company to Bluebeard glances of frightful intensity.

Phew! if we had only known!...

Finally one of the Indians took out the diamond from its case—which had been brought from the strong-room a few minutes before. It was a wonderful thing, I suppose, of quite unusual size, and it sparkled and gleamed in the sunlight streaming through the open porthole in an absolutely dazzling fashion. I had ranged myself close beside Nahèmah. Each of us was permitted to handle the stone. It was I who passed it to her, Mr. Rawlingson having passed it to me. She held it in the palm of her little hand, and her eyes sparkled with childish delight as she bent to examine the gem. Then a very strange thing happened.

From somewhere behind me—I was sitting with my back to the porthole—a dull gray object came leaping and twirling; and a scorpion— I have never seen a larger specimen—fell upon Nahèmah's wrist!

She uttered a piercing cry, dropped the diamond and brushed the horrid insect from her wrist; then fell swooning into my arms....

A scene of incredible confusion followed. The four Indians, ignoring the presence of the scorpion, dropped like cats upon the floor, seeking for Lure of Souls. Mrs. Patterson and I carried Nahèmah to the sofa hard by and laid her upon it. Just as we did so the scorpion darted from between the end of the sofa and the wardrobe, and the chief officer put his foot upon it.

Ensuing events were indescribable. Since the diamond had not yet been picked up, obviously the cabin door could not be unlocked; so in the stuffy atmosphere of the place it was a matter of some difficulty to revive Nahèmah. Meanwhile, four wild-eyed Indians were creeping about amongst our feet—like cats, as I have said before.

In the end, just as the girl began to revive somewhat, it became evident that Lure of Souls was missing. A pearl shirt button, the ownership of which we were unable to establish, was picked up, but no diamond.

The chief officer showed himself a man of priceless tact. He rang for the stewardess, and the ladies were shepherded to a neighboring, vacant cabin. Then the door was relocked, and Mr. Brodie proceeded to strip, placing his garments one by one upon the little folding table for examination. He was not satisfied until every man present had overhauled them. We all followed his example, the Rev. Mr. Rawlingson last of all ... and Lure of Souls was still on the missing list!

Then we gave the chief officer's cabin such a turnout as it had never had before, I should assume. Our quest was unrewarded. Meanwhile, the ladies had been submitted to a similar search in the adjoining cabin; same result.

With great difficulty we succeeded in hushing up the matter to a certain extent; but the captain's language to the chief officer was appalling, and the chief officer's remarks to Hamilton were equally unparliamentary; whilst Hamilton seemed to consider that he was justified in placing the whole blame upon me, which he did in terms little short of insulting. The four Indians apparently regarded all of us with equal suspicion and animosity.

I could not foresee the end. The thing was so sudden, so serious, that at the time it banished even thoughts of Nahèmah from my mind. I anticipated that we should all find ourselves arrested when we reached Port Said.

Later in the day Hamilton walked into my cabin and placed a little cardboard box upon the dressing-table. It contained the crushed body of the scorpion.

"Where did that scorpion come from?" he demanded abruptly.

It was a question which already had been asked fully a thousand times, yet no one had discovered an intelligent reply.

I shook my head.

"It came from the open porthole," he replied, "and as it's a thousand to one against a scorpion being aboard, somebody was *carrying* it for this very purpose—somebody who was on the deck outside the chief officer's cabin *and who threw the scorpion* into the cabin."

"But such a deadly thing...."

"Have a good look," said Hamilton, turning the insect over with a lead pencil; "this one isn't deadly at all. See!—his tail has been cut off!"

I looked and stifled an exclamation. It was as Hamilton had said. The scorpion was harmless.

I never once set eyes upon Nahèmah again until we arrived at Port Said. Then I saw her preparing to go ashore in one of the boats. I managed to join her, ignoring the scowls of her one-eyed attendant, and we arrived at the quay together. Right there by the water's edge a most curious scene was being enacted. Surrounded by two or three passengers and a perfect ring of uniformed officials, Hamilton, very excited, watched his baggage being turned out upon the ground. He saw me approaching.

"Hang it all, Fane," he cried, "this is disgraceful!—I don't know upon whose orders they are acting, but the beastly police are searching my baggage for the diamond...."

I thought it very extraordinary and said as much to the Rev. Mr. Rawlingson, who was one of the onlookers.

"It is very strange indeed," he said mildly, turning his gold-rimmed spectacles in my direction.

A moment later, to my horror and indignation, Nahèmah was submitted to the same indignity! The crowd had been roped off from the part of the quay upon which we stood, and I could see that the whole thing had been arranged beforehand in some way, probably by wireless from the ship. Curiously, as I thought at the time, my own baggage was not examined in this way, but I was detained long enough to lose sight of Nahèmah and her one-eyed guardian. When I got to the hotel I indulged in some reflection. It occurred to me that Hamilton was bound for Colombo, which made it rather singular that he should have had his baggage put ashore at Port Said.

I should have liked to have searched the town for my lady of the *yashmak*, but having no clue to her present whereabouts, realized the futility of such a proceeding. My last thought before I fell asleep that night was that some day in the near future I should visit Damascus.

III

I saw very little of Port Said, for we had arrived in the early morning and I was departing for Cairo by a train leaving shortly before midday. I wandered about the quaint streets a bit, however, and wondered if, from one of the latticed windows overhanging me, the dark eyes of Nahèmah were peering out.

Although I looked up and down the train fairly carefully, I failed to find among the passengers anyone whom I knew, and I settled down into my corner to study the novel scenery uninterruptedly. The shipping in the canal fascinated me for a long time as did the figures which moved upon its shores. The ditches and embankments, aimlessly wandering footpaths, and moving figures which seemed to belong to a thousand years ago, seized upon my imagination as they seize upon the imagination of every traveller when first he beholds them.

But, properly speaking, my story jumps now to Zagazig. The train stopped at Zagazig; and, walking out into the corridor and lowering a window, I was soon absorbed in contemplation of that unique town. Its narrow, dirty, swarming streets; the millions of flies that boarded the train; the noisy vendors of sugar cane, tangerine oranges and other commodities; the throng beyond the barriers gazing open-mouthed at me as I gazed open-mouthed at them—it was a first impression, but an indelible one.

I was not to know it was written that I should spend the night in Zagazig; but such was the case. Generally speaking, I have found the service on the Egyptian State Railway very good, but a hitch of some kind occurred on this occasion, and after an hour or so of delay, it was definitely announced to the passengers that owing to an accident to the permanent way, the journey to Cairo could not be continued until the following morning.

Then commenced a rush which I did not understand at first, and in which, feeling no desire to exert myself unduly, I did not participate. Half an hour later I ascertained that the only two hotels which the place boasted were full to overflowing, and realized what the rush had meant. It was all part of the great scheme of things, no doubt; but when, thanks to the kindly, if mercenary, offices of the International Sleeping Car attendant, I found myself in possession of a room at a sort of native *khân* in the lower end of the town, I experienced no very special gratitude towards Providence.

I have enjoyed the hospitality of less pleasing caravanserai since, but this was my first experience of the kind, and I thought very little of it.

My room boasted a sort of bed, certainly, but without entering into details, I may say that there were earlier occupants who disputed its possession. The plaster of the walls—the place apparently was built of a mixture of straw and dried mud—provided residence not only for mosquitoes, but also for ants, and the entire building was redolent of an odor suggestive of dried bones. That smell of dried bones is characteristic, I have learned, of the sites of ancient Egyptian cities (Zagazig is close to the ruins of ancient Bubastis, of course); one gets it in the temples and the pyramids, also. But it was novel to me, then, and not pleasing.

I killed time somehow or other until the dinner hour; and the train, which now reposed in a siding, became a rendezvous for those who desired to patronize the dining-car. Evidently no sleeping-cars were available (or perhaps that idea was beyond the imagination of the native officials), and having left a trail of tobacco smoke along the principal native street, I turned into my apartment which I shared with the ants, mosquitoes—and the other things.

An examination of my rooms by candle-light revealed the presence of a cupboard, or what I thought to be a cupboard, but opening the double doors I saw that it was a window, latticed and overlooking a lower apartment; so much I perceived by the light of an oil lamp which stood upon the table. Then, stifling a gasp of amazement, I hastily snuffed my candle and peered down eagerly at that incredible scene....

Nahèmah, longer veiled, was sitting at the table, and opposite to her was seated the hideous wall-eyed attendant!

They were conversing in low tones, so that, strive as I would, I could not overhear a word. You ask me why I spied upon the lady's privacy in this manner? For a very good reason.

Midway between the two, upon the rough boards of the table, lay Lure of Souls, twinkling and glittering like a thing of incarnate light.

I observed that there was a door to the room below, almost immediately opposite the window through which I was peering ... and this door was opening very slowly and noiselessly. At least, *I* could hear no noise, but the one-eyed man detected something, for suddenly he started up and did a remarkable thing. Snatching up the diamond from the table, he clapped it into the eyeless cavity of his skull and turned in a twinkling to face the intruder.

Then the door was thrown open, and Hamilton leapt into the room.

I could scarcely credit my senses. Honestly, I thought I was dreaming. Hamilton's whole face was changed: a hard, cunning look had come over it, and he held a revolver in his hand. Nahèmah sprang to her feet as he entered, but he covered the pair of them with his revolver, and pointing to the one-eyed man muttered something in a low voice. Rage, fear, rebellion chased in turn across the evil features of One-eye; but there was something about Hamilton's manner that cowed.

Manipulating the sunken eyelids as though they had been of rubber, the guardian of the veiled lady slipped the diamond into the palm of his hand and tossed it, glittering, on to the table.

Hamilton's expression of triumph I shall never forget. One step forward he took and was about to snatch up the gem when—out of the dark cavity of the doorway behind him stepped a second intruder.

It was the Rev. Mr. Rawlingson!

The reverend gentleman's behavior was most unclerical. He leapt upon the unsuspecting Hamilton like a panther and screwed the muzzle of a revolver into that gentleman's right ear with quite unnecessary vigor.

"You have been wasting your time, Farland!" he snapped in a voice that was quite new to me. "That is, unless you have turned amateur detective."

He made no attempt to reach for the diamond, but just held out his hand, and with his eyes fixed upon Hamilton, silently commanded the latter to hand over the gem. This Hamilton did with palpable reluctance. Mr. Rawlingson, who, though still clerically garbed, had discarded his spectacles, slipped the stone into his pocket, snatched the revolver from Hamilton's hand and jerked his thumb in the direction of the open door. Hamilton shrugged his shoulders and walked out of the room. For scarce a moment did Rawlingson's eyes turn to follow the retreating figure, but the chance was good enough for the wall-eyed man.

He launched himself through space like nothing so much as a kangaroo, bearing Rawlingson irresistibly to the floor! With his lean hands at the other's throat he turned his solitary eye upon Nahèmah, muttering something gutturally. After a moment's hesitation she ran from the room.

Twenty seconds later I was downstairs, and ten seconds after that was helping Rawlingson to his feet. He was considerably shaken and boasted a very elegant design in bruises which was just beginning to reveal itself upon his throat; but otherwise he was unhurt.

"I have lost her, Mr. Fane!" were his first words. "She knows this part of the world inside out. I have no case against Farland, but I am sorry to have lost the woman."

Was my mind in a whirl? Did I think that madness had seized me? Replies both in the affirmative; I was simply staggered.

I always go to pieces with this part of the yarn, being an unpractised narrator, as I have already explained; but I may relieve your mind upon one point. I never saw Nahèmah and the one-eyed man again, nor have I since set eyes upon Hamilton. Mr. Rawlingson, the last time I heard from him, was in similar case.

The explanation of the whole thing was something of a blow to me, of course. The lily of Damascus who had fascinated me so hopelessly was no Eastern at all; you will have guessed as much. She was a Frenchwoman, I believe; at any rate they had a long record up against her in Paris. She had gone out after Lure of Souls, and very ingeniously had made me her instrument. As Mr. Rawlingson explained to me, what had probably taken place was this:

The harmless scorpion, specially brought along for some such purpose, had been thrown into the chief officer's cabin from the open porthole by the one-eyed villain. That had been the cue for Nahèmah to drop the shirt button, and, whilst the occupants of the cabin were in confusion, to toss the diamond out on to the deck where her accomplice was waiting. The search of their effects had been futile, of course; no one had thoughts of searching the eye-cavity of her Eastern companion.

Where did Hamilton come in? Hamilton was one James Farland, an American crook of the highest accomplishments, known to the police of the entire civilized world. He, too, had gone out for Lure of Souls, but the woman, his professional competitor, had proved too clever for him.

The Rev. Mr. Rawlingson? He was Detective-Inspector Wexford of New Scotland Yard. Yes, it's a rotten story, from a romantic point of view.

III

THE SECRET OF ISMAIL

I

Mustapha Mirza knew it—Mustapha Mirza, the blind Persian who makes shoes hard by the Bâb ez-Zuwêla and in the very shadow of the minarets of Muayyâd; Hassan es-Sîwa of the Street of the Carpet-sellers in the Mûski, Hassan, who, where another man has hands, has but hideous stumps, knew it, and because of him it was that Abdûl Moharli sought it—Abdûl the mendicant who crouches on the steps of the Blue Mosque muttering, guttural, inarticulate, and pointing to the tongueless cavity of his mouth. Now I know it; but not from Abdûl Moharli: may Allah, the Great, the Compassionate, defend me!

I say "May Allah defend me," yet I am no Moslem; I have no spot of Egyptian blood in my veins. No, I am a pure Greek of Cos, of Cos the home of the loveliest women in the world; and my mother was one of these, whilst my father was a Cretan, and a true descendent of Minos. My story perhaps will not be believed, for always it has been my fate to be maligned. You will ask, perhaps, what I was doing in the Mâzi Desert between Beni Suêf and the Red Sea, but I reply that my cotton interests—for I have cotton interests in the Delta—often lead me far afield. You do not understand the cotton industry or this explanation would be unnecessary. It is only those who do not understand the cotton industry that speak of *hashish. Hashish!* I leave it to the Egyptians and the Jews to deal in *hashish*; I am neither a Jew nor an Egyptian, but a Greek of Cos, who would not soil his hands with such a trade—no.

Upon my business, then, my legitimate business, I found myself with a small company of servants encamped by the Wâdi Araba. At the Wâdi Araba I had a commercial acquaintance, a sheikh of the Mâzi Arabs. Those villains who say that he was a "go-between," that my business was not with him, but through him with a port of the Red Sea, dare not say as much to my face; for there is a law in the land— even in the land of Egypt, now that the British hold power here.

I had reached the point, then, whereat it was my custom to meet my business acquaintance and to discuss certain affairs in which we were interested. My servants had erected the tent in which I was to sleep, and the camels lay in a little limestone valley to the west, their eyes mild because they knew that the day's work was ended; for it is a foolish mistake to suppose that the eye of a camel is mild at any other time. The camel knows the secret name of Allah—and that name is Rest.

The violet after-glow, which is the most wonderful thing in Nature, crowned the desert with glory right away to the porphyry mountains. I stood at my tent door looking westward to the Nile. I stood looking out upon the waste of the sands, the eternal sands which are a belt about Egypt; and my thoughts running fleetly before me, crossed the desert, crossed the Nile, and came to rest in the verdant, fertile Fàyûm, its greenness sweet to look upon in the heat of such an evening, its palms fashioned in ebony black against the wondrous sky. Yes, I, who am a Greek, love the Fàyûm more than any spot on earth; the modern clamor and dust of Cairo are hateful to me, although my business often takes me there, and also to Alexandria, the most European city in the East, and to me the most detestable. But my business is in the Delta and it is a good business, so why should I complain?

I stood at my tent door, and I thought of many things, though little of the matters which had brought me there; a faint cool breeze fanned my brow, and about me was that great peace which comes to Egypt with the touch of night. My servants were silent in their encampment, and the shrieking of the camels had ceased. About me, then, all was sleeping; only I was awake, only I was there to receive Abdûl Moharli and his secret—the secret of Ismail.

By the pattering of his bare feet upon the sand, I first learned of his coming, but for a long time I could not see him, for his way led him through the valley where the camels slept, and a mound obscured my view. But presently I heard his panting breaths and his little delirious cries of fear, which were like sobs, and presently, again, I saw him staggering over the slope. At the sight of me he uttered one last gasping cry and fell forward on his face unconscious—like a dead man.

I hurried to him, stooped and raised him. His face was dreadful to look upon. His eyes were sunken in his skull, and his flesh shrivelled as by long fasting. His beard was filthy, knotted and unkempt, and his hair a black mat streaked with dirty gray. He was thin as a mummy and the bones protruded through his skin. He was as one who is dying from excess of *hashish*.

Ah! I know how they look, those poor fools who poison themselves with the Indian hemp. I wonder Allah does not strike down the villain who places that poison within their reach. I use the term "Allah" because my business brings me much in contact with the natives, but I am no Moslem, as I have related. Father Pierre of Alexandria can tell you how devoted a Christian I am.

Drink and food revived him somewhat; and as I sat beside him in my tent that night he babbled to me, half deliriously; he raved, and to another it might have seemed the fancies of a poor madman which he poured into my ears. For he spoke of a secret oasis and of a sheikh who had lived since the days of Sultan Kalaûn; of a treasure vast as that of Suleyman—and of magic, black magic; of the transmuting of gold and the making of diamonds.

But I, who am a Greek, and one who has lived all his life between Alexandria and the Red Sea; I who know the Garden of Egypt as another knows the palm of his hand—I detected in this delirium the shadow of a truth. To me it became evident that this wretched being who had fled, a hunted thing, over the trackless desert for many days and nights—it became evident to me, I say, that he spoke of the far-famed secret of Ismail.

You would ask: What is the secret of Ismail? I would tell you, ask it of Hassan the Handless, of Mustapha, the blind Persian of the Bâb ez-Zuwêla; better still, ask it of any son of the Fàyûm, of any man of the Mâzi. None of them will answer you, for none save Hassan and Mustapha knows the strange truth—Hassan and Mustapha, and Abdûl Moharli ... and no one of these three knows all, nor will reveal what he knows.

Ah! how my heart leapt and how my eyes must have gleamed in the darkness of the tent, yet how cold a fear clutched at the life within me. The night seemed suddenly to become a thin curtain veiling eyes that watched, the empty desert a hiding-place for unseen multitudes that listened; the faint breeze raising the flap of the tent, ever so gently, ever so softly, assumed the shape of a malignant hand that reached for my throat, that sought to stifle me ere the secret, the deathly secret of Ismail should be mine.

Abdûl Moharli was the name of this wanderer; and as he spoke to me, gulping down great draughts of water between the words, ever he glanced to right and left, over his shoulder and all about him.

"It is four days from here," he whispered hoarsely; "due south in the direction of the porphyry quarries and the Mountain of Smoke. There is a tiny village and all the inhabitants are of the race of Saïd Ebn al As, being descendants of the companion of the prophet. I had long supposed that this race of heretics was extinct; but it is not so, O my benefactor; with these eyes, have I seen the houses wherein they dwell. By the strategy of which I have spoken did I penetrate to their secret dwelling-place and win their unsuspecting love."

And then, clutching me to him with his bony hands, he spoke in hushed and fearful tones of the house of the Sheikh Ismail Ebn al As. It was the fabled treasure of this holy man which had been the lodestone drawing Abdûl Moharli out into the desert. Something of his fear, of his constant apprehension seized upon me too; and as he glanced tremblingly first over this shoulder and then over that, so likewise did *I* glance, until I seemed to crouch in a world of spies listening to a secret greater than that of the Universe.

I pronounced the *Takbîr*, "Great is the Lord!"—a superstitious custom which I have acquired from my business acquaintances. I made the sign of the Cross and called upon the name of the Holy Virgin. Almost I feared to listen further, yet I lacked the courage to abstain.

"Not with mine eyes have I beheld the treasure of Ismail," he whispered to me, this shadow of a man, this living mummy, those same eyes rolling in their sunken sockets; "nor with mine ears have I heard it named. These hands have never touched it; yet the secret of Ismail is *my* secret."

So far he had proceeded and no further, when a slight noise, that was not of my imagination, came from immediately outside the tent. On the instant I sprang forth ... but no one was there and nothing now disturbed the solitude of the desert about me. A moment I stood, peering to left and right, into the void of the velvet dusk; no more than a moment, I can swear, yet long enough for that dreadful thing to happen—that thing which sometimes haunts my dreams.

Shrill and awful upon the silence it burst; the scream of a stricken man. It stabbed me like a knife; and as a creature of clay I stood, unable to stir or think. It died away, in a long wail of pain, that gave place to a guttural, inarticulate babbling—a choking, sobbing sound indescribable, but that may not be forgotten once it has been heard.

No living thing, as I can testify, entered or left the tent; so far the evidence of my senses bears me. But that one had entered and left it, unseen, I learned, when, throwing off this palsy of horror, I staggered back to the side of the one who knew the secret of Ismail.

He lay writhing upon the ground; blood issued from his mouth. The tongue of Abdûl Moharli had been torn out!

II

Three weeks later I had my first sight of the secret oasis. The fate from which Abdûl had fled had overtaken him as I have related, in my tent, and from that moment until we parted company—for this poor wretch survived his mutilation—not another hint could I glean from him respecting the discovery for which he had paid so terrible a price.

In the first place, he lacked the accomplishment of writing and in the second place his fear of the vengeance of Ismail had become a veritable madness. I left him at Beni Suêf, filled with a determination to probe this mystery for myself. Suitably prepared for such an undertaking I set out alone from Dér Byâd, and undertook the four days' journey which I had planned.

In a little gorge, arid, shadeless, in which only a few stunted tamarisks grew, but affording a sort of hiding-place for myself and my camel, I made my base of operations. Provisions of a sort I had plenty, but for water I must depend on the secret oasis, which I estimated to be not more than four miles distant. In the dead of night I set out, making for a series of mounds or hillocks rising up from the rocky face of the plateau. Cautiously I ascended their slopes, ever watchful and with eagerly beating heart; and it was lying prone upon the crest of the greatest of these that I first saw the village and the oasis.

There was nothing extraordinary in the appearance of the village; it presented to the eye the usual group of small, squat houses clinging to the trunks of the palm trees and surrounding a shrine or mosque boasting a wooden minaret. There were tilled fields and palm groves to the left of the village and a large house surrounded by white walls embracing extensive gardens. My spirits rose high. Within that house lay the secret of Ismail.

I determined to approach from the left, where I should be able to take advantage of the far-cast shadows of the palm groves and of the direction of the faint breeze; for most of all I feared the dogs, without which no Arab village is complete. Sure enough, although I had elected to approach the left of the village and although I crawled laboriously upon hands and knees, the accursed brutes apparently scented me or heard me and made night hideous with their clamor.

Flat upon the ground I lay, awaiting the dogs who bore down upon me snarling, their fangs bared. I had come prepared for this; but, mysteriously, at a point by the end of the palm grove and some twenty yards away from me, the pack halted, and after a time became silent. This was unaccountable but fortunate; and after waiting a while longer to learn if anyone had been aroused by the outcry, I advanced towards the wall of the garden, passing stealthily from palm to palm.

I observed that the mosque was a more important building than I had supposed, with a tomb on the right of the entrance surmounted by a white dome. A passage leading to the courtyard, which presented a charming picture in the moonlight, its fountain overshadowed by acacias, reminded me very much of that in the Mosque of Muayyâd in Cairo. As in the latter, a double arcade surrounded it on three sides and the columns were of some kind of marble and sculptured with inscriptions in Arabic. I had a glimpse of a blue-tiled sanctuary, through a fine *mushrabîyeh* screen beneath the pointed arches. Arabesques in colored glass rendered the windows very beautiful to look upon. Nothing stirred within the village, as I crept along the narrow lane separating the mosque from the wall of the garden. Beyond prospecting the ground, I had no definite plans for to-night; but Fate had willed it that I was to become more deeply involved in the affair than I had designed or intended.

A side door opened from the garden at a spot nearly opposite the little wooden platform which served as the minaret of the mosque; and the mud bricks of the porch were so broken and decayed by time that I perceived here an opportunity of mounting to the top of the wall, an opportunity of which I instantly availed myself.

Yes, in spite of my peaceful calling (I have explained that I have cotton interests in the Delta) my life has not been unadventurous nor have I ever hesitated to incur risk where profit might be gained. Therefore, having climbed to the top of the wall, unmolested, and perceiving at a spot some little distance to the right a sort of trellis overgrown with purple blossom, I did not hesitate to make for it and to descend into the garden. I had just completed the descent, and stood looking cautiously about me, when a sound disturbed the silence—a sound so entirely unexpected, in that place, at such an hour, that it turned my blood cold, bringing to my mind all those stories of the black magic for which the people of this oasis were famed.

It was the sound of a woman singing; and although the song she sang was a familiar Arab love song and the voice of the singer was sweet, if very mournful, the effect, as I have said, was weird to a degree.

> *Ashik yekul l'il hammám hát le genáhak yom*
> (A lover said to a dove, "Lend me your wings for a day," etc.)

Overcoming the fear and astonishment which momentarily had deprived me of action, I advanced with the utmost caution in the direction from whence this mysterious singing seemed to proceed. Passing an angle of the house, where the stucco wall ran sheerly up to a *mushrabîyeh* window, I perceived before me a smaller, detached building in the form of a sort of pavilion. Some fine acacias overhung its white and glistening dome, in which were little windows of colored glass. Concealed in the shadow of the house, I stood looking towards this smaller building, observing with astonishment that it possessed a massive, bronze-mounted door.

Indeed, in many respects, and in spite of the charming picture which its jeweled appearance presented, it might well have been the tomb of some holy Sheikh. But seated on an old-fashioned *mastabah* before the entrance were two huge negroes of most ferocious aspect, armed with scimitars which glittered evilly in the light of the moon!

I drew back sharply into the shelter of the projecting wall. One of the negroes seemed to slumber, but the wicked black eyes of his companion were widely open and he revealed his ivory teeth in a frightful leer. The beating of my heart almost suffocated me, for I ascribed that ghastly grimace to the fact that the negro had detected my presence and was already gloating over the pleasing prospect of my swift and bloody despatch. For many agonized moments I lurked there, one hand clutching the stucco wall and the other resting upon the butt of a new Colt magazine pistol which I had taken the precaution to purchase in Alexandria a week earlier.

When again I ventured to protrude my head, I learned how groundless my fears had been; I realized that the loathsome contortion of the negro's countenance represented a smile of appreciation. He was listening to the unseen singer whose voice now stole again upon the silence of the night! His blubber lips drooped open cavernously and his fierce little eyes blinked in stupid rapture.

It appeared to me, now, that the sweet voice proceeded from some subterranean place: I thought that I was listening to the song of a *ginneyeh*. I remembered how the Sheikh Ismail was reputed to be the son of an *Efreet* and an Arabian princess, and to have lived in that oasis for generations, since the reign of the Sultan Mohammed Nâsir ibn-Kalaûn, who had expelled him from Cairo as a magician. He was said to possess the secrets of Geber and of Avicenna—the great Ibn Sina of Bokhara; to possess the Philosophers' Stone and the *Elixir Vitæ*. In this pavilion with the bronze door I beheld the magician's treasure-house, guarded, within, by a *ginneyeh* and, without, by ghouls or black *Efreets*!

You will understand that these childish superstitions sometimes overcome me, because I have lived so long among those who believe them; but to me, a Greek, possessing the consolation of the true religion, it was only momentary, this cold fear which belongs to ignorance and is bred in the blood of the Moslem but finds no place in the heart of a true Christian.

And now the Fates again took a hand in the game. The pack of curs in the distant palm grove set up a sudden tempest of sound, so that they seemed to have become possessed of a million devils. It was a disturbance infinitely louder and more prolonged than that with which the dogs had greeted my appearance, and I had barely time to throw myself flat in the depths of a black and friendly shadow ere the two negroes, monstrous in the moonlight, passed me silently and trotted off in the direction from whence the uproar proceeded. You will say, no doubt, that a madness as great as that of the dogs possessed me; but because what I tell you is true, you must not be surprised to find it strange.

Allowing the negroes time to reach the gate for which I divined them to be making, I ran across the moon-bathed garden to the door of the pavilion.

You must understand that my madness was not entirely without method; for I had a vague plan in my mind: it was to ascertain the character of the lock upon the bronze door (for you must know that I am skilled in the craft of the locksmith), and then, passing beyond the pavilion, which I was assured was the treasure-house of Ismail, to make my escape over the garden wall at some point to the west and return to my base in the desert ravine armed with a knowledge of the enemy's dispositions.

But, as I have said, the Fates took a hand. The sweet-voiced singer ceased her song as I approached the pavilion; and, at the moment that I set foot upon the lower step, her voice—by Allah! whose Name be exalted, it was sweet as honey!—addressed to me these words:

"O my master, at last thou art come! Here is the key! enter ere they return."

Whilst I stared blankly upward to the open lattice from whence the invisible speaker thus addressed me, an antique key wrapped in a piece of perfumed silk, fell almost upon my head!

III

Dazed though I was by the complete unexpectedness of this happening I doubt if I should have had the temerity to pursue the matter further that night but for the sound of fleetly running footsteps of which at this moment I became aware.

My escape was cut off! If I endeavored to pass around the pavilion in accordance with my original plan I should undoubtedly be perceived. My only hope lay in accepting the invitation so singularly given. With trembling hands I fitted the key to the cumbersome lock, opened the door, and entered the pavilion. My presence of mind had not completely deserted me and before closing the door I withdrew the key.

I found myself in a saloon of extraordinary magnificence, furnished with mattresses covered with silk and lighted by hanging lamps and by candles, and having at its upper end a couch of alabaster decorated with pearls and canopied by curtains of satin peacock-blue. From a carved wooden archway draped with cloth of gold there leaped forth a girl of such surpassing loveliness that her image must forever reside in my heart together with those of the saints.

Conceive all the dark-eyed beauties of Oriental poetry, of Hafiz, of Omar, of Attâr, and from each distil the very essence of female loveliness; though you combine them all in one rapturous vision of delight you will have conceived but a feeble shadow of shadows of this wondrous reality who now stood panting before me, her red lips parted and her bosom tumultuous.

I think if the light in her eyes had been for me I could gladly have died for her and found death sweet; but as her gaze met mine a pitiful change took place in that lovely countenance. Her color fled and she swayed and almost fell.

"Oh," she whispered, "thou art not my beloved! O Allah! this is some snare that Ismail hath set for my feet! Who art thou? who art thou?"

But because of the excess of the loveliness of the speaker, from whom I could not remove my eyes, and because as I stood in that perfumed apartment it seemed to me that I was no longer a real man, but a figment of some *Efreet's* dream, I found myself incapable of both speech and action.

Yet I was speedily to know that the Fates, which had thrust me into that saloon—nay, which had brought me across the desert to that secret oasis—were not yet wearied of their sport.

A soft call, a lover's signal (for no true Believer will whistle at night, since to do so is to summon the evil *ginn*) sounded from immediately outside the bronze door, followed by a muffled rapping upon the door itself!

"Saîd, my beloved!" cried the girl wildly, and ran towards the door.

At that very moment, and whilst I stood there like a man of clay, I heard the negro guardians returning to their posts; I heard the clatter of their sandals and I heard their guttural cries of rage! Uttering a long tremulous sigh, the beautiful occupant of the pavilion fell swooning upon the floor.

A loud imperious voice now rose above the sounds of conflict which had commenced outside the pavilion; I heard the sound of many running feet, and—my blood turned to ice—that of a key being inserted in the lock of the bronze door! Power of action returned to me, though I confess that I now grew sick with dread. Only one hiding-place was possible: the first I could reach.

I leaped across the lovely form extended upon the floor and dropped, almost choking with emotion, behind the alabaster couch. I had barely gained this cover when the door was hurled open and a tall, excessively gaunt, and hawk-faced old man entered, his eyes blazing, his thin nostrils quivering, and his lean hands opening and closing at his sides in a sort of clutching movement horribly suggestive and terrifying.

He was followed by the two negroes, who were dragging between them a young Egyptian of prepossessing appearance down whose pale face blood was pouring from a wound in the brow.

Several other persons, principally servants of the *harêm*, brought up the rear.

Towering over the recumbent body of the girl, the terrible old man—in whom I could not fail to recognize the Sheikh Ismail—glared down at her for some moments in passionate silence; then he made as if to spurn her with his foot; then he clutched his long white beard with both hands and plucked at it frenziedly, whilst tears began to course down his furrowed cheeks, which had the frightful appearance of those of a mummy.

"O light of mine eyes!" he exclaimed; "O shame of my house! O reproach of my white hairs!"

He recovered himself by dint of a stupendous effort and turning a fiery glance upon the captive:

"Cast him down upon the floor," he cried, "that I may spit upon him, who is a scorn among swine and the son of a disease!"

To my unspeakable horror, the Sheikh then strode across the saloon and seated himself upon the alabaster couch! I almost choked with fear; I felt my teeth beginning to chatter and the beating of my heart sounded in my ears like the throb of a *darâbukeh*. The Sheikh, fortunately ignorant of my proximity, thus addressed the unfortunate young man who lay at his feet:

"Know, O disgrace of thy mother, that thy death hath been decided upon, and it shall visit thee in a most painful and unfortunate manner. O thou spawn of offal, learn that I have been aware of thy malevolent intentions since first thou didst seek to penetrate into my secret. What! am I heir to all the wisdom of the ages, that I should remain ignorant of the presence of such as thee, O thou gnat's egg, in my house? When the partner in thine infamy didst steal the key of the door from me, thinkest thou that mine eyes were blind to the theft, O thou foredoomed carrion? It was in order that thy culpability should be made manifest that I permitted thee to enter. Thy double stratagem for quelling and then exciting the dogs, in order that the guards might be drawn from their posts, was known to me, and the negroes had received my orders to run to the gate in seeming accordance with thine accursed desires,

O filthy insect!"

Throughout the time that this dreadful old man thus addressed his victim, the latter crouched upon the floor, apparently paying no heed to his words but keeping an agonized glance fixed upon the lovely form of the girl. I was now in a condition of such profound and dejected fear as I had never known before and trust I may never know again. The Sheikh continued:

"Learn of the fate of some of those who sought the secret of Ismail before thee. One there was, Mustapha Mirza, a Persian, who came hither to despoil me. With his eyes did he behold my treasure. To-day *he hath no eyes*! And there was one Hassan of the Khân Khalîl. He dared to lay violent hands upon the treasure of my house—the 'treasure' not of gold nor jewels but of fairest flesh and blood. To-day *he hath no hands*! Wouldst like to know of Abdûl Moharli, who learned much of this "secret" of mine, and would have spoken of it? His tongue I threw to the carrion crows! *Thou*, O sink of iniquity, hast not only seen with thine eyes, heard with thine ears and laid thy filthy hands upon the treasure of Ismail: thou hast approached thy foul lips to this peach of Allah's garden! thou hast...."

He choked in his utterance and seemed upon the point of hurling himself upon the young man before him: but again he recovered his composure after a great effort and proceeded:

"The unpleasant punishments visited upon those others shall likewise fall to thy portion, since thou hast committed like crimes; but this shall only be in order to prepare thee for a most protracted and painful death. Bear him forth into the courtyard."

As one who dreams an evil dream, I saw the company stream out of the saloon, the wretched prisoner in their midst. When at last the bronze door was reclosed and I found myself alone with the swooning girl, I could scarce believe that even this respite was mine.

I offered a prayer to St. Antony of the Thebäid—*my* patron saint—as I listened to the sound of their receding footsteps; when I was aroused from the lethargy of fear into which I had fallen by a distant scream— a long wailing cry....

I have often asked myself: How did I make my escape from that dreadful village? You will remember that I had the purloined key of the bronze door in my possession? Then it was to this in the first place that I owed my preservation. To regain the garden was a simple matter, for the Sheikh and his bloodthirsty following were engaged in the courtyard of the house, but to St. Antony be all praise for the circumstance that the little door opposite the mosque had been left

open—possibly by the unhappy Saïd,—and to St. Antony be all praise
that a second time I avoided the dogs....

Dawn found me staggering down into that friendly ravine which
sheltered my camel. I was utterly exhausted, for I bore a burden, but
triumphant, delirious with joy and rapture, because my burden was so
sweet. You may question me of these matters, and I shall reply: As well
as my cotton interests I have now another interest in the Delta—the
lovely "Secret" of the Sheikh Ismail Ebn al As!*

* Readers of *Tales of Abû Tabâh* will recognize Mizmûna, "The Lady
of the Lattice," the story of whose recovery by the bereaved Sheikh
has already been related.

IV

HARÛN PASHA

I

I will tell you this story (said Ferrier of the Egyptian Civil) with one reservation; comments are to be reserved for some future time. I can only tell you what I saw with my own eyes and heard with my own ears; I offer no explanation; I pass on the story; you can take it or leave it.

Some of you will remember Dunlap—I don't mean Robert Dunlap, who is chief officer of the *Pekin*, but Jack Dunlap his cousin, the irrigation man who used to be stationed at Assuan.

You remember the build of the beggar?—the impression of scaffolding his figure conveyed? I always used to think of him as an iron framework, and he had the most hard-bitten head-piece I have ever struck; steel blue eyes and a mouth that was born shut. The dash of ginger in his hair, complexion, and constitution made up a Scotch brew that was very strongly flavored.

He came down to Cairo one spring, and a lot of us got together in the club—on a Sunday night, I remember, it was. The conversation got along that silly line; what we were all doing, and why we were doing it, what we had really intended to do, and how Fate had butted in and made sailors of those that had meant to be parsons, engineers of the poets, and tramps of the chaps who had proposed to become financiers.

Well, we had traveled up and down this blind alley for hours, I should think, when Dunlap mounted on his hind legs and took the rug with the proposition that nothing—*nothing*—was impossible of achievement to the man of single purpose. Someone put up an extreme case; asking Dunlap how he should handle the business of the son of a respectable greengrocer who, with singleness of purpose, proposed to become king of England.

He said it was not a fair case, but he accepted the challenge; and the way this junior greengrocer, under Dunlap's guidance, plunged into politics, got elected M.P., wormed himself into the confidence of the entire Empire by a series of brilliant campaigns conducted from John o' Groats to Van Diemen's Land; induced the reigning monarch, publicly, to advocate his own abdication; established a sort of commonwealth with his ex-Majesty on the board and Dunlap occupying a post between that of a protector and a Roman Cæsar—well, it was wonderful.

Of course, you can judge of the lateness of the hour from the fact that a group of moderately intelligent men tolerated, and contributed to, a chat of this nature. But what brings me down to the story is the few words which I exchanged with Dunlap at the break-up of the party, when he was leaving.

His cousin Robert, as you know, is well on the rippity side; but Jack, with all his fine capacity for heather-dew, had always struck me as something of a psalmster. I've heard that Bacchus holds the keys of truth, and it may be right; for out on the steps of the club, I said to Jack Dunlap:

"It seems you don't practise what you preach?"

"Don't I?" he snapped hardly. "What do you suppose I am doing here?"

"Engineering, I take it. Do you aspire to a pedestal beside De Lesseps?"

"De Lesseps be damned!" he retorted sourly. "Look at these."

He held out his hands, hardened with manual toil—the hands of a grinder.

"Clearly you are a glutton for work," I said.

"I am aiming at never doing another hand's stroke in my life," he replied, with an odd glint in his blue eyes. "My idea of life—*life*, mind you, not mere existence—is to be a pasha—one of the old school, with gate porters, orange trees, fountains, slaves, mosaic pavements, a marble bath."

He mixed his ambitions oddly.

"Someone to do all the shifting for me, and even the thinking; to hold a book in front of me if I wanted to read, to poke my pipe in my mouth, and to take it out when I wanted to blow smoke rings—and to *know* when I wanted it taken out without being told."

"On your showing, you are traveling by the wrong road."

"Am I?" he snapped viciously. "Just wait awhile."

That was all the indication I had of Dunlap's ideas, and remembering the time of night and other circumstances, I did not count upon it worth a brass farthing; putting it down to the heather-dew rather than to any innate viciousness of the man. But listen to the sequel, which shifts us up just about twelve months, to the spring of the following year, in fact.

II

I had seen no more of Dunlap, and concluded that he was back in Assuan, or somewhere on the river, foozling with his irrigation again. I never had the clearest conception of the work of his department, by the way. An irrigation man once started to explain to me about his section, mixing up surveying paraphernalia in his talk, telling me something about an allowance of half an inch variation in half a mile of bank, or chat to that effect; but I couldn't quite make it out. My impression of Dunlap at business was very hazy; I pictured him measuring the bank of the Nile with a six-foot rule, and periodically kneeling down in the smelly mud to footle with a spirit-level. But he was a Senior Wrangler, as you remember, and a man, too, of more substantial accomplishments, and he drew five hundred a year from the Egyptian Government; so that probably I underestimated his usefulness.

At any rate, I had forgotten his iron framework and mahogany countenance, together with his response (under the afflatus of heather-dew) at the time of which I am now speaking.

A little matter had cropped up which touched me on a weak spot; and with a mob of jabbering Egyptians and one very placid Bedouin flooding my room, I found myself thinking again of Dunlap and envying him his intimate acquaintance with Arabic.

Although I had been in the country quite twice as long as Dunlap, my Arabic was far from perfect, for I have always been a rotten linguist. Dunlap, as I now remembered, might have passed for a native (excepting his Scottish headpiece), and I ascribed his proficiency to an inherent trick of mimicry. There was something of the big ape about him; and after one function at which we both were present, I remember how he convulsed the entire club with an imitation of a certain highly placed Egyptian dignitary, voice and gesture being equal in comic effect to Cyril Maude at his best. In fact, if you notice, you will find that the best linguists, as a rule, have a marked apish streak in their composition.

Well, here was I at my wits' ends to grasp twenty points of view at one and the same time; no two expressed in quite the same dialect, and each orator more excited than another. You know the brutes?

That got me thinking of Dunlap, and even after the incident was closed, I found myself thinking of him. Some friends from home were staying at Shepheard's, and of course they had claimed me as dragoman; not that I objected in the least, for one of the party—when it was possible to dodge her mother—was, well, a very agreeable companion, you understand.

On this particular morning we were doing the bazaars. I have found by comparison that the average tourist knows far more of the Mûski than the average resident; in the same way, I suppose that for information regarding the Tower of London or the British Museum, one must go, not to a Cockney, but to an American visitor. At any rate, my party told me more than I could tell them, and my job degenerated into that of a mere interpreter. In the matter of purchases, I possibly saved them money, but their knowledge of the wares was miles ahead of my own. These up-to-date guide books must be very useful reading, I think.

Although I had tried hard to rush them past that dangerous quarter, the *Gôhargîya*, the ladies of the party had discovered a shop where little trays of loose gems, turquoises, rubies, bits of lapis-lazuli, and so forth, were displayed snarefully.

After that I knew where I could find them up to any time before lunch; I knew they were safe enough for the rest of the morning; and accepting my defeat at the hands of the jewel merchant who turned his slow eyes upon me and shrugged apologetically, I drifted off, after a decent interval (leaving young Forrest, who, mysteriously, had turned up, to do the cavalierly), intending to visit my acquaintance, Hassan, in the *Sûk el-Attârin* (Street of the Perfumers), not twenty yards away.

You know Hassan? A large, mysterious figure in the shadows of his little shop, smoking amber-scented cigarettes as though he liked them, and turning his sleepy eyes slowly upon each passer-by. Well, I drifted around in his direction.

Right at the corner of the street, a big limousine was standing; an up-to-date car, fawn cushions, silver-plated fittings, and simply stuffed with fresh-cut flowers. A useful-looking Nubian was chauffeur, and on the step squatted a fat and resplendent being in all the glory of much gold braid.

These *harêm* guards are rarely seen in Cairo nowadays—they belong to the other picturesque Oriental institutions which have begun to fade with the crescent of Islâm. There was something startlingly incongruous about this full-grown specimen, that bloated representative of Eastern despotism squatting on the step of an up-to-date French car.

It was a kind of all-round shock; I cannot describe how it struck me. It was something like running into Martin Luther at the Grand National or Nero, say, at an aviation meeting.

This was a frightfully hot morning, and the adipose object on the car step was slumbering blissfully. A moment later I spotted the charge which he was guarding with such sedulous care. She was seated in Hassan's shop—well back in the shadows—a gauzy white vision, all eyes and *yashmak*. A confidential female servant accompanied her. They made a pleasing picture enough, and a more suitable setting could not well be found. It was an illustrated page of the *Arabian*

Nights, and it appealed strongly even to my jaded perceptions.

Of course, I was not going to interrupt the *tête-à-tête*; but from where I stood I could observe the group very well whilst remaining myself unobserved. It presently became evident that the lady of the *yashmak*, under the pretence of purchasing perfumes, was merely killing time, and my interest increased as the hour of noon grew near and the artistic group remained unbroken. You know the Mosque of El-Ashraf by Hassan's shop? Its minaret almost overhung the place. Well, in due course, out popped the *mueddin*.

"*La il aha illa Allah....*"

There he was a very sweet-voiced singer, as I noted at the time, telling them there was no God but God, and all the rest of it; and presently he worked round to the side of the gallery overlooking Hassan's shop.

Then I could see which way the wind blew. He seemed to be deliberately singing *at* the picturesque trio—and the dark eyes of the lady of the *yashmak* were lifted upward—in reverence, perhaps; but I hardly thought so.

There was no doubt about the *mueddin's* final glance, as he turned and retired from the gallery. I remained where I was until the *yashmak* left the shop; and as she had to pass quite close to me in order to rejoin the waiting car, I had a good look at her.

It was just an impression, of course, an impression of red lips under the white gauze, an oval Oriental outline, with very fine eyes—notably fine, where fine eyes are common—and a little exquisitely chiseled nose; a bewitching face. Just that one glimpse I had and a vague impression of rustling silk with the tap of high heels. A faint breath of musk still proclaimed itself above the less pleasing odors of the street; then, the female attendant having cuffed the slumbering Silenus into wakefulness, the car moved off and this *harêm* lily vanished from the bazaar.

I knew that my party was safe for another half an hour, at any rate, so I nipped along to Hassan's shop. Of course, he began brazenly by declaring that no ladies had been there that morning. I had expected it, and the attitude confirmed my suspicions.

Presently, when his boy had made fresh coffee, and Hassan, from the black cabinet, had produced some real cigarettes, we got more intimate. There was a scarcity of European visitors that morning; and excepting one interruption by a party of four American ladies, I had Hassan to myself for half an hour.

He raised his fat finger to his lips when I pressed my question, and rolled his eyes fearfully.

"She is from the palace of Harûn Pasha," he whispered with more sidelong glances. "Ah! *effendim*, I fear...."

We smoked awhile; then—

"The Pasha's wife?" I inquired.

"It is the Lady Zohara," he said.

This did not add greatly to my information; but I continued: "And the *mueddin*?"

"Ah!—do not whisper it.... That is my brother, Saïd!"

"He raises his eyes very high?"

"Not so, *effendim*; it is she who raises her eyes. I fear—I fear for Saïd. The Pasha ... you have heard of him?"

"I may have heard his name," I replied; "but I am quite unfamiliar with his reputation."

Hassan shook his head gloomily.

"He is the last of his race," he explained; "the race of the Khalîfs. He inhabits the ancient palace—but much has been rebuilt, and much added—in Old Cairo, close behind the Coptic Church...."

"I did not know that such a palace even existed."

Again Hassan raised his finger to his lips.

"He is not like the other pashas," he said; "in the house of Harûn Pasha are observed to-day all the old customs as in the day of his great ancestor Harûn al-Raschîd."

"But a motor-car!"

"Ah, *effendim*, he does not scorn to employ modern comforts, nor do I mean that he is a strict Moslem. But you saw the one who sat upon the step? The *harêm* of the Pasha is well guarded; not only by such as he, but by the Nubians and by the other mutes."

"Mutes!"

"He has many slaves. His agent in Mecca procures for him the pick of the market."

"But there is no such thing as slavery in Egypt!"

"Do the slaves know that, *effendim*?" he asked simply. "Those who have tongues are never seen outside the walls—unless they are guarded by those who have no tongue!"

It was a curious sidelight upon a more curious possibility and I was much impressed.

"Your brother——"

"Alas! I have warned him! I fear, most sincerely I fear, that one dark night the same will befall him that befell the son of my cousin, Ali."

"And what was that?"

"He climbed the wall of the Pasha's garden. There is a fig tree growing close beside it at one place. Someone assisted him to descend on the other. But he had been betrayed; the Nubian mutes took him—and they——"

He bent and whispered in my ear.

"Impossible!" I cried—"impossible! *báss! báss!*"

"Not so, *effendim*—nor was that all. After that they——"

"Enough, Hassan, enough!" I cried. "*Usbûr!*"

Hassan sighed, raising fearful eyes to the minaret.

III

There has been nothing you are likely to disbelieve so far; but now—well, I specified at the beginning—no comments. Let me tell the story in my own way, and you have permission to *think* what you please.

There was a dance at Shepheard's that night, and young Forrest rather interfered with my plans again as to one of the members of the English party; I think I have referred to her before? That sent me home in a bad humor—at least not home; for as I was standing over by the Ezbekîyeh Gardens, wondering whether to go along to "Jimmy's" or not, I formed a sudden determination to go and have a look at the abode of Harûn Pasha instead!

Mind you, I was not surprised to have lived in Cairo all these years without having heard of the place; I had learned things about the Mûski in the morning, from my tourist friends, which had revealed to me something of my pitiable ignorance. But I was determined to mend my ways, so to speak, and I thought I would turn my restless mood to good purpose, by improving my knowledge of my neighbors.

I induced the torpid driver of an *arabîyeh* to drive me out to Old Cairo. He obviously considered me to be even more demented than the rest of my countrymen, but since the fare would be a substantial one, he tackled the job. Mad expedition? Quite so; but you appreciate the mood?

After we had passed a certain quarter—a quarter which never sleeps—there was nothing livelier than decayed tombs *en route*. In the chill of the evening I began to weigh up my own foolishness appreciatively, but having got so far as the Coptic Church—you know the church I mean?—I was not going back unsatisfied; so I told my man to wait, and started off to look for the famous palace.

I must say the scene was impressive; a sky full of diamonds and a moon just bursting with light. The liquid night—sounds of the Nile alone disturbed the silence, and the buildings might have been made of mother-o'-pearl, so flawless and pure did they seem, gleaming there under the moon.

Well, I wandered up some narrow streets—past ruins of former important houses, and all that—until I found myself in the shadow of a high wall which obviously was kept in good repair. I followed this for some distance, and I could see trees on the other side; at one place a perfect mat of those purple flowers hung over the top; gorgeous things; the name begins with a B, but I can never remember it. This seemed promising, and as there was not a soul in sight, nor, on the visible evidences, a habitable building near me, I began to fossick for a likely place to climb up.

Presently I found the spot, and at the same time confirmation of my belief that these were the precincts of the Pasha. A fig tree grew beside the wall, affording an admirable means of reaching the top—a natural ladder. In a jiffy I was up ... and overlooking one of the most glorious gardens I had ever seen or dreamt of!

It must have been planned by an artist simply soaked in the lore of the Orient. It set me thinking of Edmond Dulac's illustrations to the *Arabian Nights*. Apart from those pages, you never saw anything like it, I swear. The position of each tree was a study; the arrangement of the flowerbeds was poetic—that is the only word for it; there was a pond with marble seats around and a flight of steps with big copper urns filled with growing flowers, mosaic paths, and lesser pools with fountains playing. I peered down into the water, and the moon rays glittered magically upon the scales of the golden carp which darted there. And all this fairy prospect was no more than an introduction, as it were, a sort of lead-up, to the Aladdin's Palace beyond.

I saw now that what with palms and the natural rise of the land back from the Nile, the wonderful palace, with its terraces and gleaming domes, must actually be invisible from all points; a more secret locality one could not well imagine.

As to this magician's abode, which lay before me, I shall not attempt to describe it. But turn to the illustrations which I have mentioned, or to those of Burton's big edition; I will leave it to the artist's and your imagination to fill up the canvas.

Lights shone out from a hundred windows. Out of the ghostly, tomb-like silence of Old Cairo, I had clambered into a sort of fairyland; I stood there with the spray from a fountain wetting me, and rubbed my eyes. Honestly, I should not have been surprised to find myself dreaming. Well, you may be sure I was not going back yet; there was not a living soul to be seen in the gardens, and I meant to have a peep into the palace, whatever the chances.

The likeliest point, as I soon determined, was to the west—where a long, low wing of the building extended, and was lost, if I may use the term, in a great bank of verdure and purple blooms. I took full advantage of the ample shadow cast by the trees, and came right up under the white wall without mishap.

To my right, the wall was obviously modern, but to my left, although in the distance and under the moon it had seemed uniform, it was built of sandstone blocks and was evidently of great age. The palace proper, you understand, was fully forty yards east; the place before me was a sort of low extension and evidently had no real connection with the residential part.

Just above my head was a square window, iron-barred, but this did not look promising, and cautiously, for I was hampered by the creepers which grew under the wall, I felt my way further west. Presently I encountered a pointed door of black, time-seared wood, and heavily iron-studded. Then, with alarming suddenness, the quietude of my adventure was broken; things began to move with breathless rapidity.

A most dreadful screaming and howling split the stillness and made me jump like a startled frog!

The sound of a lash on bare flesh reached me from some place behind the pointed door. Screams for mercy in thick, guttural Arabic, mingled and punctuated with horrifying shrieks of pain, informed my ignorance unmistakably that mediæval methods yet ruled in the civilized Near East.

Screams and supplications merged into a dull moaning; but the whistle of the lash continued uninterruptedly. Then that too ceased, and dimly came the sounds of a muffled colloquy; a sort of gurgling talk that got me wondering.

I had just time to creep away and conceal myself behind a thick clump of bushes, when the door was thrown open, and the most gigantic negro I have ever set eyes upon appeared in the opening, outlined against the smoky glare from within. He had one gleaming bare arm about the neck of an insensible man, and he dragged him out into the garden as one might drag a heavy sack; dropping him all in a quivering heap upon the very spot which I had just vacated!

The negro, who was stripped to the waist and whose glistening body reminded me of a bronze statue of Hercules, stood looking down at the insensible victim, with a hideous leer. I ventured to raise myself ever so slightly; and in the ghastly, sweat-bedaubed face of the tortured man—whose bare shoulders were bloody from the lash—I recognized the Silenus of the limousine!

In response to a guttural inarticulate muttering by the black giant, a second Nubian, of scarcely lesser dimensions, emerged from the dungeon with a jar of water. He drenched the swooning man, evidently in order to revive him; and, when the wretched being ultimately fought his way back to agonized consciousness—to my horror he was seized, dragged in through the doorway again, and once more I heard the whistle of the lash being applied to his lacerated back, the skin of which was already in ribbons.

I suppose there are times when the most discreet man is snatched outside himself by circumstances? The door of this beastly torture-room had not been reclosed, and before I could realize what I was about, I found myself inside!

The wretched victim had been hauled up to a beam by his bound wrists, and the huge Nubian was putting all his strength into the wielding of the cat-o'-nine-tails, drawing blood with every stroke; whilst his assistant hung on to the rope running through a pulley-block in the low ceiling.

All in a sort of whirl (I was raving mad with indignation) I got amongst the trio, and landed a clip on the jaw of the son of Erebus which made his teeth rattle like castanets.

Down came the fat sufferer all in a heap in his own blood. Down went my man, and began to cough out broken molars. Then it was my turn; and down *I* went with the second mute on top of me, and the pair of us were playing hell all about the blood-spattered floor—up, down, under, over—straining, punching, kicking ... then my antagonist introduced gouging, and I had to beat the mat.

It had been a stiff bout, and the stinking shambles were whirling about me like a bloody maelstrom. When things settled down a bit, I found myself lying in a small cell skewered up like a pullet, and with a prospect of iron grating and stone-flagged passage before me. I was more than a trifle damaged, and my head was singing like a kettle. If I had thought that I dreamed before, it was a struggle now to convince myself that this was not a nightmare.

Amid the rattling of chains and dropping of bars, a fantastic procession was filing down the passage. First came a hideous, crook-backed apparition, hook-nosed, and bearing a lantern. Behind him appeared two guards with glittering scimitars. Behind the guards walked a fourth personage, black-robed and white-turbaned—a sort of dignified dragoman, carrying an enormous bunch of keys.

The iron grating of my dungeon was unlocked and raised, and I was requested, in Arabic, to rise and follow. Realizing that this was no time for funny business, I staggered to my feet, and between the two Scimitars marched unsteadily through a maze of passages with doors unlocked and locked behind us, stairs ascended and stairs descended.

From empty passages, our journey led us to passages richly carpeted and softly lighted. By a heavy door opening on to the first of the latter, we left the squinting man; and, with the two Scimitars and Black Robe, I found myself crossing a lofty pavilion.

The floor was of rich mosaic, and priceless carpets were spread about in artistic confusion. Above my head loomed a great dome, lighted by stained glass windows in which the blue of lapis-lazuli predominated. By golden chains from above swung golden lamps burning perfumed oil and flooding the pavilion with a mellow blue light. There were inlaid tables and cabinets; great blue vases of exquisite Chinese porcelain stood in niches of the wall. The walls were of that faintly amber-tinted alabaster which is quarried in the Mokattam Hills; and there were fragile columns of some delicately azure-veined marble, rising, graceful and slender, ethereal as pencils of smoke, to a balcony high above my head; then, from this, a second series of fairy columns crept in blue streaks up into the luminous shadows of the dome.

We crossed this place, my heel taps echoing hollowly and before a curtained door took pause. An impressive interval of perfumed silence; then in response to the muffled clapping of hands, the curtain was raised and I was thrust into a smaller apartment beyond.

I found myself standing before a long *dîwan*, amid an opulence of Oriental appointment which surpassed anything which I could have imagined. The atmosphere was heavy with the odor of burning perfumes, and, whereas the lofty pavilion afforded a delicate study in blue, this chamber was voluptuously amber—amber-shaded lamps, amber cushions, amber carpets; everywhere the glitter of amber and gold.

Amid the amber sea, half immersed in the golden silks of the daïs, reclined a large and portly Sheikh; full and patriarchal his beard, wherein played amber tints, lofty and serene his brow, sweeping up to the snowy turban. From a mouthpiece of amber and gold he inhaled the scented smoke of a *narghli*. Behind him, upon a cushioned stool, knelt a female whose beauty of face and form was unmistakable, since it was undisguised by the filmy artistry of her attire. With a gigantic fan of peacock's feathers, she cooled the Sheikh, and dispersed the flies which threatened to disturb his serenity. A second houri received in her hands the amber mouthpiece as it fell from her lord's lips; a third, who evidently had been playing upon a lute, rose and glided from the apartment like an opium vision, as I entered between the guardian Scimitars.

I found myself thinking of Saint Saen's music to *Samson and Delilah*; the barbaric strains of the exquisite *bacchanale* were beating on my brain.

Black Robe advanced and knelt upon the floor of the *dîwan*.

"We have brought the wretched malefactor into your glorious presence," he said.

The Pasha (for I knew, beyond doubt, that I stood before Harûn Pasha) raised his eyes and fixed a stern gaze upon me. He gazed long and fixedly, and an odd change took place in his expression. He seemed about to address me, then, apparently changing his mind, he addressed the recumbent figure at his feet.

"Have the slaves returned with the female miscreant and her partner in Satan?" he demanded sternly.

"Lord of the age," replied the other, rising upon his knees, "they are expected."

"Let them be brought before me," directed the Pasha, "upon the instant of their arrival. Has Misrûn confessed his complicity?"

"He fainted beneath the lash, excellency, but confessed that he slept— that pig who prayed without washing and whose birth was a calamity— on several occasions when accompanying the lady Zohara."

"Leave us!" cried the Pasha. "But, first, unbind the prisoner."

He swept his arm around comprehensively, and everyone withdrew from the apartment, including the Scimitars (one of whom cut my lashings) and the lady of the fan. I found myself alone with Harûn Pasha.

<h2 style="text-align:center">IV</h2>

"Sit here beside me!" directed the Pasha.

Being yet too dazed for wonder or protest, I obeyed mechanically. My exact situation was not clear to me at the moment and I was a long way off knowing how to act.

"I am much disturbed in mind, and my bosom is contracted," continued the Pasha, with a certain benignity, "by reason of a conspiracy in my *harêm*, which came to a head this night, and which led to the loss of the pearl of my household, a damsel who cost me her weight in gold, who entangled me in the snare of her love and pierced me with anguish. Know, O young Inglîsi, that love is difficult. Alas! she who had captivated my reason by her loveliness fled with a shame of the Moslems who defamed the sacred office of *mueddin*! In truth he is naught but the son of a disease and a consort of camels. My soul cries out to Allah and my mind is a nest of wasps. Relate to me your case, that it may turn me from the contemplation of my sorrows. At another time, it had gone hard with you, and penalties of a most unfortunate description had been visited upon your head, O disturber of my peace; but since this child of filth and progeny of mules has shattered it forever, your lesser crime comes but as a diversion. Relate to me the matters which have brought you to this miserable pass."

There was some still little voice in my mind which was trying to speak to me, if you understand what I mean. But what with the suffocating perfume of ambergris (or it may have been frankincense), my incredible surroundings, and the buzzing of my maltreated skull, I simply could *not* think connectedly.

A memory was struggling for identification in my addled brain; but whether it was due to something I had seen, heard, or smelled, I could not for the life of me make out. I heard myself spinning my own improbable yarn as one listens to a dreary and boresome recitation; *I* didn't seem to be the raconteur; my mind was busy about that amber room, furiously chasing that hare-like memory, which leaped and doubled, dived under the silken cushions, popped up behind the Pasha, and flicked its ears at me from amid the feathers of the peacock fan.

I driveled right on to the end of my story, mechanically, without having got my mind in proper working order; and when the Pasha spoke again—there was that wretched memory still dodging me, sometimes almost within my grasp, but always just eluding it.

"Your amusing narrative has diverted me," said the Pasha; and he clapped his hands three times.

It never occurred to me, you will note, to assert myself in any way; I accepted the lordly condescensions of this singular personage without protest. You will be wondering why I didn't kick up a devil of a hullabaloo—declare that I had come in response to screams for assistance—wave the dreaded name of the British Agent under the Pasha's nose, and all that. I can only say that I didn't; I was subdued; in fact I was down, utterly down and out.

Black Robe entered with eyes averted.

"Well, wretched vermin!" roared the Pasha in sudden wrath; "do you tell me they are not here?"

The man, with his head bumping on the carpet, visibly trembled.

"Most noble," he replied hoarsely, "your lowly slave has exerted himself to the utmost——"

"Out! son of a calamity!" shouted the Pasha—and before my astonished eyes he raised the heavy *narghli* and hurled it at the bowed head of the man before him.

It struck the white turban with a resounding crack, and then was shattered to bits upon the floor. It was a blow to have staggered a mule. But Black Robe, without apparent loss of dignity, rose and departed, bowing.

The Pasha sat rocking about, and plucking madly at his beard.

"O Allah!" he cried, "how I suffer." He turned to me. "Never since the day that another of your race (but, this one, a true son of Satan) came to my palace, have I tasted so much suffering. You shall judge of my clemency, O imprudent stranger, and pacify your heart with the spectacle of another's punishment."

He clapped his hands twice. This time there was a short delay, which the Pasha suffered impatiently; then there entered the squint-eyed man, together with the two Scimitars.

"I would visit the dungeon of the false Pasha," said my singular host; and, rising to his feet, he placed his hand upon my shoulder and indicated that we were to proceed from the apartment.

Led by Crook Back, in whose hand the gigantic bunch of keys rattled unmelodiously, and followed by the Scimitars, we proceeded upon our way; and it was beyond the powers of my disordered brain to dismiss the idea that I was taking part in a Christmas pantomime. Many steps were descended; many heavy doors unbolted and unbarred, bolted and barred behind us; many stone-paved passages, reminding me of operatic scenery, were traversed ere we came to one tunnel more gloomy than the rest.

Upon the right was a blank stone wall, upon the left, a series of doors, black with age and heavily iron-studded. The only illumination was that furnished by the lantern which Crook Back carried.

Before one of the doors the Pasha paused.

"In which is Misrûn?" he demanded.

"In the next, excellency," replied the jailer—for such I took to be the office of the hunchback.

As he spoke, he held the lantern to the grating.

I found myself peering into a filthy dungeon, the reek of which made me ill; and there, upon the stone floor, lay poor Silenus! He raised his eyes to the light.

"Lord of the age," he moaned, lifting his manacled wrists, "glory of the universe, sun of suns! I have confessed my frightful sin, and most dire misfortunes. Of your sublime mercy, take pity upon the meanest thing that creeps upon the earth——"

"Proceed!" said the Pasha.

And with the moaning cries of Misrûn growing fainter behind us, we moved along the passage. Before a second door, we halted again, and the jailer raised the lantern.

"Look upon this!" cried the Pasha to me—"look well, and look long!"

Shudderingly I peered in between the bars. It had come home to me how I was utterly at the mercy of this man's moods. If he had chosen to have me hurled into one of his dungeons, what prospect of release would have been mine? Who would ever know of my plight? No one! And beyond doubt I was in the realm of an absolute monarch. I silently thanked my lucky stars that my lot was not the lot of him who occupied this second dungeon.

As the dim light, casting shadow bars across the filthy floor, picked out the features of the prisoner, I gave a great start. Save that the beard was more gray, longer, filthy and unkempt, and that, in place of the nearly shaven skull, this unhappy being displayed dishevelled locks, the captive might easily have passed for the Pasha.

I met the eye of this terrible despot.

"Look upon the false Pasha," he said; "look upon the one who thought to dispossess me! For years, by his own miserable confession, he studied me in secret. When I journeyed to my estates in Assuan" (I started again) "he was watching—watching—always watching. His scheme, which was whispered into his ear by the Evil One, was no plant of sudden growth, but a tree, that, from a seed of Satan planted in fertile soil, had flourished exceedingly, tended by the hand of villainous ambition."

I clutched at the bars for support. The stench of the place was simply indescribable; but it was neither the stench nor the bizarre incidents of the night which accounted for my dizziness: it was the sudden tangibility of that hitherto elusive memory.

In build, in complexion, in certain mannerisms underlying the dignified assumption, Harûn Pasha might well have been the twin brother of Jack Dunlap!

A frightful possibility burst upon me like a bomb; clutching the bars with quivering hands, I stared and stared at the wretched impostor in the cell. *Could* it be? Had he been mad enough to make some attempt upon the Pasha? And was this his end?

I looked around again. I searched the bearded features of the Pasha with eager gaze. Good God! either I was going mad, or incredible things had been done, were being done, in Cairo.

I had not seen Dunlap for a year, remember, and in the ordinary way I did not see him more than half a dozen times in twelve months, so that, all things considered, it was not so remarkable that I had overlooked the resemblance. A full beard and mustache, artificially darkened eyelashes, a shaven head and a white turban, are effectual disguises; but if you can imagine Dunlap—the Dunlap you remember— so arrayed, then you have Harûn Pasha. Imagine Harûn Pasha, dirty, bedraggled, a hopeless captive ... and you have the prisoner who crouched upon the straw in that noisome dungeon!

For the second time that night I was lifted out of myself. I turned on the man beside me in a blazing fury.

"You villain!" I shouted at him, and clenched my fists—"do you *dare* to confine a Britisher in your stinking cellars. By God! sir...."

Harûn Pasha clapped his hand over my mouth; the two guards had me by the arms from behind. But my cries had aroused the man in the dungeon, and, as I was dragged down the passage, these moaning words reached me, spoken in Arabic:

"Help! help! Englishman! A crime has been committed! I appeal to Lord——."

A door was slammed fast with a resounding bang, and the rest of the captive's appeal was lost to me. One of my guards had substituted his hand for that of the Pasha, but now it was removed; and, speechless with rage, I found myself being thrust up stone stairs—and I realized that by a moment's indiscretion, I had ruined everything.

Back in the amber apartment once more, with the two Scimitars at the door and Harûn Pasha reclining upon the cushions, I found speech.

"What are you going to do with me?" I demanded.

"My son," replied the Pasha with benignity, "I pardon all! Your great courage and address, together with the modesty of your deportment, and the spirit of adventure which has brought you to your present unfortunate case, plead for you in a manner which my clemency cannot resist. It is my unhappy lot often to be called upon to punish. To-night, those gloomy dungeons which you have seen will echo, alas, with the howls of miserable wretches who are responsible for the loss of the pearl of my soul; for I am persuaded that she has fled with the son of offal who profaned the words of Allah from the minaret. This being so, I would temper my proper severity with a merciful deed. You shall never speak of what you have seen within these walls, save in terms suitably disguised. You shall never seek to return, nor, by speech with any man, to confirm whatsoever you may suspect. Upon this warranty, you shall depart in peace."

He clapped his hands twice, and a houri of most bewitching aspect glided into the *dîwan*.

"Bring sherbet!" ordered the Pasha.

The maiden departed; and whilst I was yet trying to come to a decision (the Pasha had mentioned no alternative, but my imagination was equal to the task of supplying one!) she returned with a tray upon which were porcelain cups and two vessels of beautifully chased gold.

Harûn Pasha decocted a sparkling beverage, and, with his own hands, passed the brimming cup to me.

I knew you would not believe it; but I warned you, and I made a stipulation. Your idea is that I must be a poor sort of animal to accept so dishonorable a compromise? I agree. But the situation was even more peculiarly difficult than is apparent to you at the moment. Without *seeking* the information, I learned from Hassan of the Scent Bazaar that his brother had indeed fled with the beauteous Lady Zohara, no one knew whither; and this confirmation of the Pasha's sorrows touched a very tender spot in my heart!

Then there is another little point.

When the Pasha removed the elaborate stopper from the first of the golden vessels to which I have just referred, *my* eye alone perceived that a bottle, bearing a familiar black and white label, was contained in this golden casing. The flavor of the decoction with which we sealed our infamous bargain clinched the matter.

I was absolutely thrust out of the presence chamber before I had time for another word; but, looking back from the door and meeting the eye of the Pasha, I encountered a most portentous wink. Therefore I have stuck to my bargain.

Oh! I have not given much away. The Pasha is not called Harûn, and the palace is nowhere near the Coptic Church in Old Cairo. Because, you see, I only knew one man who winked in quite that elaborate fashion—and his name was Jack Dunlap!

V

IN THE VALLEY OF THE SORCERESS

I

Condor wrote to me three times before the end (said Neville, Assistant-Inspector of Antiquities, staring vaguely from his open window at a squad drilling before the Kasr-en-Nîl Barracks). He dated his letters from the camp at Deir-el-Bahari. Judging from these, success appeared to be almost within his grasp. He shared my theories, of course, respecting Queen Hatasu, and was devoting the whole of his energies to the task of clearing up the great mystery of Ancient Egypt which centres around that queen.

For him, as for me, there was a strange fascination about those defaced walls and roughly obliterated inscriptions. That the queen under whom Egyptian art came to the apogee of perfection should thus have been treated by her successors; that no perfect figure of the wise, famous, and beautiful Hatasu should have been spared to posterity; that her very cartouche should have been ruthlessly removed from every inscription upon which it appeared, presented to Condor's mind a problem only second in interest to the immortal riddle of Gîzeh.

You know my own views upon the matter? My monograph, "Hatasu, the Sorceress," embodies my opinion. In short, upon certain evidences, some adduced by Theodore Davis, some by poor Condor, and some resulting from my own inquiries, I have come to the conclusion that the source—real or imaginary—of this queen's power was an intimate acquaintance with what nowadays we term, vaguely, magic. Pursuing her studies beyond the limit which is lawful, she met with a certain end, not uncommon, if the old writings are to be believed, in the case of those who penetrate too far into the realms of the Borderland.

For this reason—the practice of black magic—her statues were dishonored, and her name erased from the monuments. Now, I do not propose to enter into any discussion respecting the reality of such practices; in my monograph I have merely endeavored to show that, according to contemporary belief, the queen was a sorceress. Condor was seeking to prove the same thing; and when I took up the inquiry, it was in the hope of completing his interrupted work.

He wrote to me early in the winter of 1908, from his camp by the Rock Temple. Davis's tomb, at Bibân el-Mulûk, with its long, narrow passage, apparently had little interest for him; he was at work on the high ground behind the temple, at a point one hundred yards or so due west of the upper platform. He had an idea that he should find there the mummies of Hatasu—and another; the latter, a certain Sen-Mût, who appears in the inscriptions of the reign as an architect high in the queen's favor. The archæological points of the letter do not concern us in the least, but there was one odd little paragraph which I had cause to remember afterwards.

"A girl belonging to some Arab tribe," wrote Condor, "came racing to the camp two nights ago to claim my protection. What crime she had committed, and what punishment she feared, were far from clear; but she clung to me, trembling like a leaf, and positively refused to depart. It was a difficult situation, for a camp of fifty native excavators, and one highly respectable European enthusiast, affords no suitable quarters for an Arab girl—and a very personable Arab girl. At any rate, she is still here; I have had a sort of lean-to rigged up in a little valley east of my own tent, but it is very embarrassing."

Nearly a month passed before I heard from Condor again; then came a second letter, with the news that on the eve of a great discovery—as he believed—his entire native staff—the whole fifty—had deserted one night in a body! "Two days' work," he wrote, "would have seen the tomb opened—for I am more than ever certain that my plans are accurate. Then I woke up one morning to find every man Jack of my fellows missing! I went down into the village where a lot of them live, in a towering rage, but not one of the brutes was to be found, and their relations professed entire ignorance respecting their whereabouts. What caused me almost as much anxiety as the check in my work was the fact that Mahâra—the Arab girl—had vanished also. I am wondering if the thing has any sinister significance."

Condor finished with the statement that he was making tremendous efforts to secure a new gang. "But," said he, "I shall finish the excavation, if I have to do it with my own hands."

His third and last letter contained even stranger matters than the two preceding it. He had succeeded in borrowing a few men from the British Archæological camp in the Fáyûm. Then, just as the work was restarting, the Arab girl, Mahâra, turned up again, and entreated him to bring her down the Nile, "at least as far as Dendera. For the vengeance of her tribesmen," stated Condor, "otherwise would result not only in her own death, but in mine! At the moment of writing I am in two minds what to do. If Mahâra is to go upon this journey, I do not feel justified in sending her alone, and there is no one here who could perform the duty," etc.

I began to wonder, of course; and I had it in mind to take the train to Luxor merely in order to see this Arab maiden, who seemed to occupy so prominent a place in Condor's mind. However, Fate would have it otherwise; and the next thing I heard was that Condor had been brought into Cairo, and was at the English hospital.

He had been bitten by a cat—presumably from the neighboring village; and although the doctor at Luxor dealt with the bite at once, traveled down with him, and placed him in the hand of the Pasteur man at the hospital, he died, as you remember, in the night of his arrival, raving mad; the Pasteur treatment failed entirely.

I never saw him before the end, but they told me that his howls were horribly like those of a cat. His eyes changed in some way, too, I understand; and, with his fingers all contracted, he tried to *scratch* everyone and everything within reach.

They had to strap the poor beggar down, and even then he tore the sheets into ribbons.

Well, as soon as possible, I made the necessary arrangements to finish Condor's inquiry. I had access to his papers, plans, etc., and in the spring of the same year I took up my quarters near Deir-el-Bahari, roped off the approaches to the camp, stuck up the usual notices, and prepared to finish the excavation, which, I gathered, was in a fairly advanced state.

My first surprise came very soon after my arrival, for when, with the plan before me, I started out to find the shaft, I found it, certainly, but only with great difficulty.

It had been filled in again with sand and loose rock right to the very top!

II

All my inquiries availed me nothing. With what object the excavation had been thus closed I was unable to conjecture. That Condor had not reclosed it I was quite certain, for at the time of his mishap he had actually been at work at the bottom of the shaft, as inquiries from a native of Suefee, in the Fáyûm, who was his only companion at the time, had revealed.

In his eagerness to complete the inquiry, Condor, by lantern light, had been engaged upon a solitary night-shift below, and the rabid cat had apparently fallen into the pit; probably in a frenzy of fear, it had attacked Condor, after which it had escaped.

Only this one man was with him, and he, for some reason that I could not make out, had apparently been sleeping in the temple—

quite a considerable distance from Condor's camp. The poor fellow's cries had aroused him, and he had met Condor running down the path and away from the shaft.

This, however, was good evidence of the existence of the shaft at the time, and as I stood contemplating the tightly packed rubble which alone marked its site, I grew more and more mystified, for this task of reclosing the cutting represented much hard labor.

Beyond perfecting my plans in one or two particulars, I did little on the day of my arrival. I had only a handful of men with me, all of whom I knew, having worked with them before, and beyond clearing Condor's shaft I did not intend to excavate further.

Hatasu's Temple presents a lively enough scene in the daytime during the winter and early spring months, with the streams of tourists constantly passing from the white causeway to Cook's Rest House on the edge of the desert. There had been a goodly number of visitors that day to the temple below, and one or two of the more curious and venturesome had scrambled up the steep path to the little plateau which was the scene of my operations. None had penetrated beyond the notice boards, however, and now, with the evening sky passing through those innumerable shades which defy palette and brush, which can only be distinguished by the trained eye, but which, from palest blue melt into exquisite pink, and by some magical combination form that deep violet which does not exist to perfection elsewhere than in the skies of Egypt, I found myself in the silence and the solitude of "the Holy Valley."

I stood at the edge of the plateau, looking out at the rosy belt which marked the course of the distant Nile, with the Arabian hills vaguely sketched beyond. The rocks stood up against that prospect as great black smudges, and what I could see of the causeway looked like a gray smear upon a drab canvas. Beneath me were the chambers of the Rock Temple, with those wall paintings depicting events in the reign of Hatasu which rank among the wonders of Egypt.

Not a sound disturbed my reverie, save a faint clatter of cooking utensils from the camp behind me—a desecration of that sacred solitude. Then a dog began to howl in the neighboring village. The dog ceased, and faintly to my ears came the note of a reed pipe. The breeze died away, and with it the piping.

I turned back to the camp, and, having partaken of a frugal supper, turned in upon my campaigner's bed, thoroughly enjoying my freedom from the routine of official life in Cairo, and looking forward to the morrow's work pleasurably.

Under such circumstances a man sleeps well; and when, in an

uncanny gray half-light, which probably heralded the dawn, I awoke with a start, I knew that something of an unusual nature alone could have disturbed my slumbers.

Firstly, then, I identified this with a concerted howling of the village dogs. They seemed to have conspired to make night hideous; I have never heard such an eerie din in my life. Then it gradually began to die away, and I realized, secondly, that the howling of the dogs and my own awakening might be due to some common cause. This idea grew upon me, and as the howling subsided, a sort of disquiet possessed me, and, despite my efforts to shake it off, grew more urgent with the passing of every moment.

In short, I fancied that the thing which had alarmed or enraged the dogs was passing from the village through the Holy Valley, upward to the Temple, upward to the plateau, and was approaching *me*.

I have never experienced an identical sensation since, but I seemed to be audient of a sort of psychic patrol, which, from a remote *pianissimo*, swelled *fortissimo*, to an intimate but silent clamor, which beat in some way upon my brain, but not through the faculty of hearing, for now the night was deathly still.

Yet I was persuaded of some *approach*—of the coming of something sinister, and the suspense of waiting had become almost insupportable, so that I began to accuse my Spartan supper of having given me nightmare, when the tent-flap was suddenly raised, and, outlined against the paling blue of the sky, with a sort of reflected elfin light playing upon her face, I saw an Arab girl looking in at me!

By dint of exerting all my self-control I managed to restrain the cry and upward start which this apparition prompted. Quite still, with my fists tightly clenched, I lay and looked into the eyes which were looking into mine.

The style of literary work which it has been my lot to cultivate fails me in describing that beautiful and evil face. The features were severely classical and small, something of the Bishârîn type, with a cruel little mouth and a rounded chin, firm to hardness. In the eyes alone lay the languor of the Orient; they were exceedingly—indeed, excessively— long and narrow. The ordinary ragged, picturesque finery of a desert girl bedecked this midnight visitant, who, motionless, stood there watching me.

I once read a work by Pierre de l'Ancre, dealing with the Black Sabbaths of the Middle Ages, and now the evil beauty of this Arab face threw my memory back to those singular pages, for, perhaps owing to the reflected light which I have mentioned, although the explanation scarcely seemed adequate, those long, narrow eyes shone catlike in the gloom.

Suddenly I made up my mind. Throwing the blanket from me, I leapt to the ground, and in a flash had gripped the girl by the wrists. Confuting some lingering doubts, she proved to be substantial enough. My electric torch lay upon a box at the foot of the bed, and, stooping, I caught it up and turned its searching rays upon the face of my captive.

She fell back from me, panting like a wild creature trapped, then dropped upon her knees and began to plead—began to plead in a voice and with a manner which touched some chord of consciousness that I could swear had never spoken before, and has never spoken since.

She spoke in Arabic, of course, but the words fell from her lips as liquid music in which lay all the beauty and all the deviltry of the "Siren's Song." Fully opening her astonishing eyes, she looked up at me, and, with her free hand pressed to her bosom, told me how she had fled from an unwelcome marriage; how, an outcast and a pariah, she had hidden in the desert places for three days and three nights, sustaining life only by means of a few dates which she had brought with her, and quenching her thirst with stolen water-melons.

"I can bear it no longer, *effendim*. Another night out in the desert, with the cruel moon beating, beating, beating upon my brain, with creeping things coming out from the rocks, wriggling, wriggling, their many feet making whisperings in the sand—ah, it will kill me! And I am for ever outcast from my tribe, from my people. No tent of all the Arabs, though I fly to the gates of Damascus, is open to me, save I enter in shame, as a slave, as a plaything, as a toy. My heart"—furiously she beat upon her breast—"is empty and desolate, *effendim*. I am meaner than the lowliest thing that creeps upon the sand; yet the God that made that creeping thing made me also—and you, you, who are merciful and strong, would not crush any creature because it was weak and helpless."

I had released her wrist now, and was looking down at her in a sort of stupor. The evil which at first I had seemed to perceive in her was effaced, wiped out as an artist wipes out an error in his drawing. Her dark beauty was speaking to me in a language of its own; a strange language, yet one so intelligible that I struggled in vain to disregard it. And her voice, her gestures, and the witch-fire of her eyes were whipping up my blood to a fever heat of passionate sorrow—of despair. Yes, incredible as it sounds, despair!

In short, as I see it now, this siren of the wilderness was playing upon me as an accomplished musician might play upon a harp, striking this string and that at will, and sounding each with such full notes as they had rarely, if ever, emitted before.

Most damnable anomaly of all, I—Edward Neville, archæologist, most prosy and matter-of-fact man in Cairo, perhaps—*knew* that this nomad who had burst into my tent, upon whom I had set eyes for the first time scarce three minutes before, held me enthralled; and yet, with her wondrous eyes upon me, I could summon up no resentment, and could offer but poor resistance.

"In the Little Oasis, *effendim*, I have a sister who will admit me into her household, if only as a servant. There I can be safe, there I can rest. O *Inglîsi*, at home in England you have a sister of your own! Would you see her pursued, a hunted thing from rock to rock, crouching for shelter in the lair of some jackal, stealing that she might live—and flying always, never resting, her heart leaping for fear, flying, flying, with nothing but dishonor before her?"

She shuddered and clasped my left hand in both her own convulsively, pulling it down to her bosom.

"There can be only one thing, *effendim*," she whispered. "Do you not see the white bones bleaching in the sun?"

Throwing all my resolution into the act, I released my hand from her clasp, and, turning aside, sat down upon the box which served me as chair and table, too.

A thought had come to my assistance, had strengthened me in the moment of my greatest weakness; it was the thought of that Arab girl mentioned in Condor's letters. And a scheme of things, an incredible scheme, that embraced and explained some, if not all, of the horrible circumstances attendant upon his death, began to form in my brain.

Bizarre it was, stretching out beyond the realm of things natural and proper, yet I clung to it, for there, in the solitude, with this wildly beautiful creature kneeling at my feet, and with her uncanny powers of fascination yet enveloping me like a cloak, I found it not so improbable as inevitably it must have seemed at another time.

I turned my head, and through the gloom sought to look into the long eyes. As I did so they closed and appeared as two darkly luminous slits in the perfect oval of the face.

"You are an impostor!" I said in Arabic, speaking firmly and deliberately. "To Mr. Condor"—I could have sworn that she started slightly at sound of the name—"you called yourself Mahâra. I know you, and I will have nothing to do with you."

But in saying it I had to turn my head aside, for the strangest, maddest impulses were bubbling up in my brain in response to the glances of those half-shut eyes.

I reached for my coat, which lay upon the foot of the bed, and, taking out some loose money, I placed fifty piastres in the nerveless brown hand.

"That will enable you to reach the Little Oasis, if such is your desire," I said. "It is all I can do for you, and now—you must go."

The light of the dawn was growing stronger momentarily, so that I could see my visitor quite clearly. She rose to her feet, and stood before me, a straight, slim figure, sweeping me from head to foot with such a glance of passionate contempt as I had never known or suffered.

She threw back her head magnificently, dashed the money on the ground at my feet, and, turning, leaped out of the tent.

For a moment I hesitated, doubting, questioning my humanity, testing my fears; then I took a step forward, and peered out across the plateau. Not a soul was in sight. The rocks stood up gray and eerie, and beneath lay the carpet of the desert stretching unbroken to the shadows of the Nile Valley.

<h1 style="text-align:center">III</h1>

We commenced the work of clearing the shaft at an early hour that morning. The strangest ideas were now playing in my mind, and in some way I felt myself to be in opposition to definite enmity. My excavators labored with a will, and, once we had penetrated below the first three feet or so of tightly packed stone, it became a mere matter of shoveling, for apparently the lower part of the shaft had been filled up principally with sand.

I calculated that four days' work at the outside would see the shaft clear to the base of Condor's excavation. There remained, according to his own notes, only another six feet or so; but it was solid limestone— the roof of the passage, if his plans were correct, communicating with the tomb of Hatasu.

With the approach of night, tired as I was, I felt little inclination for sleep. I lay down on my bed with a small Browning pistol under the pillow, but after an hour or so of nervous listening drifted off into slumber. As on the night before, I awoke shortly before the coming of dawn.

Again the village dogs were raising a hideous outcry, and again I was keenly conscious of some ever-nearing menace. This consciousness grew stronger as the howling of the dogs grew fainter, and the sense of *approach* assailed me as on the previous occasion.

I sat up immediately with the pistol in my hand, and, gently raising the tent flap, looked out over the darksome plateau. For a long time I could perceive nothing; then, vaguely outlined against the sky, I detected something that moved above the rocky edge.

It was so indefinite in form that for a time I was unable to identify it, but as it slowly rose higher and higher, two luminous eyes—obviously feline eyes, since they glittered greenly in the darkness—came into view. In character and in shape they were the eyes of a cat, but in point of size they were larger than the eyes of any cat I had ever seen. Nor were they jackal eyes. It occurred to me that some predatory beast from the Sûdan might conceivably have strayed thus far north.

The presence of such a creature would account for the nightly disturbance amongst the village dogs; and, dismissing the superstitious notions which had led me to associate the mysterious Arab girl with the phenomenon of the howling dogs, I seized upon this new idea with a sort of gladness.

Stepping boldly out of the tent, I strode in the direction of the gleaming eyes. Although my only weapon was the Browning pistol, it was a weapon of considerable power, and, moreover, I counted upon the well-known cowardice of nocturnal animals. I was not disappointed in the result.

The eyes dropped out of sight, and as I leaped to the edge of rock overhanging the temple a lithe shape went streaking off in the greyness beneath me. Its coloring appeared to be black, but this appearance may have been due to the bad light. Certainly it was no cat, was no jackal; and once, twice, thrice my Browning spat into the darkness.

Apparently I had not scored a hit, but the loud reports of the weapon aroused the men sleeping in the camp, and soon I was surrounded by a ring of inquiring faces.

But there I stood on the rock-edge, looking out across the desert in silence. Something in the long, luminous eyes, something in the sinuous, flying shape had spoken to me intimately, horribly.

Hassan es-Sugra, the headman, touched my arm, and I knew that I must offer some explanation.

"Jackals," I said shortly. And with no other word I walked back to my tent.

The night passed without further event, and in the morning we addressed ourselves to the work with such a will that I saw, to my satisfaction, that by noon of the following day the labor of clearing the loose sand would be completed.

During the preparation of the evening meal I became aware of a certain disquiet in the camp, and I noted a disinclination on the part of the native laborers to stray far from the tents. They hung together in a group, and whilst individually they seemed to avoid meeting my eye, collectively they watched me in a furtive fashion.

A gang of Moslem workmen calls for delicate handling, and I wondered if, inadvertently, I had transgressed in some way their iron-bound code of conduct. I called Hassan es-Sugra aside.

"What ails the men?" I asked him. "Have they some grievance?"

Hassan spread his palms eloquently.

"If they have," he replied, "they are secret about it, and I am not in their confidence. Shall I thrash three or four of them in order to learn the nature of this grievance?"

"No thanks all the same," I said, laughing at this characteristic proposal. "If they refuse to work to-morrow, there will be time enough for you to adopt those measures."

On this, the third night of my sojourn in the Holy Valley by the Temple of Hatasu, I slept soundly and uninterruptedly. I had been looking forward with the keenest zest to the morrow's work, which promised to bring me within sight of my goal, and when Hassan came to awaken me, I leaped out of bed immediately.

Hassan es-Sugra, having performed his duty, did not, as was his custom, retire; he stood there, a tall, angular figure, looking at me strangely.

"Well?" I said.

"There is trouble," was his simple reply. "Follow me, Neville Effendi."

Wondering greatly, I followed him across the plateau and down the slope to the excavation. There I pulled up short with a cry of amazement.

Condor's shaft was filled in to the very top, and presented, to my astonished gaze, much the same aspect that had greeted me upon my first arrival!

"The men——" I began.

Hassan es-Sugra spread wide his palms.

"Gone!" he replied. "Those Coptic dogs, those eaters of carrion, have fled in the night."

"And this"—I pointed to the little mound of broken granite and sand—"is their work?"

"So it would seem," was the reply; and Hassan sniffed his sublime contempt.

I stood looking bitterly at this destruction of my toils. The strangeness of the thing at the moment did not strike me, in my anger; I was only concerned with the outrageous impudence of the missing workmen, and if I could have laid hands upon one of them it had surely gone hard with him.

As for Hassan es-Sugra, I believe he would cheerfully have broken the necks of the entire gang. But he was a man of resource.

"It is so newly filled in," he said, "that you and I, in three days, or in four, can restore it to the state it had reached when those nameless dogs, who regularly prayed with their shoes on, those devourers of pork, began their dirty work."

His example was stimulating. *I* was not going to be beaten, either.

After a hasty breakfast, the pair of us set to work with pick and shovel and basket. We worked as those slaves must have worked whose toil was directed by the lash of the Pharaoh's overseer. My back acquired an almost permanent crook, and every muscle in my body seemed to be on fire. Not even in the midday heat did we slacken or stay our toils; and when dusk fell that night a great mound had arisen beside Condor's shaft, and we had excavated to a depth it had taken our gang double the time to reach.

When at last we threw down our tools in utter exhaustion, I held out my hand to Hassan, and wrung his brown fist enthusiastically. His eyes sparkled as he met my glance.

"Neville Effendi," he said, "you are a true Moslem!"

And only the initiated can know how high was the compliment conveyed.

That night I slept the sleep of utter weariness, yet it was not a dreamless sleep, or perhaps it was not so deep as I supposed, for blazing cat-eyes encircled me in my dreams, and a constant feline howling seemed to fill the night.

When I awoke the sun was blazing down upon the rock outside my tent, and, springing out of bed, I perceived, with amazement, that the morning was far advanced. Indeed, I could hear the distant voices of the donkey-boys and other harbingers of the coming tourists.

Why had Hassan es-Sugra not awakened me?

I stepped out of the tent and called him in a loud voice. There was no reply. I ran across the plateau to the edge of the hollow.

Condor's shaft had been reclosed to the top!

Language fails me to convey the wave of anger, amazement, incredulity, which swept over me. I looked across to the deserted camp and back to my own tent; I looked down at the mound, where but a few hours before had been a pit, and seriously I began to question whether I was mad or whether madness had seized upon all who had been with me. Then, pegged down upon the heap of broken stones, I perceived, fluttering, a small piece of paper.

Dully I walked across and picked it up. Hassan, a man of some education, clearly was the writer. It was a pencil scrawl in doubtful Arabic, and, not without difficulty, I deciphered it as follows:

"Fly, Neville Effendi! This is a haunted place!"

Standing there by the mound, I tore the scrap of paper into minute fragments, bitterly casting them from me upon the ground. It was incredible; it was insane.

The man who had written that absurd message, the man who had undone his own work, had the reputation of being fearless and honorable. He had been with me before a score of times, and had quelled petty mutinies in the camp in a manner which marked him a born overseer. I could not understand; I could scarcely believe the evidence of my own senses.

What did I do?

I suppose there are some who would have abandoned the thing at once and for always, but I take it that the national traits are strong within me. I went over to the camp and prepared my own breakfast; then, shouldering pick and shovel, I went down into the valley and set to work. What ten men could not do, what two men had failed to do, one man was determined to do.

It was about half an hour after commencing my toils, and when, I suppose, the surprise and rage occasioned by the discovery had begun to wear off, that I found myself making comparisons between my own case and that of Condor. It became more and more evident to me that events—mysterious events—were repeating themselves.

The frightful happenings attendant upon Condor's death were marshaling in my mind. The sun was blazing down upon me, and distant voices could be heard in the desert stillness. I knew that the plain below was dotted with pleasure-seeking tourists, yet nervous tremors shook me. Frankly, I dreaded the coming of the night.

Well, tenacity or pugnacity conquered, and I worked on until dusk. My supper despatched, I sat down on my bed and toyed with the Browning.

I realized already that sleep, under existing conditions, was impossible. I perceived that on the morrow I must abandon my one-man enterprise, pocket my pride, in a sense, and seek new assistants, new companions.

The fact was coming home to me conclusively that a menace, real and not mythical, hung over that valley. Although, in the morning sunlight and filled with indignation, I had thought contemptuously of Hassan es-Sugra, now, in the mysterious violet dusk so conducive to calm consideration, I was forced to admit that he was at least as brave a man as I. And he had fled! What did that night hold in keeping for me?

I will tell you what occurred, and it is the only explanation I have to give of why Condor's shaft, said to communicate with the real tomb of Hatasu, to this day remains unopened.

There, on the edge of my bed, I sat far into the night, not daring to close my eyes. But physical weariness conquered in the end, and, although I have no recollection of its coming, I must have succumbed to sleep, since I remember—can never forget—a repetition of the dream, or what I had assumed to be a dream, of the night before.

A ring of blazing green eyes surrounded me. At one point this ring was broken, and in a kind of nightmare panic I leaped at that promise of safety, and found myself outside the tent.

Lithe, slinking shapes hemmed me in—cat shapes, ghoul shapes, veritable figures of the pit. And the eyes, the shapes, although they were the eyes and shapes of cats, sometimes changed elusively, and became the wicked eyes and the sinuous, writhing shapes of women. Always the ring was incomplete, and always I retreated in the only direction by which retreat was possible. I retreated from those cat-things.

In this fashion I came at last to the shaft, and there I saw the tools which I had left at the end of my day's toil.

Looking around me, I saw also, with such a pang of horror as I cannot hope to convey to you, that the ring of green eyes was now unbroken about me.

And it was closing in.

Nameless feline creatures were crowding silently to the edge of the pit, some preparing to spring down upon me where I stood. A voice seemed to speak in my brain; it spoke of capitulation, telling me to accept defeat, lest, resisting, my fate be the fate of Condor.

Peals of shrill laughter rose upon the silence. The laughter was mine.

Filling the night with this hideous, hysterical merriment, I was working feverishly with pick and with shovel filling in the shaft.

The end? The end is that I awoke, in the morning, lying, not on my bed, but outside on the plateau, my hands torn and bleeding and every muscle in my body throbbing agonisingly. Remembering my dream—for even in that moment of awakening I thought I had dreamed—I staggered across to the valley of the excavation.

Condor's shaft was reclosed to the top.

VI

POMEGRANATE FLOWER

I

There are not so many *Antereeyeh* (story-tellers) in Cairo now (said my acquaintance, Hassan of the Scent Bazaar, staring, reflectively, at two American ladies paying fabulous prices for the goods of his mendacious neighbor on the left). They have adopted other, and more lucrative, professions; but in my father's time, it was an excellent business.

For one thing, the stories which you call the *Arabian Nights* are no longer recited, because they are said to be unlucky. This has considerably reduced the story-teller's stock-in-trade; for unless a man is blessed with much originality, he cannot well refrain from using in his narratives some part of the thousand and one tales.

To this day, however, there is in the city of Cairo a tale-teller of much repute. With his tale-telling he combines the profession of a barber; and like the famous barber of the *Arabian Nights* bears the nickname Es-Samit (the Silent). An old man is this Es-Samit, who no more will know his ninetieth year, of dark countenance, and white beard and eyebrows, with small ears like the ears of a gazelle, and a long nose like that of a camel, and a haughty aspect. This barber enjoys every comfort in his declining years by reason of his amusing manner, and because his ridiculous stories and disclosures respecting his six brothers (for in all things he resembles, or claims to resemble, his famous namesake) divert all who hear them, causing him whose bosom is contracted with woe to swoon with excessive laughter, and filling the saddest heart with joy; such is the absurd loquacity and impertinence of the barber called Es-Samit, the Silent.

It chanced one day that I found myself at the wedding festivities of a prosperous merchant distantly related to me; and for the entertainment of his guests, this wealthy man, in addition to the usual dances and songs, had engaged Es-Samit to divert us with one of his untruthful stories. In order to refresh the *Anteree's* mendacity, the host thus addressed the barber—

"O Es-Samit, thou silent one! it hath come to my ears that in thine exceeding paucity of speech thou hast omitted, hitherto, to relate the story of thy seventh brother. Since thou hast a seventh brother, let not thy love of silence (in thee even greater than in thy famous ancestor) deprive us of a knowledge of his depravity, but acquaint us with his case."

"O Merchant Prince!" replied the barber, "to none other than thyself—so handsome, so liberal, and of such excellent morality—would I break my vow, to speak of that wretched villain, that malevolent mule, that vilest of the vile, my twin brother Ahzab."

My cousin, feigning astonishment at the manner of his speech, said—

"Thy twin brother, O Es-Samit, was not, like thee, a man of rectitude, of exalted mind, and of enlightened intelligence?"

"Alas!" replied the barber, "he was a dog of the most mongrel kind. My bosom is pierced when I utter his accursed name! At the hands of Ahzab, my twin brother, I met with every indignity, and with penalties of a most unfortunate description."

When the host heard this, he laughed exceedingly, saying—

"Acquaint us, O Es-Samit, with his shameless misdeeds."

The barber, sighing as though his soul sought rest from all earthly afflictions, proceeded as follows:

Know, O light of my eyes! that my other brother, Ahzab, was born in the city of Cairo, and his birth was unattended by a darkening of the sun and other unpleasant calamities only by reason of the fact that *I* was born in the same hour!

My twin brother, Ahzab, was blessed with handsome stature, an elegant shape, a perfect figure, with cheeks like roses, with eyebrows meeting above an aquiline nose brightly shining. In short, this shame of my mother was endowed with all those perfections which Allah (whose name be exalted) had also bestowed upon me; but his heart was the heart of a serpent, and he lacked the nobility of mind which thou hast observed in thy servant, O Paragon, of wisdom!

When we were yet in the bloom and blossom of handsome youth, a dispute arose between us, and for many moons I saw not Ahzab, but pursued my occupation as a barber and teller of wonderful stories in a distant part of the city. In this way it befell that I knew of his state only by report, until one day as I sat before my shop observing if the ascendent of the hour were favorable to one who waited to be shaved, there came to me a negro most handsomely dressed, who said:

"My Master, Ahzab the Merchant, desires that you repair as soon as possible to his magazine. He hath urgent need of thee."

Upon hearing these words, and observing the richness of the negro's apparel, I perceived that those reports which had come to me, respecting Ahzab's wealth, were no more than true; and I spoke thus to myself:

"Within the vilest heart may bloom the flower of brotherly affection. Ahzab desires to share with me, the most enlightened of his family, this good fortune which hath befallen him."

Accordingly, I shut up my shop, dismissing the one who waited to be shaved, and followed the black to the Khân Khalîl, where were the shops of the wealthy silk merchants. My brother received me affectionately, embracing me and saying:

"O Es-Samit, ever have I loved thee. Lo! Thou growest more like myself each year. Save that thou art more dignified and noble. Enter into this private apartment with me, for it is important that no one shall see thee."

Much surprised at his words, I followed him to an elegant apartment above the shop, and there he ordered the servants to roast a lamb and to bring to us fruit and wine; and while we thus pleasantly employed ourselves, he unfolded to me his case.

"Know, O my brother, that I have accumulated great wealth; and this I have done by observing those wise precepts of conduct laid down by thee. By the charm of my speech, which I have fashioned upon thine, and the elegance of my manner, in which I have, though poorly, imitated thine own, and by the dignity and the modesty of my conduct, I have endeared all hearts and am esteemed above all the other merchants in Cairo.

"It is necessary that I repair to Damascus, and during my absence I wish nothing better than that thou shouldst take my place here. This will be favorable to both of us; for I will reward thy services with five hundred piastres and an interest in my affairs, and thou wilt pass for me; for all will say, 'Lo! Ahzab the Merchant waxes more handsome each day; such is the benign influence of righteous prosperity and conscious rectitude!' My affairs stand thus and thus, and my steward, who will be in our confidences, will acquaint thee with all matters necessary. Thou wilt wear my costly garments, and sit in my shop. Each evening thou wilt secretly repair to thine own abode."

Upon hearing those words, my bosom swelled with joy; for I observed that Ahzab had not failed to perceive my exalted qualities. We sat far into the night in conversation respecting our plans; and on the following day, Ahzab having departed secretly for Damascus, I repaired to his shop, as arranged, and took my seat there.

But the number of the persons who saluted me, and by the manner of their speech, I perceived, more and more, the great prosperity of my brother; and being of a thoughtful mind, I passed the days very pleasantly in contemplation of my good fortune.

Upon the fourth day after the departure of my brother, as I sat in his shop, there came past a damsel accompanied by female attendants. This damsel was riding upon a mule with a richly embroidered saddle, with stirrups of gold, and she was covered with an *izar* of exquisite fabric; and about her slender waist was a girdle of gold-embroidered silk. I was stricken speechless with the beauty and elegance of her form; and when she alighted and came into the shop, the odors of sweet perfumes were diffused from her, and she captivated my reason by her loveliness.

Seating herself beside me, she raised her *izar*, and I beheld her black eyes. And they surpassed in beauty the eyes of all human beings, and were like the eyes of the gazelle. She had a mouth like the Seal of Suleyman, and hair blacker than the night of affliction; a forehead like the new moon of Ramadan, and cheeks like anemones, with lips fresher than rose petals, teeth like pearls from the sea of distraction, and a neck surpassing in whiteness molten silver, above a form that put to shame the willow branch.

She spoke to me, saying:

"O Ahzab! I have returned as I promised thee!"

At the sound of her voice, by Allah (whose name be exalted!) I was entangled in the snare of her love; fire was burning up my heart on her account; a consuming flame increased within my bosom, and my reason was drowned in the sea of my desire.

Perceiving my state, she quickly lowered her veil in pretended displeasure, and desired to look at some pieces of silk. While she thus employed herself, she surpassed the branches in the beauty of her bending motions, and my eyes could not remove themselves from her. I thus communed with myself:

"O Es-Samit, thou didst contract with thy brother to do this and that, and to render unto him a proper account of thy dealings. But though he hath made thee no mention of his affair with this damsel— it is important that thou conductest this matter as he would have done, so that he cannot reproach thee with negligence!" For I was ever a just as well as a discreet and silent man.

Accordingly I spoke as follows:

"O my mistress, who art the most lovely person God has created, rend not my heart with thy displeasure, but take pity upon me. Know that love is difficult, and the concealment of it melteth iron and occasioneth disease and infirmity. Thou hast returned as thou didst promise; therefore I conjure thee, conceal not thy face from thy slave!"

The damsel thereupon raised her head and put aside her veil, casting a glance upon me and looked sideways at the attendants, and placed one finger upon her lips; so that I knew her to be as discreet as she was lovely. She laughed in my face, and said:

"I will take this piece of embroidered silk that I have chosen. What is the price?"

And I answered:

"One hundred piasters; but I pray thee let it be thine, and a gift from Ahzab!"

Upon this, she looked into my eyes and the sight of her face drew from me a thousand sighs, and took the silk, saying:

"O my master, leave me not desolate!"

So she departed, while I continued sitting in the market-street until past the hour of afternoon prayer, with disturbed mind enslaved by her beauty and loveliness. I returned to my house and supper was placed before me, but reflecting upon the damsel, I could eat nothing. I laid myself down to rest, but passed the whole night sleepless, communing with myself how I could best carry out this affair and obtain possession of the damsel ... for my brother, Ahzab!

II

Scarcely had daybreak appeared when I arose and repaired to the market-place and put on a suit of my brother's clothing, richer and more magnificent than that I had worn the day before; and having drunk a cup of wine, I sat in the shop. But all that day she came not, nor the next, but upon the third day she came again, attended only by one attendant, and she saluted me and said in a speech never surpassed in softness and sweetness:

"O my master, reproach me not that I thus reveal the interest I have in thee, but I could not speak to thee when my women were in hearing; and this one is in my confidence. I have told thee that my father will never give me to thee because of my rank, but thou hast wounded my heart, and more and more do I love thee each day—for each day thou growest more beautiful and elegant. Forever I must be desolate. Alas! I have placed thy letter in the box thou didst give me, and no day passes that it is not wet with my tears. Farewell! O my beloved!"

On hearing this, my love and passion grew so violent that I almost became insensible. The damsel rose to leave the shop, and the one who was with her spoke softly in her ear; but she shook her head, expressing displeasure, and went away.

When I perceived that indeed she was gone, verily the tears descended upon my cheek like rain, and my soul had all but departed. My heart clung to her—I followed in the direction of her steps through the market-place, and lo! the attendant came running back to me, and said:

"Here is the message of my mistress: 'Know that my love is greater than thine, and on Friday next my servant will come to thee and tell thee how thou mayest see me for a short interview before my father comes back from prayers.'"

When I heard these words of the girl, the anguish of my heart ceased, and I was intoxicated with love and rapture, and in my joy and longing, I omitted to ask the girl the abode of her mistress—neither did I know the name of my beloved; but reflecting upon these matters, I returned to my brother's shop, and sat there until late, and then I repaired secretly to my abode.

I paused in a quiet street, and seated myself upon a *mastabah* to scent the coolness of the air, and to abandon myself to exquisite reflections.

But no sooner had I thus seated myself than a negro of gigantic stature, and most hideous aspect, suddenly appeared from the shadow of a door, and threw himself upon me, exclaiming:

"This is thine end, as it was written, O Ahzab the Merchant!"

By Allah! (whose name be exalted) I thought it was even as he said; and none but myself had fallen into sudden dissolution, but that everything slippery is not a pancake, and the jar that is struck may yet escape unbroken.

So it befell that by great good fortune and by the exercise of my agility and intelligence, I tripped the negro and his head came in contact with the *mastabah*, and before he could recover himself, I held to his ebony throat the blade of a razor which, by the mercy of God, and because it was a custom of my profession, I carried in my *kamar*.

"O thou dog!" I exclaimed, "prepare to depart to that utter darkness and perdition that awaits assassins! For assuredly I am about to slay thee!"

But he humbled himself to the ground before me, and embraced my feet, crying:

"Have mercy, O my master! I but obeyed the commands!"

"Of whom, thou vile and unnamable vermin?" I asked of him.

"Of whom else but Abu-el-Hassan, the son of the Kadî! For hath he not revealed to thee that for what has passed with Jullanar (Pomegranate Flower), the daughter of the Walî, he will slay thee?"

"He hath revealed this to me?" I asked of him, astonished at his words.

And he replied: "Thou knowest, master, it was by my hand that the message was borne."

Whereupon I praised Allah (whose name be exalted) and spurned the slave with my foot, saying:

"Depart, O thou black son of filth, and report that I am dead. I give thee thy wretched life; depart!"

But when he had gone, I again lifted up my voice in thanksgiving. And having come to my abode, I performed the preparatory ablution, and recited the prayer of night-fall; after which I recited the chapters "Ya-Sîn" (The Cow) and "Two Preventatives." For I perceived that this was the true purport of my brother's absence, and that in his love and affection he had resigned to me this affair, well knowing that I should perish!

It was by the mercy of Allah, the Compassionate, the Merciful, that my case was not as he had foreseen. The damsel called Jullanar, daughter of the Walî, was famed from Cairo to the uttermost islands of China for her elegance and loveliness, and I knew that my beloved could be none other than she, and that Abu-el-Hassan, son of the Kadî, could be none other than the betrothed chosen of her father the Walî.

I slept not that night, but passed the hours until sunrise reflecting upon this matter, and upon the dangers which awaited my father's handsome son on Friday. And I went not to the market on the next day, but sent a message to my brother's steward saying that I was smitten with sickness and enjoining him to acquaint the girl, who presently would come, where I was to be found.

Thus it befell that at noon on Friday the same girl that had been with Jullanar came to me, sent thither from the shop of Ahzab by the steward, saying:

"O my master, answer the summons of my mistress. This is the plan that I have proposed to her: Conceal thyself within one of the large chests that are in thy shop, and hire a porter to carry thee to the house of the Walî. I will cause the *bowwab* to admit the chest to the apartment of the Lady Jullanar. She doth trust her honor to thy discretion, by reason of her love for thee, and because she will die if she see thee not to bid thee farewell. I will arrange for thee to be secretly conveyed from the house, ere the Walî returns."

And at her words I was like to have swooned with ecstasy; and I forgot, in the transport of love and delight, the black assassin and the threatened vengeance of Abu-el-Hassan. I set at naught my fears at trusting my father's favorite son within the walls of the Walî's house. I thought only of Jullanar of the slender waist and heavy hips, of the dewy lips, more intoxicating than wine, and the eyes of my beloved like wells of temptation to swallow up the souls of men.

I shaved and went to the bath, and repaired to the shop of Ahzab. My brother's steward was not there, whereat I rejoiced, and arrayed myself

in the most splendid suit that I could find, and having perfumed myself
with essences and sweet scents, I summoned a boy and said:

"Go thou and bring here a porter. Order him to carry yon large chest
to the house of the Walî, near the Mosque of Ibn-Mizheh, and ask for
the lady Jullanar who hath purchased this box and a number of things
which are in it. See that he be a strong man, for the box is very heavy."

The boy replied, "On the head," and departed on his errand.

Thereupon I commended my soul to Allah, and entered the box,
closing the lid upon me. Scarcely had I concealed myself, when the
porter entered and lifted the chest. The boy assisted him to take it
upon his back, and he bore it out into the market-street.

"Now by the beard of the Prophet (on whom be peace)," I exclaimed
to myself, "it is well that I am named Es-Samit, the Silent; for had it
been otherwise, I must have lifted up my voice against this son of
perdition who carries me with my soles raised to heaven!"

The porter conveyed me for some distance, panting beneath the
weight of the box, and, presently, coming to a *mastabah*, dropped one
end of the box upon it, whilst he rested himself.

"Now as Allah is great, and Mohammed his only prophet," I said in
my beard, "I am fortunate in that I have acquired a paucity of diction.
There is no other in Cairo, but the joy of my mother, that could refrain
from speech when dropped upon his skull on a stone bench!"

After a while, the porter raised the chest again, and resumed his
journey, presently coming to the house of the Walî, and dropping the
box into the courtyard.

"Allah be praised!" I said. "For if this porter, whose name be accursed,
did but carry me a quinary further, my silence would become even
more surprising than it is; for my affair would finish, and I should
speak no more to any man!"

The *bowwab* now cried out:

"What is in this chest?"

"Purchases of the lady Jullanar," said the girl, whom I recognized by
her voice. "Permit the porter to carry it to her apartments."

"I must obey the orders of the Walî my master," replied the door-
keeper. "The box must be opened."

I was bereft of the power to control myself, and seized with a colic
from excess of fear; I almost died from the violent spasms of my limbs.

"O Es-Samit!" I said, "this is the reward of him whom love leads to
the house of the Walî!"

I felt certain that my destruction approached. The intoxication of
love now ceased in me, and reflection came in its place. I repented of
what I had done, and prayed a happy solution of my dangerous case.

Whether as a result of my prayers, I know not, but some arrangement was come to, and the porter once more raised the chest, and, striking my head upon the end of it at each step, bore me up to the apartments of Jullanar, which I thus entered feet first.

He deposited the box, lid downward, upon the soft mattress of a *dîwan*, so that I found myself upon all fours, like a mule with my face between my hands! Ere I could break my habitual silence, he lifted some heavy piece of furniture—I know not what—and placed it on top of the box!

A voice sweeter than the songs of the Daood spoke:

"Slave! what art thou doing!"

"I *am* thy slave!" spoke another voice, at the accursed sound whereof I almost died of spleen. "Knowest thou me not, my beloved? I have devised a new stratagem and come to thee in the guise of a porter! But lo! beneath my uncomely garments, I am Ahzab, thy lover!"

III

As a man who sleeps ill after a protracted feast, I heard her answer, saying:

"Is it true thou hast come to me, or is this a dream?"

"Verily, it is true!" answered the accursed, the vile, the unspeakable Ahzab, my brother—for it was he. "From the time when I first saw thee, neither sleep hath been sweet to me, nor hath wine possessed the slightest flavor! I have come to thee thus, fragrant bloom of the pomegranate, because I would not have thee see me in a posture so undignified as that of one crouched in a box! So that thy people might be compelled to give me access to thine apartments, I have put a mendicant in my place, rendering the chest heavy!"

And she said, "Thou art welcome!" and embraced him.

By Allah (whose name be exalted), I gnawed my beard until I choked!

"Thou art changed, beloved!" she said to him; "thou art always beautiful, but to-day thou seemest less rosy-cheeked to mine eyes!"

The accursed Ahzab, like an enraged mule, kicked the box wherein I dissolved in flames of wrath.

"I am burnt up with love and longing for thee!" he replied. "O my love! how beautiful thou art!"

Whereat my command of silence forsook me! As Allah is the one god, and Mohammed his only Prophet, I became as one possessed of a devil!

"Robber!" I cried; and my words lost themselves within the box. "Cheat! accursed disgrace of my father! infamy of my race! O dog! O unutterable dirt!"

Jullanar cried out in fear, but my accursed brother took her in his bosom, soothing her with soft words.

"Fear not, O my beloved!" he said. "I gave the mendicant wine that his heart might warm to his lowly task, but I fear he has become intoxicated!"

"O thou liar!" I cried. "O malevolent scoundrel! O son of a disease!" And with all my strength I sought to raise the weight that bore me down; but to no purpose.

"Know, my beloved," continued my thrice-accursed brother, "what I have suffered on thy account. But three days since I was attacked by four gigantic negro assassins despatched by Abu-el-Hassan to slay me! But I vanquished them, killing one and maiming a second, whilst the others escaped and ran back to their wretched master."

"O unutterable liar!" I groaned. For I was near to hastening my predestined end both from suffocation and consuming rage. "Thou didst fly, thou jackal! from that peril, and reapest the fruits of my courage and dexterity! O, mud! O, stench!"

"Lest he should despatch a number too great for me to combat, I have lurked in hiding, delight of souls! in a most filthy hovel belonging to a barber!"

"May thy tongue turn into a scorpion and bite thee!" I cried. "My abode is as clean as the palace of the Khedive! Thou hast never entered it, O thou gnat's egg! Thou hast hidden in I know not what hole, like the unclean insect thou art, until thy steward (may his beard grow backward and smother him!) informed thee of this! O Allah! (to whom be ascribed all might and glory) give me strength to move this accursed box that I may crush him!"

Scarce had I uttered the last word, when a girl came running into the apartment, crying: "Fly, my master! O my mistress! The Walî! the Walî!"

Upon hearing these words, my rage departed from me and in its place came excessive fear. My breath left my body, and my heart ceased to beat.

"He that falleth in the dirt be trodden on by camels," I reflected. "It is not enough, O Es-Samit, that thou hast suffered the attack of the assassin; that thou hast all but died of fear at the door of the Walî's house; that thou hast been torn from the arms of the loveliest creature God hath created; thou are destined, now, O most unfortunate of men, to be detected by the Walî in his daughter's apartments, concealed in a box!"

And I pronounced the *Takbîr*, crying, "O Allah! thy ways are inscrutable!"

"Fly, my beloved!" cried Jullanar to Ahzab. "My women will conceal thee!" Wherewith she swooned and fell upon the floor senseless.

"Quick! follow me closely, O my master!" cried the girl, and I heard my perfidious brother depart from the room by one door, as the Walî entered by another.

"Ah!" cried the Walî, clapping his hands. "Slaves! what is this?"

And people came running to his command; some carrying out the lady Jullanar to her sleeping apartment, and sprinkling rose-water upon her, and some remaining.

"What is in this box upon the *dîwan!*" demanded the Walî. "Bring it hither and open it!"

At that I knew that I was lost, and my soul as good as departed, and I bade farewell to life and invoked Mohammed (whom may God preserve) to intercede for me that I might die an easy death.

The chest was dragged into the middle of the floor and thrown open.

"Name of my mother!" exclaimed the Walî. "It is Ahzab the Merchant! It is the villain who hath presumed to make love to my daughter! O Allah! my daughter hath disgraced me! By the beard of the Prophet, I can no more hold up my head among honest men!"

And he slapped his face and plucked his beard, and fell insensible upon the floor. As he did so, I leaped from the box and would have escaped, but two blacks seized me; and the noise, or the refreshing quality of the rose-water with which the women were sprinkling him, revived the Walî, who recovered, fixing upon me a terrible gaze.

"O thou dog!" he said; "thou who hast wrought my disgrace! As thou didst enter my house in yonder box, in yonder box shalt thou quit the world! Cast him back again, fasten the box with ropes, and throw it into the Nile at nightfall!"

IV

Now were my powers of silence most surprisingly displayed. For I spoke no word, but dumb as a tongueless man, I allowed myself to be knocked backward into the box. The lid closed upon me, ropes bound about the box, and the seal of the Walî affixed to it. Negroes carried it out, and threw it into some cellar to await nightfall.

"O Es-Samit!" I said, "this is the end that was appointed to thy father's wisest son! To this pass thy silence and wisdom have brought thee! O Allah (to whom be all glory), grant that one of the fishes that eat me in the Nile shall be served up to Ahzab, my twin brother, and choke him!"

And then my thoughts turned to Jullanar, and I sighed and groaned; and the torments I suffered through lying drawn up in the box were delights to the agonies that my reflections respecting her case occasioned in me; so that, with the excess of my woe and misery, I became insensible. How long I remained so I know not, but I was awakened by a knocking at the lid of the box, and the voice of the Walî spoke, saying:

"Prepare to die, O wretch! for my servants are about to convey thee to the river and cast thee in! Thou dog! who didst presume to raise thine eyes to my daughter!—know that this is the reward of such malefactors; for assuredly if thou escapest alive, thou shalt wed Jullanar!"

Whereat he laughed until he almost swooned and kicked the box until I thought he had burst it. Blacks raised me, and I was borne down a long flight of steps and onward in I know not what direction.

"From here?" said one of them, and through a crack in the lid, I saw the light of a torch, and the whispering of the river came to my ears.

"Yes!" replied another.

And I commended my soul to Allah as the box was swung to and fro and hurled through the air. With a sound in my ears as of the shrieking of ten thousand *efreets*, I was plunged into the water!

Far under the surface I went and knew all the agonies of dissolution; but the box was strongly and cunningly made and rose again; then it began to fill and sink once more, and again I tasted of the final pangs. Throughout all this time, a strong current was bearing the box along, and presently, as, for the fiftieth occasion, I was seeking to die and to end my misery, I heard voices.

The most miserable life is sweet to him who feels it slipping from his grasp, and I summoned sufficient strength to raise a feeble cry.

"O Allah!" I cried, "if it be thy will, grant that these persons whose voices I hear take pity upon my unfortunate condition, and draw me forth."

Even as I spoke, something stayed the onward progress of the box. It was a fisherman's net! And the fishermen began to draw me into the boat, I praising Allah the while.

But when they had the box upon the edge of the boat, and heard my voice proceeding from within, and saw the Walî's seal upon the lid—"By the beard of the Prophet!" cried one, "this is some evil *ginn* or magician whom the Walî hath imprisoned in this chest! Allah avert the omen! Cast him back, comrades!"

Alas! I could find no words wherewith to entreat them to take pity; never had paucity of speech served me so ill! A great groan issued from my bosom as I was consigned again to the Nile!

Allah is great, and it was not written that I should perish in that manner. For another current now seized upon the box, and just as I was on the point of dissolution, cast it upon a projecting bank, where it was perceived by a band of four robbers, who derived a livelihood from plundering such vessels as lay unprotected in the river.

These waded out and dragged the box ashore. I was too near my end to have spoken had I desired to speak, but from my unfortunate adventure with the fishermen, I had learned that silence was wisdom, now as always. Thus I lay in the box like a dog that has been all but drowned, and listened to the words of my rescuers.

These were arguing respecting the contents and value of the box, one holding this opinion and another that. One, who seemed to be their leader, was about to unfasten the ropes, but another claimed that this was his due. So, from angry words, they came to blows, and by the grace of God (whose name be exalted) they drew their knives, and three of the four were slain. The fourth removed the ropes and opened the box, thinking to enjoy, alone, the treasures which he supposed it to contain.

Whereupon I uprose and looked up to where Canopus shone, and said:

"There is no God but God! Praise be to Allah who has preserved me from an unfortunate and unseemly end!"

At that, the robber, with wild cries of fear, turned and ran, and I saw him no more. Such, O bountiful patron, is the disgraceful story of the dog Ahzab, my seventh and twin brother. But all that which I endured happened by Fate and Destiny, and from that which is written there is no escape nor flight.

Our worthy host (concluded Hassan) laughed heartily at this story, saying:

"O Es-Samit, it is evident to me that thy paucity of speech alone preserved thee from drowning! But acquaint us, I beg, with the fate of thy dog of a brother, and of thy beautiful Pomegranate Flower."

"O glory of beholders!" replied the barber, "by the mouth of the girl who was in Jullanar's confidence—Ahzab, that shame of mules, learned, whilst in hiding, how the Walî had said in the presence of many witnesses: 'Assuredly if thou escapest alive, thou shalt wed Jullanar.'"

"Tellest thou me that he had the effrontery to demand the fulfilment of a pledge so spoken, O Es-Samit?"

"Alas!" replied the barber, with tears pouring like rain down the wrinkles of his aged cheek, "he lived with her the most joyous, and most agreeable, and most comfortable, and most pleasant life, until they were visited by the terminator of delights, and the separator of companions!"

THE END

Sax Rohmer Bibliography
(1983-1959)

Pause! (1910) [essays, monologues & dramatic sketches, published anonymously]
Little Tich (1911) [autobiography of the Music Hall entertainer ghost-written by Ward]
The Sins of Severac Bablon (1914; stories)
The Romance of Sorcery (1914; nonfiction study of the occult)
The Exploits of Captain O'Hagan (1916; stories)
Brood of the Witch Queen (1918)
Tales of Secret Egypt (1918; stories)
The Orchard of Tears (1918)
The Quest of the Sacred Slipper (1919)
The Dream Detective (1920; Moris Klaw stories)
The Green Eyes of Bâst (1920)
The Haunting of Low Fennel (1920; stories)
Tales of Chinatown (1922; stories)
Grey Face (1924)
Moon of Madness (1927)
She Who Sleeps (1928)
The Emperor of America (1929)
Yu'an Hee See Laughs (1932)
Tales of East and West (1932; stories)
The Bat Flies Low (1935)
White Velvet (1936)
Salute to Bazarada (1939)
Egyptian Nights (1944; US Title: Bimbashi-Baruk of Egypt; stories)
Hangover House (1949)
Wulfheim (1950; originally credited to Michael Furey, later printings listed as by Sax Rohmer)
The Moon is Red (1954)
The Secret of Holm Peel and Other Strange Stories (1970)
The Green Spider and Other Forgotten Tales of Mystery & Suspense (2011)
The Leopard Couch and Other Stories of the Fantastic & Supernatural (2012)
The Complete Cases of the Crime Magnet (2012; stories)

Fu Manchu series
The Mystery of Dr. Fu-Manchu (1913; US Title: The Insidious Dr. Fu-Manchu)
The Devil Doctor (1916: US Title: The Return of Dr. Fu-Manchu)
The Si-Fan Mysteries (1917; US Title: The Hand of Fu Manchu)
The Daughter of Fu Manchu (1931)
The Mask of Fu Manchu (1932)

The Bride of Fu Manchu (1933; original US Title: Fu Manchu's Bride)
The Trail of Fu Manchu (1934)
President Fu Manchu (1936)
The Drums of Fu Manchu (1939)
The Island of Fu Manchu (1941)
The Shadow of Fu Manchu (1948)
Re-enter: Fu Manchu (1957; UK Title: Re-Enter: Dr. Fu Manchu)
Emperor Fu Manchu (1959)
The Wrath of Fu Manchu and Other Stories (UK: 1973; US: 1976; 12 stories
    including four previously uncollected Fu Manchu stories)

Gaston Max series
The Yellow Claw (1915)
The Golden Scorpion (1919)
The Day the World Ended (1930)
Myself and Gaston Max (a series of six BBC radio plays, 1942)
Seven Sins (1943)

"Red" Kerry series
Dope (1919)
Yellow Shadows (1925)

Paul Harley series
Bat-Wing (1921)
Fire Tongue (1921)
The Voice of Kali: The Early Paul Harley Mysteries (2013)

Sumuru series
The Sins of Sumuru (1950; US Title: Nude in Mink)
The Slaves of Sumuru (1951; US Title: Sumuru)
Virgin in Flames (1952; US Title: The Fire Goddess)
Sand and Satin (1954; US Title: Return of Sumuru)
Sinister Madonna (1956)

Related Works:

Bianca in Black by Elizabeth Sax Rohmer (1958; Rohmer's wife)
Master of Villainy: A Biography of Sax Rohmer by Cay Van Ash and Elizabeth
    Sax Rohmer, edited by Robert E. Briney (1972)
Ten Years Beyond Baker Street: Sherlock Holmes Matches Wits with the
    Diabolical Dr. Fu Manchu by Cay Van Ash (1984)
The Fires of Fu Manchu by Cay Van Ash (1987)
The Terror of Fu Manchu by William Patrick Maynard (2009)
The Destiny of Fu Manchu by William Patrick Maynard (2012)
The Triumph of Fu Manchu by William Patrick Maynard (2015; unpublished)